PRAISE FOR BAR

"*Ambush* truly kicks butt and takes names, crackling with tension from page one with a plot as sharp as broken glass. Barbara Nickless is a superb writer."

—Steve Berry, #1 internationally bestselling author

"A nail-biter with some wicked twists . . . Fast-paced and nonstop . . . Sydney is fleshed out, flawed, gritty, and kick-ass, and you can't help but root for her. Nickless leaves you satisfied and smiling—something that doesn't happen too often in this genre!"

—*The Bookish Biker*

"*Ambush* has plenty of action and intrigue. There are shoot-outs and kidnappings. There are cover-ups and conspiracies. At the center of it all is a flawed heroine who will do whatever it takes to set things right."

—BVS Reviews

"*Ambush* takes off on page one like a Marine F/A-18 Super Hornet under full military power from the flight deck . . . and never lets the reader down."

—*Mysterious Book Report*

"*Ambush* is modern mystery with its foot on the gas. Barbara Nickless's writing—at turns blazing, aching, stark, and gorgeous—propels this story at a breathless pace until its sublime conclusion. In Sydney Parnell, Nickless has masterfully crafted a heroine who, with all her internal and external scars, compels the reader to simultaneously root for and forgive her. A truly standout novel."

—Carter Wilson, *USA Today* bestselling author of *Mister Tender's Girl*

"Exceptional . . . Nickless raises the stakes and expands the canvas of a blisteringly original series. A wholly satisfying roller coaster of a thriller that features one of the genre's most truly original heroes."
—Jon Land, *USA Today* bestselling author

"*Ambush* . . . makes you laugh and cry as the pages fly by."
—Tim Tigner, internationally bestselling author

"A stunner of a thriller. From the first page to the last, *Blood on the Tracks* weaves a spell that only a natural storyteller can master. And a guarantee: you'll fall in love with one of the best characters to come along in modern thriller fiction, Sydney Rose Parnell."
—Jeffery Deaver, #1 international bestselling author

"Beautifully written and heartbreakingly intense, this terrific and original debut is unforgettable. Please do not miss *Blood on the Tracks*. It fearlessly explores our darkest and most vulnerable places—and is devastatingly good. Barbara Nickless is a star."
—Hank Phillippi Ryan, winner of Anthony, Agatha, and Mary Higgins Clark awards and author of *Say No More*

"Both evocative and self-assured, Barbara Nickless's debut novel is an outstanding, hard-hitting story so gritty and real you feel it in your teeth. Do yourself a favor and give this bright talent a read."
—John Hart, multiple Edgar Award winner and *New York Times* bestselling author of *Redemption Road*

"Fast-paced and intense, *Blood on the Tracks* is an absorbing thriller that is both beautifully written and absolutely unique in character and setting. Barbara Nickless has written a twisting, tortured novel that speaks with brutal honesty of the lingering traumas of war, including and especially those wounds we cannot see. I fell hard for Parnell and her four-legged partner and can't wait to read more."
—Vicki Pettersson, *New York Times* and *USA Today* bestselling author
of *Swerve*

"The aptly titled *Blood on the Tracks* offers a fresh and starkly original take on the mystery genre. Barbara Nickless has fashioned a beautifully drawn hero in take-charge, take-no-prisoners Sydney Parnell, former Marine and now a railway cop battling a deadly gang as she investigates their purported connection to a recent murder. Nickless proves a master of both form and function in establishing herself every bit the equal of Nevada Barr and Linda Fairstein. A major debut that is not to be missed."

—Jon Land, *USA Today* bestselling author

"*Blood on the Tracks* is a bullet train of action. It's one part mystery and two parts thriller with a compelling protagonist leading the charge toward a knockout finish. The internal demons of one Sydney Rose Parnell are as gripping as the external monster she's chasing around Colorado. You will long remember this spectacular debut novel."
—Mark Stevens, author of the award-winning
Allison Coil Mystery series

"Nickless captures you from the first sentence. Her series features Sydney Rose Parnell, a young woman haunted by the ghosts of her past. In *Blood on the Tracks*, she doggedly pursues a killer, seeking truth even in the face of her own destruction. The true mark of a heroine. Skilled in evoking emotion from the reader, Nickless is a master of the craft, a writer to keep your eyes on."

—Chris Goff, author of *Dark Waters*

"Barbara Nickless's *Blood on the Tracks* is raw and authentic, plunging readers into the fascinating world of tough railroad cop Special Agent Sydney Rose Parnell and her Malinois sidekick, Clyde. Haunted by her military service in Iraq, Sydney Rose is brought in by the Denver Major Crimes Unit to help solve a particularly brutal murder, leading her into a snake pit of hate and betrayal. Meticulously plotted and intelligently written, *Blood on the Tracks* is a superb debut novel."

—M. L. Rowland, author of the Search and Rescue Mystery novels

"*Blood on the Tracks* is a must-read debut. A suspenseful crime thriller with propulsive action, masterful writing, and a tough-as-nails cop, Sydney Rose Parnell. Readers will want more."

—Robert K. Tanenbaum, *New York Times* bestselling author of the Butch Karp–Marlene Ciampi legal thrillers

"*Blood on the Tracks* is a superb story that rises above the genre of mystery . . . It is a first-class read."

—*The Denver Post*

"Nickless's writing admirably captures the fallout from a war where even survivors are trapped, forever reliving their trauma."

—*Kirkus Reviews*

"Part mystery, part antiwar story, Nickless's engrossing first novel, a series launch, introduces Sydney Rose Parnell . . . Nickless skillfully explores the dehumanizing effects resulting from the unspeakable cruelties of wartime as well as the part played by the loyalty soldiers owe to family and each other under stressful circumstances."

—Publishers Weekly

"An interesting tale . . . The fast pace will leave you finished in no time. Nickless seamlessly ties everything together with a shocking ending."

—RT Book Reviews

"If you enjoy suspense and thrillers, then you will [want] *Blood on the Tracks* for your library. Full of the suspense that holds you on the edge of your seat, it's also replete with acts of bravery, moments of hope, and a host of feelings that keep the story's intensity level high. This would be a great work for a book club or reading group with a great deal of information that would create robust dialogue and debate."

—Blogcritics

"In *Blood on the Tracks*, Barbara Nickless delivers a thriller with the force of a speeding locomotive and the subtlety of a surgeon's knife. Sydney and Clyde are both great characters with flaws and virtues to see them through a plot thick with menace. One for contemporary thriller lovers everywhere."

—Authorlink

GONE TO DARKNESS

ALSO BY
BARBARA NICKLESS

Blood on the Tracks
Dead Stop
Ambush

GONE TO DARKNESS

BARBARA NICKLESS

THOMAS & MERCER

Text copyright © 2020 by Barbara Nickless
All rights reserved.

Published by Thomas & Mercer, Seattle

www.apub.com

Amazon, the Amazon logo, and Thomas & Mercer are trademarks of Amazon.com, Inc., or its affiliates.

ISBN-13: 9781542092869
ISBN-10: 1542092868

Cover design by Kirk DouPonce, DogEared Design

Printed in the United States of America

To Kristin Mueller, Leslie Alpin Wharton, and the Wonderful Waldo Women.
We helped each other rise from the ashes and find our wings again.
And most especially to Susan Ruane McConnell: my dear friend, you flew all too briefly.

THE COMING DARK

He loved that the room was always cold.

He loved that down here, far below the cheer of man's normal haunts, the air carried a bite like the bright edge of a knife. Down here, his fingers turned clumsy, snot dripped from his nose, his breath hung in the air from the bellows of his lungs.

Sometimes, the room seemed alive. As if he stood inside a beast of stone and steel. Water seeped down the concrete walls. Pipes groaned overhead. Bare bulbs cast a weak light, while the walls gathered shadows to themselves. A rusty drain in the middle of the floor emitted a sharp stink that caught in his throat and made his eyes water. Far below, something long dead still lay rotting in the dark, dense earth.

Here, in this room, anything felt possible.

Here, everything was right.

And so he made the room a shrine.

Taped to the walls: newspaper clippings, articles from the internet, files from hacked databases. There were illegally obtained service records and transcripts from phone calls. He'd spent months collecting every scrap he could.

So he could take her in.

So he could *inhale* her.

He'd arranged everything in chronological order. From her late teens—sporting events, prom, graduation—through her Marine career and into her time with the railroads. A life recently made public in the Denver papers, which had made his job easier.

> Dynamic Duo: Missing Girl Found by Railroad Cop and
> K9 Partner

> Heroes Ride Again: Railroad Cop and K9 Partner Solve
> Wartime Mystery

> Our Heroes: Railroad Cop and K9 Partner Leave the
> Rails, Join Denver Police

> Rising Heroes: Railroad Cop and K9 Partner Join Denver
> Major Crimes Unit

Then there were the photographs. She gazed at him from every surface.

Some pictures were from the papers. Another was her boot-camp photo. He had pictures from the media announcement when she'd been plucked from the obscurity of the rails and promoted to the Denver Major Crimes Unit as the chief's golden girl.

But most of the photos were from his private collection. The ones *he'd* taken.

Those were his favorite.

Here she was, sweaty and breathless, returning to her fuckboy's house from a run in the park. A few photos showed her dining out, others caught her sitting on her deck, and in another picture, he'd snapped her as she exited her police-issued Chevrolet Tahoe. He had two from when she'd walked nude past her bedroom window. And he had a single picture from the party the railroad had thrown for her just the night before, taken from his dimly lit place at the end of the bar.

He breathed with the room. With the drain and its stench. The thrum of the pipes. Lust raged inside him. He understood that hunger as clearly as if it had come straight from God.

Take. Use. Destroy.

Hers was a life on the rise. And the higher they flew . . .

"Like Icarus." He nodded to himself. "And we all know how that turned out."

The room swallowed his words. The shadows rustled, disturbed.

The dog was a problem. He was still working on that. But for every problem, there was a solution.

He stepped into the middle of the room, straddling the drain with its putrid stench, and turned in place. Dreaming. Imagining.

In the far corner he'd placed a cot, a large, easy-to-clean plastic bucket, and a storage tub with assorted tools—screwdrivers, pliers, clamps, duct tape. He also had power tools. His favorite was the Craftsman twenty-volt half-inch drill. His mind lingered over the word *craftsman*. He was a craftsman. He was an artist.

He also loved the portable band saw. For when they reached the end together.

He had handcuffs welded to the ceiling, plastic sheeting on the floor. An industrial hose.

It was all so perfect.

His eyes came to rest on the media photo of her standing behind a dais next to the chief. She was smiling, even if something in her eyes suggested she wasn't entirely certain about her change in affairs.

"Crash and burn, baby," he whispered. "Just like Icarus. Crash and burn."

CHAPTER 1

To hell with their laws and restrictions. You have a great and wise heart, Sydney Rose. And that makes for a much better guide to what's wrong and what's right.

—Effie "Grams" Parnell. Private conversation.

My first official homicide investigation began without a corpse.

An actual body is what triggers a murder case. It's straightforward—in order to prove that a murder occurred, you must have a dead person. *Corpus delicti*, the courts call it. Latin for *body of the crime*.

All I had on that foggy, still-dark morning as my K9 partner and I drove through the outskirts of Denver was a message on my phone from a railroad cop named Heinrich. And a bad feeling—after our brief conversation, Heinrich had stopped answering his phone.

Next to me in the console, a cup of 7-Eleven coffee steamed into the air. Ray Wylie Hubbard sang on the radio about righteous killing. I drove with both hands on the wheel, as patches of the highway were slick with black ice. When I test-tapped the brakes, the Chevy Tahoe skated sideways.

Beside me, Clyde made a noise in his throat.

I dropped my speed.

"Easy, pal," I said.

Oncoming headlights flared against the windshield, skirted off the side windows, then vanished behind us, taillights aglow like baleful eyes.

The date was March 15.

The Ides of March. When assassins bare their knives.

◆ ◆ ◆

My first exchange with Special Agent Heinrich that day had been at 3:14 a.m.

This was after I discovered he'd pilfered my blue-and-silver detective's shield. A group of us from the railroad had gone out the night before to celebrate my promotion from patrol to homicide. Heinrich was there. My former boss, Deputy Chief Mauer, too. And about twenty railroaders I'd worked with during my two years as a cop with Denver Pacific Continental. It was a damn weird party—half celebration for my success and half mourning that my promotion meant I'd likely never return to the railroads. I think a few of us cried. Or maybe it was just me, three drinks in and still hung up on whether I'd made the right choice to put the railroads in my past.

In Denver PD, I was the golden girl on the fast track. Six months in patrol and now three weeks into my on-the-job training as a homicide detective with the Denver Major Crimes Unit. My serendipitous rise had coincided with a nasty series of sexual harassment charges inside the department. The chief needed to show the good citizens of Denver that their police had a zero-tolerance policy toward caveman behaviors.

And that they enthusiastically promoted women.

Which was where I came in. Sydney Rose Parnell. Poster child.

I test-tapped the brakes again, felt the tires grip, and rewarded myself with a one-handed sip of coffee. I was officially on probation for three more months. Screw up, and I'd be back in patrol, the promotion of women be damned.

The night before, I'd given my wallet to Heinrich to spot him a twenty, and he'd filched my shield as a joke, the son of a bitch. I hadn't noticed until oh-dark-thirty, after a case of nerves had gotten me up hours before the alarm and I'd spotted the voice mail from Heinrich: *So sorry, it was a joke, didn't mean to leave the bar with your badge.* I'm sure my counselor would say that my carelessness with my badge was indicative of my ambivalence toward my new career. When I phoned Heinrich to arrange a meet, he was already on his way east, answering a call from dispatch. An engineer running a train through the area had spotted a trespasser standing near the tracks, a woman.

Maybe the woman was just a poor insomniac, night-haunted like so many of us. But the nearest homes and businesses were miles away. So it was possible she was a jumper. Maybe even a terrorist with derailment in mind.

Heinrich—along with my shield—had gone to investigate.

Now I was also on my way east to get it back before anyone found out I'd lost it. With Denver PD in the crosshairs of local politicians, the new lieutenant was a take-no-prisoners commander who operated on the broken-window theory—any mistake, however minor, was an indication the entire department was going to the dogs. If Lobowitz learned I'd lost my badge, she'd make a note in my file. Two more infractions, and she'd drop me from the detectives' room to the dreary dullness of midnight patrols in Green Valley Ranch.

I could hear the chatter already. A woman. A railroad cop. Couldn't hold on to her badge.

Not figuratively.

Not literally.

On the radio, Hubbard moved on from death to dying. The windshield wipers scraped against the glass. Something else scraped the inside of my skull.

"Blue Train cocktails," I muttered to Clyde, who was comfortably buckled shotgun. "Whoever got the numbskull idea to ruin champagne with fruit syrup should be shot."

My partner tipped his velvet-soft ears at me and managed an expression that looked like the K9 equivalent of an eye roll. Belgian Malinois are good at that. You don't need a guilty conscience when you have a maligator. Someone might put pineapple juice in Clyde's bowl, but that didn't mean he'd drink it.

"I know what you're thinking," I went on.

His brow furrowed.

"No one held a gun to my head, right? That's what you'd say if you could. But I got you there, pal. Gift of gab."

Clyde yawned and returned his gaze out the window, putting me in my place. Mals are good at that, too.

There wasn't much to see outside the cab. Dawn was still a couple of hours away, and springtime in the Rockies had pinned a thick, cottony fog to the bounds of earth. The beams of my headlights looked like underwater ectoplasm.

From the highway I drove north and east along a series of increasingly smaller roads until eventually I hit a dirt track. I buzzed Heinrich again to tell him that I was probably fifteen minutes out. Just in case he was playing choke the chicken and needed to hurry and finish.

But he didn't pick up.

A herd of pronghorn zipped out of the night, their slender bodies darting through the swirling mist as they sprinted by. I hit the brakes; the antiskid light glowed. We watched the antelope disappear into the gloom, and I eased back onto the gas, wondering what had spooked them enough to get them up and moving in the dark.

I tried Heinrich again. Five rings and then voice mail.

A familiar, years-old worry ignited in my gut. The sense that things weren't going down the way they should. The faith that they would only get worse. My time in the Marines serving in Mortuary Affairs had honed my natural sixth sense for trouble into the psychological equivalent of a map and a road sign: **DISASTER AHEAD**.

I reminded myself that my early warning system was as likely to trigger on a missed dentist appointment as any real threat.

"Just breathe," I said out loud.

Clyde glanced at me. I ruffled his ears.

"It's me, buddy. You're breathing fine."

Five minutes later, I spotted a diffuse glow that morphed into the twin beams of stationary headlights. As I drew nearer, I made out the shape of a blue SUV with the words DENVER PACIFIC CONTINENTAL RAILWAY POLICE stenciled in reflective paint on the side. Heinrich's Expedition. No other lights or vehicles were visible. I eased off the road into the weeds and parked a short distance away, mindful of not disturbing any tracks or footprints. Just in case my gut was right.

"Special Agent Heinrich," I whispered. "If you are out taking a dump in the weeds, I am seriously gonna hurt you."

I slid on a headlamp, flicked the switch to low beam, then did a press check on my Glock to confirm I had a round chambered. I holstered the gun and unbuckled Clyde before I stepped out into the morning's frosty soup. Clyde hopped down beside me. He pricked his ears, and his tail came up. I watched him for a moment, but he didn't go into high alert.

"Gib acht," I said softly in German as I snapped on his lead. *Watch out.*

I scanned the road for evidence that someone aside from Heinrich had been here, but a dry winter and spring had turned the ground to hardpan.

My headlamp picked out a few shapes. On the far side of the SUV, a stand of winter-chewed cottonwoods thrust bony fingers through sections of rusting, broken-down fence. Beyond the fence ran an empty stretch of train tracks—two faint lines of water-beaded iron that gleamed when my light struck.

All around, frost glittered in the field's dips and hollows. The musty-tart smell of juniper mixed with the cold damp, as bracing as a lungful of menthol.

Clyde and I approached Heinrich's vehicle. The outside of the SUV sparkled with moisture; the mirrors threw back only a glaze. The driver's door was flung open, the engine still running. Beyond that persistent purr, the world was still and silent.

I shone my light through the Expedition's passenger-side window.

A DPC baseball cap. Leather gloves. An open can of Red Bull in the drink holder. And my badge.

Clyde and I walked around the front of the vehicle. I reached into the cab, turned off the engine and headlights, and grabbed my shield. I clipped it on my belt and pocketed Heinrich's keys.

Into the dark, wet silence, a crow croaked.

Then the radio on the Expedition's console static-buzzed into life.

"Unit One, what is your status?"

I leaned in and keyed the mic. "This is former Special Agent Parnell. I'm at Heinrich's vehicle now. The officer has vacated the vehicle. I'm going to look for him."

"Roger that. Good to hear your voice, Sydney. You need backup from Denver PD?"

I sure hoped not. "I'll let you know."

After I signed off, I watched Clyde for a minute to make sure he hadn't transitioned into red alert. He was taking in the world—an aromatic smorgasbord of jackrabbits, prairie dogs, pronghorn. But nothing of concern. He met my gaze as if to ask when we were going to get a move on.

"Greg!" I shouted.

On the cottonwood trees, moisture collected and dripped, the world caught between freeze and melt. The air bit through my wool jacket.

I leaned again into Heinrich's vehicle and grabbed one of the leather gloves. Then I pulled Clyde's Kong from my pocket, waving the hard rubber toy that signaled it was time to get to work. Clyde wagged his tail.

"Let's do this, boy." I held out Heinrich's gloves and gave Clyde a good whiff. Then I raised my arm.

I often used a mix of English, German, and Hebrew commands with Clyde—it was a good way to confuse the bad guys. Now I cried, "Seek!"

Clyde thrust his nose into the air. He was an air-sniffing dog, not a ground tracker. But he soon lowered his head and began to sample closer to the ground. Humidity pushed odors toward the earth. Foggy, windless days distributed a person's scent over a wide area. Not ideal conditions.

But a minute later Clyde had something and took off.

The cotton-shrouded world jumped and swayed in the beam of my headlamp as I followed him, his long lead firmly in my grasp. He made a beeline for the tracks, then just before the fence he veered right, his path paralleling the rails.

Night and fog swallowed our vehicles. Clumps of winter-gold grass crunched beneath our feet. Although it was March, Mother Nature cared nothing for a human's idea of springtime. The fog was denser here than on the highway, a gray-white clot reflecting a mysterious luminescence. Trees and hillocks popped up like fright-house wonders and vanished almost as we walked by.

Clyde slowed. He trotted forward, then back, then struck off at an angle. He disappeared into the fog, his lead trailing after him like one of those toy leashes that seemed linked to an invisible pet. Then his lead quivered and went slack.

He'd found something.

I plunged into the white shroud after him, the beam from my headlamp bouncing against the fog and refracting at weird angles. The light caught Clyde first, then illuminated the sprawled, motionless form of a man lying on his back. Particles of light hit on the Denver Pacific Continental patch on the sleeve of his jacket.

Greg Heinrich.

I closed the space between us.

"Pas auf," I said to Clyde. *Guard.*

I knelt, touching two fingers to Heinrich's neck. A steady pulse beat beneath his cold skin. Gently I turned his head and found a lump the size of a baby's fist above his right ear. I did a quick survey of his body but found no other injuries. I called in a Code Nine for medical assistance—dispatch took the details of Heinrich's injuries and location and routed an ambulance in our direction.

"Heinrich!" I snapped. "Wake up."

No response. I peeled back each eyelid with my thumb and shined my headlamp on the irises. The pupils were of equal size and contracted nicely.

I released his lids. "Greg!"

He moaned. "The hell?"

"We got you, buddy," I said. "Help is on the way. Can you hear me?"

"Dear God," he whispered. He opened his eyes, winced at the light. I aimed my headlamp away. "Sorry."

"I feel like shit."

"You look worse. You got hit pretty hard."

"By what?"

"I was hoping you could tell me."

He raised a hand toward his head. "Hurts like a mother."

I caught his fingers. "Wait for the EMTs."

"I was on a call." He frowned. "Wasn't I?"

"I figured you were off sneaking a smoke."

"Dispatch sent me. I remember that. Then . . ." He closed his eyes, opened them. "How bad's my head?"

"You've got a knot the size of Rhode Island up there. But that's good. Means the swelling is going out instead of putting pressure on your brain. You remember seeing a woman?"

"A woman? Was that the call?" His freckles were dark against his pale skin. "Ah, shit. If I was clocked by a woman, I'm going to look like an idiot."

"You don't need a woman for that. Do you remember her?"

"I don't even remember getting hit. I must have blacked out. That's not a good sign, is it?"

"You got a concussion. Doesn't mean it's long-term serious. Speech is good, eyes are good. But my guess is you were out for ten minutes or more. You feel all your fingers and toes?"

He moved around. "Yeah."

"You want to try sitting up?"

He levered himself onto his elbows and tried to work his way up to a sitting position. His face went from the color of old ice to new snow.

"We'll wait a bit on that, Lone Ranger." I slid out of my jacket, folded it, and used it to prop up his head and shoulders. "Let's stay horizontal for now."

"Mauer is going to fire my ass."

"Nah. He'll just run your ass through a thresher," I said.

"Wait." Heinrich tried again to sit up. "Is my truck still here?"

I put my hands on his shoulders. "It was ten minutes ago."

"I left it running, didn't I?"

"You must have seen something. Exited the vehicle in a hurry."

"My truck—"

"It's fine."

"What would make me do that?"

"Question of the hour." I turned his hand over and dropped the keys into his palm. "Now will you take a minute? I need to think."

Heinrich closed his eyes.

"But don't sleep."

"No." Heinrich opened his eyes.

I rocked back on my heels, shivering in the cold. Whoever had thumped Heinrich was long gone, I figured. Hitting a cop, even a railroad cop, was a good way to three squares and a long-term piece of solitary real estate. Any self-respecting criminal would be miles away by now.

But maybe he—or she—had left a clue.

"I'm going to take a look around," I said. "But let's get you to your truck first. You think you can walk?"

"You aren't supposed to do my job."

"Someone has to."

Sweat popped on Heinrich's forehead. "I'm gonna puke."

I helped him turn his head, and he vomited onto the grass. Gently I settled him back down.

"Maybe help me to my truck in a little bit," he said.

"Sure. You all right if I leave you for a few minutes? Where's your phone?"

"Coat pocket."

I found it and placed it in his hand. "I'll be back in twenty. Call me if you feel worse. Or if you hear or see anything."

For a moment he looked panicked. "You think he's still here?"

"So maybe it was a he?"

"Big motherfucker. That's my story."

"Well, there's no vehicle. And Clyde's calm. I think it's just us. You got your gun?"

His right hand fumbled down to his holster. "Yeah."

"We won't be long. Hang tight. And don't shoot us when we come back."

I got to my feet, took Clyde's lead, and, knowing I could do nothing more for Heinrich at the moment, headed out. I directed my partner toward the train tracks, and when my headlamp picked out the iron railings, we made our way over the broken-down fence and walked parallel to the tracks. We stayed a safe distance away, mindful that a train could appear at any moment.

Fifty yards on, Clyde slowed and hesitated. His ears swiveled, and his nose came up. I signaled through the lead for him to stop, and then I turned slowly in a circle, watching for the headlamp to catch something.

There. A flash of gold in the grass.

Clyde barked. Sudden shapes materialized in the fog. One prong-horn and then another leapt past. Maybe the same herd we'd almost crashed into earlier. We'd crept upon them from downwind, and now they bolted, heading away from us and from Heinrich, vanishing into the darkness, a rush of hooves and horns and the smell of wildness.

I listened to them flee, my heart slamming up somewhere near my throat.

When they were gone, I looked back at the ground.

The light struck a small, upright cross made of two unbent paper clips held together by a rubber band and pushed into the ground. Coiled around the cross was a gold pendant, strung by a loop onto a thin gold chain. Chain and pendant were spattered with red.

I crouched and leaned in. The medallion showed an image of a woman. At the top were the words *Our Lady of Guadalupe*. At the bottom, *Pray for us*.

Not just any woman. The Virgin Mary.

Smears of red darkened her face.

Behind me, Clyde gave a soft whine. I looked over my shoulder at my partner. He'd lowered his tail and pinned his ears to his skull.

A shiver slipped down my spine. "What is it, boy?"

But he was staring past me. I pivoted. There was only the fog. It swirled and eddied around us, pushed by nothing that I could detect.

After hundreds of patrols in hostile territory, my partner had returned from Iraq with a direct channel to a world I couldn't see. A brilliant canine intuition built on smells and sounds and God knew what else. All of it hidden to humans.

This was Clyde's gift from the war. Much like my own gift, which was visitations from the dead. Ghosts from Iraq, and from the more recently deceased.

Clyde's behavior now—the shivering, the tucked tail—struck me as the death fear. As if he'd caught a scent of something once terrible that was no longer here.

I stood, and the headlamp tossed shadows across the grass. A fly rose into the air, a dance of iridescent blue moving in and out of the light. On the ground below lay a ripped piece of peach chiffon fabric ornamented with lace and pearls. Another fly crawled along the edge, sluggish in the cold.

The cloth glimmered with fresh blood.

Clyde leaned into me while I played the light back and forth between the cross and the cloth. Taken together, the items formed an eerie tableau—as if someone was trying to send a message.

A cry for help, mute and unnoticed.

Save for the passage of a train.

CHAPTER 2

*Inside me is a monster. It allows me to see the monster in oth-
ers. The drunk at the end of the bar with the scraped knuckles.
A hot-eyed man sliding into an alley. Combat veterans with
one too many tours. Random people passing on the street.*

When our eyes meet, I see the startle of recognition on their faces.

It is never a happy acknowledgment.

—*Sydney Parnell. Personal journal.*

I spun slowly, taking in the surrounding field.

The beam from the headlamp danced over the grasses, lighting on
the ruined fence, where a crow perched. He cocked his head and held
one eye on me, then lifted weightily from the post and flapped into the
dark with the rustle of wings.

Clyde shivered against my legs.

"Damn," I said.

I looked at the cross, the gold necklace, and the length of fabric.
Mentally, I measured the distance from the cloth to the train tracks.

Now I said, "Shit."

I approached the tracks, expecting to find blood and broken bone,
a ruin of flesh that had been hidden by the darkness and the fog. An
added reason for Clyde's unease.

But the tracks were clean.

I walked east and then west along the rails for a few hundred yards but found nothing more than the desiccated carcass of an antelope. I circled back to the cross and the fabric.

A woman, the engineer had said. Standing near the tracks. There and gone as the train whipped by.

Suicide or homicide? Victim or predator?

Heinrich was six feet three. It would take a hell of a tall woman to land a blow on his skull, big a target as it was.

So where was she?

"We've got ourselves a mystery," I said to Clyde.

He looked as unhappy as I felt.

We returned to Heinrich, shouting to let him know of our approach. He'd managed to wrestle up to a sitting position, and his face had regained its color. I checked his pulse and pupils again, then went to my truck to get him some water. When I returned, I crouched and passed him the bottle.

"Sip it slowly. You still nauseous?"

"Not bad." He licked his lips, uncapped the bottle. "Did you find anything?"

"A cross. A broken necklace. And a piece of bloody fabric with two bottle flies that ought to be dead in this cold."

He narrowed his eyes at me. "What does all that mean?"

"Beats the hell out of me." I kept going back to Clyde's behavior before we found the fabric. "I don't like it."

Heinrich took a long drink. "Think it's a jumper?"

"Not unless she jumped right onto the train. I checked the tracks. You remember seeing any vehicles when you approached?"

"I—no. I mean, it's pretty fuzzy. But I would have looked around when I drove up. 'Course with the fog, there could have been a damn T. rex on the road." He frowned. "Everything after I turned onto the dirt road is a blank."

"You remember the phone call from dispatch?"

"Most of that's come back." He sipped the water. "Deke Willsby was running the southbound out of Nebraska. Said he saw a series of flashing lights, then spotted a woman standing near the tracks. I think it was a little before three a.m. when he put in the call. You know that with all the Homeland Security stuff they have to report any trespassers."

"He find the source of the lights?"

"Not that I know."

"How long was his string?"

"Information's on my phone." He tapped the screen, brought up Denver Pacific's tracking software. "A hundred and twenty-three cars. A mixed string but mainly commodities."

"Any empties?"

"A few, looks like."

I was running scenarios in my mind. "The train make a stop near here?"

Heinrich nodded, then groaned at the motion. "About ten minutes after he saw the woman, Willsby made a planned stop for a crew while they finished installing a joint bar to repair a bad piece of track. So if you're wondering, the last third of the train would have been stopped in this area for around twenty minutes. He would have pulled out just before I got here."

"So you didn't see the train?"

"I can't—" He balled his fists. A flash of panic showed in his eyes. "It's all a blank."

"That's normal, Heinrich. Blow like that. It'll come back to you." I looked at the display on his screen. The train was now at the rail yard in Denver and scheduled to move out in thirty minutes.

I handed back his phone and stood. I checked in with dispatch. The ambulance was ten minutes out. There had been a lot of accidents that morning, with the ice. Nonpriority cases were lagging.

"What are you going to do?" Heinrich asked.

"Call out the dogs. Then I'm going to head back to where I saw the cross. See if I spot anything else."

He made an effort to get his legs under him. "I'm coming, too."

"Not today, cowboy. The ambulance is almost here. And we have to call a tow for your vehicle."

He glared up at me. "Now who's being the Lone Ranger?"

I laughed. "You really do care."

Heinrich flushed. "Fine." He tossed my coat to me. "You're shivering."

"Thanks." I shrugged into the warmth. "I find anything else, I'll let you know."

As Clyde and I headed back toward where I'd found the cross, I glanced at the time on my phone's display; the night-shift unit wouldn't officially hand over responsibility for two more hours. But there was no point in getting them involved this close to the end of their shift.

"You sure about this, Clyde?"

Clyde stared into the fog, his ears now up and tipped forward.

I pushed aside any lingering doubts and made a quick series of calls.

First, I dialed Denver PD Crime Scene to ask the on-call detective to come to my location. Detective Ron Gabel's voice was thick with exhaustion when he picked up, but he promised to arrive within the hour.

Next, I woke my old boss, Deputy Chief Mauer. I told him about Heinrich and asked him to delay the train. Mauer's sleep-addled voice expressed concern about Heinrich. But he was also beside himself at what the delay would cost, all because of a cross made out of paper clips and a piece of fabric. When I pointed out that Heinrich's assailant—or a clue to her whereabouts—might be on the train, Mauer groused another minute, then ended the call with, "Consider it done. But, Parnell?"

"Yeah?"

"Don't be wrong."

With the two easiest calls out of the way, I stopped walking and stood at the line I'd mentally drawn around the crime scene, the line where crime scene tape would go. Clyde stopped next to me and took in the air. Still on guard.

I hesitated, my index finger poised over the number for my trainer-slash-partner in the Major Crimes Unit.

The faint trace of a breeze sighed past, cooling the sweat on my face.

Detective Len Bandoni had carried a hate for me for over a year. We'd met when he was my lover's partner and I was a railroad cop pulled into their murder case. Bandoni saw me as nothing more than an uppity security cop. The fact that he neither liked nor trusted women merely strengthened his animosity. In my dark moments, I figured Lieutenant Lobowitz's decision to pair us up was meant to test me and punish the antifeminist Bandoni. In even darker moods, I was certain that Lobowitz wanted to drive out the previous lieutenant's golden girl and Bandoni was the perfect man for the job.

I lifted my chin and tapped my partner's number on the screen.

He answered with a growl. "The fuck?"

I wondered if he'd bothered to check caller ID before answering. "It's Parnell."

"I got eyes," he said. "You've decided to quit?"

"Only after you're a broken man."

There was a long enough pause that I wondered if he'd set down the phone and wandered away. But then I heard him breathing.

"Bandoni, we've got something."

"What?"

I filled him in on what had happened—the woman seen by the engineer, Heinrich's assault, the cross, the necklace, and the bloody fabric. The fact that the train had been stopped in the area for half an hour.

"Those flies," I said. "They had to come off the train. They'd be dead otherwise. As soon as the crime scene detective gets here, I'm heading to DPC's rail yard to look over the train."

"Look it over for what?"

I blinked.

He said, "You think whoever nailed your railroad cop will be sitting on the caboose, painting her nails and waiting for you to show up?"

"There aren't cabooses anymore."

"Screw the caboose. What's your point?"

"My point is that maybe we're looking for another victim, in addition to Heinrich," I said. "Maybe someone hurt or killed the woman and placed her on the train."

"Murder? How do you get murder out of a couple of paper clips and a piece of, what did you call it, *peach chiffon*?"

"And blood."

"And *maybe* blood."

I kicked at a clump of grass. I hadn't expected Bandoni to pat me on the back. But I hadn't expected him to fight me, either.

"We can't just ignore this," I pressed. "This woman could be—"

"Stop." Bandoni gusted a sigh that would have rattled oaks. "I ain't faulting your enthusiasm. You're young. You're new. You've got a lot to prove. I get that. But it's not our job to find people. Not dead people and not live people. The way it works is, someone finds a body. Or someone sees someone get whacked. And they pick up the phone, and they call us. *Then* we go and check it out. You get what I'm saying? So if there's a body on that train, someone will find it. And then they'll call us."

"If we don't search the train while it's stopped in Denver, *days* could go by before someone finds the body."

"*If* there's a body. What you've got, Parnell, is peach chiffon. We want to stop and search a train? Then we need probable cause to get a warrant. Or permission from the railroad. I'm sure they told you about that in cop school."

I watched the mist thin to the weight of spider silk while Bandoni launched into a lecture about reasonable suspicion versus probable cause. He was being an asshole, hammering home things I already knew.

"*And*," he went on, "*if* there *is* a body, by then it will be in someone else's jurisdiction."

Now he was testing me. If someone had been killed in Denver, it was Denver's case. And no self-respecting murder cop would try to pass the buck. For detectives, finding a killer was a moral obligation.

I kept kicking at the grass while my pulse jackhammered under my jaw. I wanted to tell Bandoni about my sixth sense, my war-given superpower. And about Clyde's canine clairvoyance. But doing so would be like handing Bandoni a shovel while I stood next to an open grave.

"What's up with you playing pass the buck?" I said, calling him on his bluff.

"The hell's that supposed to mean?"

Under the force of my kicks, the dirt around the grass came loose in clots. "I mean why do you want to dump this on a department in another jurisdiction? Even if it's only an assault, it's our assault."

"What's up with *me*? You need to pull your head out of your pretty little ass. We got a caseload longer than my dick, and you call me at five in the morning to tell me you've spotted a unicorn you want to chase instead of doing the work that is *already on your desk*."

His voice boomed over the speaker. Clyde looked up, a frown between his dark eyes.

My shoulders came up. "You know damn well that if we wait, it's going to be that much harder to find Heinrich's assailant. Not to mention a killer, if that's what we've got. We won't be *hours* behind. Whoever catches this will be *days* late. And we both know what that means when it comes to solving cases."

Another long silence on the phone. Far away but coming closer, the call of a siren rose and fell. I stared across the field at the necklace with its ugly, red spatter of blood. At the torn cloth.

Bandoni said, "How do you even know it's blood?"

I took that as victory. "There are flies all over it." Two flies, perhaps, did not count as a multitude. But I didn't elaborate.

"Chocolate looks just like blood."

"That's why I called Crime Scene. To tell us if it's blood. And if it's human."

"Ah, Jesus."

"Someone knocked a railroad cop unconscious," I reminded him.

"Probably thought it was you," Bandoni muttered.

"Excuse me?"

"Look, Parnell. I'm not arguing that there was a crime. The assault on the railroad bull for starters. Felony right there. I get that you're all hot under the collar to find whoever nailed your friend. But there's no body. Even if it's blood, that dress could be from ages ago. Or maybe the mysterious woman spotted by your engineer cut herself shaving. Maybe she sliced her wrists, and when it didn't take, she drove herself home. That would make the most sense, right? She got into her car instead of on a train." He grunted. "You got to have more dots before you start connecting them."

I opened my mouth. Closed it. Acknowledged to myself that an unconscious cop, an anxious dog, and a piece of bloody fabric did not a murder make.

"Start thinking like a cop," he said. "Turn it over to the guys handling assaults. If someone finds a corpse while that train's still in Denver, then it'll be ours."

"But—"

"Or go right on down to the rail yard. Poke around to your heart's content. See if I give a fuck. Then explain it all to the lieutenant when you finally get in to work."

He hung up.

I looked at Clyde, who returned my gaze with a furrowed brow.

"You think I'm crazy, partner? If I'm wrong about what we're looking at, this could end our career before it even starts."

Clyde leaned against me. I rested my hand on the curve of his skull. Dogs were more honest than people, more in touch with the things we tried to explain away. As far as Clyde was concerned, *something* had gone down here.

But Bandoni was right. No body, no missing-persons report, no witnesses other than a sleepy engineer working the midnight shift who might have been making mermaids out of manatees.

I had only my partner. And my gut.

And sometimes that was all you had.

Because sometimes people just . . . vanished.

And not of their own volition.

I couldn't let it go.

CHAPTER 3

I don't need saving. I can be my own damn white knight.

—*Sydney Parnell. Conversation with Detective Michael*
Cohen.

Detective Ron Gabel of the Denver Crime Lab arrived five minutes after the ambulance left with Heinrich. Clyde and I went to greet him as he pulled in next to my Tahoe.

Gabel unfolded his lean body from behind the steering wheel and stepped into the predawn. A tall man with close-cropped gray hair, focused blue eyes, and a lively expression, Gabel had been a cop for longer than I'd been alive, even if he didn't carry himself like a man twice my age. Marathons. Fourteeners. He was the starting pitcher for the department's baseball team—Crime Scene dicks against detectives from Major Crimes. Crime Scene always won, and Gabel was the biggest part of that.

He had bags under those baby blues now, though. And he'd skipped the shave.

I said, "I got you out of bed, I hope."

"Sofa. I was taking twenty."

We shook hands, and then he squatted and gave the fur along Clyde's neck and back a good roughing.

I was anxious to get to the crime scene. But I let Gabel set the tempo.

"Busy night?" I asked.

"A stabbing outside a bar on Eleventh. You know the place with the mechanical bull and two-dollar drinks from ten to midnight? I don't know if it's the alcohol or the bull that turns men into either poets or fighters. Then I caught a hit-and-run on Downing." He closed the car door, moved toward the trunk. "Don't take this wrong, Sydney, but I'm hoping you've got a whole lot of nothing."

"You talked to Bandoni."

"He said you were a little uncertain about the evidence."

"I'm guessing those weren't the words he used."

Gabel smiled and popped the trunk. "I got the gist."

He rummaged a headlamp out of a plastic crate, then passed a large canvas bag to me. I heard the clink of stakes as I swung the strap over my shoulder. Gabel grabbed a silver-sided case and closed the trunk.

"Look," I said. "If it's nothing, then all we've lost are a few hours and a little sleep. Right?"

I didn't mention the delay-of-train costs.

"Spoken like a detective," Gabel said. "Why don't you show me what you've got."

I gestured in the direction of the tracks. "This way."

Ron Gabel was one of the best crime scene guys working for Denver PD, according to pretty much everyone. I knew this personally from our brief encounters when I'd been a railway cop, and also from our conversations around the project I'd been assigned as part of my three-week training period: processing years-old rape cases that had never been solved. Gabel had agreed to help me with the backlog of rape kits, and he both guided me through the process and shared the load. In his late fifties, he'd been around long enough to see things change in the department. Not just new technology, he told me, but a changing culture. Like new dress codes and the rule against cursing in the detectives' room. We'd gone from being cowboys to toe-the-line professionals. No one was sure if the change was for the best.

I stopped next to the clump of grass I'd destroyed earlier and pointed.

"I figured we'd run tape here," I said. "The soiled cloth and the rest of it is just over that rise."

"Seems about right." He paused long enough to push a single stake into the ground. "Let's get closer."

With the world growing lighter, the makeshift cross seemed even more forlorn than before. Weightless, almost invisible. I imagined the woman bending down, pushing the thin wire into the hard earth. Removing her necklace just before someone grabbed her dress and ripped it.

Gabel's voice brought me back. "You make that mark?"

I followed the direction of his finger. On the far side of the cross, a section of the soil had been smoothed flat, with a little ridge of dirt on each side.

I shook my head. "I didn't get that close."

"Sure looks like someone scraped across the ground with the toe of their shoe. Or a boot, rather. That might be a bit of a waffle pattern." Gabel squatted, let his hands dangle between his knees. "But there's something else there as well. Part of a word, maybe. You see? The only thing left is at the end of the scrape. Looks like part of a capital letter *T*. Or maybe an *L*. Even a *P*."

"She wrote something."

"Could be."

"Then someone wiped it out."

"Might be one and the same person." He pulled his silver case close and popped the lid. "You find any other footprints?"

"No. And I was careful."

"Maybe you should have another look around. For footprints. For anything else."

"Right." I stared at the cloth. "Does it look like blood to you? On the necklace and the fabric?"

"Let's find out. I'll run a presumptive." He pulled out a camera, snapped photos of the fabric, then removed four dropper bottles.

"The Kastle-Meyer test," I said.

"You were paying attention in class." He placed a drop of water on a swab, then leaned over the fabric and dabbed the swab on a corner of the stain. He next added a drop of ethanol to the swab, followed by phenolphthalein and a drop of hydrogen peroxide.

The swab turned pale pink.

I released the breath I'd been holding. "It's blood."

"Mammalian." He nodded. "I'll run a precipitin test as soon as I'm back in the office to see if what we've got is animal or human. That will get us over the next hurdle." He closed up the bottles and rubbed his jaw. "I'm going to start by taking photos. Why don't you string tape? When we're done here, you can show me where the railway cop was assaulted."

Forty-five minutes later, Gabel had taken photographs of both scenes, and I'd strung crime scene tape after doing another search for prints. I'd found nothing. This area of eastern Denver consisted of grass, cactus, and antelope droppings, with very little exposed dirt.

"What do you think?" I asked when he rejoined me.

"No way to tell right now," he said, taking the roll of remaining tape. "I've learned the hard way not to pass judgment too soon."

"Unlike Bandoni."

"Don't let him get under your skin. He's got a big bark, but his bite isn't bad. He listened to what you found, and now he's looking for the simplest solution."

"Occam's razor. He brings it up all the time."

"It works pretty well."

The crow was back at the fence. It gave a deep caw that rattled my spine.

"Don't start second-guessing yourself now," Gabel said. "This is normal procedure, Parnell. You're doing it right."

"From your lips to the lieutenant's ears."

He laughed.

"You get down to the rail yard," he said. "If you find anything, let me know, and I'll come back out here with the van. For now, I'm going to take a few samples and bag everything. I'll be in touch later today."

The fog thinned as Clyde and I walked back to the truck, and the world shouldered into view as a series of low hills. Light simmered along the ground. The fog changed from the color of ashes to pearl and then to opals, as if the world were dragging itself up from hell.

Away from the crime scenes, Clyde became pure dog. His tail swished, his tongue lolled. He nudged up against me, then bounded ahead in the direction of the vehicle. He bore only a faint limp from when he'd been shot six months earlier by a man trying to keep secrets from the world.

My sense of service—instilled by the Marines—was one reason I'd switched from railroad bull to murder cop. But Clyde was an even bigger reason. My original, post-Iraq decision to work on the trains had been meant to provide the two of us enough quiet and space to heal from the war. But things hadn't worked out that way, and Clyde had been injured twice. My lover, Detective Michael Walker Cohen, assured me that being a murder cop was nothing like what you saw on TV. It was more a matter of single-minded persistence, sitting in front of a computer screen or working the phone. Making the occasional walk across the plaza to the crime lab. Lots of paperwork, lots of witness interviews. Lots of time spent waiting.

As I watched my canine partner celebrate the day, all that sounded pretty good.

I reached for my phone, wanting to call Cohen. To get his advice. But I hesitated. Cohen had transferred to the sex crimes unit three months ago—he had his own caseload to deal with. Plus, I'd promised myself I'd make it on my own and not lean on my boyfriend. I didn't want to succeed because I had a former murder cop in my back pocket.

I let my hand drop.

My counselor had pointed out something when I told him about my career change. That perhaps I hoped to find in the police department that same sense of family I'd had with the Marines.

That sounded good, too, if I could work my way past Bandoni.

But I missed the trains.

Clyde came running back. I dropped my hand to his head, ran my fingers along the sensitive edges of his ears.

Then I let all my doubts about pursuing this new path roll over me. I breathed in the cold prairie air and imagined the rumble of a train. I held myself still for two minutes. Five.

Then I let it go. However this worked out, we'd manage. The only way to get through this world was to keep moving forward, doing your best not to trip.

A flat, silver sun heaved itself above the horizon, unspooling a line of mercury where earth met sky.

"Let's get to work, boy."

CHAPTER 4

In war, there is no future. You do not count on another sunrise, another birthday, old age. You take only that day.

None of us knows what lies ahead. But war rolls up the horizon and sets it down right outside your door.

—*Sydney Parnell. Personal journal.*

I dialed Bandoni as I drove. By now, the workday was underway, and my absence from the office would be obvious.

"I'm on my way to the rail yard," I said.

"Not going to let it go, are you?"

"Not until I'm sure."

"I heard a lot of veterans are suicidal."

"It's the company they keep."

"Ha ha." Another of his gusting sighs. "I'm throwing up a smoke screen for you, partner. But you should know that the sergeant's been asking when you'll be in. So has the Lobster. I don't know if she's just checking up on you or if there's something else going on."

Lieutenant Lobowitz, a.k.a. the Lobster. One of the detectives had given her the nickname because of the way she turned bright red when she was angry. Which was often. My mind flashed to the stack of rape kits on my desk, and unease fluttered in my chest. "She say anything specific?"

"Nope. I told her you were working something, and you'd be in as soon as you could."

"Thanks."

"There's your one pass, gift-wrapped with a bow. What did Gabel say about the scene?"

"Too soon to tell. Except the stain on the fabric is mammal blood."

"You take my advice and call someone about your buddy with the dent in his skull?"

The rising sun bounced off the rearview mirror. I tilted it. "A detective is going to the hospital to talk to him."

"And he's still drawing a blank?"

"So far."

"Fucking railroad cops. For the record, Parnell, you are one pain in the ass. I'll keep you covered with the Lobster. But either move fast or bring us something."

That shaved a few ounces off the ten-pound stone in my stomach. "Will do. And thanks."

"Don't thank me. If this turns out to be nothing, you're gonna have your own personal blood-spatter problem. The sergeant's up in arms, and the lieutenant's giving me the evil eye. And there's the fact we got real work to do. Starting with those rape kits the chief is asking for. The *chief*. Remember him? Guy who signs your paychecks."

He hung up.

◆　◆　◆

Half an hour later I walked into the control tower at Denver Pacific Continental to get a feel for the magnitude of our problem and see if I could rustle up some help.

DPC's yardmaster was a taciturn Russian American named Sergei Illych. His parents had fled the USSR for the US in the late fifties, when Sergei was twelve. I knew this because Sergei and I had gotten drunk one night at Joe's Tavern after a company holiday party, and he'd been in a rare, whiskey-induced mood to talk. He was well more than twice my age, but we got along fine due to a shared love of fine spirits and a vast experience with trauma. Ever since that night, I think he had a special fondness for me, as he would for anyone who could hold both her liquor and his secrets.

When Clyde and I entered the control room, he was staring out at the morning sun, a cup of some ill-smelling brew raised halfway to his lips, the steam curling up like a question mark. Through the glass, the yard was mostly quiet. My train, the train that might or might not hold a body, sat idle. In contrast to the rest of the yard, the roundhouse on the south end of the yard was bustling. As DPC faced budget cuts due to the reduction of long-distance freight, we—*they*—depended more and more on patching up the old trains.

"You see that coupler on Big Red," Sergei said without preamble. He could read trains the way a radiologist read MRIs. "Looks like a crack."

I stared. "I don't see anything."

"Your eyes are untrained." He sipped from his cup and finally glanced at me. "The look on your face. I would say you had a fight with your best friend, but he's right over there, watching you. Man's best friend. Woman's, too, I think."

"I've only officially been a detective for three weeks, and I'm going to get busted back down to patrol."

He raised an eyebrow. "Tell me."

"I need a dead person on that train."

"So very Russian." The other eyebrow went up. "There are ways."

"Put away your Makarov, Boris." I gestured out the window. "How many cars?"

"Deputy Chief Mauer did the calculations and determined which cars were most likely in the area when the train was stopped. That brings it down to maybe forty cars."

"Tell me about those forty."

"Half of them are refrigerated cars coming out of Nebraska. Packed to the gills with chickens. Or rather, packed to the wattles. Also, we have fertilizer. And paper and lumber all the way from Canada. A few empties."

"Box or flat?"

"Box."

I perked up. I'd mentally eliminated the refrigerator cars—they would be sealed by plug doors, which required special equipment to open. And while the cars with fertilizer and the other commodities deserved a look, they would likely be too full to accommodate an injured woman. Or a corpse.

But the empties were another matter.

I made my voice soft and sweet. "Sergei."

"Whatever it is, the answer is no."

"You have a few track laborers or repair guys you can spare?"

"Look at these bags under my eyes. Do I look like I have *anything* to spare?"

"Next two rounds at Joe's Tavern are on me."

He eyed me. "You would make a good Russian. In the mother country, everything is barter." He set down his cup. "The crew that was on the line earlier is coming in, probably holding their dicks in one hand and their lunches in the other. I can start them on the far end."

"Tell them to focus on the empties."

"And that we are looking for Jimmy Hoffa?"

"Who?"

"A corpse."

"Yes." I nodded. "Or someone hurt. Or signs of either of those. Basically, tell them to look for anything that doesn't look like it should."

He picked up the phone, yelled something to whoever answered about checking out the train with their lazy, fat heads and not their lazy, fat asses, threw in some Russian to make it sound intimidating, then hung up and gave me a honeyed smile that was completely at odds with the vitriol he'd just been spewing.

"No problem," he said.

"What's your favorite vodka?"

"I hate vodka."

"You're Russian."

"Vodka is the opium of the masses. It explains everything that happened after the revolution. I can't even look a potato in the eye. In a manner of speaking."

"Single malt, then. Cheers."

His grin transformed his face. *"Na Zdorovie."*

I found my old boss down in the yard. Deputy Chief Jim Mauer had pulled coveralls over his DPC uniform and now walked alongside the train, rattling handles and peering underneath the carriages.

"I am too damn old for this," he said when I approached.

"A little exercise is good for you."

"What's good for me is trains that run on time. Much better for my blood pressure. Did you know I have high blood pressure?"

"I suspected."

"And that you're a big part of that?"

"Think of me as your inducement to start an exercise program."

"Bah."

Mauer and I had a long history of him applying the brakes to my runaway train. A Chicago boy, he had adapted well to Denver and established himself as a good boss and even better mentor. It had been Mauer who encouraged me to stretch myself by going into homicide.

By that measure, he was only getting what he deserved.

Mauer scratched a willing Clyde behind the ears, then reached into the pocket of his overalls and came up with a doggy biscuit. Clyde's eyes lit up.

"Softie," I said.

Mauer tossed the biscuit, and Clyde snatched it out of the air.

"He looks thin. You been feeding him?"

"Vegan kibble."

Mauer narrowed his eyes at me before recognizing the sarcasm. He scowled, planted his hands in his lower back, and leaned into the arch of his spine. He stared down the length of the train. "Couldn't stay away, could you?"

"I knew you'd miss me."

"You have any idea what this is costing?"

"Almost exactly." I kicked at the gravel with my fresh-out-of-the-box sensible pumps, now stained with grass and mud. My new job dictated a wardrobe of somber-colored pantsuits and equally somber blouses, shoes, and belts. Somber as a fashion statement was right up my alley. But I missed my steel-toed boots and the mindless consistency of a uniform.

I said, "Sergei's pulling in some crewmen to help."

"Good." Mauer finally took a good look at me. He opened his mouth. Shut it. Surprised by the suit, I suppose. He said, "You'll get filthy in that getup. Go back inside and find yourself some coveralls. Then why don't you and Clyde take the far side?"

Twenty minutes later I'd broken two fingernails while pulling myself up to examine something on the side of a car, and turned my ankle when I stepped off the ladder in my sensible pumps.

All for nothing. By the time Mauer and I caught up with the repair crew working their way toward us, my heart had clawed its way into my throat and put up a no vacancy sign.

"Anything?" I asked the men as they approached.

"Nothing but train," said a man with a red bandanna tied around his neck. He appeared to be the lead of the three-man crew.

I said, "You looked in every empty?"

"That's what we were told to do. That's what we did."

"You see anything at all?"

"Graffiti. Two empty liquor bottles and a beer can. That any help?"

They were pissed about using their break for a snipe hunt. I wondered if they'd complain to the union.

"What about the flatbeds? Any chance that—"

"Tight as a drum. No movement." He glared. "Okay with you if we take our break now?"

"One second."

I felt Mauer's gaze on me. I didn't look at him—I couldn't take either his pity or his anger.

"And the refrigerator cars," I said. "Those were sealed?"

"Sure," said the man.

"You checked?"

"Didn't have to. You can't have a plug door that ain't sealed."

Modern-day refrigerator cars used plug doors. Heavier than normal doors, the plugs were designed to roll shut either vertically or horizontally along a track and then move inward to form a tight seal. It was a violation to move plug-door cars with the doors open—the cars were checked by the shipper and the crew before the train departed. And on the off chance that a door was left open, the motion of the train would almost certainly close it.

"I want to confirm it," I said.

"Sydney—" Mauer began.

"If I'm going down, I'm going down swinging."

"One of them did stink," one of the men volunteered. A big-boned guy with a Santa Claus beard. "Like chicken left out to spoil."

My heart, still somewhere in my throat, gave a little kick. I gestured down the length of the train. "Show me."

"I didn't smell nothing," said Red Bandanna.

"That's 'cause you need to give up the smokes. You can't smell shit when you're in the bathroom."

◆ ◆ ◆

We caught the stench before the car came into view. A putrid smell like what you got if you tossed chicken scraps in the trash. Only much worse.

Santa Claus grinned. "Smell it now?"

"Damn eyes are watering," Red Bandanna said.

At the car, we stopped to take in the scene.

The importance of first impressions was drilled into detectives during training. You only got your first view of a crime scene once. After that, your brain started sorting everything, deciding what was important and what wasn't. This subconscious process could give you tunnel vision. So I took a moment to study the boxcar. It was typical for its kind—white with a horizontal sliding plug door set in the middle. A logo on the car's side indicated the unit was owned by ColdShip Distributors, a hub-to-hub refrigerated-boxcar service that provided warehouse-to-train cargo transfer across the US. ColdShip had a hub in North Platte, Nebraska, which meant the frozen chickens had probably originated from a poultry-processing facility nearby.

Vandals had hit the car somewhere along the route. Recently, judging by the brightness of the paint. The graffiti was to the left of the door, a stylized design of uncertain meaning, spray-painted in black, blue, and yellow.

"I hate taggers," Mauer said.

I nodded. While taggers consider themselves artists and daredevils, to the railroad companies they are a hazard and an expense.

I thought of the woman spotted by the engineer. A tagger equipped with spray paint who just happened to be in the middle of nowhere when a train came to a halt? Not impossible—taggers went to great lengths to find a place where they could practice their art undisturbed. Some even listened to railroad communications on a scanner so they would know when and where trains would be stopped on their routes.

But it was a long shot. And it didn't explain everything else I'd found.

Even so, I took a picture of the car along with a close-up of the graffiti. Then I turned to Red Bandanna. His name was embroidered over a pocket of his coveralls.

"Tabor," I said. "Can you request a door buster please?"

He looked at Mauer, who nodded.

Tabor shrugged. "Sure, if that's what you want."

Ten minutes later, one of the track laborers drove up in a forklift, a door buster mounted on the forks.

Tabor raised his voice. "Everyone stand back. If that door's been damaged, the whole thing could come off."

We moved away and watched while the driver used the portable bully plug and wench to turn the handle and then pull the door open along its track. The door didn't fall or buckle. But as it opened, a tide of stench washed over us.

"That is some bad shit," Tabor said.

Clyde wagged his tail.

The driver backed the forklift away and turned off the engine but left the cable in place, holding the door open. An incessant hum filled the air; after a moment, I realized it was the sound of flies. Confirming that the two I'd seen earlier were escapees.

My phone buzzed. Bandoni. I refused the call, then ordered Clyde to stay while I approached the open door.

The sun hung in the morning sky, and since we were on the west side of the train, the door yawned into shadows. I yanked on my headlamp and stepped closer, peering inside.

Fiberboard cartons filled the interior. All of them were wet and dripping slime, testament to Nebraska's unusual heat wave. The boxes were soggy, the cardboard disintegrating, and the stacks had begun to collapse. There was enough space in the car that some of the boxes had fallen and smashed open on the floor, scattering shrink-wrapped chickens that continued to seep slime.

A strange mix of relief and disappointment hit me along with the odor.

No body. No murder.

I stepped away from the car.

"Nothing but chickens?" Mauer asked.

I nodded. The adrenaline I'd felt at the discovery subsided to a dull wash of agitation that popped and sizzled in my blood.

"You had to check," Mauer said without conviction.

I nodded. Equally without conviction. I pulled out my phone to return Bandoni's call, let him know I'd been wrong, wondering if I should just go ahead and resign.

I hesitated with my finger poised.

If the door had been closed the entire time, then the refrigeration unit must have failed. But how had the flies escaped?

I glanced at my partner. He'd stopped wagging his tail. His ears were back.

Cohen's voice rose in my mind. I'd been struggling with a murder case I was reviewing in a textbook. No matter how many times I looked at the photographs, I couldn't see anything but a woman who'd been snatched by the bad guys, stripped naked, mutilated for fun, then dumped outside of town. She was sprawled on her back, her legs spread apart. Her clothes were scattered along a dirt road, as if the bad guys had tossed them out the window as they drove away.

You're making assumptions, Cohen had told me. *Look at the injuries again. Widen the scene. Look at the surroundings. Keep your mind as open as your eyes.*

He'd been right. Which I'd realized once I noticed the prints in the snow and reexamined the woman's throat. She'd fallen victim, not to human predators, but to a pair of wolf dogs.

I removed a sealed package of gloves and a packet of booties from my new leather satchel—a farewell gift from my railroad friends.

"What are you doing?" Mauer asked.

"Just going to take a closer look."

"Yeah?"

"Yeah."

"Sure you don't want an oxygen mask?"

I studied the door track for a moment. Scratch marks—faint but new looking—marred the bottom of the track.

Interesting.

I used the grip bar to pull myself into the train. Once inside, I stared around at the disintegrating boxes. The car had been poorly loaded, and the cargo had shifted as the train went through the normal motions of braking and acceleration. Not only had the cargo been poorly stacked, the boxes hadn't been placed in receptacles or strapped to the locking rings on the wall that were designed to hold cargo in position. I made a mental note to check who at ColdShip had loaded the cargo.

I made a second mental note to tell Mauer about it instead. Not my job anymore.

I closed my eyes, focusing. I caught the faintest whiff of something beneath the reek of thawing chickens.

Excrement. Coupled with the vinegary stink of urine. And the ancient, iron-dark smell of blood.

I opened my eyes and flicked on the headlamp.

Shadows jumped and swayed as I picked my way across the slime-slick floor and along the corridor formed by the slumping walls of boxes. The place looked like it had been raided by the proverbial fox in the henhouse, with thawed chickens tossed left and right.

Except in this case, the fox hadn't taken something away. The fox had perhaps left something.

My pulse thumping in my neck, I shoved a box out of my way and moved to the far end of the car. The light caught on a shape half-hidden by the boxes and chickens. It took a second for me to realize what I was looking at.

A pair of naked human feet.

My heart did a backflip off the diving board of my breastbone.

I took two more steps and moved the beam of light up a pair of pale, hairy legs—a man's legs. Then came swirls of pale chiffon fabric, bloodied and torn, twisted around the legs and torso. A pair of large-knuckled hands. A hint of solid chest near the neckline of the ruined dress.

And finally, the head.

Or what was left of it. The skull was crushed, the face destroyed.

A horde of flies swarmed the corpse.

I jumped back, slipped in the ooze, went down on one knee.

My nostrils filled with grains of desert sand, my ears with the thump of helicopter rotors. I heard my commanding officer, the Sir, shouting orders. A shaft of moonlight dropped through a break in the clouds and illuminated a row of body bags. I reached to grab the end of one of the bags, to lift it onto the gurney as I squinted against the backwash from the rotors.

Far away, Clyde barked. Once. Twice. I blinked and returned to the boxcar with its piles of thawing chickens.

And a dead man.

"Damn it," I whispered.

I got to my feet and stumbled back through the boxes to the door. I jumped down from the train.

"Parnell?" Mauer's voice broke through my dismay. "You okay?"

I held my filthy gloved hands out to my sides as I bent at the waist and sucked in air. Clyde broke his stay and came to my side.

When I was sure the world wasn't going to go black, I straightened.

Tabor was watching me closely. "Guess there's something in there 'sides chickens."

Mauer set a hand on my shoulder. "What is it?"

"Your rail yard is about to turn into a circus." I stripped off the gloves and let them drop to the ground, then pulled out my phone and hit redial.

Bandoni answered with, "You must just love patrol. I'm thinking Green Valley Ranch again."

"Corpus delicti," I said and hung up.

CHAPTER 5

Peter: You do know that working in homicide means viewing corpses.

Sydney: This is me, rolling my eyes.

Peter: What I mean is, you've been making real progress. Dealing with death on a daily basis could be . . . counterproductive. And I'm not talking just any death. This is the worst kind.

Sydney: I've already seen the worst kind.

Peter: You said you wanted that behind you.

Sydney: In Iraq, I handled our dead with profound respect. But—there's a difference.

Peter: Tell me.

Sydney: Back then, I couldn't get the motherfuckers who killed them.

—Conversation with Peter Hayes, Clinical Therapist, VA Hospital.

Within an hour, the crime scene detectives, the medical examiner and her crew, and the great Detective Leonard Bandoni himself had descended on Denver Pacific Continental's rail yard. Bandoni took lead while I watched and learned. My partner could be less than pleasant, but when he was working a crime scene he turned into a man of thrilling grace. Pointing here, directing there. Assessing, guiding, questioning, analyzing.

Bandoni conducted our somber band like a maestro.

Once the ME, Emma Bell, had removed the body, Bandoni gave Mauer permission to disconnect the car and relocate it to the shelter of the roundhouse so that the rest of the train could get underway. I broke free to get additional information from Sergei about the train—points of origin for the various commodities and a timeline for the refrigerator cars. Then I stripped off the coveralls, cleaned my filthy shoes with paper towels in the women's restroom, and washed up in the sink.

A cautious sniff suggested I wasn't entirely free of *odeur de poulet*. Clyde found my shoes particularly entrancing. But at last, semiclean and somewhat composed, I told Clyde to act like a Malinois instead of a pointer, and we went to find the man who'd been driving the train, Deke Willsby.

Deke sat at a folding table in the basement-level employee lounge, nursing a cup of coffee in the otherwise deserted room. A career engineer in his sixties, Deke sat hunched in his chair like he was braced for bad news and halfway on his knees in preparation. He'd looked that way the last time I'd seen him—after his train had struck and killed the victim of a kidnapping.

Ah, damn, I thought. *No one told him.*

He straightened and released the cup as I dropped into a chair across from him. I leaned over the table and took his cold fingers in my own.

"You didn't hit anyone," I said.

He lifted his gaze. "Say again?"

"Someone either climbed into that car or was placed there. A man. His death had nothing to do with your train." I squeezed his fingers, then released them. "I'm sorry you thought it did."

Deke's eyes cleared slowly, like fog burning off. After a moment, he picked up the cup, drained the contents.

"Well." He cleared his throat. "That's something, then."

I busied myself finding coins in my satchel, ignoring the sudden sheen in his eyes. "More coffee?"

"Black, please." He puffed air. "This is a load off, I have to tell you."

"I bet." I bought two coffees at the vending machines, excused myself while I filled Clyde's water bowl, then resumed my seat. By then, Deke was himself again.

"This have anything to do with the woman I saw?" he asked.

"That's what we're trying to determine." I set my phone on the table and got Deke's permission to record our conversation. I also pulled out a notebook and pen. First rule when interviewing witnesses: don't count on the technology.

I began. "Why don't you walk me through last night and this morning? Start with where you picked up the string."

"That was yesterday, at the Bailey Yard in North Platte. The string originated in Columbus, but the Bailey was where I came in. They added fifty cars there."

"Including the refrigerator cars?"

"Yep. All the reefers came from a local warehouse, where they'd been cross docked—trucks to boxcars. A twenty-four-hour stay at the warehouse in between. Picked up some empties, too. I ran all the normal safety checks and headed out before dark."

"This was after you got the go-ahead from the yardmaster?"

"Sure."

"Bailey's a busy yard."

"Always is."

"Once your string was built, do you know who did the inspection?"

Deke shook his head. "Only person I talked to was the yardmaster."

"He seem distracted?"

A shrug. "He was busier than a one-legged man in an ass-kicking contest, that's for sure. But it's always like that."

I made a note. An overworked yardmaster and crew could explain how an open plug door was missed. But not how the door managed to stay open long enough for all the chickens to thaw. And for our victim to get inside.

"How many stops did you make before you got to Denver?"

"Two. First was Ogallala. That's where we picked up the fertilizer."

"Anything unusual about the pickup?"

"Nope. Went right as planned. The second was the one you know about. The delay for the repair."

"Tell me about that."

"Just outside Sterling I got word from dispatch that a crew was installing a joint near Denver. When I got the first notice it was just an FYI. They expected to be finished with the repair before I came through. But you know how it goes."

Whenever a section of rail is damaged, a repair crew has to cut a new piece to patch the gap. The workers burn or drill holes at the ends of the rails, then bolt the new joint bar in place. If the weather is bad or if the track is in worse shape than expected, delays occur.

I made a note to get a copy of the work order for our records. But joint-bar installations were common; I didn't expect the order to reveal anything.

I said, "What happened next?"

"I got the word from dispatch that I'd definitely be making a stop. So I started keeping an eye out. Especially in the kind of fog we had last night. If you know there might be crew on the track, you have to be vigilant."

"Is that how you happened to see the woman?"

"Yep. If not for that planned stop, I probably would have missed her. Before I saw the woman, though, I spotted lights."

"Heinrich mentioned that."

Deke nodded. "Up ahead, pretty dim in the fog. Couldn't tell what they were."

"Moving or stationary?"

"Moving. A cluster of them. Five or six, I'd guess. They were well away from the tracks, but soon as I saw them, I started braking, worried dispatch had given me the wrong location."

"Headlights? Flashlights?"

"Could have been either. Or both. Could have been a UFO for all I know. But they were bright enough for me to pick them out over the glare of my running lights."

The compressor on one of the vending machines clanked on, echoing in the low-ceilinged space. I took in the odor of overheated plastic wrap and warmed leftovers—a mix of tomato sauce and beans and tuna casserole. My stomach rumbled, a reminder that I hadn't eaten since last night's dinner.

My gastronomic bar was set pretty low.

Under the table, Clyde snored softly, oblivious. His bar was set higher.

I made a note about the lights, then spent the next few minutes clarifying timing, rate of speed, and other details with Deke. When I was satisfied with the timeline, I said, "So you had already started braking before you saw the woman. Because of the lights."

He nodded. "Afraid it might be the crew."

"And where was the woman?"

"Standing just north of the tracks. Out of range of the ditch lights and the event recorder. But still too damn close."

North. That would place her on the side of the tracks where the road ran. I made another note. "It was dark. And foggy. How were you able to see her?"

"Fog was pretty bad," Deke admitted. "But she had a flashlight. Probably one of the lights I saw. And the way she was holding it was strange."

"In what way?"

"Well, if she was a railfan, just someone who wanted to see the train, she would've held the light away from her, right? Maybe pointed it toward the ground so she wasn't half-blind." Deke's gaze had gone somewhere else as he slipped into the memory. "But she was holding the flashlight under her chin. Made it so it lit up her face. Put me in mind of how we used to tell ghost stories as kids."

Interesting. "Do you think she wanted you to see her?"

"That's for sure how it seemed."

"And you saw her face clearly?"

"Yeah. Well, sort of. It was so quick. She was there and then gone. I was still going pretty fast at that point."

"What else did you notice?"

"She was a bitty thing. Skinny. And I got the sense she was short."

"You saw more than her face, then?"

"I guess I must've. I noticed that flashlight. It was a doozy."

"What do you mean?"

"It looked like my big tactical light. Long and heavy."

I flashed to the lump on Heinrich's skull. "Did you see the other lights again?"

"Maybe. Off in the distance. But maybe they were just ghost lights. Will-o'-the-wisps." He flushed, then shrugged apologetically. "Easy to get superstitious on midnight runs."

"Tell me what the woman looked like. Her face."

He finished his coffee and pushed away the cup. His gaze went toward the ceiling as he thought back. "She was Mexican. Or whatever they call themselves these days. Hispanic."

"It depends on where they're from."

"What?"

"What they call themselves depends on where they're from. Anyway, what makes you say she was from south of the border?"

"Black hair. Brown skin." He shrugged. "You know."

"Young or old?"

He laughed, gave a soft shake of his head. "These days, anyone who doesn't have to tweeze their nose hairs looks twelve to me."

"A teenager maybe?"

He considered. "Older than that. But not by a lot. Early twenties. A little younger than you, would be my guess."

"What about clothes? Did you see what she was wearing?"

He shook his head. "Too dark."

"Anything else? Take your time, Deke. Close your eyes, see if you can pull up her image."

We were in dangerous waters. I didn't want to steer Deke into creating false details merely because of the normal human desire to please the interviewer.

But I needed information.

Deke did as I asked, tilting his chair back so it rested on two legs and closing his eyes. After a moment he let the chair fall forward, opened his eyes, and rested his palms on the table. "That's as much as I got, Sydney. Sorry."

"No, this is all great, Deke. Thanks."

"Yep." His phone buzzed, and he glanced at it. "Looks like they're ready for me to haul that train on down the road."

We both stood. Clyde woke, lifted his head. Across the room, Bandoni appeared in the doorway.

I said, "When you get back to Denver, Deke, why don't you plan on coming down to the station? I'll get in a sketch artist, see if we can give this woman a face."

"Sure." He nodded. "I'll be back in Denver late this afternoon."

"I'll arrange something for this evening and give you a call with the time."

We shook hands. Deke gave Bandoni a nod as the two men passed each other.

Bandoni gripped a chair across from me and gave it a shake as if to confirm it would hold his weight. When he lowered his bulk into the seat, Clyde moved out from underneath the table and sat next to my chair.

Bandoni looked amused. "Dog doesn't much like me, does he?"

"He's a good judge of character."

Bandoni put his cop's eyes on me, and for a moment I saw myself as he must. Young. Ignorant. Foolish. And female. My fears no doubt aligned with his—that I'd fail spectacularly and bring us both down.

I said, "Are you done with the scene?"

"Just about. I've asked the ME to delay before moving the body. I want to make sure we get all possible microscopic evidence. Too easy to lose shit during transport." Bandoni jerked a thumb over his shoulder in the direction Deke had gone. "That the engineer?"

I gave Bandoni a rundown of my conversation with Deke.

"Good idea to have him meet with a sketch artist," he said. A rare dollop of praise. "Our victim's a white male. Midtwenties to midthirties. Dead four or five hours. Gay, tranny, something, based on that dress he's wearing. I'm thinking we're looking at a hate crime."

Something shifted inside me. Small, but also seismic. Man's murderous ways toward man. "What about the fact that his face was obliterated? Does that also go to your hate-crime theory?"

Bandoni worked something out from beneath a fingernail. "Don't read too much into that. A blow to the head is always ugly. It destroys flesh and breaks bones. But it doesn't mean the murder was personal. Could be our killer is a stone-cold psychopath."

With appreciation for how forthcoming Bandoni was being, I picked up my pen. "Cause of death?"

"Don't quote me, but the blow to the head's at the top of my list. Won't know for sure until after the autopsy."

"Identification?"

"Total John Doe. No wallet, so no driver's license. No passport, no dog tags. If we're lucky, his fingerprints will be in the system."

"Be nice if the department had a mobile print identifier. We'd already know."

"Be nice if we had a lot of things." Bandoni grunted. "Whole budget has gone to hell with the shit that's happened."

The sexual-harassment scandals, he meant. A society that didn't trust its police force didn't award the department with money and grants.

I waited for Bandoni to continue, but he stared past me with eyes gone bleary with age and overwork. He looked like he took the department's troubles personally. And maybe he did. He'd been with the Denver PD for over thirty years, working his way up from patrol through the motorcycle squad, then riding high on a stunning series of successes, including identifying the Capitol Hill Killer and running down a psychopath who'd spent five years robbing liquor stores and kneecapping the owners. Cohen had shown me a picture of Bandoni in his prime—a startlingly handsome man in a black trench coat and good suit, his tousled hair falling over a high forehead. With his intense blue eyes, square jaw, and cleft chin, he was just what a 1950s casting director would have demanded for his lead.

But somewhere in the stretch of highway between fifty and sixty, he'd hit some speed bumps—cases that dragged out, a dispute with his lieutenant. Then, hard after that, came potholes and a broken axle or two. A divorce, a headliner case that went wrong. Too many days looking evil in the eye and too many nights alone with the bottle.

Too many nights fighting himself.

He was still a huge man, tall and broad across the beam. But the muscle had gone soft, and instead of dominating a room with his size, he carried his bones like a curse—shoulders slumped, the large round head sunk into the flesh of his neck as if he'd been handed a thirty-pound bowling ball in lieu of the ten pounder he'd been promised. The perpetual grimace on his face suggested he was still pissed about it.

Pissed about everything.

He heaved himself out of his chair, went to the vending machine, and pressed the button for a package of chocolate doughnuts.

He resumed his seat and ripped open the cellophane. His thinning hair was cut in a short burr that showed his scalp. His tie was pulled loose and askew, and a coffee stain marred the rumpled whiteness of his shirt. His hands still had a residue of talc from the latex gloves he'd worn at the scene.

I felt a flare of pity. "You okay?"

He ignored that. "Can you explain something to me? As a railroad cop?"

"Former railroad cop."

"Tell me how a body that ain't even a day old got into a car that was sealed shut three days ago."

"You got a timeline."

"Courtesy of the Russki."

"Sergei Illych. And he's American."

"Once a Red, always a Red, in my book."

I sighed. "You want Occam's razor?"

"That's funny, Parnell. You gonna say *I told you so*, too?"

I picked up my pen, wrote the word *theories* in my notebook. "If we figure that the chickens went bad because the refrigeration unit failed or the seal broke, then the simplest scenario is that our victim is a hobo, and he was alive when he got on the train in Nebraska. He would have entered after the car was loaded and before the door was shut, trapping him inside. The boxes weren't restrained, and during the journey they fell on him, crushing his skull."

"What do you think those boxes weigh?"

"Not enough."

"That ain't Occam's razor. That's just a bad hypothesis."

"Fair enough." I drew a box around the word *theories*. "Here's another one."

He popped a doughnut in his mouth, waved his hand in a go-ahead gesture.

"He was assaulted near where the car originated and then placed inside," I said. "Again, before the door was closed."

"Still alive."

"But just barely. He survived for almost three days and died in transit."

Bandoni swallowed. Grunted. Freed a second doughnut from the plastic wrapping and waved it toward me. He must have seen something in my face because he pushed the package in my direction.

I tugged one out. "Thanks."

"Sharing a little cholesterol. I can't see our victim holding on for three days with his skull crushed."

"Maybe he didn't," I said, talking around a mouthful of chocolate. "Third hypothesis. Maybe he was alive and well when he got on the train. But he didn't get on alone."

"Someone hit him in transit?"

"Right."

"Then where's our killer? The door had to be closed the entire trip. It takes special equipment to open it. That's why everyone figures something went bad with either the seal or the refrigeration system. And why our dead guy ain't a human Popsicle."

"The railroad will get a mechanic to take a look. If the door and the refrigeration unit check out mechanically, and I think they will—"

"Now you've got psychic powers, too?"

"The flies, Bandoni."

"They probably got in when the car was loaded."

"In. But not out."

He stared at me a moment. "You saw flies at the little shrine."

I nodded. "The only way the flies could have gotten out is if the door was open when the train stopped. And the only way the door could have been open when Deke stopped the train—"

"—was if it was already open. Forget it, rookie. The guys out there swore that wasn't possible. Even if the loaders left the door open, it would have closed with the train's motion."

"When I first entered the reefer, I saw what looked like fresh scratches in the door track."

A light flickered in Bandoni's eyes. He plucked out a third doughnut. "Go on."

"Those plug doors weigh a thousand pounds. Every once in a while when the cars are being loaded, if something jolts the car and the cam locks aren't properly positioned, the door closes when it shouldn't and kills someone. This is especially true with older cars like the one we're dealing with. So loaders sometimes jam a piece of pipe or a tool—whatever they have on hand—into the door track to keep the door from closing."

Bandoni's eyes lit up. "Meaning the door is wedged open, and our hobos can get in at any point."

I nodded. "The poultry was loaded into the refrigerator car at a ColdShip distribution warehouse in North Platte before the cars were taken to the Bailey Yard. Let's figure a loader at ColdShip was scared of the door and jammed it open. The open door could have been missed in North Platte, where the yardmaster and the rest of the yard crew were overwhelmed. That's why the poultry thawed. After our two hobos got in a fight, the killer grabbed the pipe—or whatever was holding the door open—and used it to kill our John Doe."

Bandoni chewed thoughtfully, then scowled. "Won't work. As soon as the killer removed the pipe, the door would close, trapping our killer inside along with his victim. Am I right?"

"That's true only if the train is moving."

Bandoni frowned.

I said, "It's physics. An object at rest stays at rest until acted upon by some force. If the train was stopped when the pipe was removed, then the door would remain open until something jolted it."

"Fucking physics," he grumbled.

"Worked for Newton."

Bandoni snapped his fingers. "Our two guys are fighting. The train stops for the repair, and our murderous asshole grabs the pipe, kills his pal, and flees. Then the door closes when the train starts up again."

"Where it gets a little muddied is that the engineer saw lights near the tracks *before* he stopped."

"Fuck me, what lights?"

"Headlights or flashlights. Deke wasn't sure."

"It was the woman."

I nodded. "And possibly others."

"But nothing to do with our case."

I shrugged.

Bandoni said, "So who *were* those people? Partiers out in the middle of nowhere?"

"That's easy."

He wrestled the last doughnut free. "Fill me in, Sherlock."

"They hopped off an earlier train and were waiting for their next ride."

"There was an earlier train?"

"If not that night, then the day before. Hobos are used to waiting."

"Fun life."

"For some."

"Okay, that could work." Bandoni nodded. "The train stops. This second group of hobos sees the murder. They make a—what'd you call it, a shrine—for the dead guy. The woman shines a light on her face hoping the engineer will see her and call it in and then the police will find the body."

"Which we did."

He gave me a sharp glance, probably looking for sarcasm.

"But," I said. "Again, it doesn't work. The woman had the light on her face *before* the train stopped. She couldn't have known yet about the body."

"Ah, fuck me again." He palmed his balding head. "I'm getting a headache."

I sympathized. But I had momentum, and I plowed on. "It's still likely she was a hobo, shining the light on her face to acknowledge the engineer. Nothing to do with the murder. Some of the riders are just like that. A nod to the railroaders. Then after the train stops, the hobos see the murder. Or at least they spot the victim while the murderer flees in the fog, coldcocking Heinrich on his way out."

"And the woman makes the shrine before she and the hobos ride the train into Denver. But why bother with a shrine?"

"Maybe it was a simple act of kindness." The thought eased the ache in my heart.

"It would also mean the killer hung around for a while after nailing our victim. Long enough for the cop to get there. That seems a little odd."

"Agreed. But I'm at the end of my hypothesizing."

He grunted. "This all feels shaky. Too many what-ifs and why-the-hells."

I couldn't argue with that. "Why don't I start by pulling video from the Bailey and Ogallala Yards and maybe from ColdShip, if they have cameras. We get lucky, we'll find footage of our riders."

"We'll have to go through the North Platte detective's bureau to get a warrant for the recordings."

"Not if I ask nicely. Railroad cop to railroad cop."

"Former railroad cop," he growled. "Might be better to play it by the book." He wadded up his trash, tossed it toward the can. Missed. "Speaking of railroad cops, how is that guy? Heinrich. How's he doing?"

"He's scheduled for an MRI. That's all I know at the moment."

"He remember anything yet?"

"Not the last I spoke with him."

"Our closest witness, and he's no good to us."

I flashed to Heinrich's wound. "You leave your heart at home this morning?"

He shot me a look. "I don't care about being nice right now. I care about solving this case."

We glared at each other, our momentary ease gone. Then I sucked in a breath and forced myself to think like my partner.

"Okay," I said, putting personal feelings aside. "How long until they start the autopsy?"

"Doc says this afternoon. First thing is to get his prints during the external exam. We learn his name, then we got something to go on." Bandoni flicked his wrist so that the sleeve of his suit rode up, revealing a once-fine watch scratched and dinged with age. "It's past noon. Why don't you head into the squad room, start making calls, and work on the warrants. I'll meet you there in a couple of hours. I'm going to finish here, then probably check out the scene with the cross."

"There won't be much to see by now. Gabel was going to bag everything."

He shrugged. "I like to take in the ambiance."

We stood. Clyde got to his feet, his tail swishing, ready to move. I grabbed my coffee cup, picked up the empty doughnut package from the floor, and tossed all of it into the trash.

On our way to the door, Bandoni stopped and looked at me. "What made you so sure there'd been a murder?"

"I wasn't."

"But still, you ignored my advice and stopped the train."

"Yes."

"You could have put serious brakes on your career right there."

"I know."

"So why?"

I looked down at Clyde while my mind ran through a list of acceptable answers. Telling Bandoni the truth was out. My reasoning would make no sense to him. He lived in a linear world where one thing led logically to the next. A, then B, then C. Probably that made him a great detective.

It was too soon to know how my more chaotic thinking would fare. Maybe our differences would make us great partners. Then again, maybe we'd kill each other.

I settled on a half truth.

"Woman's intuition," I said. "Got you beat there."

CHAPTER 6

Remember that fierceness you had as a kid? That bring-it-on feeling that was yours before you knew the world would punch you back?

You still got it. Along with a bigger fist.

—*Sydney Parnell. Conversation with a friend.*

By the time we drove through traffic and parked, the day had warmed into the upper fifties with a clear sky and a light breeze. Clyde and I were enjoying our walk across the plaza toward police headquarters when my phone rang.

I didn't recognize the number, but answered with the title I was still adjusting to. "Detective Parnell."

"This is Denise Jackson, Detective. I got your number from Rachel Gibbons."

I stopped so quickly that Clyde had to backtrack.

One of the rape kits Detective Gabel and I were processing involved a sexual assault at an assisted-living facility. The woman, Carolyn Jackson, had been a healthy eighty-seven-year-old at the time of the rape. She was now in her nineties and suffering dementia. Two weeks ago, I'd obtained warrants to collect DNA swabs from every male worker who'd been employed at the home at the time of the rape. Uniformed officers were collecting the samples, and Gabel was sending them to the lab as they came in. He was looking for a match between the new swab and our original DNA.

So far, nothing.

But when we reran her rapist's DNA in CODIS, the Combined DNA Index System, we got a match between her rapist's DNA and the DNA from a more recent attack. It was progress.

Although we still had no name.

"Detective Parnell? Are you there?"

I pushed aside my impatience at getting derailed and led Clyde out of the flow of pedestrian traffic. Denise Jackson was Carolyn's daughter. She deserved my respect.

"Ms. Jackson," I said. "I appreciate your call. But you need to direct any questions through Ms. Gibbons. She's your mother's victim advocate. She can answer any questions you have."

"I understand. But the way I hear it, you're the one leading the investigation. And my mother and I need answers."

Investigation wasn't the right word. The Denver PD had been ordered to work through the backlog of rape kits—more than three thousand. Funding was coming, and once it was approved, the Colorado Bureau of Investigation would take over. But in the meantime, the chief himself had decided my first task as a new detective would be to select those kits with the best chance for closure. My job amounted to identifying kits with at least a minimally detailed report, a victim who was still alive, and DNA samples that either hadn't been tested or hadn't found a match in CODIS at the time of the crime.

So far, I'd raced my way through more than five hundred kits, scanning and digitizing the information as I went. Of those five hundred, I'd reviewed fifty more closely. And of those fifty, thirty-two had met our requirements. Carolyn Jackson's assault was one of them.

But I couldn't share any of this with the woman on the other end of the call.

I said, "I'm handling certain aspects of your mother's case, Ms. Jackson. But it's against procedure for the two of us to have a conversation without the presence of the victim advocate. If you wish to talk, why don't you arrange a meeting through Ms. Gibbons?"

"Please," she said. "I'm right here."

Clyde came to his feet, and I turned. A sixty-something woman in a red pantsuit and short afro with a cell phone pressed to her ear waved at us. Her nails were long and as cherry red as her suit. When our eyes met, she lowered her phone and powered in our direction.

I signaled Clyde to sit.

"You're Detective Parnell," the woman said when she reached us. "And this handsome animal is Clyde. I recognize you from the newspapers."

"As accused," I said.

"I'm Denise Jackson."

We shook hands, and I explained that Clyde was on duty and couldn't shake paws. I glanced at my phone to note the time, then took a breath and mentally settled in. Now that Denise Jackson was standing right in front of me, I would hear her out.

"What can I do for you, Ms. Jackson?"

"Please, call me Denise."

She smiled again, open and friendly. I had to admire someone who could maneuver so neatly into my space. But the firmness in her eyes told me she wouldn't be shrugged off or mollified.

"Tell me how I can help, Denise."

"You know the details of the case," she said. "But what I'm sure those police reports don't tell you is that my mother has not been the same woman she was before she was assaulted."

"No one would—"

Denise rolled right over me. "The attack confirmed everything she'd come to believe about herself. That she's an old, worthless, half-senile woman, loved only by her daughter. After that assault, she went from having a mild case of dementia to hardly being herself anymore." Her eyes flashed. "I lost my mother in that attack, Detective Parnell. And I would like to see some justice. For her and me both."

"I am sorry for what you and she have suffered."

"You know what's worse than all of that?" Her hands fisted and moved to her hips. "What's so much worse? The fact that weeks after the assault, her case was dropped. Like none of it mattered. She was just an old black lady, not worth anybody's time." Denise frowned, all the niceties gone. "What you can do for me, Detective, is tell me what you've learned. Who did this to her?"

"First, my apologies that it has taken us so long to find a way to reopen your mother's case. At the time of her assault, a DNA profile was created, and we searched a nationwide database for a match. But we didn't get a hit."

"A hit. What's that mean, exactly?"

"DNA from your mother's swabs was used to create a DNA profile of the suspect. That profile, called a forensic unknown profile, is run against all DNA databases in the hope of finding a match. In the case of your mother's assailant, there was no candidate match at the time of her assault."

"But now there is?"

"I'm not at liberty to say."

"Meaning yes."

"Please talk to your mother's advocate."

"Playing pass the buck?" Jackson tapped her foot angrily on the concrete. "So why?"

"Why what?"

"Why did you call us when you have nothing new to share?"

"It's policy to notify someone when their case is reopened."

"Why is that?" Her voice shook with indignation. "Just so you can rip open wounds that might finally be healing?"

I couldn't argue with her. The policy had never struck me as wise.

"I know it's painful, Ms. Jackson," I said. "Please try to be patient a little while longer. We're working angles, hoping to find a different way to link the assailant's name with his DNA."

"What kind of different way?"

"I can't go into the details. When we know more—*if* we know more—Ms. Gibbons will contact you."

Denise leaned back, looked me in the eye. "Have you ever been raped, Detective Parnell?"

I held her gaze. "No."

"Then maybe you're not the person who should be handling this. I've heard about the backlog of rape cases. Runs right across all fifty states. Lots of buried hurt. Takes compassion to do that right."

I considered her words. "The fact that I have not been raped doesn't mean I don't understand trauma. And it certainly doesn't mean I won't do my best."

She glared at me. I waited her out, and at last she softened.

"I'm sorry," she said. "Like I said, I read about you in the paper. I know what you went through." She held out her hand, and we shook. "Thank you for your service."

I nodded. "Ms. Gibbons will be in touch."

I signaled Clyde through his lead, and we stepped around her and strode toward headquarters. My hands were shaking, and I forced myself to slow down and breathe. I knew Denise Jackson was only trying to be kind with her words about my service. Most people were. But they had no idea the kind of shit they brought up for veterans and service members by tossing out a casual thanks. Some of us had done things they couldn't even imagine.

They wouldn't thank us if they knew.

◆ ◆ ◆

There was a chicken sprawled across my desk when I walked into the empty detectives' room.

My desk—as befitting the newest and least experienced member of the squad—sat directly beneath a wall-mounted television that blared the news 24-7, bouncing between CNN and Fox depending on the proclivities of the on-duty sergeant. The desk had belonged to a detective named Bill Gorman—his because even with his seniority he was known for being a fuckup. Denver didn't have detective grades like a lot of departments. But everyone knew who was good and who was a lazy hanger-on riding out their days until retirement.

The desk was an indication of exactly where a detective stood on the totem pole.

When Cohen transferred to sex crimes, Gorman had claimed his desk, vacating this one. I'd accepted the crappy location as my lot and settled in. The only personal thing I'd put on the desk was a photo of Cohen. I'd meant it as a reminder to myself to have a personal life and not get buried by the job. But it didn't take long for me to realize that the other detectives saw it as my way of saying I was untouchable. Cohen had been a valued member of the squad, and they thought I was trying to stand in his sunshine.

I'd finally slid Cohen's laconic smile into a drawer. Now the only thing marring the clean sweep of faux wood was the stack of reports from the rape kits.

And the rubber chicken. Someone had pinned an index card to the breast and written **CHICKEN MAN INVESTIGATION** in all caps.

"Funny," I said. Clyde heard the sharpness in my voice and cocked his head. "That's right, pal. Don't think for a second that label won't stick. Our first case has been named in perpetuity after poultry. Which means you and I are now the Chicken Man detectives."

Clyde didn't look bothered.

I clicked off the television set. My fellow detectives were either in court, out on cases, or grabbing lunch. With relief I noted that the lieutenant's office was closed and dark. I had no good answer for the question she would inevitably ask: What had I been doing in Denver's farthest reaches at zero-dark-thirty?

I hung up my coat, shoved my satchel under the desk, and downed Clyde in his designated place to my right, a wedge of space complete with dog bed and bowls for food and water. Unlike me, my K9 partner had been an instant hit with the squad—with everyone but Bandoni, anyway. Maybe it had to do with the mysteries of male bonding. Now Clyde settled into the spot I'd made for him and rested his head on his paws. A minute later he was zonked out and snoring.

My war buddy.

I phoned the forensic artist and scheduled a meet between her and Deke. Then I stuffed the rubber chicken in a drawer and powered up my computer. I worked on the online incident report while I ate the PB&J I'd packed that morning when I'd planned on going straight to the office after meeting Heinrich. When I'd filled in what I could on the report and emailed it to Bandoni, I made a new pot of coffee in the break room, then returned to my desk and scanned my email. Mauer had come through. A message from him carried an attachment with the video from the train's event recorder. Another file contained the work order for the installation of the joint bar. A third email confirmed that the door, the seal, and the refrigeration unit were all mechanically sound.

Mauer also said he was working to get the recordings from the Bailey Yard and Ogallala. But the yard where the reefer had originated was owned by ColdShip. He had no sway there.

I read the work order and then watched fifteen minutes of the train recording, focusing on Deke's approach to Denver. There was nothing new or enlightening on either one.

I leaned back, sipping my coffee. The mechanical soundness of the refrigerator car meant that the door had been open for the entire trip, and that meant our hobo—or hobos—could have hopped on at any point. Maybe they'd been so drunk or stoned they hadn't cared about the oozing chicken slime.

Or they could have gotten on before the great thaw and just ridden it out.

I pulled up the North Platte facility on a satellite image. ColdShip consisted of a single large metal-roofed warehouse. There was a parking lot to the south and fields and a dirt road to the north. Also to the north was a picnic table set on a concrete patio next to an outdoor ashtray. Along the western side of the building ran two parallel railroad tracks, which ultimately joined in with Denver Pacific's line. At the junction, the ColdShip reefers would be added to an existing train and hauled to the Bailey Yard for sorting.

There had been two train cars sitting at the warehouse when the satellite image was taken. Probably the entire west side of the building sported docks where the reefers were loaded.

It was a perfect setting for stowaways. They could have come in on a train or rubber tramped—hitchhiked—into the area. Nearby trees and structures offered places to hide until it was possible to slip aboard.

Bandoni was right that we'd probably need a warrant to get ColdShip's recordings. But going through the North Platte police, district attorney, and a judge would take time. Why not try a little honey before applying the vinegar? Detectives did it all the time.

A receptionist answered at ColdShip Distributors in North Platte. I asked for the manager. While I waited, I listened to hits from the eighties and contemplated how forthcoming I should be in my approach. I heard Cohen's voice in my head: *Except for those times when we get to lie to the scum of the earth to help a case, be honest. Any conversation you have could end up in court.*

The phone clicked. "This is Gene Vacek."

Presumably Vacek wasn't scum of the earth. I introduced myself and gave the manager an abbreviated version of the incident. I finished with a request for any video recordings that showed the reefer being loaded.

"A murder," Vacek said. "Dear God."

"Hard to imagine," I agreed.

"I just—I don't see how we could have left a door open. We have rules the employees are required to follow. There are safeguards. And now we have all that lost product . . ."

His voice trailed into silence, no doubt contemplating the cost per pound of frozen chicken.

"Maybe something went wrong at a different point and not at your facility," I said. "I'd love to get ColdShip off my radar. Video recordings would go a long way toward making that possible."

"I don't . . . I don't know that we actually have cameras. That's a security issue. I don't manage those kinds of concerns."

To my credit, I didn't roll my eyes. "Who is your security guy?"

"That would be Martin Chase."

I got a phone number for Chase, then thanked Vacek for his time. "I'll be in touch."

He cleared his throat. "Detective Parnell, I guess I have a question. What is it exactly you're looking for? Are you wanting to question our workers?"

"Should I?"

A pause. "I can't see why. It's not like it's one of ours you found on that train. So why do you want the recordings? Is it about the door?"

"I'm looking for trespassers, Mr. Vacek. I would imagine that might be important to us both."

I hung up and dialed Martin Chase. Straight to voice mail. Was Vacek already on the phone with his security man? Bandoni had said that it might be better to play it by the book. Uneasily, I left a message asking Chase to call me at his earliest convenience.

I typed up a request for North Platte PD to issue a search warrant and forwarded it to Bandoni. The request would have more weight coming from him. I had moved on to researching Lady of Guadalupe necklaces on the internet when Clyde bounded to his feet, tail wagging. I looked up. Clyde's favorite man, Detective Michael Cohen, was weaving his way toward us through the desks.

I smiled and stood as Cohen approached. If I had a tail, no doubt it would be wagging. Cohen was my favorite man, too.

"You slumming?" I said as he came within earshot.

The skin crinkled around his eyes as he offered his own smile. "Never seen the place so empty. You scare everyone away?"

"The rumor of my near arrival was sufficient, apparently."

A foot away, Cohen stopped as if he'd walked into a wall. "What is that?"

"What is what?"

"That smell."

"Clyde's favorite. *Odeur de poulet.*" I waggled my eyebrows. "You like it?"

"Now I know why everyone's gone." He backed up a step. "Why don't we take it outside?"

"Pie at Tom's?"

"Anything. As long as it's not chicken."

The three of us cut across North Washington and made our way to Colfax Avenue and Tom's Diner. Tom's was a local landmark, a 1970s-style diner with decent food and a waitstaff that made sure you never saw the bottom of your coffee cup. Midafternoon, the place was empty. We settled in our favorite booth near the windows and ordered apple pie à la mode and coffee. The stink from my clothes—while not defeated—was mitigated by the odors of grease and fried foods.

Clyde stretched out beneath the table and fell asleep on our feet.

"Heard you and Bandoni caught a case," Cohen said when we were halfway through our respective slices and had come up for air.

I nodded. "Guess I'm now officially a homicide dick."

"What I actually heard was that you hunted it down, shot it, and dragged it back."

"Bandoni?"

"Gabel. I stopped at the lab to talk to him about one of my cases."

"So, what? I'm not supposed to follow up on things? I was right."

"You *were* right," Cohen said mildly.

I *hated* when I got defensive. This job was going to involve a constant struggle to separate my lack of confidence from simple inexperience.

"Tell that to your old partner," I said. "Maybe he'll listen to you."

A smile. "Why would he suddenly start doing that?"

Cohen had transferred into sex crimes at the encouragement of Division Chief Trujillo, who was head of all investigations including Major Crimes, the Forensics and Evidence Division, Special Operations, and Investigative Support. Trujillo wanted Cohen to get a broad base of experience—no doubt grooming him for a future high-level position. If it came to that, Cohen wasn't sure what he'd do. He was a street cop at heart. A man of the people who believed in the mission: serve and protect. But for now, he was ready for a change. My move to the department gave him all the push he needed.

Friendship between detectives was encouraged. Sex, not so much.

For my part, I was glad that sex with me trumped looking at dead people.

I put aside my annoyance with Bandoni and smiled at my man. He looked good with his close-cropped hair and well-fitted suit, the lean angles of his face accented in the afternoon sun. Today he also looked rakish—a scruff of beard told me he'd probably left the house in a hurry, and not long after I did.

"Tell me about your case," I said. "The one that sent you running out the door today."

He raised a brow. "Keeping yours close to the vest?"

I dug my fork into the pie again. "Not much to tell. We're waiting for the autopsy and an ID."

"I hope you aren't going to play hard to get. I need my murder fix." He pushed away his now-empty plate, and my glance caught the scars on the fingers of his left hand. The nails had grown back, but raised red lines still marred the surrounding skin.

A reminder that six months earlier he had been tortured on my account during my hunt for a killer responsible for monstrous war crimes.

Cohen swore he'd moved on, and I'd done my best to do the same. But with this morning's victim weighing on my mind, I found myself in a melancholic mood.

Too much pain in the world.

I forced lightness into my voice. "Your murder fix? You know how sick that sounds?"

"Pot calling the kettle. Don't make me go begging to Bandoni for the details."

I hesitated before reminding myself that this was about a dead man, not my ego. I should be willing to take whatever help I could get. So I told Cohen what we knew so far. He listened intently, but didn't comment other than to acknowledge that Bandoni could be a pain in the ass and I'd done well to stand up to him. He then told me about his case, a woman who'd been raped and beaten and dumped in an apartment parking lot in University Hills, where a resident found her and called the police. The woman had initially told the police her boss had assaulted her. She agreed to a rape kit. But halfway through the exam, she'd retracted her accusation and refused to press charges. It was just a misunderstanding, she said.

"She's scared," I said, then fell silent when the waitress came by and refilled our coffees.

After she left, Cohen dumped sugar and cream in his cup and stirred the now-noxious brew. "My guess is she's undocumented and terrified she'll lose her job."

"Even though her boss is a rapist. Dear God. Where does she work?"

Wrinkles folded around Cohen's eyes as he sighed. "No idea. But she smelled like pine cleaner." A soft shake. "Fucking pine cleaner. I didn't know if it was from her job or if she'd tried to purge the assault."

I stroked the back of his hand. "Keep your chin up, Warrior Detective. This is why we do what we do. Maybe her advocate will convince her to press charges."

We were quiet for a few minutes. Then, beneath the table, Cohen nudged me gently. "I have a surprise for you."

"A Caribbean vacation?"

"Better. My cousin is coming to town. From my mother's side. He'll be here for a linguistics conference."

My coffee curdled in my gut. "Okay."

"I want you to meet him."

Family. I set down my coffee. "I don't know if I'm ready for that, Mr. Michael Walker Cohen of the fabulously wealthy Walkers. I'm not exactly Walker material. The idea of meeting your family gives me hives."

He shot me a grin. "Evan's a Wilding, not a Walker. And he's used to troglodytes. He consults on the FBI's worst cases."

"Which makes me look what—almost normal?"

"If he squints. Anyway, Evan is very nonjudgmental. You'll love him. Plus, he's going to stay at Grandma Walker's mansion, so he'll be right next door to us. You can't avoid him."

"That's . . . fabulous."

"I thought you'd see it that way. Shall I arrange dinner for two nights from now? The Barolo Grill?"

"Let's go Ethiopian. That way he won't be shocked when I eat with my fingers."

CHAPTER 7

All I got is my life, and it ain't worth much.

Can't get more free than that.

—Kevin "Rotten" Russell. Conversation with Sydney
Parnell.

Gutter punks weren't hobos.

They were a hobo's evil twin.

Young, rebellious, carrying a grudge with the explosive power of an atomic bomb, these street kids and runaways caught out on trains because it was free. They couldn't give a shit about the hobo tradition. Their idols were drugs, concerts, and anarchy. Everything else came in a distant second.

If it came in at all.

A railroad bull could spot these so-called crusties or traveler kids in a New York minute. Filthy T-shirts and camo pants, ratty dreadlocks and a general aura of viciousness. And some serious body art. A crustie had enough homemade tattoos to qualify as a walking skin infection. Stoner eyes, too. Half the time I encountered these kids, they were so high it was a wonder their brain stems remembered to ask for air.

I had one contact in the crustie community—a traumatized seventeen-year-old runaway who went by the moniker Rotten. A little digging on my part filled in Rotten's past. His birth name was Kevin

Russell, and throughout his childhood there had been so many domestic-violence charges brought against his parents that social workers finally plucked nine-year-old Kevin from their loving arms and dropped him into the foster system. He ran away from every home until he turned fifteen, and then he ran away for good. Rotten had vowed that if he was ever forced home, he would kill himself.

But first he would slit his parents' throats.

Rotten's miserable past and his determined defiance were why I alternated between wanting to give traveler kids a good spanking and wanting to take them home for milk and cookies.

The kids were on my radar now for two reasons. A crustie was more likely than a traditional hobo to hit a railroad cop. And a lot of them wore Doc Marten boots with waffle soles—something like the print Gabel had found at our first crime scene.

Of course, around thirty thousand pairs of Doc Martens had been sold in Colorado the previous year, so the boots didn't exactly whittle down the suspect pool. But it was something.

Denver's collection of gutter punks mostly hung out at the 16th Street Mall in Lower Downtown because of its proximity to Union Station and the generally solid panhandling opportunities in this wealthy part of Denver. I parked in one of the garages that served the area, and Clyde and I made our way to the pedestrian walkway.

Finding the crusties took under three minutes. They were stirring up trouble along Market Street.

Clyde and I watched them. Six grimy white boys jitter-walking up and down the sidewalk, accosting tourists and suit-clad business folks. The passersby were having none of it. Probably they knew that pulling out their wallets would invite the hyenas to circle and attack. The pedestrians averted their eyes and speed-walked on by to shouts of derision and the occasional shove meted out by the punks.

I didn't see Rotten in the crew. Clyde and I skirted the gang and a block farther along spotted a girl sitting cross-legged on the sidewalk, panhandling solo. She probably figured she'd have better luck going it alone than mobbing it with the more aggressive members of her pack. It seemed to be working. Unlike the guys, she had a nice pile of cash in her bowl. If she wasn't careful, another crustie or an enterprising junkie would make off with it.

The girl didn't yet have the street-hardened look. Her torn jeans were dirty but not filthy, and her lavender I♥NY T-shirt still had most of its sequins. The tips of her dirty-blond dreadlocks were bright purple—a recent dye job. She wore pink lipstick and oversize sunglasses. Just like any girl her age might.

The cardboard sign propped in front of her read **NEED $ FOR TRAIN HOME.**

If she was new to the community, she wouldn't know many folks. But she might be more willing to talk. And maybe I could give her a nudge in the direction of a shelter.

I approached and held out a twenty-dollar bill. She grabbed for it without looking up, and I pulled my hand back.

I said, "I'll trade it for answers to a few questions."

She wiped her nose with the back of a dirty hand. "Give me the dub and fuck off."

Ballsy. Given her chosen line of work, that was a good thing. "A few answers, and you get not only the twenty bucks, but a good meal. And a safe place to stay, if you want it."

"You a fucking lesbo?"

"Just a person in need of information."

She lifted her eyes, took in my suit and shield. Her pink lips curled into a snarl. "You're a cop."

Couldn't fool these kids.

She grabbed her bowl and stood, preparing to flee. But then she saw Clyde. She froze, a moment of indecision.

She wiped her nose again. "He yours?"

"We're partners."

She reached a tentative hand toward Clyde.

Gently, I blocked her. "Better not."

"Will he bite?"

"He's on duty. But if you let me buy you lunch, you can pet him. He'll be on break."

◆ ◆ ◆

We walked to Union Station, the multihub train and bus depot. The girl waited outside while I ordered a couple of burgers, fries, and a milkshake. When I came back out, she was sitting on a bench near the rail lines watching a departing passenger train and chewing her lower lip. I knew what she was thinking.

Crusties hopped coal bins. Rich people rode Amtrak. Just the way it was.

I sat next to her on the bench, comfortable knowing for the first time that day that my reek of chicken slime couldn't hold a candle to weeks of street living.

I handed her the paper bag. "You got a name?"

"Purple."

"A real name?"

"Purple." She opened the bag. "This all for me?"

"However much you want."

The first burger was gone almost before she unwrapped it. She took the second burger more slowly.

"He's a mal, right?" she asked between bites. "I had a mal when I was a little girl. Or my stepdad did. Tom was an asshole, but Loki was a good dog."

I motioned Clyde to sit, then unbuckled his vest, signaling a break from his workday. The girl wiped her greasy hands on her pants, and I showed her how to introduce herself, then scratch Clyde under the chin. Clyde rolled his eyes at me, but he tolerated the girl's attention like a pro.

Purple rubbed Clyde's shoulder. "How do you get a dog like this one?"

"He's a former military working dog. Sometimes people can adopt them."

"Not street kids."

"You need a stable home first."

Purple gave Clyde a final pat, then leaned back on the bench and chewed through the french fries. When they were gone, she pushed her sunglasses up on her head. Her expression was soft and loose—food and a little time with an animal can do that.

"You could go almost anywhere from here, couldn't you?" Her voice was wistful.

I nodded. "Anywhere a train goes."

"Wish I had money to buy that kind of ticket."

"My dad used to ride the rails. He taught me how to catch out when I was just a kid."

She blinked. "No shit?"

"No shit. You from Denver?"

"California. I've been in Denver a couple of weeks. I'm gonna catch out pretty soon."

"Any place in particular?"

"There's a rock festival in North Carolina next month. Might go there."

"Long way to go for a concert."

"I like the music scene." She gave a shrug with one skinny shoulder, and a tattooed butterfly on her neck fluttered briefly. "I'm gonna settle down one of these days. Get a grown-up life. A house with a yard and a dog. A mal, like yours. Kids. Some guy who thinks I'm amazing. He and I can make the kids eat their vegetables and argue about who's going to pick up the dog shit. Normal stuff, you know?"

She hugged herself, rubbing her hands up and down her bare arms. When her face softened, she looked like the teenager she was. Someone who should be painting her nails at a sleepover and giggling over her latest crush.

Few things were harder than pretending to be tough when the street hadn't yet kicked you across that line.

I pulled out a business card for a friend of mine who ran a shelter and offered it to her.

Purple took it, shrugged, stuffed it in her back pocket. "Why you being so nice?"

I showed her the photo on my phone of the tagging on the refrigerator car. "Have you seen this tag before?"

She took the phone, spread her thumb and forefinger to enlarge it. "It's the tag for a punk band. Kill the Normies."

"Sounds ominous."

She rolled her eyes at me. "It's a *band*, not a threat."

"They play in Denver?"

"They're on tour. They play at Leopard's Den tomorrow night. Is that the secret information you were looking for?"

"You know who made this tag?"

The wariness snapped back into place like a visor. "I look like a rat to you?"

"The people I'm looking for aren't in trouble, Purple. I just want to talk to them."

"That's what cops always say." She handed the phone back to me. "They're vandals."

"I don't care about that. But whoever did the tagging might have seen something."

Purple sucked in her lower lip and narrowed her eyes, like she was doing some heavy thinking. Then she puffed out a breath. "Something like murder, you mean?"

"What would make you say that?"

She looked at Clyde. "Is he really a hero dog?"

"He's saved people's lives. A lot of lives."

She watched Clyde a moment longer. Then she stared out at a train on the far side of the tracks. Finally, she turned back to me.

"Okay," she said. "I might have heard some talk."

◆　◆　◆

Twenty minutes later, Clyde and I were back in the car, and I was on the phone with Bandoni.

"The girl heard other punks talking about two men hitching a ride on a freight who claim they saw someone get killed," I told him. "She didn't have names, and she wouldn't look at mug shots. But she—"

"You could have brought her in on a panhandling charge. Gotten her to look at photos."

I put the phone on speaker and started to back out of the parking space. I heard the shatter of breaking glass and stopped. *Crap.* I turned off the engine.

"If I'd brought the girl in," I said, opening the door, "she would have lied, then bolted as soon as we cut her loose. She's not a big fan of police, and she doesn't want to be a rat." I walked around to the rear of the Tahoe. Shards of brown glass glittered on the asphalt. Someone had placed a beer bottle behind my tire.

"Shit," I said.

"Shit what?"

"Nothing." I went back to the cab for work gloves. "Anyway, she said the witnesses are likely the taggers, and they're in Denver to see a band. Group's playing tomorrow night at Leopard's Den."

"You get descriptions?"

"The main tagger is a guy who calls himself Damn Fox. He has crosses and Bible verses tattooed on his arms. Travels with a five-foot-two punk with a green rooster tail who goes by the name Street Cred. I asked another group of punks about them, but the kids scattered soon as I mentioned Damn Fox. His reputation precedes him, apparently."

"You know these kids. You think a guy in peach chiffon would be part of that scene?"

"No." I found gloves and pulled a paper bag from my satchel. "But our victim could have hopped on board the train for the same reason college kids do it. They don't want the life, they just want a thrill."

"Would him muscling in on that scene get him killed?"

"These kids are fiercely protective of their territory. And with that dress . . ."

"Hate crime."

"Most of those kids are just lost souls from broken homes. But some of them are really messed up." I crouched next to the rear tire and reached for the glass. At least the tire looked okay.

"Murderously messed up?"

"It happens."

A grunt. Then Bandoni said, "Not too shabby, Parnell."

I hated how good his praise felt. "Thanks."

"Even a blind squirrel can find a nut. Where are you now? The PM starts in half an hour."

Postmortem. "I'm in LoDo. I'll see you in thirty."

I disconnected and kept picking up glass, pissed that someone had decided to share their black mood by adding to mine. I reached out an arm for the last bit of glass, and my fingers knocked against something. I peered under the Tahoe.

A naked, blond Barbie doll hung from the chassis. I pulled her free and turned her in my hands. Her breasts had been painted red, and she had a ribbon around her neck that looked disconcertingly like a hangman's noose.

I stared into the vacant, plastic eyes for a moment and tried not to think about how adding this bit of weirdness to my day made me feel.

I stuffed the doll into the bag with the glass, unsure what it meant, and got to my feet.

All around, the garage was filled with echoing sounds. Tires screeching on the turns. Car doors slamming. Voices. A blue cargo van came around the corner, heading toward the exit, tailgated by a man in a cherry-red Porsche.

As near as I could tell, no one lurked in the shadows to watch the results of their handiwork.

I rolled closed the top of the bag. Just my luck to be the random target of some pissed-off freak. I returned to the cab, tossed the bag behind my seat, then looked at my partner as I got in.

"A weirdo born every minute, right?"

Clyde shook himself. His tags jingled.

I backed up again and headed for the exit. As we pulled into the sunshine, I forced aside thoughts of the glass and the doll and turned my mind to more important matters. Like the PM.

A vision of our John Doe's faceless corpse rose in front of me.

My fellow Mortuary Affairs Marines and I had worked hard to compartmentalize the carnage we saw. We learned to mentally separate the ruin in front of us from the person he or she had been before the bomb or the bullets. Most of us got pretty good at it, and those who didn't were allowed to transfer out. No harm, no foul.

But even with rigid discipline, there were some things that managed to break through the walls we built.

My gut told me our John Doe was a wall breaker.

CHAPTER 8

I always worked backward from the remains, trying to piece
a Marine together by imagining where he'd been inside the
Bradley or in the Humvee. How close he'd been to an IED
during a foot patrol. In my mind, I re-created the man as he'd
been before the bomb. His hair and eyes, his hands and face.

His bones unshattered, his skin unburned.

That is how I found my ghosts.

—*Sydney Parnell. ENGL 0208 Psychology of Combat.*

The afternoon was flat and cool, the sky the tepid color of weak tea in a
sun-bronzed wash of clouds. I parked across the street from the Denver
Office of the Medical Examiner—a long, low gray building topped with
a bright-blue roof. A garbage truck grumbled past as I stepped out of
the truck, and Canada geese winged overhead with a whispered stroke
of feathers.

Bandoni leaned on the railing near the front doors. He had a can
of Mountain Dew in his left hand, and a cigarette curled smoke from
between his fingers.

I made sure Clyde was comfortable in the back of the Tahoe—no
dead bodies for him—then crossed the street and jogged up the concrete steps to my human partner.

I said, "It's kind of late in the day to start an autopsy."

"The stiff don't mind." He dropped the half-smoked cigarette on the concrete, ground it under his shoe. "But Bell's doing us a favor, scheduling it an hour before closing. She knows we need that ID."

I stood at the railing next to him and looked for the geese. They were nothing more than black pinpricks, stubble against the skin of clouds. "Is someone here from the crime lab?"

"Miller. He's already inside."

Bandoni seemed in no hurry to follow suit. He took a long swallow of the soda.

I said, "What are the chances we'll get an ID with fingerprints?"

"Who knows? If you're the praying kind, start now. Even putting a rush on the DNA means we're looking at twenty-four to thirty-two hours. And if the powers that be decide there's no good reason to rush? Christ, I'll be retired."

He tapped the rail with the flat of his free hand and narrowed his eyes, as if trying to follow the birds. But they'd been swallowed by the clouds.

Cohen had told me that Bandoni was one of the rare detectives who stayed for the entire autopsy. Most cops left after the external examination, heading out as soon as they had an idea about trace evidence and the level of injuries. It was easy enough to read the details later, in the medical examiner's report.

But Bandoni stayed, and during all the years of his partnership with Cohen, he had refused to offer an explanation.

Maybe it was his way of sitting with the dead.

He smacked the railing. "I hate that name, Chicken Man."

Surprised, I said, "Finally, something we have in common."

He grunted. "Hell of a small thing to share." But there was almost humor in his voice. "How about we just keep it at John Doe until we know who he is?"

"That works."

I watched Bandoni surreptitiously. His face was a collection of pouches—under his eyes, along his jaw. A pocket of flesh rolled over the collar of his shirt. Other than two spots of red in his cheeks, his skin carried a dull-gray pallor.

I opened my mouth before I knew I was going to speak. "You look like you're two steps from a gurney yourself."

A little color came back. He swigged the Mountain Dew. "You that eager for a new partner?"

"God. I didn't mean to say that."

"No?" He pulled out a roll of antacids, popped two in his mouth. Around the tablets he said, "It's the truth, so it's okay."

"No. It's not."

"I only *look* like shit." His mouth crooked up in a half smile. "I feel a hell of a lot worse."

We were silent for a moment, this time both of us staring into the sky, maybe willing the geese to return.

Finally I said, "We should go in."

"Yep." He drained the soda and picked up the smashed cigarette, shoving it into the can. "Let's get this show on the road."

We signed in and picked up badges, then followed the hallway down to the autopsy suite. A glance through the windows showed John Doe already wheeled in, the gurney slotted to the workstation in one of the bays. Our victim was still just a shape inside the body bag, but Emma Bell stood next to him, arranging items on a stainless-steel cart. Dan Miller, the crime-lab detective, was inside the room, talking to a tech in a lab coat.

The other bays were empty save for another tech washing instruments.

Bandoni and I slipped on disposable paper masks from a shelf in the hall. As soon as he opened the door to the suite, a wave of cool air washed over us, acrid with chemicals.

Bell waved us over, and we gathered with Miller and the tech in a loose horseshoe around the gurney.

"I just finished with the X-rays," she said. "It looks like the decedent has a hairline fracture of the left temporal bone. He also has complex, depressed fractures of both sides of the frontal bone along with breaks that continue down through the anterior facial skeleton. I'll be able to provide more detail when I look inside. But injuries of this nature are often associated with substantial damage to the brain."

Bandoni's normal boom was softened by the mask. "Meaning the blow to the head killed him?"

"Blows. I think we have two separate injuries, although again, I need to look inside to be sure. But unless I find something unusual or if something shows up in the tox, I'm guessing the cause of death will be blunt force trauma to the head."

While the tech snapped photos, Bell clipped the red seal—used to show that the body had not been disturbed since being placed in the bag—and pulled down the zipper.

My gaze went to what was left of John Doe's skull and face. In my mind, I heard the Sir's voice telling me the same thing he'd said every day when we served together in Iraq.

Body's got anything missing—a hand or a foot or head—you shade it black in the paperwork.

I blinked. Bell stood by the victim's right hand, removing the cinched bag that had been placed over it at the crime scene to preserve evidence. After she photographed and examined John Doe's hand and forearm and clipped his fingernails, she gave Miller the go-ahead to create a fingerprint card.

"No defensive wounds," she said.

Bandoni nodded. "He was surprised."

"Or intimidated," I said.

Bell continued her exam. "There's a pair of tattoos on the inside of his upper right arm."

She turned the arm so that we could see one of the tats—a two-inch-long line ending with a hook. It looked like a shepherd's staff. The line was set inside a tattooed triangle.

Bandoni leaned in. "Never seen that before."

"That symbol might have been at the crime scene," I said. "Next to the fabric. It looked like words had been scratched in the dirt, then mostly scuffed out. Gabel thought it was a capital letter. Possibly a *T* or an *L*. But it could also be this symbol."

"The tattoo is only a week or two old." Bell gently stretched the skin. "You see how the skin is flaking? And here"—she pointed—"the red streaking?"

We nodded.

"The tattoo was in the itchy phase, which occurs seven to fourteen days after the skin is inked. The red marks show he was scratching himself." She lifted John Doe's arm higher. "This second tattoo is newer."

We leaned closer. The second design was larger and looked home-made. It consisted of the universal symbols for men and women stacked on top of each other.

"Antemortem?" Bandoni asked.

"Correct. But it's fresher. There is oozing and swelling. My guess is that it happened only a day or two before he died."

We took photos of the tattoo, then focused on the ripped and bloody dress. The way it had twisted around his legs, presumably in the last moments of his life, the fabric so saturated with blood that it had stiffened into a rigid coil.

"The dress is a poor fit," Bell said.

"So maybe not something he picked out himself?" Bandoni said.

"You're the detectives."

When we'd noted most of the damage, the technician turned the body—still in the bag—so that Bell could unzip the dress.

She paused with the zipper halfway down and frowned.

"What?" Bandoni said.

"Just a minute," she said, "and I'll show you."

She and the tech tilted and rolled the body to remove the dress, then laid the garment out on a plastic-covered gurney.

"No underwear," Bell said.

We stared at the corpse, which—stripped—displayed a vivid array of bruises along the torso and thighs.

"He was beaten," I said.

"And worse." Bell gestured to the tech. "Let's turn him over."

When I saw what had caught Bell's attention, my chest began to burn.

"Oh, Lord," Miller whispered.

Bandoni said, "Fuck me."

Someone had carved words into John Doe's flesh. They'd started with the skin between his shoulder blades and cut all the way down to the base of his spine. The wounds were deep but precise, etched with a tool or a very sharp blade. Whoever did this had taken their time, carving slowly, meticulously slicing a message into their victim's flesh.

BETRAY ME WITH A KISS

Then a deep slash across his midback, left to right, as if to separate the messages. And the words LIFE OF THE FLESH IS IN THE BLOOD.

Only the word *Life* was carved. The rest of the message was written in black ink. As if the scribe had grown weary of the work.

"The hell does it mean?" Bandoni muttered.

Miller cleared his throat. "The part about betraying with a kiss. That's from the Bible. Judas kissed Jesus to signal to the soldiers which man they should arrest."

Bandoni snapped his fingers. "Judas. Right." He had his phone out. "The hell is the exact quote?"

We looked at Miller, who said, "Sorry. I've lapsed."

Bandoni typed and scrolled. He said, "Fucking fat fingers." Then: "Got it. King James version. The exact words are, 'But Jesus said unto him, Judas, betrayest thou the Son of man with a kiss?'"

"This asshole thinks he's the son of man?" Miller's voice cracked on the last word.

The tech spoke up. "What about the other words? What are those from?"

"The life of the flesh is in the blood." Bandoni looked at Bell. "You're the doc. What does it mean?"

"Unless you're looking for a literal explanation," she said dryly, "I'm not the person to ask. My knowledge is limited to hearing the quote in a hematology class."

But this one I knew.

When I was little, my parents had sent me to Sunday school, even though they weren't churchgoers. Maybe they figured if I had a place in heaven, I'd help them trade up. I recognized the words on John Doe's back because we'd been forced to memorize them, and they had scared the crap out of me.

"Those words are from the Bible, too," I said.

Bandoni's eyes above the mask were intent. "Go on."

"Leviticus." I closed my eyes, summoning the memory. "It goes something like this. For the life of a creature is in the blood, and I have given it to you to make an atonement for your souls upon the altar, since it is the lifeblood that makes atonement."

I opened my eyes. Bell, Bandoni, and Miller were staring at me.

Miller whistled. "You're like a quotation book."

"Just a weird childhood." I looked at our victim. The words on his skin seemed to convulse as we moved in and out of the glare from the ceiling-mounted surgical light. "Betrayal and atonement. This guy wants to even some score."

"I hate religious nuts more than just about anything." Bandoni glowered. "Quoting from the Bible."

"He's on a mission," I said. "Ordained by God."

"Or the devil," Miller said.

"Your gutter punk." Bandoni's faded-blue eyes sparked. "The guy who calls himself Damn Fox. Didn't your source say he has Bible verses tattooed on him?"

"That's right."

"We gotta find his righteous ass."

"We'll get him at Leopard's Den," I said. "At the concert."

"That's twenty-four hours from now." He scowled.

Bell had continued her external exam during our back-and-forth. Without looking up she said, "I did hear that quote in medical school, as I mentioned. Although I didn't know it was from the Bible. Blood was considered all powerful by the early physicians. If you were sick or in an ill humor, it was because your blood was out of whack."

"Then maybe a medical student?" I ventured. "Or a doctor?"

"Or a coroner." Bell's flat voice betrayed nothing.

Bandoni said, "Tell me he did this after our John Doe was dead."

"I could, but I'd be lying." She had moved on to John Doe's feet. "It's definitely antemortem. I'd estimate a day or two, based on the amount of scabbing. Around the same time the tattoo was done."

"So maybe the killer did both?"

"The cuts look similar. He was likely either drugged or strapped down. There's gray, sticky residue on his wrists and ankles."

"Duct tape," Miller said.

"That would be my guess."

"Fuck me," Bandoni murmured again, almost like a prayer.

"And there's more," Bell said. "There was violent anal penetration."

I forced myself to stand steady. To give away nothing. But inside, microscopic fissures fanned out through my heart like ice fracturing.

Bandoni, though, actually looked happy. "We'll get DNA maybe."

"I'll take swabs. But from the injuries, I'd guess he was penetrated with something inorganic. The internal examination will show exactly how violent the assault was."

"It couldn't have been self-inflicted?" Bandoni asked.

Her gaze was level. "No."

"It's not uncommon for gay-bashers to sodomize gay men," I said. "Or trans individuals."

Bandoni nodded. "Some warped idea of making the punishment fit the crime."

"An eye for an eye." I glanced at the words on our victim's back. "Like in the Bible."

"Boy who did this had some serious hate going on."

We waited while Bell and the assistant tipped the body left and then right as they slid the bag away. The tech examined the corners of the bag for any additional evidence while Bell washed the body. They took more photos, then placed blocks under the neck and between the shoulder blades to raise the upper torso and head.

When Bell began a coronal mastoid incision across John Doe's skull, my gaze returned to the ruin of his face. It was impossible to guess what he'd looked like before his killer found him. We had no photo yet with which to fill in the blanks. All I knew was that he was roughly my age. That he was pale and a little pudgy and had black hair.

Without even knowing what he'd looked like, my mind began to build an image of who he had been before his death. I imagined him standing tall, ducking through rain, laughing at something he'd heard. His dark hair lifted in a breeze, his hands folded around a cup of coffee or a dog's leash or a book.

He was a man who should have had a long life in front of him. A life in which to struggle and make mistakes. And also a life with which to succeed in ways that mattered to him. To love someone and be with them. To have children, if that was his wish. To take his dog to the park or play video games or hike fourteeners. To have a beer with a friend, a glass of wine with his lover.

I dug my fingernails into my palms to stop myself.

"I'm just going to use the ladies'," I said to Bandoni.

I did not need another ghost.

I shoved through the morgue's two sets of doors almost at a run, blasting into daylight. I grabbed the railing as the world tipped, and for a horrible moment I thought I would vomit.

I closed my eyes. I was no stranger to violent death. No brand-new rookie showing up for her first autopsy. I knew all too well the myriad ways men hurt each other, the countless variations on pain. Death is a song with a million melodies that always ends on the same discordant note.

So why this?

I pushed my mask down around my neck and gulped in one breath, then another. There came a shimmer of air, and I closed my eyes, unwilling to see.

Breathe, Parnell, I told myself. *Our ghosts are merely our guilt.*

After a moment, I said, "It's been a while."

He said, "You haven't needed me."

I opened my eyes and looked at the dead man standing next to me at the railing.

The Sir. My murdered commanding officer. He'd been my mentor while he lived, my restless conscience ever since.

"What makes you think I need you now?" I asked.

"Love."

"Love?"

He nodded his ghost-gray head. "That's right."

"Pardon the fuck out of me, Sir. But I don't get it."

92

"You're living for something bigger now. And that's good."

I was thinking of Cohen. Of Clyde. But I didn't think that was what the Sir meant. "Are you talking about our John Doe?"

"Love your fellow man. Sixties tripe." He tapped his hand on the railing, a mimicry of Bandoni's earlier action. "Except it's true. More now than ever."

"You're telling me I should love a dead man. And that will fix . . . what, exactly?"

"Your heart," the Sir said. "You're doing good so far, Corporal. Don't screw it up."

"A dead man is telling me not to screw up," I said. "That's rich."

But he was gone.

Behind me, the door opened and closed. I looked over my shoulder. Bandoni. Probably come to tell me to grow a pair.

Angrily, I patted my pockets for a cigarette. Then remembered I'd quit.

"Here," Bandoni said, passing me his half-empty pack.

"Thanks." I shook one out. Bandoni passed over his plastic lighter. We both lit up and smoked in silence for a few minutes.

"You here to give me shit?" I asked.

"Nope."

I glanced sidelong at him. He was watching the heavens again.

The nicotine hit my blood, and tension oozed out of my pores like sweat. "How many times have you quit?"

"God knows." He tapped ash onto the concrete. "I don't have a fucking clue."

"I thought I'd forever quit."

He laughed, then sobered. "If you're going to be a murder cop, you can't let the cases get to you. Not even the nasty ones."

"Who says they are?"

"Parnell."

"You're my mother now?"

"If I have to be. Rookie."

I looked at him. He rolled his eyes.

I breathed in, exhaled. Watched the smoke linger in the still air. A motorcycle revved its engine somewhere nearby, and the sound of traffic on the interstate thrummed. Clyde was invisible in the back of the Tahoe, probably taking a nap.

"That's the nicest thing you've said to me, Bandoni."

"Don't mean we're engaged. Just saying, if you aren't careful, this job will kill you."

I raised an eyebrow at him as we both tapped ash onto the ground. "You and irony? I never would have guessed."

"You'll have to talk simple. Keep it at my level."

I laughed despite my mood.

He said, "How many autopsies you seen?"

"This is my fifth. But I've handled plenty of dead people."

"I know that. It's not the same."

Bandoni walked down to a picnic bench where morgue staff probably took their lunches on nice days. I followed. He heaved his bulk onto the center of the table and set his feet on the bench. "In Iraq, you were treating those men and women with complete respect. Here, you must feel like we're doing more damage than the killer."

By now, Bell would have peeled John Doe's scalp from his skull, opened the bone, and would be lifting out his traumatized brain.

"You're right," I said. "An autopsy is another intrusion."

"Don't sound so surprised. It's the shits, this job. Sometimes. Sometimes it's fucking fantastic."

"When you find the killer?"

"Not that. Or not *just* that, anyway. The pure, sweet rush of drugs in your veins comes when you nail 'em in court."

I remembered the big case Bandoni had lost, long before my time. The one that had fallen apart in court.

"What happens when you lose in front of the judge?" I asked.

"I don't. Not anymore." He stabbed his cigarette at me. "So don't do anything stupid, rookie. Or my advice to the lieutenant will be to bust you all the way down."

One thing with Bandoni—at least you knew where you stood.

"I've been thinking about the ink on his arm," he said. "We'll need someone to look through that tattoo mug book."

I only had to give it two seconds of thought. "Gorman isn't on a case right now, is he?"

Bandoni grinned. I think it was the first time I'd seen his upper teeth.

"Gorman." He nodded. "No job too small."

I sucked in a lungful of smoke and released it. "Where do you think they took him to hurt him like that?"

"Our job to figure it out."

He pushed himself off the picnic table. The slick soles of his cheap dress shoes slapped the concrete. We both crushed out our cigarettes.

"You ready?" he asked.

"Lead on, Macduff."

"Sometimes I have no fucking idea what you're saying."

"Shakespeare. *Macbeth.* Give it a try."

"Shakespeare." He opened the door. "He as good as Louis L'Amour?"

"Who?"

"Louis L'Amour. The Sacketts." He clapped my shoulder almost cheerily. "Gap in your knowledge base, rookie. Better work on it."

CHAPTER 9

Perhaps we are not cursed by war and what we've seen.

Perhaps we are holy.

—Peter Hayes, *Clinical Therapist, VA Hospital.*

When Clyde and I stopped at headquarters, the detectives' room was quiet. A light glowed in the lieutenant's office, but her blinds were drawn, and I hoped she was gone for the day. I needed to type up the incident reports. Paperwork was every cop's nemesis.

One hour, I promised myself. Then home.

I filled Clyde's water bowl, and my patient partner settled into his usual spot as if he was far more adjusted to the career change than I was. I kicked off my shoes, made a note to buy a case of blister bandages, then typed up my interview with the gutter punk, Purple, and my observations from the autopsy. Once Bell supplied us with her own report, I'd link the files. By then we would hopefully have a name to attach.

My phone buzzed as I was finishing up. The forensic artist had sent me the composite sketch from her meeting with Deke. I studied the image. Definitely Latina. Dark hair and eyes, a sweet, uncertain expression. She did not look like killer material.

"Where are you?" I said out loud.

I forwarded the text to Bandoni, then tried again to reach the security guy from ColdShip. Martin Chase. Still no answer. I left another message explaining how important it was that he contact me. I didn't mention we'd requested a warrant.

I finished out the hour by looking at my email. I had a message from Ron Gabel. He'd eliminated another potential suspect from the rape of Denise Jackson's mother. Tired as I was, anger did a quick boil in my blood. Too many times these creeps climbed out of the swamp, ruined someone's life, then disappeared back into the murk.

I had just shut down my computer when Clyde lifted his head and footsteps scuffed the carpet behind me.

"Parnell."

I swiveled my chair. Lieutenant Lobowitz leaned against Detective Shultz's desk, her arms folded, her expression unreadable. Lobowitz wasn't physically imposing, but she radiated a cross-this-line-you-die vibe. No one wanted to draw her ire. Not fresh-faced patrol FNGs. Not crusty old homicide dicks who'd faced the most violent dregs of humanity.

And especially not me.

Lobowitz hooked one ankle over the other. Despite her stylish high heels, it didn't look as if her feet hurt. I wondered if it would be bad form to ask her secret.

"You're making a late night of it," she said.

I refrained from pointing out that I wasn't the only one. "I was just finishing up our reports. I'm heading out now."

"And your partner?"

Hopefully settling in with a beer and March Madness. But discretion is the better part of valor. "Finishing up at the morgue."

"You make me nervous, Parnell."

"Ma'am?"

"Your previous cases. The ones you handled while you still worked for Denver Pacific. Pretty damn impressive. Catching killers, solving a

97

ten-year-old cold case. Saving a kidnap victim. Not too many cops have a record like that."

Sensing a trap, I waited.

"So I'm impressed," she went on. "That's the good news."

I knew my line like I'd seen it written in a script. "And the bad news, ma'am?"

"You're a cowboy, Detective Parnell." She uncrossed her ankles and leaned in to rest a hand on my desk. Her breath smelled strongly of coffee, as if she'd just downed a gallon of the stuff. "Calling your own shots. Ricocheting solo around the city like an out-of-control pinball. Maybe that was fine with the higher-ups at Denver Pacific. But we can't afford that. *I* can't afford that. Do you want to know why?"

My mama didn't raise no fool. Not on most days, anyway.

I nodded.

"Because right now, every eye in the city is on this department. Civilians. Our fellow cops. And city officials, right on up to the mayor. A lot of those people want me to fail simply because I'm a woman. They are *looking* for something to go wrong on my watch. Something they can point to and say, 'Our bad, promoting females. Won't make that mistake again.'"

If it's so tough for women, I wanted to say, *shouldn't we be on the same side?*

Lobowitz straightened and tapped her palm against my desk. Her wedding band ticked against the metal trim. "If you learn anything at all during your probation period, make it this. You aren't a one-man show anymore. No heroics. No knight-in-shining-armor bullshit. There's a lot of talk about women empowerment. But the Denver PD is not the place where you decide you can scrap the rules. Better to think of yourself as being back in the Marines, when you couldn't blow your nose without some officer's say-so."

"Initiative—"

She held up a hand. "Is good when you have enough experience. Not now. You're to be on Bandoni's ass like wet toilet paper. Unless he specifically tasks you with something, you don't do it. You especially don't do it if it's *your* idea and he hasn't okayed it."

I resisted saluting. Or bolting for the door.

"Are we clear on that, Parnell?"

Clear as the business end of an assault rifle. "Perfectly, ma'am."

"I don't have your back. I am not your friend. And if I catch even a whiff of any more cowboying, I will make sure your detective days are gone forever."

Lobowitz pushed herself off the desk, rubbed her neck. "Bandoni told you to finish the reports tonight?"

Underneath the desk, I crossed my fingers. "Yes, ma'am."

"Are you finished?"

"I am."

"Then go home." For a moment, her face softened. "Work-life balance, Parnell. Keep that fixed in your headlights. This job will eat you alive if you let it."

I nodded.

"How's Bandoni?" she asked.

"Fine," I said, because I knew that was what Bandoni would want me to say. The gray skin. The exhaustion. Whatever he was sitting on, if it was anything at all, it was his secret for now.

"Okay, then. I'll see you tomorrow."

She threaded her way through the desks but stopped at the door.

"Good job this morning," she said. "But don't ever do it again."

◆ ◆ ◆

The drive home was a good opportunity to begin the separation of work and the rest of my life. As night settled over Denver, I found U2 on the radio, and Clyde and I rocked along with Bono as we made our way through rush-hour traffic on the interstate. Or I rocked, and Clyde managed to look like he was enjoying himself.

We exited at US 285 and headed west. A few minutes later, I turned into the entrance to Cherry Hills—the location of Cohen's home and one of the most exclusive neighborhoods in all of Denver. Not to mention the United States. I pulled up to the guard's gate and rolled down my window.

Bill Major stepped out of his shack and propped his arms on the Tahoe's door. "Ms. Parnell. And my pal Clyde. How are you two this cold evening?"

"Happy to be home, Bill. How's your day been?"

"No complaints. 'Cause who'd listen, anyway?" He grinned and stepped back, smacking the roof of the Tahoe with his open palm. The gate swung grandly open. "Enjoy your evening, Detective."

"You, too, Bill," I said, vaguely astonished, as always, that I wasn't turned away at the gate.

I checked my rearview as I drove through the gateway—a habit left from my days driving on and off the forward operating base in Iraq. Eyes in the back of your head.

Outside the entrance and across the street, a dark-colored cargo van pulled to a stop beneath a streetlight. In the light's yellow glow, it was impossible to tell if the vehicle was blue or black.

A memory surfaced—a van like this one had driven past in the parking garage right after I'd finished stuffing a naked Barbie doll into a paper bag along with broken glass.

I pulled over inside the gate and parked. I don't know what I was thinking—that I'd approach the driver and ask if he'd tied a doll to the Tahoe's chassis? But as I opened the driver's door and stepped out, the van pulled into traffic and vanished into a stream of headlights.

I slid back into the Tahoe and looked at Clyde. He was half-out of his seat, ready to tackle whatever had caught my attention.

"Let's go home, boy," I said. "It was just a case of paranoia."

◆ ◆ ◆

Thirty minutes later, I sat across from Cohen at the kitchen table. Thelonious Monk played softly on the speakers, and two fingers of Macallan glowed like topaz in the cut-crystal glasses he'd set in front of us. Clyde sprawled at my feet, chewing rawhide.

"How was the rest of your day?" Cohen asked. He was freshly showered after a run, and his damp hair clung to his forehead. In his long-sleeve T-shirt and sweats, his bare feet propped on the chair next to his, he looked like a model for an ad in a men's magazine—the sexiness of casual wear.

"It was fine," I said.

He raised an eyebrow. "Okay."

Work-life balance, I reminded myself. Then I thought, *fuck it.*

"Would you look at something?" I asked.

The other eyebrow came up. Something sparked in his eyes. "What did you have in mind?"

I grabbed a pad of paper from the junk drawer and drew the inverted triangle with the shepherd's staff inside that had been tattooed on John Doe's arm. "You ever see this?"

Cohen looked disappointed for just a second before he turned his attention to the drawing. After a moment he shook his head. "You look in the tat book?"

"Bandoni's got Gorman on it." I took the paper back and drew the other odd symbol that had also been on John Doe's arm, the traditional symbols for male and female, with a line in between. "There was this, too. Probably placed on our victim by his killer. You think maybe it suggests a person with both male and female characteristics?"

"It's close to one of the symbols used by an intersex person." Cohen made another drawing and pushed the pad back to me. The image showed a single circle with both the female cross and the male arrow emanating from it.

"You're the sex guy now," I said. "What's an intersex person?"

"It means someone who has physical aspects of both male and female. It can be as obvious as female breasts and a penis or as subtle as contradictory sex hormones."

"But the tattoo on our victim keeps male and female separated. Divided by the line."

We studied the drawing. Cohen said, "Maybe it's part of a hate-crime pattern. That man is rightfully over woman."

That sounded right. "And our victim, by being gay or by cross-dressing or whatever was going on here, maybe telling people he was intersex . . ."

Cohen waited.

I plowed on. "Maybe his actions made the killer decide to assert male dominance and punish someone who didn't follow the so-called natural order."

"Wasn't there a woman at the crime scene?"

"Sometimes women buy into the male-superiority thing."

The corners of Cohen's mouth tipped up. "Wise of them."

I tossed the notepad at him. "That's the last time I let you be on top."

He leaned across the table. The candlelight glinted in his gray eyes. "Prove it," he said.

In the middle of the night, while both my men were snoring, I came wide awake.

I tossed and turned for a time before I gave up on sleep and eased out of bed, phone in hand. Clyde lifted his head as I stirred, but I signaled for him to stay and went out of the room.

A soft glow from the outdoor lights on Grandma Walker's mansion next door filtered through the windows, brushing silver strokes onto a gray world. I grabbed a throw blanket from the couch and went out onto the deck.

An owl loosed its lonely call, and the boughs of nearby firs whooshed in the wind. Frost sparkled on the planks of the deck, burning against my bare feet. But I didn't step away. It was one of a hundred small punishments I pressed upon myself. For surviving.

For other things.

I sucked in cold air. The world was caught between winter and spring, and at night, winter still held sway. I sat on one of the deck chairs and checked my phone. Mauer had gotten the recordings from the Bailey Yard and forwarded them to me. I played through the footage from the time the refrigerator cars arrived in the yard through their transfer to Deke's train, and the departure.

No hobos. No gutter punks. At least none caught by the cameras.

I looked at my voice mail. Nothing from ColdShip.

I slipped the phone into the pocket of my sweats and leaned back in the chair. Overhead, stars blazed. The night was deep and dark, and I was alone inside it.

Or perhaps not. Nearby, a car door slammed, followed by the grumble of an engine. I waited for the sound of a vehicle pulling away, but the night stayed quiet. And weighted. As if someone else was awake with me in the darkness.

I closed my eyes. Unbidden, an image of the dark-colored van pulling under a streetlight rose in my mind.

There'd been a similar van two months earlier, I now recalled. In a grocery store parking lot. I'd left Clyde at his trainer's and decided to pick up a few things at the store. It was the middle of winter, bitterly cold, and dark had arrived with the suddenness of a hammer blow. I was loading groceries into the back of the Tahoe when a man approached.

"Help you with those?" he asked.

I straightened and gave the man my full gaze, trying to gauge if he was a threat. Cops aren't always popular, and I was still in uniform from the day's shift.

"Evening," he said.

He was tall and muscular. White. Dressed in jeans and a parka. His age was indeterminate—he'd wrapped a scarf around his lower face, and his eyes were invisible in the gloom. He stood with his legs planted wide and his shoulders up and back, his head tipped ever so slightly to one side in a gesture that inexplicably suggested menace. As if I were nothing but a curiosity, a bug under glass. Beyond him, at the outer reaches of the lights from the store, a dark-colored van idled, exhaust blooming into the night.

The rest of the parking lot was all but empty. Only an elderly man twenty spaces over, easing his thin body into a truck.

"I'm good," I said firmly. My hand went to the butt of my gun.

"Just trying to be helpful, Officer." Then: "You aren't wearing a wedding ring."

"Why don't you move along, sir."

"Thought maybe you'd let a gentleman take you for a drink." His voice was low and heavy. Like silt from an ancient riverbed.

"You need to leave," I said.

His eyes flashed. Maybe it was nothing more than lights from the store catching his irises, but the sudden gleam made the hair rise on the back of my neck.

Behind us, laughter rose as a group of teenagers spilled from the store, shouting at each other as they made their way out into the parking lot.

The man kept his eerie, sidelong gaze on me for a few more seconds, then spun on his heel and strode away, slipping into the van on the passenger side. I watched while whoever was behind the wheel drove away.

The van had no plates.

A minute later, the night swallowed it as completely as if I'd imagined the entire encounter.

Now, on Cohen's deck, I opened my eyes.

I'd forgotten all about that night. Was it possible there was a connection between the man and the Barbie doll? With the van idling outside Cherry Hills?

A veil of clouds drifted over the stars. The lights at the Walker mansion clicked off on a timer, and the night turned utterly black.

Sensing something, I jerked upright as goose bumps rose on my skin.

A man—unearthly, insubstantial—stood at the far end of the deck, turned away from me, his hands gripping the rail as he lifted his broken face to the night. He was nude from the waist up, his back carved with words of blood and betrayal.

I pulled the blanket tight around my shoulders.

Our John Doe had no face. But still I had not been able to stop myself at the autopsy. As much as I could, I did for him what I do for all the dead. I restored him to what he'd been before violence broke him apart. I cleaned away the blood and reshaped his ruined skull and made his chest rise and fall once more. I placed a pulse in his wrists and ankles and neck.

But I did not give him a face. And I did not make him smile.

For if the dead smile, they don't do so in the places where I meet them.

CHAPTER 10

What greed, to think others can belong to us. That we can belong to them.

It's like trying to hold the universe in your pocket.

—*Sydney Parnell. Personal journal.*

At six in the morning, Bandoni phoned.

"We got an ID," he said. "Our victim's a local boy."

Cohen and I were sitting on the deck, surrounded by trees and birdsong and the remnants of breakfast. After I'd signed on with Homicide, Cohen had decided that we should start our days with a good meal whenever our caseloads allowed. Today he'd outdone himself. Egg and vegetable frittata with toast and blueberries. Fresh-squeezed orange juice. Coffee from Saint Helena.

An hour steeped in indulgence before we moved on to sex and murder.

"Go on," I said.

A grunt from Bandoni. I suspected there was an entire language buried in Bandoni's nonverbal sounds. Like dolphin clicks. Or whale song. Maybe someday I'd figure out the code.

"Victim is Noah Asher, twenty-five years old," he said. "He lived alone in University Hills, so clearly not doing badly for himself. No wants, no warrants. Not so much as a traffic ticket. I just texted you his

DMV photo. Kid looks like a choir boy. You want to tell me what he was doing on a train out of Nebraska?"

"That's why it's called a mystery." I opened Bandoni's text. He was right. Pale-moon face, gentle eyes. A cowlick. I passed the phone to Cohen so he could look at the photo. "When can we get in his house?"

"Soon as we get there."

"I can meet you in—"

"But." A sigh. "My fucking take-home car won't start. I'm having it towed to the police garage."

I gulped down the last splash of coffee. "Why don't I pick you up, and we'll head over?"

"Long as I don't have to sit in the back with Fido."

"No worries," I said. "Fido always gets the front seat."

Forty minutes later, I pulled up in front of the Wingate apartments and texted Bandoni that Clyde and I had arrived.

The apartments, a collection of bland, beige buildings with dark-brown trim, had seen better days. Broken screens, a pitiful-looking playground featuring a single swing, wooden railings that looked like they'd fly apart in the next breeze. A strip of grass marred the otherwise flawless expanse of pitted and crumbling tarmac. The entry gates were propped open, and it looked like someone had taken a baseball bat to the code box.

I half regretted the fact that I'd driven my city-issued car instead of my old Land Cruiser. Bandoni was sure to be unhappy with my ride, a blinged-out black Chevrolet Tahoe equipped with a passenger-seat K9 belt and a temperature-controlled dog crate in the rear. But the Tahoe had come to the Denver PD free of charge—an anonymous donation by someone who said they'd read about my role in recovering a kidnapped child and wanted to make sure Clyde and I were safe in our new position.

While the cars issued to detectives by the city were decent, they weren't fancy. And when they broke down, the cop had to get a car from the carpool, which meant driving around a piece of junk. Which meant I was grateful for the SUV. But I also knew it was another black mark in an ever-lengthening column whose heading read *Golden Girl*.

Bandoni emerged from his building brushing crumbs from the front of his suit jacket. He looked unkempt and harried and pissed off at the world.

In other words, exactly like himself.

"Good morning, partner," I said when he opened the passenger door.

His scowl deepened. "Who sprinkled fairy dust on your cereal?"

"Same guy who peed in yours."

"Ha."

Bandoni hauled himself into the front seat—freshly dehaired just for him—and examined the car's features as I pulled out of the parking lot and into traffic. The donor had added every imaginable upgrade, from heated leather seats to Bluetooth.

Bandoni glared. "You're probably scared to eat in here."

I wasn't about to admit that, even though it was true. "Car's got a self-cleaning function."

"Good." His grin was pure evil. "Let's go through the drive-through at Mickey D's. It's gonna be a three–Egg McMuffin day."

A while later, the Tahoe redolent with the smell of sausage, I turned into a neighborhood of homes dating from the 1950s. I parked in front of a single-story redbrick home with dark-green shutters and a matching door. The door was blocked by crime scene tape, and a locksmith called by the Denver PD had placed a coded lockbox on the knob.

I glanced down the street. No weedy yards, no cans at the curb. Lots of birdbaths and minivans.

"Respectable little neighborhood," Bandoni said.

"Not exactly the place for a young man hoping to hook up," I said. "Nearest nightlife is miles away."

"Yale Station and the light-rail is only two blocks over," Bandoni pointed out. "It's a good starter home. Especially if you're thinking family. Or if you travel. Lots of stay-at-home moms to keep an eye on your place."

There was a certain wistfulness in his voice. After seeing Wingate, I could understand.

I pushed my sunglasses up on my head. "If we're lucky, one of them will have seen or heard something."

"Uniforms are canvassing later."

We got out, and while Clyde watered the bushes, Bandoni and I studied the house.

The place was shabby genteel. The yard—still dormant after winter—was groomed but not fancy. A yard designed to meet the local homeowners' covenants without any undue effort. A large fir in the front yard blocked half of the house from view. On the walk-up porch, two chairs and a bistro-style table sat near one of the windows. On the north side, a lane led toward the back and an unattached garage.

I looked up and down the neighborhood and inhaled the scent of composting leaves and still-brown grass. No gardeners. No joggers. There was a sign asking drivers to slow for playing children and a pedestrian crossing at the end of the street. The kids would be in school by now, one or both parents at work.

Clyde rejoined us, and we walked around to the back. A single-car garage took up a third of the yard. The DMV had a Saab 9-3 registered in Noah's name, but a peek through the window showed an empty bay.

"We need to put out a BOLO for Noah's Saab," I said.

Bandoni rattled the handle on the garage door. It didn't budge. "You know what would make me happier than a pig in mud? If we found his car, and his cell phone was in the glove box."

"If it's an iPhone, finding it will be as useful as picking up a brick."

"Way to think positive. You ever leave your phone in your car?"

"There was one time, a couple of years ago."

"Like all you millennials." He grunted. "We'll get the records."

An alleyway ran behind Noah's garage and those of his neighbors. A trashcan and a recycling bin were inside his chain-link fence, the gate padlocked shut. I peered into both cans. Empty. I made a mental note to find out when the trash went out.

Back at the front, Clyde and I followed Bandoni up the porch steps. He punched the code to the lockbox, then sliced open the crime scene tape.

"Not like the old days," he said. "We used to have to break windows."

Once inside, we both signed the form on the clipboard Bandoni had brought. He left it near the front door for the forensics detectives.

"Let's see what we got," he said.

An empty home feels like just that—empty in a way that makes the air echo with loneliness, as if the very molecules had too much weight to bear and had slunk away. Walk into the home of a dead person, and the sense of wrongness threatens to steal your breath.

Bandoni and I slipped on booties and gloves, and I cinched booties onto Clyde's paws. We did a walk-through to allow Clyde to sniff for weapons or illegal substances while Bandoni and I got a feel for the place, which had that new-house smell of paint and resin. The front of the house consisted of living and dining rooms. A hallway led to the kitchen, half bath, a bedroom and master bath, and a door to the basement. Nothing caught Clyde's attention. At the very back of the house was an art studio with a large drafting desk and bookshelves filled with bottles of ink, stacks of sketch pads, and mason jars crammed with brushes, pens, and pencils. An impressive array of ink sketches covered the walls all the way to the ceiling.

I stared up at them. The drawings were brilliantly done. Whatever else Noah had done in his life, he'd left behind a kind of legacy.

We returned to the living room, and I downed Clyde near the front door.

The entire home had been renovated. The attic had been displaced by a high-beamed ceiling. Wide-plank wood floors ran throughout the house. The fireplace boasted freshly painted white brick, and the kitchen mixed white cabinetry with granite and stainless steel. Except for the art studio, furnishings consisted of a blend of metal and wood tables and consoles, a sofa and chairs with stilt legs, and brightly colored geometric rugs.

The furniture looked like the same vintage as that in my childhood home. Except it was sparkling and fresh. Not a single cigarette burn or whiskey ring that I could detect.

"This guy have a time machine?" I wondered out loud.

"Mid-century modern," Bandoni muttered.

"What?"

"It's the thing now. Copying furniture from the fifties. Like that show. *Mad Men*. The fifties are back, Parnell. Vintage modern. Welcome to the Cleavers'."

"The who?"

"Wally and the Beav. Check it out sometime."

The Beav. Made me glad I'd missed the fifties. "So the furniture is new? It's just designed to look old?"

"Like I said, it's a thing."

"I have a new appreciation for you, Bandoni."

"Save the sweet nothings for Cohen. Bottom line, our boy was fashionable."

I nodded, but what did I know about fashion? Before Cohen waltzed into my life and carried me off to his castle, I was living in my grandmother's home. My bedroom hadn't changed since I was a teenager.

"Let's start with the basement," Bandoni said.

I followed him down a narrow staircase into the unfinished basement—bare concrete floor and walls with a single garden-level window shrouded in cobwebs. Other than a pantry with a second refrigerator, a small storage closet, and an old futon, the place was taken up by folding tables covered with computers and odd parts. There were laptops, tangles of cords, SD drives, piles of hard drives, speakers, and stacks of computer manuals.

Most of it looked brand new and top dollar, including three large-screen monitors occupying a single table.

Bandoni whistled. "This shit'll keep the computer forensics guys busy for weeks."

He tapped a flat silver trackpad next to one of the monitors. The center console lit up, revealing the cartoon image of a scantily clad woman walking toward us, ass swaying, breasts swinging, her expression come-hither. The image enlarged until only her breasts showed, then the image rewound and she began her seductive walk anew. When Bandoni tapped again, a password box appeared.

"Not what I would have expected for a gay guy," Bandoni said.

"You're hung up on gay. Or maybe there's a roommate."

"Not according to the DMV, for what that's worth."

Bandoni watched the woman sashay again. After two more passes, he sighed and turned away.

The other screens remained dark when he touched their trackpads.

Another table held six laptops. All were powered on, and all were password protected.

"Who the hell needs six laptops?" Bandoni muttered. "Notepad and pen is good enough for me."

"There's this thing called the internet now. You should give it a try." But I wondered the same thing.

While Bandoni looked around the rest of the space, I returned to the main table with its three large monitors. Taped to the wall above the center console was a piece of paper torn from a legal pad. Written on it in red felt-tip pen was a single line.

OUR ANGER IS RIGHTEOUS

"What's that?" Bandoni asked.

"His mantra?" I shrugged. "His brand?"

"'Our,' though. Sounds like he's part of a group."

Paperwork next to the computer caught my eye. I picked up the top sheet, and a spider skittered away. "Maybe this one."

It was an invoice from Water Resources, Inc. with Noah's name typed at the top. The invoice showed two weeks' worth of billable hours for work on a project called Water Assets Development DB.

I studied the numbers. Noah was very well paid.

"One mystery solved," I said, handing the invoice to Bandoni. "Our guy was a software geek. *DB* is probably *database*."

Bandoni scanned the page. "Explains all the computers. Maybe those words are the motto of the group he works with. Doesn't seem real business friendly, though, if he's on their payroll. And what about water would piss a guy off?"

"That there's not enough of it?" I got on my phone, looking for information on the company. "Water Resources Incorporated is a hydrology business. Offices throughout the West. They seem more interested in turning water into money, not conserving it."

"Bet the environmentalists love that," Bandoni said.

I looked at the words again. *Our anger is righteous.* "Maybe Noah was on their side."

We considered the implications of that while we finished looking around. Bandoni found an accordion folder with more invoices, which showed Noah had been employed at Water Resources for a little over a year.

The room yielded nothing else of immediate interest.

Back upstairs, we went more slowly through the rooms, starting with the kitchen.

Wolf appliances. Crate & Barrel dishes. An extensive collection of glassware, from whiskey tumblers to brandy snifters.

The refrigerator revealed what I would have expected—shelves filled with boxes of takeout. Chinese, Italian, Ethiopian, some of it well past its shelf life. My fridge used to be its twin. There was a cardboard box of beer from a local brewery, one end ripped open, two cans gone.

The room also held a well-stocked liquor cabinet, and the stuff was high end. I recognized some of the bottles from the scotch in Cohen's grandmother's collection. The old woman's cellar held the kind of liquid ambrosia that would lure the gods down from Olympus.

"He had expensive taste," I said. "Hundreds of dollars for some of these bottles."

Bandoni shot me a look of surprise. "I thought you grew up on the other side of the tracks."

As a flush rose in my face, I busied myself reading labels.

But Bandoni's surprise settled into a knowing grin. "Cohen. Whole new world, huh, kid?"

The best defense is a good offense. "You were his partner for how many years? You learn *anything* from hanging out with him?"

"Relax, Parnell. You want boundaries, we got boundaries. It's the secret to a successful partnership. Didn't work so well with my ex, but . . ." He moved the bottles around with his gloved hand. "Two inches gone from one bottle. Maybe one from another. The rest hasn't even been opened."

In the master bedroom, I took the closet while Bandoni headed toward the dresser.

Noah's walk-in was meticulously arranged. Shirts and pants on the left, finely tailored suits and jackets on the right, shoes arrayed on metal racks. There wasn't a single dress or pair of high heels or anything else to suggest Noah had a secret life. I glanced at some of the clothing labels. I knew enough from Cohen's wardrobe to realize I was looking at tens of thousands of dollars' worth of clothes.

My guess was when we got to Noah's banking records, we'd be equally impressed. Software development sure beat the hell out of a cop's salary.

A gym bag sat on the floor next to the shoe racks. I knelt and unzipped it. Neatly folded gym clothes, a stainless-steel water bottle, and in the side pocket, a membership card to a national fitness chain.

Pushed into a back corner of the closet was an unsealed cardboard box. Inside were faded, ratty sweatpants, a couple of hoodies, and a slew of T-shirts with the necks stretched out of shape and holes under the arms. The tees had tech logos, and a couple were from COMDEX. I looked it up on my phone—COMDEX was a Las Vegas hi-tech conference.

I stared at the old clothes for a moment. Out with the old and in with the new. Noah Asher was shedding feathers, molting into something new and shiny. Or at least vintage and cool.

But he hadn't gotten to enjoy his transition for long.

I straightened, stretched my back.

Was Noah's transformation a conscious change from stereotypical computer geek to man of the world? Or a sexual outing from straight to gay? Had his killer been part of that metamorphosis? Maybe resented it?

I stepped out from the closet and turned toward Bandoni where he was bent over the dresser's open drawers.

"Anything?" I asked.

"Gym clothes," Bandoni said. "Socks. Underwear. Some nice fleece pullovers. But mostly gym clothes. And a stash of cash. Five hundred dollars in twenties."

"He was a member of a local fitness center."

"We'll get someone from the squad to pay a visit. Maybe he tried to make a move on someone in the locker room."

"What gives you that idea?"

He snorted. "'Cause he was fucking gay. You ever seen a man's bedroom this organized?"

I rolled my eyes.

On each side of the neatly made bed was a nightstand. One held cold medicine. The other an unopened box of condoms—a sign of optimism or an indicator of regular use? No phone or calendar. A graphic novel lay on one nightstand, a bookmark halfway through. The novel appeared to be about a future in which women had taken over.

While I went into the master bathroom and examined an awe-inspiring array of grooming lotions and gels, Bandoni headed toward the hallway.

"Check this out," he called a minute later.

I closed the medicine cabinet and followed Bandoni's voice to the back of the house.

"One mystery solved," he said as I entered the room. "Or deepened."

The art studio. The room was large and filled with light from the back windows. The drafting table occupied the center of the room, white task lamps clamped to each end. A stool was tucked beneath the desk, while on top lay a single sketchbook.

Bandoni had opened the book. Now he pointed to a drawing. "There she is."

The sketch showed a Latina sitting at a bistro table in an ice cream shop. She had long, dark hair, soulful black eyes, and a fierce expression. She wore a tight-fitting T-shirt and was tilting the straw in a milkshake glass to her lips. The milkshake was complete with whipped-cream swirls and a cherry on top.

"She looks like Deke's composite drawing," I said.

"Spitting image. She's your engineer's mysterious woman. And look at her T-shirt."

Emblazoned on the tee was an inverted triangle containing the shepherd's staff.

"It's the tattoo," I said. "The one on Noah's bicep."

"Gorman promised to look through the book this morning. Cross your fingers."

Behind the lady with the milkshake, another Latina leaned against the wall, her hair spilling out of a ponytail, her hands clutched tight around the handle of a mop. She stared at the other woman—the Milkshake Lady—with exhausted but hopeful eyes.

I lifted my gaze to the wall beyond the desk. The entire space was covered with page after page of both ink and colored drawings of the woman mixed in with sketches of trains, orphan waifs, and barely clad blond women serving—and sometimes servicing—handsome men. There were sketches of men holding assault rifles. One drawing showed men rioting in the street with women cheering them on. There were also sketches of a seriously-pissed-off-looking guy with yellow eyes, his face all but hidden in the shadow of a hoodie.

A smorgasbord of artistic curiosity, lust, and empathy.

The indecipherable mind of Noah Asher.

"Writing code paid for his Gucci loafers," I said. "But this art is what mattered to him."

We went over everything carefully, looking for some indication of who the woman was. We found receipts for his art supplies, tickets to comic conventions, books on how to illustrate, ink, and color graphic novels, and letters of encouragement from other writers and illustrators as he pursued a career in comics.

Bandoni found a manila folder filled with photographs of teens and young adults. He spread the pictures out on the drafting table.

"What do you make of these?" he asked.

I looked at each one. Dreadlocks. Homemade tattoos. One kid had his middle finger in the air. Another was sitting in a boxcar, playing a guitar. I glanced at the drawings on the walls, and understanding dawned. Not orphan waifs.

Kids like Purple.

"They're gutter punks," I said. "Like the girl I talked with yesterday. Noah wasn't trying to muscle in on their territory. He was drawing them."

"Some of these kids look hard-core. Maybe they weren't too crazy about the idea."

"Maybe. But I don't see anyone in these photos who matches the descriptions Purple gave for Damn Fox and Street Cred."

"Maybe those two didn't know him. Just witnesses, like they claimed."

"It still doesn't explain why Noah was in that dress."

We took the photos of the kids and kept searching. But we found no hint to the woman's identity.

"Hell, we don't even know if she's real," Bandoni said with disgust. "Maybe the resemblance between the woman Deke saw and this woman is nothing but coincidence."

"I don't like coincidence."

"It happens. 'There are more things in heaven and Earth, Horatio . . .'"

"Are you spouting *Hamlet*?" I laughed, and he looked wounded.

"Fuck you," he said. "I'm not a complete troglodyte. You look up L'Amour?"

"Twentieth-century writer of frontier novels. But I can't quote him. You win this one, Bandoni."

The wounded look shifted to a certain smugness.

But he was right. Our Milkshake Lady was perhaps nothing more than Noah's fantasy, a woman created for his comics. Maybe Noah was catering to new markets, finding his readers among women and minorities.

But whatever strangeness existed in the world, I still hated coincidences. And there was something about the woman in the illustrations. She didn't look like the overly stylized women I'd seen in comics drawn by men. Her breasts were large, but not to a degree that defied physics. Her face was full and round rather than classically beautiful, and her features were far from perfect. Her hair, thick and dark, was her best feature.

She looked real.

Unlike the sweet-faced woman in Deke's sketch, though, the Milkshake Lady looked angry. And tough. Like she could kick anyone's ass.

My mind flicked back to the piece of paper downstairs. *Our anger is righteous.*

Bandoni rubbed the back of his neck, turning his head back and forth as if something hurt. "You know anything about comics?"

"Just that I loved them when I was a kid. Superman. Batman. Supergirl. I especially loved the creepy comics. Tales from the Crypt. Boris Karloff. Scared the crap out of me." I shook myself. "Those were good times."

"Sounds like a happy childhood. Now you're about to learn a whole lot more about comics, starting as soon as we finish here." He looked up at the wall of drawings again, crossed his arms, and frowned. "Noah Asher didn't have a shortage of interests."

I nodded. "Starting with that train and the punks."

"And all those men with guns."

"And the hot babes."

His frown deepened. "Doing things their mamas wouldn't approve of."

"It's a lot of crazy pieces."

"And the thing is . . ." He narrowed his eyes at the artwork. "I'm not sure the pieces even come from the same puzzle."

"Maybe he was searching for something. Trying to find himself."

"With sex and guns?" He grunted. "I'll say one thing."

"What's that?"

"When I look at all this shit . . ."

"Yeah?"

"Makes the hair rise on the back of my neck."

We spent another hour in the house, and the surprises kept coming.

The living room held an L-shaped sofa in black leather, a glass-topped coffee table covered with a fan of *GQ* magazines, and floor-to-ceiling built-ins—open bookshelves with closed cabinets at the bottom. The mantel above the fireplace was covered with a series of photographs, a timeline that marched from left to right. On the far left, the pictures were black and white, showing a stern couple in wedding clothes followed by an equally stern couple with a baby girl. The next generation was the little girl—I presumed—all grown up. Several photos in, she was pregnant and starting a family of her own. The photos after that showed two babies becoming toddlers, teenagers, young men.

"Noah has a twin brother," I said.

Bandoni came over from the bookshelves and took a look. "Two peas in a pod."

Sarcasm. The boys looked nothing alike. Noah was dark haired, maybe six feet, pale with a tendency toward pudginess. His brother was several inches taller and fair, with lean features, a Cupid's-bow mouth, and intense blue eyes.

If Noah identified as straight, it must have been hard getting a date with a brother like that beaming his high-wattage smile on the girls. Assuming the brother was straight.

The final photo, and apparently the most recent, showed Noah and four other men standing in his backyard, a section of the house visible behind them. The camera had caught them clowning around, each boy-man striking a ludicrous pose—tongues out, one guy flashing a gang sign in a way only rich suburbanites can, another man air-kissing Noah's cheek. Noah's twin had his arm draped over his brother's shoulders as if to highlight the differences between them.

I picked up the photo in my gloved hands. One man stood slightly apart from the others, and unlike the rest, he didn't look like a goofy frat boy. He was tall and heavily built, and something about his pose—arms folded, a mocking look on a naturally severe face—made me think he was the group's leader. The others had on fashionable suits and flashy ties. But this man wore a plain black T-shirt and jeans. He stared directly into the camera with a look that was both commanding and arrogant.

I frowned.

He was also familiar. I took a minute to try and chase the memory before deciding I'd have to come back to it.

I pulled the photo out of the frame. On the back, someone had written **THE SUPERIOR GENTLEMEN**.

Could one of these men be Noah's killer? Other than the leader, the men in the group looked like good friends. But maybe there'd been a falling-out.

Betray me with a kiss.

I showed the photo to Bandoni—who grunted—and added it to the pile of things we would take with us. The invoices, receipts for a local comics store, bills, and credit-card statements. The photos of the gutter punks and several of Noah's sketches, including the Milkshake Lady.

"You making a note of everything on the Return on Inventory sheet?" Bandoni asked. "We'll have to run a copy over to court."

"I'm on it."

Like most of the rest of the house, the front room was neat and clean. Not the typical bachelor pad. There wasn't so much as a sheen of dust.

"Company coming maybe," I said.

Bandoni was searching the shelves next to the fireplace, which was laid with unlit logs.

"What?"

"Everything is freshly cleaned. I'll bet he was expecting company."

"Or he was OCD," Bandoni said. "Or maybe he had a cleaning lady. Don't jump to conclusions." He pointed toward the coffee table. "What do you make of the tray and decanter?"

"You asking me to jump to conclusions?" I said.

"Speculate. Not the same thing."

I looked more closely. A silver tray held a crystal decanter one-third filled with amber liquid. I lifted the stopper and inhaled. Brandy. Also on the tray were two glasses turned over on leather coasters so as not to collect dust.

"It's like it's staged," I said. "Maybe he was getting ready to put the house on the market."

"Nah." He gestured toward the mantel photos. "When you're staging a house, you hide all the personal stuff."

"Yeah?"

He shrugged and turned away. "Divorce."

On the wall opposite the front door, framing the archway that led to the rest of the house, were built-in wooden bookcases and cabinets. Modern pieces of *objets d'art* alternated with leather-bound versions of the classics. One shelf held modern mysteries and thrillers, all hardcover. There was also a series of books apparently intended for self-enrichment, each book a doorstop: *1001 Books You Must Read Before You Die*; *1001 Foods You Must Taste Before You Die*; *1001 Movies You Must See Before You Die*; *1001 Albums You Must Hear Before You Die*.

I wondered how many books and movies and albums Noah had managed to knock off his bucket list.

As Bandoni had done in the studio, I went through each book looking for notes or cards. Nothing.

"There are flyers here for a lecture series at DU," Bandoni said from where he stood at a library table at one end of the room. "And another for a film festival at that art house theater on East Colfax."

"The guy was working hard to better himself," I said.

Beneath the bookshelves were closed cabinets. I squatted and looked inside. More books. But of a very different bent. There were several paperbacks on how to attract women, a few more on how to seduce them. And a sprinkling of books with titles like *How to Get Filthy Rich Before You're Thirty*. There was also a stack of vintage *Hustler* magazines.

"Here's his secret stash," I said.

"Drugs?"

"Porn."

"Anything good?"

"Depends on your definition. But I'd say our guy is straight."

Next to the magazines was a beautiful four-by-five copper box. I opened it, then got to my feet. "Business cards."

I joined Bandoni at the library table, and together we laid out the cards. There were more than thirty. Most were for auto- or home-repair businesses along with a mix of home-remodeling companies. A couple were for managers from high-tech firms, and there were cards from headhunters—Noah's software skills were no doubt in demand. There were also two cards for housecleaning services.

"These might explain the condition of the house," I said.

"Add them to your list. He had a cleaner, she might know who came and went. Who left their toothbrush overnight."

The remaining cards were random—the kind you might pick up at a convention or at a bar during casual conversation.

Except one.

I picked up the final card—it had been at the bottom of the rubber-banded stack. It was heavy card stock, embossed, with a dark-brown background and ivory lettering. It said simply, THE SUPERIOR

GENTLEMEN. Right below was a second line, A PRIVATE CLUB. And below that was the stylized silhouette of a nude man and woman.

"Doing the dirty," Bandoni said.

There was no other information.

"The Superior Gentlemen," I said. "Like on the back of the photo."

"So these guys were in some kind of secret club involving women."

"Like a porn group, you mean?"

He shook his head. "Men don't need a special group for porn or strippers. That's just Friday night. It's something else."

"Like what?"

He kept shaking his head. "Our job to find out."

I gazed around the immaculate room, the polish, the staging. The sense it gave of a man determined to be seen a certain way. How did that mesh with gutter punks and men rioting in the streets? And the sign over his computer—*our anger is righteous.*

And how did any of this fit with the image carved on Noah's body—the symbol of a man with a line below it, and then the symbol for a woman?

I frowned. "The pieces don't fit."

But Bandoni gave a tight-lipped smile. "You'll learn, Parnell. Pick any person you pass on the street. In all this world, there's no greater contradiction than what you find in the heart of a human being."

I considered my own heart. I couldn't argue.

"The real question is . . ." Bandoni added the business card to our pile. "Which contradictory part of Noah Asher got him killed?"

CHAPTER 11

They try to step on you, Rosie girl? Then you become the gum on their soles they can't scrape off.

—Effie *"Grams" Parnell. Private conversation.*

Our task now was to build, piece by piece, a complete picture of Noah. No matter what his contradictions.

While I focused on the comics angle, Bandoni would talk to his contacts in Denver's LGBTQ community to see if anyone knew of Noah Asher. Then he'd check in with his sources in the sex business— maybe there was something on the street about the Superior Gentlemen. Forensics was on their way to Noah's home to commandeer his computers. At headquarters, a detective helping out from the Fraud Unit would start on Noah's credit cards, bank accounts, and phone records just as soon as we got the warrants.

And Smith and Wesson—Detectives Brian Smythe and Bill Weston, but they'd been saddled with the nickname as soon as they teamed up—would meet with people at Water Resources to learn what they thought of their recent employee. Smythe had a degree in geology, which gave him a scientific edge over the rest of us. If Noah's coworkers started spouting hydrology lingo, he'd at least be able to hum a few bars.

Then, if anything set off Smith and Wesson's alarm bells, Bandoni and I would march in like an army following the scouts.

Perhaps most important would be our conversation with Noah's family, once they'd been notified by a victim advocate.

I dropped Bandoni off at the police carpool so he could get a set of wheels, then stopped in at the department's print service to get copies made of Noah's drawings and the photographs of the gutter punks and the Superior Gentlemen along with their business card. While Clyde and I waited, I called the numbers on the cleaning-services business cards and introduced myself. The first place had no record of Noah Asher. But when I dialed the second business, Top-A Cleaning, a bored receptionist named Candy told me that Noah had used their cleaning service between November and February. The last cleaning they'd done for him was three weeks earlier. Which meant there should have been a little bit of dust. Unless Noah had become Mr. Domestic. Or found another service.

"How often did you clean his house?" I asked.

"He had the weekly. Everything but the basement. We also did laundry and linens."

"Do you know why he canceled your service?"

A sound that might have been gum popping. "There's nothing in the file. Usually it's a cost issue. Most people like the idea of getting their house cleaned, but after a few months they realize they can't really afford it."

"Any complaints about the work?"

"Nothing in the file."

"I'd like to talk to whoever cleaned his house."

Definitely gum popping. "Sorry," Candy said. "Can't help you with that. We don't assign our cleaners to specific clients. It's just whoever's available that day."

"Even if a client asks?"

"Even if." She sighed. "It would be too hard. Our cleaners are contractors. They come and go all the time."

"Meaning he likely didn't have the same cleaner from week to week?"

"Probably not."

I pictured the dark-haired woman with a mop in Noah's drawing of the milkshake shop. "You use a lot of minorities?"

A pause, as if she was thinking about where the conversation might be headed. "We're totally legit. If applicants don't have the right paperwork, we don't hire them. We employ a lot of white people, too. Look, I got other calls I need to get to."

Probably Grand Central station there. "All right, thanks, Candy. I'd like to talk to your manager in an hour or so. Can you set that up for me?"

"You mean Kaylee? Sure, if you really need to."

"I really do."

The comics store frequented by Noah, based on the receipts we'd found, was a place called Heroes and Villains located in the slowly gentrifying area of Denver near Tennyson and I-70. I drove past the storefront and kept circling around until I located a parking spot three blocks north by an empty lot. Worried I might need a shoehorn to get out, I wedged the Tahoe between a pickup and an aging BMW, and Clyde and I jogged back south. At least one of us was happy about it. Professional detective that I was, I was still wearing pumps.

A bell tinkled overhead as we walked in.

Inky gloom enveloped us, along with the delightful bookish funk of old and new paper, dust, and an organic underlay that made me think of the dying remnants of silverfish and carpet beetles. Comic books and graphic novels filled seven-foot-high display racks. There was a section for Marvel, another for DC, and plenty of new heroes and monsters I'd never heard of. A pair of teenagers, a boy and a girl, browsed in separate areas of the store. There was also a father with his young son rifling through a box of Archie Comics.

In the front window, a cat stirred languidly, spotted Clyde, then arched its calico back and vanished into the rear of the store.

At a counter in the back, on a stool behind an old-fashioned register, sat a heavyset forty-something woman in a Hawaiian shirt and turquoise reading glasses. As I watched, she turned the page in a paperback. She didn't look up when Clyde and I approached.

"You scared my cat," she said.

"Which would make him a scaredy-cat, right?"

She raised her eyes from the novel. She didn't look amused. "Help you?"

I showed my badge. "Detective Parnell with Denver Major Crimes. I'm trying to track down a man who was a customer here. Are you the manager?"

"Co-owner. Along with my wife. I'm Dana Gills."

I pulled out the DMV photo of Noah. "Do you know him?"

She took the picture, held it under the dim light of a banker's lamp. "That's Noah Asher. Why are you looking for him?" She squinted at my badge, clipped to my belt. "What department you with?"

"I'm investigating a murder."

"And Noah's involved?"

"He's the victim."

For a moment, her face went perfectly still, her eyes blank. As if she were the one lying on the autopsy table. Then the skin creased in harsh lines around her mouth and eyes. "Please tell me you're shitting me."

"I wish I were."

She set the picture down on the counter, folded her hands in her lap, and drew in a breath. When she looked up again, her eyes were damp behind the turquoise readers. "Now that's a damn shame. Noah was a good kid."

"You were close?"

"He was—Noah was—" Her lips and chin trembled.

"Take a minute," I said.

She nodded and looked down again. She pulled a tissue from her pocket and pressed it to her eyes. My presence felt intrusive, but I didn't look away. Interviewing 101: don't give anyone a break.

After a moment, Dana said, "Okay." She blew her nose, pitched the tissue in the trash, then looked up again. "What do you want to know?"

"How do you know Mr. Asher?"

"He worked here."

I kept my face neutral. "He did?"

"Oh, not for Marcia and me directly. He uses the back room to teach." She groaned. "*Used* the back room. Christ. The kid's been coming here since he was knee high to a grasshopper. We've known him, what, almost twenty years."

"Then he was a customer first. What did he read?"

"Everything." She smiled. "Noah was in love with all of it. He started with the superheroes, then graduated to darker stuff. First Buffy the Vampire Slayer and Jessica Jones. Then he moved on to Sandman and Preacher. Somewhere in there he started creating his own comics. Did the writing and the illustrating. Even the lettering."

"Is that unusual?"

"It's unusual for someone to be good at all those things."

"And he was?"

"You seen his stuff?"

I pulled out the laminated copies of the drawings from Noah's house and spread them out on the counter. The gutter punks and the men with guns. The man with yellow eyes and the Milkshake Lady. "Did he draw these?"

She turned the pictures around. Studied them. "I haven't seen these particular drawings, but that's his style. Although lately he's been going for something totally different. A more austere look. He said he didn't want the illustrations to get in the way of the story."

"Were his stories dark?"

"Picture the bottom of a coal mine. When Noah hit high school, he was as self-centered as any teenage boy. Turned into a real jerk for a few years. But a couple of months ago, he rejoined the human race and started growing a conscience. The latest thing he was working on had to do with street kids. He called them gutter punks. Like these drawings here." She pointed. "I tease"—she blinked—"*teased* him a lot. That he was becoming an SJW."

"SJW? What is that?"

"Social justice warrior. It's considered an insult now that the trolls have gotten hold of it. But it didn't start out that way. It just means someone who supports causes, things like feminism and cultural inclusivity. You ask me, the SJWs are a breath of fresh air in the comics world. Something different from stodgy old white guys. Superman and the like are getting a little long in the tooth."

"You mentioned gutter punks. Were there other social issues Noah was concerned with?"

She took off her readers, tapped them on the counter. "The kid cared a lot about women's issues. That's what I mean about rejoining the human race. Came from those early days with Buffy and Jessica Jones, I guess."

"He ever talk about water rights? Environmental issues, maybe?"

Her brow wrinkled. "I don't remember anything like that."

I picked up one of Dana's business cards, slid it into the pocket of my jacket. "Was Noah gay?"

Her new glare surpassed the earlier one. "What the hell does that matter?"

"It might have played a role in his death."

She held on to the glare another three seconds, and then her face sagged. "Fucking world sometimes, you know?"

"I do."

The man and his son approached the register. Clyde and I stepped aside while they bought three Archie Comics and Dana slid them into a paper bag. She watched the pair as they headed out the door.

"That father brings his son in every month," she said. "The kid has his allowance money, and he wants to spend it on comics. Sweet kid. He still thinks life is about ice cream and hanging out with your friends." She shook her head. "But pretty soon he'll graduate to all those noir Archie shows. Right around the time he decides that life is a tragedy and he's Hamlet."

I sensed a kindred spirit. But then she turned back to me and summoned up a smile. "Where were we?"

"I asked if Noah might be gay."

"Ah, right. Well, speaking as an old lesbian, Noah was straight as they come. In fact, he wanted to be the ladies' man. Nice dresser, smooth talker. Always smelled like a bank. As in *R-I-C-H* rich. He had an opening he'd use in a bar. He'd make a little sketch of the woman he was interested in. Talk about how good the woman's bone structure was and how he could tell just by drawing her that she had a good heart." Dana laughed. "He used to practice it on me. He was good enough that if I wasn't happily married, hell, I might have given him a go. Even if I am almost twice his age and gay to boot. The sad thing is, good a routine as it seemed to me, he said it didn't usually work. He said the other PUAs were better."

"PUAs?"

"I know. Alphabet soup. Pickup artists. That's what Noah called them. Guys who supposedly have a proven system for attracting and seducing women."

"He ever mention names?"

"Sorry, no." She shrugged. "I never asked."

I recalled the cardboard box of worn, discarded T-shirts in Noah's closet. "When did he get into the pickup-artist scene?"

"Hmm." She pressed her index finger to her chin. "Four months ago, maybe?"

"Any idea how seducing women for casual sex fits in with being an SJW concerned with women's issues?"

"If you're trying to understand men"—she snorted—"I'm not the person to ask."

"You ever hear of something called the Superior Gentlemen?"

A faint spark appeared in her eyes. She scratched her chin for a moment, then shook her head. "Seems kind of familiar. But I can't pull up anything."

I showed her the copy of the photo I'd taken from Noah's mantel. The one with the five men. "You know any of these guys?"

She put her readers back on. "Well, Noah, of course. And the guy with his arm over Noah's shoulders might be his brother." She set down the photo. "I don't know the others."

"You ever know Noah to be involved in anything illegal?"

"You mean like drugs?"

I sensed a new lead. "*Was* he involved in drugs?"

A small headshake. "Nah. Nothing I ever noticed."

"Anything else? Anything that seemed shady?"

Her look turned cool and assessing. "Why don't you tell me what you're digging for. 'Cause I sure can't think of anything."

"That's okay. I have to ask."

She dropped the chilly gaze. "I get it. I'm firmly on the side of no. But you might sound out his students. They're in the back now. Rivero and Markey."

"I'll talk to them." I tapped one of the pictures of the Milkshake Lady. "You ever see a woman like this with Noah?"

Another laugh, but this one carried pain. "I never saw *any* woman with Noah. It's his brother who's the real ladies' man. Noah told me Todd could walk into any bar, zero in on the best-looking woman there, and walk out five minutes later with her on his arm. A real pickup artist, that one."

"Todd is the brother?"

"Right."

"Is he part of the pickup-artist community?"

"Doubt it. But I haven't seen him years. Todd's not into comics." Her look was contemptuous. "He's like their dad, or at least that's what Noah told me. Into business. Into making money. Not so much about the arts. Good-looking guy, though, if that's him in the photo."

I touched the drawing of the woman again. "You don't think she's real?"

"If I had to guess, I'd say no."

"She seems so realistic. Not like a—" I stumbled.

"Not like Mystique? Or Black Cat? But that's a trend, too, and about time. Especially with the SJW types, who tend to create characters who are more realistic. Real women don't look like Barbie. And most of them don't want to." She looked at the drawing again and pointed at the milkshake. "You get the significance of that?"

"The drink?"

"It's another reason I don't think this woman is real. You heard of Comicsgate?"

"Enlighten me."

"A few years ago, the big comics companies like DC and Marvel started hiring women and minority artists and writers as part of a diversity campaign. Some of these newcomers are reimagining old superheroes as women or trans or minority. That got a lot of pushback from the traditionalists. Then came the day when a group of women staffers from Marvel went to have a milkshake in honor of their hero, a woman publisher named Flo Steinberg."

"Okay."

"One of the women posted their photo online. And all hell broke loose."

"Over what?"

"Over women in comics. The details are more complicated, but essentially, that's what it boiled down to. The trolls made their voices heard by the hundreds."

The bell jingled over the door. I glanced around as the teenaged boy left.

"And Noah supported diversity in comics?"

Dana gave a vigorous nod. "Only a couple of months ago I would have placed him squarely in the traditionalist category. After all, he was part of the original demographic—a young, white, socially inept male who spends his time hiding out in his parents' basement and looking at internet porn. But like I said, Noah was branching out."

"Becoming an SJW."

"That, and I think he saw the light when it comes to opening up the comics world. He's a smart kid. Probably saw there was more money to be made by diversifying."

"People get mad enough about this stuff to kill over it?"

Her eyebrows shot up. "You think that's what happened?"

"I'm just asking."

She huffed out a breath, lifting her bangs. "Some of those guys get pretty riled up. But I think most of them are web warriors. They'll troll you online and promise to eat your babies. But I've never heard of it moving into the real world."

Our anger is righteous.

"Was Noah an angry kind of guy?"

"He was pissed he couldn't get a date in a city of beautiful women. But he was over that."

"Noah's students. The ones in the back. Which category do they fall in? Social justice warriors or pissed-off trolls?"

"Those two? I don't know. They're all right. Rivero's angry, and Markey's a geek. But I wouldn't pigeonhole them." She looked at Noah's drawings again, picked up the one of the yellow-eyed man next to the train.

"What are you thinking?" I asked.

"Just that there are a lot of yellow-eyed supervillains in the comics world. This feels a little cliché for Noah."

"What villains?"

"Nightcrawler. Trigon. Gamora." She shrugged and set down the drawing. "One of the most famous is a character named Apocalypse. He was originally created as a supervillain intended to operate behind the scenes leading something called the Alliance of Evil."

"Sounds sinister."

"That's the world of comics." She leaned forward on the counter. "There is one thing you should maybe know."

I also leaned in. "What's that?"

"I might be making a bit of a stretch, here. Noah was a friend, but it's not like he confided in me."

I waited.

She pushed up her readers. "Something was bothering him lately."

"He didn't say what?"

"Like I said, he didn't confide in me." She flattened her palms on the counter and studied the backs of her hands, as if the answer lay there. "But one day, maybe a month ago, he came in dragging a serious funk. When I asked him about it, he said something about the payback."

"The payback?"

"That's right." She lifted her head. "He said that the work he was doing was going to bring some payback. At the time, I thought he was talking about getting paid. Just saying it in a strange way."

"But you don't think so now?"

"No. Because when I look back on that day, Noah wasn't just agitated. He was . . ."

"He was what, Ms. Gills?"

"Scared. I think Noah was scared."

CHAPTER 12

My counselor tells me that at my core, I am a good person.
That we all come into the world as unblemished as God made
us, and then the world starts to act on us. We can get back to
that good core, he tells me. Back to our true selves.

But I've seen too much. You can scrub all you want. But a
darkened heart will always be dark.

—*Sydney Parnell. Personal journal.*

Thoughts of a frightened Noah, pickup artists, and payback swirled through my mind as Dana Gills opened a door behind the register and ushered Clyde and me down a hall toward the back of the building.

"Noah's been teaching here for about three years," Dana said as we walked. "At one time he had almost twenty students. But then the software gig went full time, and he cut back to just these two."

"They been his students for long?"

"Rivero Martinez's been with Noah from the beginning. Markey Byron, a couple of years, I think. A long time, anyway."

She opened another door on to a concrete room starkly lit by overhead fluorescents. The back of the room overflowed with stacked cardboard boxes, along with a stained porcelain sink and a closet-size space closed off by a door marked "Toilet." The front half of the room held two plastic folding tables shoved together and covered with jars of pens and brushes, bottles of ink, and stacks of paper.

The two men sitting at the table looked up.

"Hey, boys," Dana said. "You've got company. This is Detective Parnell." To me she said, "The glowering hulk sitting on the left is Rivero Martinez. Markey Byron's the cherub on the right."

I nodded my thanks as Dana left, and Clyde and I entered the room.

The concrete walls and floor in the chilly space carried an earthy smell. The toilet emitted a faint stink, and at least one of the men gave off the aroma of unwashed flesh. I caught whiffs of paint and ink and something that might have been soot—charcoal pencils, maybe.

Rivero and Markey glared at me in silence. They both wore long-sleeve tees, down vests, dark jeans, and attitudes. Their lack of welcome radiated like gas fumes from a poorly sealed tank. Seemed I'd crossed a threshold from the colorful world of comics into a space allocated for and guarded by the men behind the art.

Women need not apply.

Then again, maybe they just hated cops.

Rivero was a strongly built twenty-something Latino with shoulder-length hair and a thick beard. His eyes glittered with subterranean emotion. He kept his eyes on me as he tipped back in his chair and folded his arms across his wide chest.

A partially finished drawing in front of him showed two men squaring off. Even in black and white, the sketch carried the motion of violence, and—in the faces of the men—anguish.

Across the table, Markey set down his pencil and casually slid a blank sheet of paper over whatever he was working on. He was also in his twenties, a white kid with shadows under his eyes and soft, brown hair that flopped over his forehead. He appeared to have trouble holding on to the scowl—his narrowed eyes and sneer seemed more an act than a conviction.

If I had to lean on these guys, Markey would take the softer touch. "Good afternoon," I said.

They nodded.

Bandoni had told me that interviewing witnesses and suspects was like inviting people to a potluck dinner. You tell them the theme of the dinner, put out a few condiments, then see what they bring to the table. I held up my badge. "I'm Detective Parnell with the Denver PD's Major Crimes Unit. My partner here is Clyde. The two of you are Noah Asher's students?"

Two nods. Rivero's scowl didn't change, but a crease appeared between Markey's eyes, which now showed a faint spark of alarm. He gripped the edge of the table. "What's this about?"

"I'm sorry to tell you that Noah Asher was found dead early yesterday morning."

Neither man moved, but they were both suddenly far away, tuned into their own thoughts. Markey went white and then red. Rivero's scowl smoothed away, like a car dropping into neutral, a powerful engine momentarily disconnected.

I let them sit with the news.

Markey broke the silence first. "What—what happened? Was it, like, a car accident?"

Rivero reconnected, foot hard on the gas. "She's from Homicide, you dumb shit." He grabbed his pencil and snapped it in two, then hurled himself out of the chair and onto his feet. "The fuck. Fuckity fuck."

Clyde stiffened beside me, his eyes on the possible threat.

"Have a seat, Mr. Martinez."

Rivero kicked the chair but then yanked it back to the table and sat.

I pulled out my notepad. Then I placed my phone on the table and tapped record.

"You guys mind if I record this?"

"Knock yourself out," Rivero said.

Markey shrugged, then nodded.

I started with the dispassionate particulars of their lives. Full name, address and phone number, how long they'd known Noah, what they did for a living. Rivero worked construction. Markey was finishing up his MFA and was applying for teaching positions. He tutored high-school students to pay the bills.

I noticed Markey's fingernails were chewed to the quick.

I rounded the corner into where they'd been two nights ago. Rivero said he'd been drinking with friends at one of their houses. Four guys, talking it up in the backyard. Markey had met a woman for happy hour, then gone home to work on job applications. He'd had a pizza delivered around 9:00 p.m. I noted the name and address of the friend, the bar, the pizza-delivery place.

I asked about Noah's former students, the ones he'd let go. No conflicts that Rivero or Markey knew about. Noah was a good teacher, great at helping his students network with other writers, illustrators, and letterers.

"He mention anyone being angry with him?" I asked.

Rivero snorted. "Noah was like a Labrador. He liked people. They liked him. Guys, anyway. He was a total fag around women."

"Noah was gay?"

"Not like that. What I mean is, he wasn't much of a man when it came to women. You know what I'm saying?"

"Talk like I'm slow," I said.

"He was a social dork." His cave eyes shone with unexpected light. "We hung out every now and then. Mostly in dive bars."

"The choice of dives yours or his?"

He shrugged. "Both. Me for the cheap beer. Noah 'cause he figured the women'd be easier. You know, desperate for any guy to buy them a drink. He used the dives to practice his spiel. And it was pretty good. He'd make little ink sketches of the women. On their forearms. Backs. Breasts if he got really lucky. A lot of times he did caricatures, but sometimes he'd put them in superhero costumes. They loved it. Only he could never close."

"Why do you think that is?"

"The truth?" He looked sincere. "No woman wants to sleep with a Labrador. Girls like huskies. Rottweilers. They dig the pit bulls, man."

"Like you?"

He bared his teeth. "Hear me roar."

"That your take on Noah, Markey?"

"Labrador." His expression carried an odd satisfaction. Maybe he liked the idea that his teacher wasn't good at everything. "Pretty much."

"You ever try to pick up women with him?"

Markey coughed. "Me?"

Rivero laughed. "Now with Markey, there, we're talking shih tzu. Soft and silky. Ooh, Markey, come sit in my lap."

Markey flushed red again. "Dive bars aren't my scene."

"What is your scene?"

"I like places that have some class."

Rivero threw back his head and laughed. "How's that working for you, lapdog?"

"Like you'd know quality if it bit your ass, Rivero." Venom pooled in Markey's voice. The lapdog, apparently, had teeth. "*C-l-a-s-s*. And I'm not talking shop class."

"Fuck you, Markey."

No love lost between these two. I wondered how Noah had handled it.

I pulled out the drawing of Noah's Milkshake Lady and placed it on the table between them. "Either of you recognize this woman?"

The men shot daggers at each other for a few seconds, then looked at the drawing. Markey shook his head. Rivero took a little longer, but then he shook his head as well.

"So he hasn't drawn her before?" I asked.

"I've never seen her." Markey fingered the edge of the blank sheet of drawing paper, rolling the corner in and out.

"It's his style," Rivero said. "I'll swear to that. And it looks like his SJW thing. But, nah. I never seen her."

I feigned ignorance. "What's SJW?"

"Social justice warrior," Markey said, brushing back a sweep of hair. "People who make themselves important by taking up some cause."

"Noah wasn't sincere?" This didn't jibe with what Dana had said.

Markey shrugged. He raised his index finger toward his mouth, stared at the ragged nail, then carefully lowered his hand.

"What kind of causes did Noah promote?" I asked.

"Bleeding-heart shit." He picked at his cuticle. "Homeless people. Minorities. Climate change."

"And women," Rivero said. He leaned in and narrowed his eyes at Markey. "Did you forget about the women, lapdog?"

A bead of blood popped out on Markey's finger. He licked it off and raised his gaze to meet Rivero's. All expression had leached out of his eyes. "You don't know anything about me."

Rivero started to laugh, then abruptly backed off. He snorted and shook his head. "Whatever."

"What about the two of you?" I asked. "You feminists?"

"I love my mama and sister," Rivero said. "That count?"

I looked at the other man. "Markey?"

His lips curled up in a parody of a smile. "I believe in equality of the sexes."

Uh-huh.

A moment's silence, then Rivero said, "Noah was into anyone who needs a white savior."

I watched his face. "You didn't approve of his causes?"

"I like what Noah stood for. I hate that sometimes it's necessary."

I took out the photo of the Superior Gentlemen and placed it on the table next to the drawing. "You ever meet any of these men?"

"Just Noah," Rivero said.

Markey said, "Right."

I narrowed my eyes. "You don't recognize any of the others?"

"Looks like a party, maybe," Markey said.

I turned the photo over and showed them the back. "Noah ever mention the Superior Gentlemen?"

The two men exchanged a quick glance, then they both said no.

I leaned in. "You two know it's a crime to impede an investigation by lying or providing false information, right?"

"It's probably a crime to make shit up, too," Rivero said. "I don't know those guys."

Markey nodded. "Me neither."

I wondered if it was time to separate them, interview them one on one. But there was no guarantee that whoever I left alone would still be waiting when I got back.

"You ever know Noah to be into anything questionable? Drugs? Prostitution?"

Rivero snorted. "Are you kidding me?"

Markey looked bruised. "No way."

"What about gutter punks?" I said. "Noah ever mention them?"

"Those kids who ride the trains?" Rivero said. "He was doing something with them. Some SJW idea he had for a graphic novel."

Markey shrugged.

"He mention any names?"

Another simultaneous headshake.

"Did Noah seem different lately? Upset about anything?"

"I didn't notice anything," Markey said.

The dark gleam left Rivero's eyes. "He was happy."

That threw me. "What?"

"He was happy about something."

"He tell you that?"

"Nah. He was just smiling all the time. Like a guy with a big check in his back pocket."

"He'd come into money?"

"Nah," Rivero said. "I don't mean like that. I'm speaking in metaphors. A metaphor is when—"

"He was happy, not scared?"

Rivero's expression softened, his gaze turned inward. "Maybe he *was* scared, in some weird way. Maybe some people are happiest when they're fighting the good fight."

"You think that's what he was doing? Fighting the good fight?"

Rivero laid his gaze on me. His eyes were sharp again. "I'd really like to think that. That Noah went down for something he believed in."

There was one thing Rivero and I had in common.

"Or maybe," Rivero said, "he was scared 'cause he had something to lose."

I leaned over to pick up the photo and the drawing. Before Markey could protest, I whipped off the concealing paper to see what he'd been working on when Clyde and I entered the room.

Cherubic Markey had sketched a naked woman kneeling in front of an equally naked man. The man looked victorious. The woman—at least from what I could see of her face—looked terrified.

In the background stood another woman. Watching.

"Nice, Markey," I said. "You always draw shit like this?"

Markey's face was so red I could have warmed my hands on it.

"It pays, you know?" he said. "It *pays*. That's the only reason I'm doing it. Until I get a regular job."

"Noah teach you how to draw like that?"

"He did it, too. What's the big deal? It's just sex. If things were fair, then sex would be something you could, I don't know, get in bulk at Costco."

Rivero threw back his head and roared. "Oh, Markey boy, that's priceless." His stomach shook. "Give me two bags of Doritos, pack of

Marlboros, and a six-pack of missionary. Oh, and I'll take some anal, too. Wait, you say there's a special on your ball-buster? Perfect! Gimme that."

Markey sat back in his chair, looking more stunned than angry. A sheen of tears made his eyes large.

Rivero took pity on him. "It's just geek porn," he said to me. "Self-indulgent shit for shih tzus."

But Markey lost whatever control he'd been clinging to. "I don't know—I don't know how I'm gonna be okay without Noah." A gulping suck of air. "Noah had contacts. He promised he'd help me. My career . . ."

Rivero rolled his eyes. "Suck it up, pasty boy. Start tutoring a few more coeds."

"Fuck you," Markey said without energy.

I gave them my business card, told them I'd be in touch again, and left. I eased the door shut, then waited outside for a few minutes, listening.

"You are such a dweeb," Rivero said. "Noah's dead, and all you can think about is your fucking career."

"What career?" Markey muttered.

"The last of the SJWs." Melancholy shifted Rivero's voice into softness.

"He maybe died for what he believed," Markey said. "That's something, isn't it?"

"That's just shit, man." The hardness was back. "Noah's dead. Deceased, cold on a slab, cadaverous. The animator is rendered inanimate."

A long pause.

"His last fucking panel, man," Rivero said. "Nothing's worth that."

CHAPTER 13

Hey, Golden Girl. Just because you're paranoid doesn't mean they're not out to get you.

—Len Bandoni. Private conversation.

My phone buzzed just as Clyde and I reached the Tahoe. A text from Candy at the cleaning company, telling me the manager could see me any time this afternoon.

I responded that I'd be there in an hour. Candy sent a thumbs-up emoji.

I considered offering my own thumbs-up in response, just to be annoying. Then I reminded myself that I was a public servant with the reputation of the Denver PD riding on my shoulders. I sent a smiley-face instead.

When Candy shot me a pink heart, I bailed.

One hour. The investigation was the priority. But my partner needed to stretch his legs. And I had to hit a drive-through before my stomach crawled into my throat and begged for a handout.

The day had turned blustery while we were in the comics store. Dark clouds scuttled overhead, and a sudden wind gusted, rattling the newly budding branches of nearby trees. I grabbed my fleece jacket from the cab and gave Clyde a few minutes to get the blood circulating and do his business in an empty lot.

After I followed Clyde into the lot and did my cleanup-crew act, I leaned against the driver's door and rubbed the back of my neck where the start of a headache snugged up against my spine.

Neither Markey nor Rivero struck me as men I'd want to hang out with. But they didn't seem like murderous thugs, either. Not that I could hang my hat on that. Plenty of people had found Ted Bundy to be a super nice fellow, and his count had been thirty.

But assuming the men weren't cold-blooded killers, there was still something off about the two of them. For one thing, there'd been that eye flash when I'd asked about the Superior Gentlemen.

And Markey's drawing rankled. It wasn't the crudity. Rivero was right about geek porn. The woman on her knees was classically beautiful in the Anglo style—tumbling blond hair, fair skin, slender with Barbie-doll breasts. She'd reminded me of the come-hither woman in Noah's screen saver—exactly the kind of woman I imagined populated Markey's fantasies.

It was the other woman who'd caught my eye—the watcher with the blank expression. Young and pretty, like the kneeling woman.

But Latina.

Like our Milkshake Lady.

Our mysterious Dark Lady, to borrow Shakespeare's imagery.

"Where are you?" I whispered. "And whose side are you on?"

The wind snatched my words and threw them into the air.

Thoughts swirled through my brain. The idea of Noah fighting for the rights of women and minorities. And his students maybe not on board with that. Which was interesting given that Rivero technically qualified as a minority. But no doubt there were shades of bias I couldn't parse. The question of the moment was if Markey and Rivero were opposed to social justice warriors, the SJWs, how much company did they have? Dana Gills had mentioned an entire army of online trolls that had risen up in protest against women and minorities in comics.

While most trolls stayed in the dank dungeon of their virtual existence, snapping at everyone whose views didn't align with their own, every once in a while one burst into the daylight—teeth bared, claws glinting, like the ogre from beneath the bridge.

And every now and again, one of them killed.

Had Noah run into the latter—someone who had lurched namelessly up from the internet's cesspool and struck before sinking back into the swamp?

My hand went to my neck again, brushing against the hair at my nape, and I finally realized what I'd been processing in the reptilian portion of my brain. It had nothing to do with Markey and Rivero. And it wasn't a headache.

I was being watched.

I lowered my hand and looked for Clyde. He was nosing through the grass, searching for the perfect place to set his olfactory mark. Nothing had alarmed him. So whoever had eyes on me wasn't close enough to be of concern to my partner.

I turned casually in place, scanning the area.

The shabby-genteel surroundings were like a lot of Denver locales where drug dens were being pushed out by hope and hard work. This was a neighborhood hauling itself up from poverty house by house and storefront by storefront. Single-story brick homes interspersed with residential-friendly businesses—bookstores and coffee shops, the occasional craft brewery. Trades that made the area chic rather than benighted.

I kept turning, keeping my motions casual so as not to spook the watcher. Was he staring at me through a window? From behind the windshield of his car?

Up the block to the west, a man in sunglasses, suit, and open-collared shirt stepped out of a shop, walked down the steps, and paused, looking at his phone. In tune with the urban-creative vibe of the neighborhood, he had silver earspools in his lobes, and the thick line of a tattoo arrowed out from beneath a sleeve of his suit coat.

He pocketed his phone and turned right onto the main street. Another man, tall and strongly built, his face hidden by a hooded sweatshirt, entered the crosswalk at the same intersection. As I stared, he glanced my way. There came an odd flash of yellow within the shadow of the hood. A light of some kind? A neon-colored scarf?

I had a sudden image of Noah's drawing of the pissed-off guy with the hood and yellow eyes.

I rotated in the man's direction, ready to call Clyde and give pursuit.

Then an engine started up somewhere to the east. When I spun back, I spotted the back end of a van as the driver turned the corner moving away from us, vanishing in a blink. The feeling of being watched lifted as suddenly as it had come.

I frowned. A dark-blue cargo van.

I reminded myself that blue cargo vans were a dime a dozen in Denver. I told myself this had nothing to do with a sinister-seeming man in a grocery store parking lot.

I whistled Clyde in and led him around to the passenger side.

And stopped.

Someone had drawn a phallus in the layer of dirt on the Tahoe's door.

I closed my eyes. Opened them. The image of the erect penis was still there. I used an oil rag to wipe the door clean, then told myself the scrawl was just some guy's bad idea of a joke. Like the Barbie doll.

"One born every minute," I said to Clyde.

But still. I rubbed the back of my neck, where an uneasy weight had settled. Perhaps I should have photographed the Tahoe door before wiping it clean. But I still had the Barbie and the broken glass. I would drop them off at the lab, ask the techs to test for DNA and fingerprints. No rush, I'd say. Just checking something out.

Picking up on my unease, Clyde stared into my face with an intensity that suggested he was examining my soul. Try hiding anything from a former military working dog.

I gave him a pat as I opened the newly clean door. "We're still good, boy."

But as we drove away, I took a last look around.

Scientists said that the eerie feeling we got of being watched was real. That it was based on subconscious cues from our eyes, which took in information beyond what was consciously processed by our visual cortex. We were aware on some level when someone was staring at us, even when they were watching peripherally, or from a distance.

Then again, maybe all this was nothing more than PTSD-fueled paranoia. During group sessions at the VA, a lot of my fellow Marines admitted to sharing the feeling. Like a phantom limb, it was the stubborn vestige of a war that demanded we scan every room we entered for possible threats. That we keep our faces toward the door. That we go into high alert at every loud bang.

I'd left the war. But it had followed me home, a dark, coiled stowaway.

"I don't understand what any of this has to do with us," she said.

Kaylee Wilkins, the supervisor at Top-A Cleaning, was one of those women who managed to look harried even when the worst thing going on—apparently—was that she hadn't been able to break for lunch. Her desk was as clear as her skin, her phone a mute, black slab encased in shimmering red, and the only other thing breathing in the building aside from Kaylee, Clyde, and me was Candy.

And I wasn't entirely sure of Candy. When I looked through Kaylee's open door toward the front office, Candy had her elbow propped on the desk and her half-lidded face propped in her hand. She looked comatose. Probably I'd feel the same way working here.

"Tell me again why you're here?" Kaylee said as I took the proffered chair in her office and Clyde settled next to me. "Candy said something about one of our clients. I do hope there haven't been any, like, official complaints?"

"Do you get a lot of those?"

"Like, no way!" She beamed. "Not one since I've been here."

Kaylee Wilkins. Valspeaking California girl. Holding back the Mongol hordes with her shiny blond ponytail and her powder-blue cashmere sweater set.

I took out my notebook. "Which is how long?"

"Five weeks. And two days." The beam dimmed slightly to a dimpled smile. "So what is this about?"

"I'm following up a lead," I said. "A man named Noah Asher used your services for a time. I'd like to know the exact dates and who cleaned his house."

She touched the computer mouse with a blue-tipped fingernail, and the screen came to life. The screen saver bore the urgent message *Make every day count!* Kaylee entered a password and a crowded desktop popped into life. Maybe she was busier than her real-world desk suggested.

She clicked and opened a folder labeled *Clients*.

"Name of the customer?" she asked.

"Noah Asher."

Kaylee typed. Her ponytail bounced as if animated by its own perkiness. A minute later a series of invoices popped up. She nodded.

"You're right! He did use our service."

And to think I'd had doubts.

She scrolled up and down the screen. "Back in February, looks like?"

"Maybe you could tell me," I said.

"What? Oh, right!" A little laugh. "We cleaned Mr. Asher's home beginning in November. Our last cleaning was on, like, February seventeenth?"

"*On* that date? Or *like* on that date? Which one?"

"What?"

I surrendered. "Nothing after February seventeenth?"

She scrolled some more. "Nope. February seventeenth was it."

"Is a reason given for the termination?"

Pink glowed in her cheeks. "It's usually a cost issue. We do good work, and we charge accordingly."

The same thing Candy had said. The party line. Which didn't make it untrue.

"No other information is given," I said.

"Nope. Sorry."

I was turning my own questions into statements to balance Kaylee's valspeak. I course-corrected. "Who did the cleaning?"

Kaylee shook her head. "Our records don't indicate that."

"Someone had to make the assignment. Who would know?"

"Like, the previous supervisor," she said. "He left six weeks ago? I took his place."

After Noah canceled his cleaning service. "Were you an internal hire?"

"Oh, no. I don't clean houses. I have an MBA."

"Who's your boss?"

"That would be Kurt Inger. He manages Top-A Cleaning. Nice guy, I guess, but a total nab. He might know who cleaned Mr. Asher's house." Her lip curled. "We're not supposed to assign specific cleaners to a customer. Strictly against policy. But sometimes Kurt does it anyway."

"Write down Mr. Inger's phone number for me, please," I said. "And I'd like copies of the invoices."

She shrugged. "Sure. Give me a minute to print them? Candy has Kurt's card."

Like pulling teeth. "Can you get that for me, please?"

"Well, all right." She pressed a few keys to close the database and then left her office. Through the open door I saw her talking to Candy, who had stirred to life when the printer did.

I looked around the office. Kaylee hadn't put much of her own mark on it. But what was there was in the tone of Norman Vincent Peale. A bookshelf filled with identical blue coffee mugs that read STAY POSITIVE! Giveaways, probably, for new clients. And a framed quote suggested that Kaylee—and everyone else, presumably—was to BE EFFECTIVE!

There were a few more items of the same ilk—water bottles, pens. A printed scarf hanging on a peg near the door—there so you could strangle yourself on positivity if it got to be too much, I supposed. I envisioned Bandoni's reaction if I showed up in a T-shirt emblazoned with the words, *I am a highly effective person!*

"What do you think, Clyde?"

Clyde huffed and settled his head on his forelegs.

"Yeah, me, too."

Kaylee bustled back in, beaming. Positivity at work. "Here you go." She handed me a sheaf of printouts and a scrap of paper on which was written the name Kurt Inger and a phone number.

"Candy didn't have Kurt's business cards, I'm afraid," she said apologetically.

"This will work. So, Kaylee." I tried my own winning smile. "It would be really helpful if you could give me the names and phone numbers of the employees who might possibly have cleaned Mr. Asher's home."

Her smile furled—packed up and stowed for better climes. "I think you need a warrant for that."

She had me there. For a moment I hesitated, thinking of Noah's dress, the words carved into his chest, and a cross and necklace in an empty field. I had to wonder what I was drilling for at Top-A Cleaning. Would finding the women who'd cleaned Noah's house months earlier shed light on his killer?

The truth was, maybe.

"I'll get a warrant," I said. "You might check in with your manager, see if he really wants it to be that difficult."

"Well." She blinked. Clearly, I'd gone off script. She said, "I really need to break for lunch. Eating at irregular times isn't healthy."

"Just a couple more things." I showed her the picture of the Milkshake Lady. "Is she in your employ?"

A headshake. "I don't recognize her."

"And these men?" I handed over the picture of the Superior Gentlemen.

She blinked. "Um, no."

That was that. "All right. Thanks for your time."

I stood. Clyde followed suit. Kaylee rose on well-oiled hinges.

"I'll walk you out," she said.

We stopped by Candy's desk. The receptionist had dyed-pink hair, a pink blouse over white jeans, and glittering pink sandals. Miniature silver-and-pink ice-cream-cone earrings hung from her lobes. I wondered if Candy was her real name or a lifestyle choice.

"I'll be back in an hour," Kaylee told her. "Just text if something important comes up."

Candy's raised eyebrow suggested the chance of something important happening lay at the intersection of two parallel lines. But she offered a nod and a thumbs-up, and Kaylee looked satisfied.

Outside, at the picnic table, which had been empty upon my arrival, were three women—one Caucasian and two Latinas. They wore matching blue polo shirts, khaki pants, and tired expressions. Kaylee gave them a wave, and they raised their hands half-heartedly.

I turned to Kaylee. "If you think of anything, or if you talk to your manager, give me a call. You have my card."

"Of course."

I waited while she slid into a white Volkswagen convertible, revved up the engine, and disappeared down the block. Then Clyde and I headed toward the picnic table.

The women looked up as we approached. I'd caught them at a lunch of filled tortillas, soup, and Cokes. They took in my suit and Clyde's K9 harness, and alarm shone in the eyes of the Latinas. The white woman—older than the other two by a couple of decades—just looked pissed.

"I'm not here about immigration," I said, showing them my badge. "I'm Detective Parnell, and this is my partner, Clyde. We're investigating a murder. I'm hoping to talk to someone who might have cleaned the victim's house."

If telling them that I wasn't with ICE was supposed to be reassuring, then the mention of murder clearly had the opposite effect. Or maybe they just didn't buy my line. The younger women put down their drinks and folded their hands in their laps. The gringa pulled a carrot out of a plastic baggie, made eye contact, and snapped off a piece with her teeth.

I got the message. Bite me.

I gestured toward the soup. *"Pozole rojo, ¿sí? Uno de mis favoritos."*

The women said nothing.

"I had *pozole verde* when I was in Mexico. At El Pozole de Moctezuma. *Mi amigo,* a *Cuerpo de Infantería de Marina,* he took me there."

"¿Pollo o cerdo?" one of the women asked.

I laughed. *"Piel de cerdo frita.* Always *cerdo.* Plus my partner here, he's partial to pork."

The women turned their attention to Clyde, who was grinning in the heat, his tongue a long strip of pink.

"Él es bello," said one of the women. *He is beautiful.*

"Don't say it too loudly," I said. "His ego is already *demasiado grande.*"

The younger women laughed. The gringa held on to her frown.

With the ice a little bit broken, I offered Noah's DMV photo to the gringa, who was nearest.

"His name is Noah Asher," I said. "He lived near Yale Station. Someone from Top-A cleaned his home and washed the linens for a few months from November to February."

The women passed around the photo. Gringa handed it back. I saw now that under their jackets they had name tags pinned near the collars of their shirts. Helen was the gringa. The other two were Erica and Lupita.

Helen said, "What happened to him?"

"His body was found inside a train car. He was beaten to death."

All three women flinched.

"Any of you know him?"

A great wall of silence rose.

"I don't care what anyone's immigration status is," I said softly. "I'm just hoping someone saw something that might help. Maybe one of the cleaners opened the door to a visitor or overheard a phone conversation. Any small bit of information could make the difference."

"Where was the house again?" This was Lupita. None of the women were big—neither tall nor heavy. But Lupita was like a songbird—petite and fragile looking with a beautiful, lilting voice.

I told them the address. The women all shook their heads.

"I've never been there," Erica said.

"Do you know who might have cleaned Mr. Asher's home?"

Helen looked at the other two, then shook her head. "I guess not. But we can ask around."

"We only clean a few houses," Erica offered. She had long, thick braids and a smoker's rasp. She'd taken off her scuffed white tennis shoes and placed them neatly next to the table.

Helen nodded. "The biggest share of our work is businesses. Office parks."

I thought of the cross in the field—two paper clips yoked together. Paper clips were found in office buildings.

But I had no idea what this might signify.

I set the picture of the Milkshake Lady on the table. "Have you seen this woman?"

The women bent their heads over the photo. A minute ticked by, then another.

"You know her," I said.

Lupita jumped and shook her head. "I thought so for maybe a minute. But no."

"Erica?"

"Sorry." She didn't meet my eyes.

Helen picked up the picture, then pulled a pair of readers out of her coat pocket. "Hmm," she said. "I don't think so."

"What about the woman standing in the background with the mop?"

"No," Erica said.

"It's important," I said. "The woman with the milkshake could be in trouble. In danger. If you know something—"

"¿Por qué?" asked Lupita, then flushed. "Why is she in danger?"

"She was seen near where Noah's body was dumped. We think she might have been trying to get a message to us."

The women remained silent.

I set the photo of the necklace on the table. "This might have been hers. Does it look familiar?"

"Lady of Guadalupe," Erica said. "Sure. A lot of the women here wear them."

"I have a Lady of Guadalupe necklace," Lupita volunteered, then looked surprised at her own boldness.

"May I ask where you got it?"

"From my *tía*. She gave it to me at my christening. Many years ago."

"And the other women? Do you know where they got theirs?"

She shrugged. "We're Catholic. Almost everyone has at least one."

My gaze went back to Helen. Her brow was furrowed, and she was worrying her lower lip.

"Helen?"

"Is that blood on the necklace?"

I nodded.

She released her lip. "If I can take a picture of that drawing with my phone, I can ask around."

I nodded, and she snapped a photo. I considered trying to push things with her. But something told me she was the kind of woman who'd go silent under pressure. I'd have to work my way back to it.

One picture to go. I set the photo of Noah and his friends on the table.

"The Superior Gentlemen. Ever hear of them?"

Once again, the women leaned over the photo. Their faces were blank canvases on which I could draw anything—surprise, ignorance, even fear.

I said, "Any of these men look familiar?"

"No," said Helen.

"They look like every other privileged white man," Erica said with unmistakable heat.

"You've had run-ins with their kind?"

"I didn't say that."

I took a small leap. "You've been harassed?"

She flushed, looked down.

"By who, Erica? Clients?"

"No one," she said. Then more firmly, "No one."

My phone rang. I went to silence it, then saw that I'd missed a call from Bandoni. A text flashed on the screen.

NOAH'S PARENTS IN TOWN. BROWN PALACE. NOW.

CHAPTER 14

That day, I sat with her and her dead son and watched as she slowly unraveled.

And I wondered, for the first time, if it was possible to resurrect the living.

—Sydney Parnell. Personal journal.

The only easy thing about my time in Mortuary Affairs was that I didn't often sit with those who had lost a loved one. The exception was whenever a Marine stumbled into our bunker, chasing a rumor that his friend hadn't made it back inside the wire in one piece. These Marines often zeroed in on me, assuming that a woman could best share their grief. And of course I sat with them. I did whatever I could—held their hands, brought them food, hugged them.

It shoved ground glass through my veins every time.

But for all the darkness of those hours, for all the memories I carried of a man weeping in despair over a body bag, the hiss of the hose against concrete and the Sir shouting, "Shade it black" as mortar fire ruptured the world outside . . . for all that, I could not imagine the agony it was to lose a child.

In this, I would gladly be a coward and let Bandoni handle the interview.

But cowardice was one thing. Shirking my job was something else entirely.

Clyde and I joined Bandoni on the sidewalk in front of the Brown Palace Hotel.

The Brown had been designed in the style of the Italian Renaissance and built in the late 1800s, during the Colorado Gold Rush, when carpenter-turned-entrepreneur Henry Brown wanted to bring luxury to the Wild West. The hotel's exterior boasted Colorado red granite and Arizona sandstone and an attentive array of uniformed doormen. As we approached, one of the doormen opened a brass-trimmed glass door and ushered us in with only a hint of disapproval at our cheap suits and the gold-and-black hairs wafting from Clyde's coat.

The doors closed, and the hush of thick carpet and thicker wallets settled over us. We took in the marble, the elegant sconces, and the ornate grillwork railings.

"Hell of a place to sit with bad news," I said as we headed across the lobby.

"The fucking Roosevelt suite." Bandoni pressed a call button for the elevator. "Every fall should have such a nice cushion."

The elevator spilled us out into softly lit opulence. Bandoni said, "Let me do the talking."

"All yours."

Our knocks were answered by a young man whom I recognized from the photo in our victim's home. Noah's utterly unidentical twin, Todd Asher.

We held up our badges.

"I'm Detective Bandoni. And this is Detective Parnell and K9 Clyde."

Todd opened the door wider. "Yes. Come in."

The door opened on to an elegantly appointed sitting room with leather furniture and paneled walls. Two Tiffany lamps were probably worth my annual salary.

A man and woman stood as we entered—Hal and Julia Asher.

"We're very sorry for your loss," Bandoni said as we all shook hands.

Like Noah, Hal Asher was meaty and solid. Unlike his son, he was well over six feet. Meeting Bandoni was probably one of the few times in his life when he had to look up to make eye contact. He had receding blond-gray hair, a day's worth of stubble below a thick mustache, and an expression that hung, perfectly poised, between disbelief and devastation.

Julia Asher looked like she'd already gone through shock and moved on to heartbreak. A slender brunette with a gentle face, she stood with her hands clasped and her shoulders down around her ankles. Her face was white except for her red eyes and her lower lip, which she kept biting.

While Bandoni went over our bona fides and offered the police chief's sympathy, I looked at Todd Asher with interest. Nearly as tall as his father, but slim in a way that managed to look aristocratic, Todd had fair, wavy hair, pale-blue eyes, and patrician features. He wore tailored slacks, a light-blue polo shirt, and a summer-weight linen jacket with the sleeves pushed up to his elbows—the very image of the leisured rich.

Noah probably hated him. *And* adored him.

"Please," Hal said to us. "Sit. Todd, why don't you get everyone water?"

"Of course." Todd disappeared through a doorway.

"We appreciate your time," Bandoni said as he perched on a leather recliner. The cushion sank beneath his weight. I took a chair across from the sofa, and Clyde lay down by my feet.

"Whatever we can do to help," Hal said. He eased his wife back onto the couch as if she were a doll, then sank next to her and took her hand between his, gently rubbing her fingers.

Todd returned with cold bottles of water, which he passed around before sitting on the sofa next to his mother. He and his father bookended the much smaller woman. I wondered if she ever felt overwhelmed by the sheer mass of her husband and sons.

Husband and *son.*

On the table stood a bottle of Wild Turkey Revival and three partially filled glasses. Outside the windows, the surrounding buildings flashed stern facades of chrome and glass, as if the Ashers' room sat in the middle of a fortress.

But a fortress served no purpose when death had already ridden in through the gate.

Julia eased her hand free from her husband's and clasped her fingers. Hal picked up the water bottle. Set it back down. Picked up the tumbler. He drank down the bourbon in one swallow.

"What happened?" he asked. "Who did this to our son?"

"That's what we're working on, Mr. Asher," Bandoni said. "We'd appreciate any information you can share about Noah."

Hal set the glass down hard on the table, picked up the water bottle. "What do you want to know?"

"First, is it okay with the three of you if we record our conversation?"

Hal nodded, and Julia whispered her okay. Todd gave a regal dip of his head. Although Hal looked more like one of Roosevelt's Rough Riders with his beefy build and old-style mustache, I wondered if Todd had been the one to request this suite. I got the impression that such things mattered to him. My first clue was the fifty-pound watch on his golden-haired wrist.

Bandoni placed his pocket recorder on the large coffee table while I pulled out my notebook and a pen. Clyde stretched out with a small sigh.

"Let's start with Noah's friends and coworkers," Bandoni said. "Who'd he hang out with?"

Hal looked relieved to have a focus. "Um, sure. You probably know he was a contractor with Water Resources, so he mostly worked from home. He'd go in for meetings, but I don't think he socialized much with his coworkers."

"That's what he told you?"

A nod. "Friendly, Noah said. But not friends." He picked at the label on the water bottle with thick fingers. "His coworkers were into the outdoors. Rock climbing. Kayaking. They all did that race in Boulder. What's it called?"

"The Bolder Boulder," Todd said.

"Right." Hal tore off a piece of the label. "That wasn't Noah's scene."

"He talk about work much? Tell you what he was doing?"

A light shone in Hal's eyes. Pride. "He was building a database for a hydrology firm. I did a bit of hydrology back in the day. Dams. Noah and I compared notes over a beer now and again."

"You're an engineer?"

"Civil." He abandoned the water bottle.

"So you and Noah talked about his work. Did he ever express any concern about the work he was doing for Water Resources?"

"Concern?" Hal rubbed his jaw, his fingers rasping against the stubble. "No."

Bandoni's gaze took in Julia and Todd. "What about the two of you? You ever hear Noah complain about work?"

Todd shook his head.

Julia said, "I remember when they got a new project and had to hire more staff. Noah found them a bigger office downtown for a better deal. His boss was really happy. He got a bonus for that."

"Okay," Bandoni said. "He ever tell you he was afraid about anything? Ever mention payback?"

Julia's eyes widened. "He never brought up anything like that."

The men nodded.

"Okay," Bandoni said again. "Who else did he hang with?"

"He was big into comic books," Hal said. "Strange thing for a grown man, you ask me. His age, I was into girls and rugby. Like Todd here."

"I play tennis, Dad." Todd pushed up from the couch and went to stand near the window.

"Same difference," Hal said. "But, of course, I supported Noah in all his interests."

"Supported him how?"

Hal waved a hand. His long fingers looked like they could span a river. "Oh, I mean I never asked him *why* he cared about all that. Ray guns. Men in tights. But I asked him questions. Showed him I cared even if I didn't understand. For his birthday, Julia and I got him tickets to Comic-Con in San Diego. That cost a pretty penny."

Bandoni shifted his bulk. "Comic-Con?"

"Where all the comic book nerds get together." Hal couldn't keep the sigh out of his voice. *So much wasted talent,* he must have been thinking. *Could have been building dams.* "You know, booths and panels. They show movies. There's a costume contest. Total—what do kids say now—total . . ." He looked at Todd.

"Geek out," Todd said.

Julia spoke up. "Graphic novels are about more than superheroes. Sometimes much more." Her voice was weary but also needled with electric current. As if she and Hal had trod this path a thousand times and this was the last time she planned to smack her head against her husband's narrow-mindedness. "A lot of the books look at social issues. Just like any good literature."

"Literature." Hal folded his arms. "Come on, Julia."

But this was exactly what the comics-store owner Dana Gills had said. Social justice warriors. I leaned forward. "Was Noah writing about social issues?"

"Yes," Julia said. "Recently he'd become interested in—"

Hal jumped in. "Things that millennials care about, I think. Climate change. And a lot of stuff about women, right, Julia? Women's issues. Gender stuff. I love my son, but he was a touch on the soft side."

"Meaning what, exactly?"

"Just . . ." Hal tightened the fold of his arms and shrugged.

Todd made a noise. Bandoni caught it. "You got anything to add to this?"

Todd had propped himself against a wall, feet spread, hands loose at his sides, graceful as a big cat.

He said, "Noah wanted to change the world."

Slanting sunlight planed the younger man's face into a Picasso-like mosaic of light and shadow. He caught me staring at the pain simmering in his eyes and held my gaze until I looked away, swamped by his glittering grief.

Bandoni said, "Change the world how?"

A shrug. "I didn't pay much attention to Noah's pet projects. Make your fortune first, I told him. After that you can think about philanthropy." The painful simmer rose to a boil. "Noah said I was being selfish."

"It's just smart," Hal said. "Idealism is great. But you've got to make your mark on the world first. I went on from dams to build my first skyscraper before I turned forty. Noah was good enough for that."

"Hal." Julia flapped a hand in the direction of her husband like she was shooing a fly.

"Will you tell me something, Detectives?" Todd asked.

Bandoni turned an expressionless face to the younger man. "If we can."

"What this . . . person did to Noah. Crushing his skull like that."

Julia turned her face into her husband's shoulder. Hal looked daggers at his son.

But Bandoni nodded. "What do you want to know?"

"Are they—do they think they have a *reason* to do that to another human being? Do they think in the dark little core of their nuclear brains that they are *justified*?"

Bandoni's expression was one of sympathy. "Sometimes, yeah. People can lash out if they figure someone has something that should be theirs. Or if they think someone has gotten in their way. Kinda like road rage on steroids. I'm not saying that's what happened with Noah. We don't know what happened, you understand? I'm just talking in general terms."

Outside, clouds wafted over the sun. The room turned gray, cool with sudden shadows. Clyde lifted his head.

From the gloom Todd said, "And if someone is capable of that kind of violence, are they also capable of remorse?"

"Real remorse?" Bandoni stretched out his legs, knocking his knees against the coffee table. "I'm an old cop. I've seen a lot. And my answer is, I doubt it. Not in any real way."

The room was silent save for Julia's soft sobs.

"And forgiveness . . . ," Todd went on. "Are they worthy of forgiveness?"

"Son," Bandoni said. "Is there something you want to tell us?"

"Todd?" That was Julia. "You want to *forgive* whoever did this?"

Sunlight whisked back in, scattering gems of light from the brilliant glass of the Tiffany shades. Todd shook himself. "No. Of course not."

"Todd's become devout," Hal said. "Redeemed Life Church. My son has a good heart."

"You and Noah were twins?" Bandoni asked.

"Brothers," Todd said. "But not biologically."

Bandoni scratched behind his ear. "How's that?"

"We'd given up on being able to have a child of our own," Julia said. "So we started adoption procedures for Noah. We knew his mother—"

"An unwed teen," Hal threw in.

"—and followed along with her through the pregnancy. We were very surprised when I got pregnant during the same time. The boys are just seven weeks apart."

"Of course, we weren't going to change our minds about Noah," Hal said. "And we raised the boys as if they were both ours."

"They *are* both ours," Julia said, her voice a knife finding its edge.

I wanted to hand her a whetting stone.

Bandoni paused until the tension damped down to a cold war. "You talk about Noah wanting to change the world. Any chance he could have offended someone?"

A strangled laugh from Hal. "Like who? He was on the side of the crazies." His eyes moved back and forth between Bandoni and me. There was a hint of challenge in his gaze.

"He ever talk about gutter punks?" I asked.

"Gutter what?"

"Kids who ride trains. He ever talk about them?"

"He drew pictures of trains . . . ," Julia offered. The men were silent.

Bandoni took off his suit coat. Rings of sweat showed under his arms despite the chilled air. "You mentioned gender stuff. Can you talk about that?"

Hal's mouth puckered in distaste before he smoothed it out again. He glanced at Julia.

"Noah was a feminist," she said. Her laugh was small and embarrassed, as if a man supporting feminism was a bad thing. Maybe it was, to her husband.

"So women's rights, things like that?"

"Noah believed every person has a masculine and a feminine side," she said. "And he believed in the feminine in everyone."

"It's from Carl Jung," Todd added. "Eros and logos."

Bandoni stared at him as if he was trying to get a finger on the guy. "He date much? Maybe have a girlfriend?"

"He spent too much time on those damn comics for that." Hal's voice held real anger. "Hung out in his basement with other loser geeks."

"Hal," Julia said.

Hal buried his face in his hands.

"What loser geeks were those?" Bandoni asked.

"They weren't losers," Julia said. "They were his friends. But—" She glanced at her husband. "We never met them."

"Names?"

She shook her head. "Noah got resentful if we asked him about his friends. He'd just say the names wouldn't mean anything since we didn't know them."

Todd spoke up. "I think they were mostly friends from the comics world. I don't know their names, either. Except his students. Noah used to talk about them. Two guys he taught drawing and writing to. Rivero Martinez and a guy named Byron. Like the poet. I can't remember his first name."

"Markey," I said. "We've talked to them."

Three sets of eyes swiveled in my direction.

"You learn anything?" Todd asked.

I kept my face blank. "Anyone else you can think of?"

Three headshakes.

Bandoni nodded at me, and I pulled out the picture of the Superior Gentlemen and set it on the coffee table.

Bandoni tapped the image. "Todd, that's you. Who are the other men?"

Todd reached over and picked up the photo. "Wow. I'd forgotten about these guys. The Superior Gentlemen."

My heart went from a stroll to a light jog.

Bandoni's face remained blank. "Why don't you tell us about them?"

"Noah's friends from the seduction community." Todd thumbed the corner of the photocopy. "This photo was taken in mid-December. Right around my birthday. I'd stopped by to have a drink with Noah, but he and his pals were getting ready to hit the clubs."

"A seduction community?" Bandoni said.

"It's a kind of secret society," Todd scoffed, dropping the photo back on the table. "Usually, guys pay a fee and join a local club to get the inside secret on how to seduce—" His eyes flicked to his mother. "On how to *date* women. Their theory is that if you say the right thing, do the right thing, women will fall over themselves to sleep—to hang out with you."

I thought of Dana Gills at the comics store. "Pickup artists."

Todd's gaze moved to me. "Right."

"And Noah joined one of these clubs?" Bandoni asked.

"Lairs," Todd said. "That's what the clubs are called."

"Lairs . . ." Bandoni let his voice trail off.

"Lame, right? But they think it sounds cool. Like they're *hunters* or something, when really, they're just sad guys who can't get a date. Noah and another guy formed their own."

"The Superior Gentlemen."

"Right." Todd looked down at the photo. Frowned. "All Noah ever told me was that he and some dude were starting a self-improvement group so they could meet women. I don't know the other guy's name, or even if he's one of the men in that photo. But the two of them formed the lair, brought in a few other guys, and I guess it was a kick for a while. But the last time I brought it up, Noah said he'd dropped out."

"He tell you why?"

"He grew up. Figured out life is about relationships, not sex."

"Very mature of him," Bandoni said.

Todd scowled. "That's right."

I snuck a glance at Noah's parents. Julia's chin was up. Hal looked confused.

Bandoni drummed his fingers along his thigh. "When did he drop out of the group?"

"About a month after this picture was taken, he told me the group wasn't really working for him," Todd said. "I don't know if he'd actually quit by then or not."

"Around mid-January, then?"

"Right."

Around the time that Noah had gotten into his social justice work, according to Dana Gills. Had he angered members of the group by leaving?

Betray me with a kiss.

"This guy he started the group with," Bandoni said. "Where'd they meet?"

"I have no idea. Just that it was in November." Todd clenched and unclenched his hands. "The only guy I know personally from the group is Riley Lynch." He pointed. "He's the short guy there on the right. With the bleached hair."

"Riley," Hal said. "I'll be damned."

Julia pulled the picture closer. "*That's* Riley?"

"Riley Lynch." Bandoni smoothed his tie with a gesture like a cat licking cream. "Tell me about him."

"Noah and Riley were friends in high school," Julia said. "Best friends. But Noah hadn't mentioned him much lately."

"They have a fight?"

Todd tilted his head against the wall. "I don't think so. Just that Riley was still into the pickup scene, and Noah wasn't. They still hung out sometimes."

Bandoni looked at Julia, who was shaking her head over the picture. "What are you thinking?" he asked.

"Just how much Riley has changed. Look at that suit! Back in high school, he was a hippie. Long, dirty hair. Scruffy clothes."

A smile touched Hal's lips. "But it wasn't like a statement. It was like he just couldn't find the energy to clean himself up."

"That *was* his statement, Dad," Todd said. "A riff against the slick and sanitized mainstream."

"Punk," I said, thinking of Damn Fox and Street Cred, guys who were all about being antiestablishment.

"Horror punk. Deathrock." Todd's pale eyes flicked with scorn. "Riley wasn't laid-back. He was subversive."

"A subversive high schooler?" Bandoni asked.

"Petty stuff. Graffiti. Dealt a little Molly. And pot before it was legal. Raised the black-power fist even though I don't think he had a single black friend. He just wanted to mess with the establishment."

Bandoni's voice was dry. "I take it the two of you didn't get along."

"What can I say?" Todd opened his arms. "I'm part of the slick mainstream."

I said, "Were Noah's students part of his lair? Rivero and Markey?"

"I doubt it," Todd said. "He wouldn't have wanted them to know he was into the pickup scene. A sad guy who can't get a date doesn't fit with his artist persona."

I tapped the image of the angry man in the dark jeans. "And this man? Did you meet him that night?"

Todd's expression narrowed with disgust. "Craze."

"Craze his first name or his last?" Bandoni asked, straight faced.

Todd's eyes flashed for just a second. "That's what they called him."

"You didn't like him?"

"Just . . . he was intense. He didn't say a lot, but the other guys hung on to every word. Like . . . disciples. He'd only been in the group a few weeks when I met him, but it seemed like he'd put himself in charge." Todd shrugged. "That might have been another reason Noah got out. The group didn't really belong to him anymore."

"What about the photographer?" Bandoni asked. "Who took the picture?"

"Another friend of Noah's. Or maybe it was a neighbor. I didn't catch his name."

"Okay," Bandoni said. "So this seduction thing is only about women?"

A crease appeared in Todd's smooth forehead. "What else would it be?"

Bandoni cleared his throat. "Any chance Noah was gay? Or maybe trans?"

Hal had looked bewildered during the talk about the Superior Gentlemen. But now heat flashed in his eyes. "No."

Bandoni saw it, too. "Mr. Asher, this is not the time for you to worry about your son's sexual preferences. Anything you share might lead us to his murderer."

A flush erupted above the collar of Hal's shirt and flamed into his cheeks. He opened his mouth in a snarl, but before he could speak, Julia laid a hand on his arm.

"Noah was seeing someone. But it was a woman."

Hal's snarl turned into surprise as he turned and gaped at his wife. Todd looked equally surprised.

Julia nodded. "It started a couple of months ago. January. He told me they were just friends. He was helping her with her art. She wanted to be a comics illustrator. But the way he drew her. He showed me." She pulled a tissue from a box on the table, blew her nose. "She was . . . special. A mother can tell. Noah was . . . he was happy."

I remembered Rivero's words at the comics store. That Noah was happy. And that he had something to lose.

"The hell, Julia?" Hal said. "Why didn't you tell me?"

Julia didn't look up from her hands. "Because you're you. And she's Hispanic."

The flush deepened. "He was dating a wetback?"

"Jesus, Dad." Todd groaned.

"That attitude is exactly why I never told you," Julia snapped.

"I don't believe it," Hal said.

But I did. I was thinking of our Milkshake Lady. Of the odd design on her shirt—the one that was also tattooed on Noah's arm.

"Do you know her name?" I asked.

"Noah called her Ami. With an *i*. Said she was from El Salvador. But he never shared her last name."

Bandoni said, "You never met her?"

While Hal glared, Julia shook her head. "No. But Noah said she was here as part of a program. IPS? TPI? I can't remember."

"Goddamn illegal," Hal said.

"TPS, maybe?" I said. "Temporary Protected Status?"

"That's it." Julia dug her eyes into her husband before turning back to me. "She was here *legally*. But she was worried that her status might change."

"What the hell is that?" Hal asked. "A TPS?"

Julia looked at Bandoni, who looked at me.

I clicked my pen closed. "Temporary Protected Status allows select migrants from approved countries to remain in the US for a time when they are at risk in their home countries. If Ami was from El Salvador, then maybe she's part of the indigenous population there. Paramilitary forces have wiped out entire villages."

Hal looked uncomfortable. Probably the first he'd heard about it.

But excitement rippled along my skin. If Ami was here under a TPS, then maybe there was a way to trace her.

Hal shook his head. "It's not right. It's just not right. I'm sorry for what's going on in these countries. I really am. But it's not our problem. We can't open our doors to everyone. We can't take care of everyone. And isn't it true that these people stay on once their visas run out?"

I spread my hands. "Sometimes. But—"

He snorted. "That makes her illegal, and Noah wouldn't do that. He was the kid who always colored inside the lines."

"You don't even know your own son," Julia said.

"Oh, but he told *you* everything?"

I cleared my throat. "You mentioned Ami was learning to be a comics artist. Did she have a regular job?"

"Cleaning houses, I think."

Hal palmed his forehead. "This just gets better."

I made a note. **AMI** _____. **TOP-A?**

Bandoni looked at Todd. "Your brother ever say anything to you about this woman?"

Todd gazed into the air as if rifling through an invisible memory deck. After a moment, he shook his head. "I wish he had."

I took Deke's composite drawing and the sketch of the Milkshake Lady from my satchel and set them on the table. "You ever see this woman?"

The three Ashers leaned over the drawings.

Hal reared back. "She's barely even pretty."

"Grow up, Hal," Julia said. Then she turned a wistful gaze on me. "That's Noah's drawing of Ami. The one he showed me."

"Did he tell you what the symbol means?" I asked, pointing at Ami's shirt. "It looks a little like a shepherd's staff."

Her hand flew to her throat. "That's his tattoo! I didn't—oh, God. I didn't put it together before. Is it important?"

"We're looking at everything," I said.

"Noah wouldn't explain it," she said and fell silent.

All three of them looked exhausted, and Bandoni gave me a faint nod, a signal that it was time to wrap up the interview. I picked up the drawings, and Bandoni shrugged into his suit coat. He said, "Is there anything else you can think of that might help? Anyone who was angry with Noah? Or maybe jealous of him?"

Todd and Julia shook their heads.

Bandoni reached into his pocket, handed out business cards. "You think of anything else, whether you believe it's relevant or not, give us a call."

"Find who did this," Hal said. "Find who killed our son."

He reached out to take his wife's hand.

She made no move at all.

Outside, we stood in the chilly shadow of the hotel. Up and down the street, lights came on against an early dusk.

Bandoni's color was high. He tugged at the knot in his tie. "Nice fucking family. Whatever the parents got left between them, this death is gonna blow them apart."

"I got the impression they haven't been all that together for a long time."

"I'll bet Hal Asher played his sons against each other every chance he got. His idea of motivation. And the mom just ducked when the dishes flew."

"Harsh."

"Call it as I see it. What'd you think?"

"We need to look into this seduction community. Talk to Riley Lynch. See if he can identify Craze and the other man in the photo."

"I start needing someone to point out the obvious, I'll get a furry partner of my own."

I patted Clyde's head. "Not sure you could keep up. We also need to find the neighbor or friend who took the photo."

"I'll get patrol to recanvass the neighborhood." Bandoni dug out a cigarette, patted his pockets for a lighter, and swore. "You got a match?"

"Sorry."

"Damn it." He shoved the cigarette back. "I had a chat with Smith and Wesson about Water Resources. Noah was a good employee. Liked by the handful of people who worked with him."

"A couple of people have mentioned Noah and climate change in the same breath. Anything threatening about their environmental stance?"

"Nah. The company seems invested in conservation and resource management. And they're careful to get input from all concerned parties before they start a project. Farmers. Recreationists. Indigenous populations." The wind ticked up, and he shoved his hands in his pockets.

"Unless something bites us in the back, it's safe to put that line of inquiry on the back burner."

"When were you going to share that with me?"

"Now. And while we're crossing our t's." He held up three fingers. "One, no one in the sex business has heard of the Superior Gentlemen. Two, Noah never made a move on anyone at his gym. Not, at least, that management got wind of. And three, none of my contacts in the LGBTQ community has ever heard of Noah Asher." He lowered his hand. "Which means we still don't know why the fuck a guy who called himself a pickup artist was wearing a dress."

"Progress by elimination?"

"What this job is."

"We know almost as little as we did at the start of all this." I zipped my coat. "Who did Noah betray? One of his so-called loser geek friends?"

"Why don't I have a chat with his students? Rivero and Markey. See if I can get a few names. And I'll get someone on the squad to check out their alibis." Bandoni absently scratched his cheek. "As for the Superior Gentlemen, our friend Riley Lynch should be able to shed some light. I want you to pull up his DMV data. And see if he's got a record. Especially for assault or battery. Or stalking. We'll have a chat with him tonight after our date with the punks. If we're lucky, we'll get him out of bed. I like witnesses when they're confused."

"Whatever you say, boss."

We started down the sidewalk. Around us, end-of-day workers streamed toward parking lots and garages, heels swapped for sneakers, briefcases and purses tucked close.

"What'd you make of Ami-with-an-i?" Bandoni said.

"Our Milkshake Lady. Maybe now we'll be able to get an ID."

"Let me see the drawing again."

I pulled out the sketch of the Milkshake Lady and passed it over.

Bandoni stopped walking and pointed at the woman in the background. The one with the mop. "Noah drew this other woman for a reason. Like maybe these women are . . . I dunno." His frown carved chasms in his face. "Before-and-after Ami? From downtrodden janitor to superhero?"

"Or maybe current-and-future Ami." I filled Bandoni in on my conversation with the women at Top-A Cleaning. "I got the sense they knew her. But they weren't going to share. If Ami works at Top-A and is worried about losing her temporary status, maybe they're protecting her."

"You told them she'd been seen near the train?"

"And showed them the Lady of Guadalupe necklace. If I had to make a guess, I'd say they're worried. But not enough to talk."

We reached an intersection, and Bandoni punched the button for the light. "Closing ranks."

"They're scared. Can't blame them. Anyway, if Ami works for Top-A, it would explain how she and Noah met. The office manager said Noah used their cleaning service from November to February. She wouldn't say who did the actual cleaning."

Bandoni rolled his eyes. "Warrant?"

"I'll get one."

The light changed. Tires squealed as drivers conceded to the law and lurched to a stop. We entered the crosswalk.

Bandoni said, "Let's run down the timeline. Last November, Noah and some guy decide to form a pickup group."

"At the same time, Noah signs up with Top-A."

Bandoni glared at an SUV nosing into the intersection. "Probably wants his house looking nice for all those babes he'll be bringing home."

"Noah invites Riley Lynch and a couple of other guys into the group."

"Including Craze."

In front of us, a woman pushing a baby carriage slowed as her leashed Pomeranian caught a glimpse of Clyde and spun around.

"Daisy!" the woman said sharply, yanking on the leash.

The dog began barking. The woman swore. I slowed and maneuvered toward the right of the woman so that I was between Daisy and Clyde.

The crosswalk sign switched from green to red. At the same time, a coolness brushed my neck. The sense of being watched. I raised my eyes. At the corner, on the other side of the intersection, a dark-blue van with a new-looking heavy-duty steel grill bolted to the front pulled to the curb.

"Hey, Bandoni," I said. "That—"

Daisy stopped barking and lunged toward Clyde. Clyde broke with his dignity long enough to release a single deep *woof* that froze Daisy in her tracks. The woman yanked on the Pomeranian's leash and shot me a glare as she race-walked toward the curb, dragging Daisy.

"What?" Bandoni said as the light changed, and we hurried onto the sidewalk.

The van had screeched around the corner, heading south. I caught a flash of brake lights, and then the van was swallowed by traffic.

"What is it, Parnell?"

"Third time I've seen that van," I said. "I think."

"The one with the T. rex–size bull bar? I can see why you'd be unsure."

"The grill looked new. You happen to catch the plate?"

"In this light?"

I watched the receding blips of red. "Right."

"Something you're worried about, Parnell? Want to issue a BOLO?"

I hesitated, then shook my head. There were thousands of blue cargo vans in metro Denver. And probably hundreds with bull bars. I started walking. "Where were we on our timeline?"

Bandoni held on to his puzzled look for a moment, then shrugged. "The Superior Gentlemen were forming their evil lair."

"Right. If Ami was cleaning Noah's house, she would have noticed his art right away. Let's figure they bond over their shared interest in comics. She tells him about the plight of immigrants, and Noah has an awakening. His art changes, according to the owner of the comics store. He begins interviewing gutter punks, looking for a social angle for his art. And teaching Ami to draw. Which maybe pisses off any of his less-liberal comics friends."

"As in a fatal piss-off?"

"Maybe."

"Then he drops the cleaning service once he starts cleaning the cobwebs with the womb broom."

I tossed him a glare. "You make that up just now?"

"Nah, it ain't original." He looked disappointed. "How about we just say when he starts plunging the porcelain?"

I massaged my forehead. Bandoni didn't go away. I said, "He drops out of the Superior Gentlemen."

"'Cause you don't need a pickup group if you're—"

"—in love," I said before he could embarrass us both.

We reached Bandoni's carpool vehicle, a nondescript Cadillac that had been new around the time Elvis hit it big. Through the window I made out crumpled fast-food wrappers and a Mountain Dew can in the console.

Bandoni said, "Maybe I need to infiltrate the seduction community."

"Don't you think you're a bit old for that scene?" I laughed. "Plus, they're peacocks."

"What do you mean?"

"Flashy. Look at their suits in the photo. You can't even."

"You got a problem with my suit, don't hold back."

"Face it. You and I aren't winning any fashion awards."

"Nothing wrong with cheap, long as we're good." He leaned against the car and folded his arms. "And speaking of cheap, you see the watch Asher junior was wearing? An Audemars Piguet. Take me a year to save up for something like that. And that's if I don't pay rent or buy groceries."

I stared. "An oh-da—what? Seriously? How do you know all this shit, Bandoni?"

He tapped his overly large skull. "Lots of real estate."

"Explains why I hear the wind whistling up there sometimes." I hunched my shoulders. "Anyway, anything about the brother seem off to you?"

Bandoni grunted. "You think maybe Todd with the Audemars Piguet and the capped-tooth smile was involved in his brother's death? All that shit about remorse and forgiveness."

"Cain and Abel? Feels a bit biblical."

Bandoni turned his head and spat into the gutter. "So were the words someone carved into his skin. Especially that bit about blood. Could be blood relations. The ME said blood used to be considered all-powerful."

"But what's his motive?"

"The father, maybe. Playing those boys against each other. And believe me, I've seen my share of fratricide. It don't take much, sometimes."

"But what about the dress and the rape? Would a brother do that?"

Bandoni opened the driver's-side door. "You really need me to answer that?"

We were silent a moment. Then I said, "I got a bad feeling. What if Ami and Noah fell afoul of the same killer? Maybe the Superior Gentlemen didn't like it when Noah got a girlfriend. Don't forget the second tattoo—the symbol of man over woman."

"But ain't getting a little sex the whole point of being a pickup artist? Why carve up a guy for scoring? And"—he aimed a finger at me—"don't go all woman solidarity on me. Maybe she *helped* the killer. Violence begins at home."

"I'm not feeling it."

"One step at a time, rookie. Punks. Then Riley Lynch. And the comics geeks."

"We're more than twenty-four hours in. And what have we got?"

Bandoni squeezed in behind the steering wheel. "We're just getting started. Rome wasn't built in a day."

"No." I looked up at the darkening clouds. "But it burned to the ground in one."

CHAPTER 15

The thing about there being hell to pay is that you can always hope the devil doesn't come to collect.

—Sydney Parnell. Personal journal.

The vice cop, Boz, leaned back in his chair and gave me a nod.

"Happy to do it," he said.

"More than happy," said his partner, Cooper. "We know about both these assholes."

We were back at headquarters, in a conference room on the fourth floor. Bandoni, Clyde and me, and the undercover cops Boz and Cooper. Newly empty pizza boxes, paper plates, and two six-packs of soda were strewn across the table. Sleet slammed the windows and formed a silver-white veil between us and the city. Every now and again, the lights flickered.

Leopard's Den, the gutter-punk hangout we were going to hit that night, was in Boz and Cooper's territory.

"We're not getting a warrant for these punks," Bandoni said. "It's strictly a friendly little chat. For the moment, they're just persons of interest."

"It's the Chicken Man case, right?" Cooper asked. He looked the part of a junkie in his ripped jeans, filthy shirt, and piercings.

"Noah Asher," Bandoni said. "Right."

"We'll go with however you want to play it," Boz said. He wore dirty camos, a watch cap, and a full beard. "But my money's on Damn Fox for doing your guy. I've just been waiting for that asshat to do something since he nudged into our territory a couple of months ago."

Bandoni popped a soda. "Tell us what you know."

Cooper tapped his laptop keyboard, and a picture of a white male appeared on the screen. "Meet Damn Fox, a.k.a. David Kelly. Twenty-eight-year-old dipshit and Colorado native."

I studied Kelly's photo. Cruel eyes. Cruel lips. Hell, even his ears looked like they were up to no good.

Cooper went on. "Classic sob-story childhood, at least according to Kelly. Not that he's a credible source, but whatever. Says he was five years old when Daddy left. Mommy turned tricks to pay the rent and buy meth. Davey boy claims that sometimes the johns came after him, and around the tender age of ten, he started dipping into Mom's drugs. Ran away from home when he was fifteen and hit the rails. Juvenile records are sealed, but he's the king of misdemeanors now—trespassing, breaking and entering. Word on the street is that he's dealing. We haven't caught him selling on our turf, but our sources say the kid has tried or sold every drug you've heard of and half the ones you haven't. His specialty, allegedly, is Molly, which he hawks at concerts."

Bandoni and I exchanged a glance. Todd Asher had mentioned that Riley Lynch dealt in Molly.

Molly, a.k.a. ecstasy, first hit the streets in the eighties and still did a solid job hospitalizing kids hoping to find chemical nirvana. The euphoria provided by Molly sometimes came with heart attacks and seizures. Especially if the dealer cut something in with the powder.

"Does he cut it?" Bandoni asked. Reading my mind.

"Does a bear shit in the woods?" Boz answered. "Christ, they all do. Baking powder. Sugar. Whatever they got in the kitchen. But a lot of times, guys like our Davey boy mix in other illegals for wealthier customers."

Cooper clicked to another photo. This one showed Kelly with shoulder-length brown hair and gold studs in his ears. "Keep in mind, these photos are a couple of years old—we got 'em from a vice guy in Colorado Springs, where these guys like to hang. Kelly could have added tattoos and piercings and God knows what else. These punks grow and cut their hair more often than the wife yells at me to stop pissing on the toilet seat."

"What do you know about his tats?" I said.

"Serious religious shit," Boz answered. "Says he found Jesus after he ran away from home, and now he's living among the poor, spreading the word. But this guy is more Charles Manson than Jesus. I think he uses the tats to convince his customers he's pure of heart. But all you gotta do is look in his eyes to see that the elevator to paradise went the wrong way."

Bandoni leaned back in his chair and planted his hands on his ample gut. "What about the other guy? Street Cred. What's his story?"

Cooper tapped a key again. Kelly's picture was replaced by that of another white guy, this one with a vacant expression and a green rooster tail. "This picture's a year old. William Patterson's story's pretty much like Kelly's, except he didn't run away until he was seventeen, which was six years ago. Rap sheet's a little shorter than his buddy's, probably 'cause he hasn't been on the road as long. Other than that and the green hair, Patterson is Kelly's clone. Don't let that dumber-than-shit expression confuse you. Guy's as nasty as they come. And street smart. Thus the name."

"Noah Asher took a lot of photos of gutter punks," I said. "You hear anything on the street about somebody wanting to turn these kids' stories into a graphic novel?"

"Me, no," Cooper said. "Boz?"

"Nope. But if he crossed paths with Damn Fox while he was walking among the lepers, it wouldn't surprise me if Kelly decided to cut him down. Kelly considers a lot of these kids his, doesn't want anyone else messing with them. Especially if it means losing customers."

"What about this? You seen a tat like this anywhere?" I showed them the tattoo of the shepherd's crook inside the triangle. The men looked at it but shook their heads.

"That was on your victim?" Boz asked.

"That one was voluntary," I said. "These weren't."

I laid the autopsy photos on the table one by one. The strange symbol. The words about betrayal and blood as the life of the flesh.

Boz whistled. "That's some nasty shit."

Bandoni opened another soda. "You seen stuff like this before?"

"Nah," Cooper said. "But we can ask around about that, too."

"Just between us chickens, though," Bandoni said.

Cooper nodded.

We spent the next fifteen minutes planning our strategy. According to Boz and Cooper, Leopard's Den would be a zoo, even with the forecasted crappy weather—Kill the Normies was a popular band. Approaching Damn Fox and Street Cred inside the club was too risky. Things could easily go sideways, especially given that most of the patrons would not be pro-police.

"Best thing to do," Cooper said, "is wait until the dickwads go outside to take a piss or have a smoke. Boz and I can let you know when we've got eyes on them, send you a photo if the guys have changed their appearance. Then you nail 'em on some bullshit charge like urinating in public."

"While we," Boz said, "simply melt away."

With a little over an hour before we were due to head out, Bandoni said he had to run an errand. He looked bad—gray and puffy, beads of sweat at his hairline. Like a guy with a 3:00 a.m. hangover who'd just been force-fed a plate of habanero chilies. I hoped he was actually heading out to steal a nap in his car.

Clyde and I walked across the plaza to drop off the Barbie doll at the crime lab, then returned to headquarters and took the stairs up to the detectives' room. Unlike the day before, business was booming, and Bandoni was the only investigator missing from our squad. Clyde got scattered cheers as we entered the room.

Detective Clark peered around his desk partition. "Hey, Parnell, he your date for tonight?"

"Beauty and the Beast," Gorman said. He put down his fly-fishing magazine and blew a kiss to Clyde. "How you doing there, beauty?"

Gorman was the incompetent cop who'd taken part of the credit for Cohen's work and mine in a previous case. I was Gorman's Achilles' heel—one of the few who knew the truth about what had gone down six months ago.

Clark shook his head. "Gorman, you shouldn't try to put the moves on Clyde like that."

Cue general laughter.

"Then again," said another detective, "Clyde's a hell of a lot better than some of the dogs I've seen him out with."

More laughter.

"Fuck you guys," Gorman said.

"Swearing on the floor," Clark said. "What the fuck?"

"Gorman," I said. "You check the tattoo book yet?"

"I'm working on it."

I looked at the fly-fishing magazine. "How about you work a little harder?"

A chorus of oohs bounced around the room. Clark grabbed his balls and turned away.

Gorman and I locked eyes, and the look he gave me made me feel like I was staring down the barrel of an RPG. I almost laughed. Can't scare a Marine with that shit. I smiled, and after a moment he spun on his heel and returned to his desk.

"Looks like Gorman's not going to get any tonight," Clark said.

"He'll be fine," called another detective. "There's a kid on the street corner with free puppies."

With the guys sidetracked razzing Gorman, I got Clyde comfortable, then powered up my computer, plugged in my headphones, and started dialing, my notebook and pen to hand.

We'd gotten the warrants for the phone and credit-card records, so I made the calls and requested records going back ninety days. I was promised I'd have them by noon the next day.

The next call was to a friend of mine in the FBI. I hoped Mac McConnell could tell me if it was even possible to get the Feds to cough up a list of immigrants who were here on Temporary Protected Status.

When Mac answered, I said, "We gotta meet at Joe's Tavern soon."

She laughed. "I'm free tonight, Parnell, if you're not just blowing smoke up my ass."

"Sadly, I'm in the smoke-blowing business right now." I told her what I needed, and she told me Temporary Protected Status was under the control of DHS—the Department of Homeland Security. But she promised to see what she could do. We promised to meet soon for whiskeys at Joe's Tavern and hung up.

After that, I called ColdShip, who still hadn't come through. My dream was to get video of Damn Fox and Street Cred somewhere, anywhere near the train where we'd found Noah. The footage would give me leverage to lean on them when we brought them in. But when the receptionist answered and I gave my name, she told me the manager was out for the day. Ditto for the head of security.

These guys were starting to seriously piss me off.

I pulled up North Platte's newspaper, the *North Platte Telegraph.* The *Telegraph* had two articles about the company. One announced the opening of the facility three years earlier. Then, two years ago, ColdShip had been raided by Immigration and Customs Enforcement. The ICE raid had revealed that the company employed undocumented immigrants and treated them poorly on a host of fronts, including providing an unsafe work environment. Penalties and criminal prosecution would be forthcoming. An immigration attorney was mentioned, John Yaeger. I entered a search for *ColdShip* and *immigrants* along with other search combinations.

But I couldn't find any follow-up.

I tilted back in my chair, planted my feet against my desk, and stared at the ceiling.

Companies couldn't be held liable by ICE if they'd done their best to verify employees' work authorizations. In fact, checking an employee's documentation too rigorously could result in discrimination charges. Employers had to walk a fine line.

But if, after the raid, ColdShip still knowingly relied on undocumented workers—cheap, willing, available—they would be highly motivated to keep any video recordings out of the hands of the authorities. My guess was that the cameras worked perfectly well. ColdShip would want to keep an eye on their employees, make sure they weren't taking too many cigarette breaks or skimming merchandise.

But they wouldn't want proof of who, exactly, was smoking those cigarettes.

I dropped my feet with a frown. Whatever ColdShip might be up to, I couldn't see how undocumented workers played into Noah's murder.

I checked the time. With half an hour to go, I generated a list of the vehicles owned by everyone in Noah's circle. Markey and Rivero. Todd Asher. Riley Lynch. A pickup, two sedans, and a BMW. No cargo vans. Then I ran a background check on Riley Lynch. Six months earlier, he'd been fined for possession of a Class IV substance. Rohypnol, the date-rape drug.

If you hadn't finessed your seduction skills, there was always Rohypnol as a fallback.

I pulled up a search engine on the computer and typed in *Superior Gentlemen*. Nothing. Then I entered *Denver pickup artists*. A website popped up advertising seminars from the previous summer—classes that promised to teach men "the game."

The instructor's name was Baron Casanova, an obvious pseudonym. I shot an email to the address listed on the seminar site. Maybe Noah had been a student. But within seconds the email bounced back with a notice that the address was no longer valid.

I widened my search. PUAs appeared to be one of several groups that were considered part of the "manosphere." There were men's-rights activists, men who advocated celibacy, and guys who figured the world would be better off without women. There were men who said you should never masturbate and others who were miserably celibate because they couldn't get a date. These celibates divided the rest of the world into Chads—men who could easily attract women—and Stacys—desirable women who slept with the Chads.

The celibates hated Chads and Stacys. They also hated pickup artists because those men—like Chads—got women.

Plenty of anger to go around.

PUAs and celibates did agree on one thing—women were props, not people. Resources to be allocated. Dating wasn't about creating a relationship.

It was a power trip.

Again, I thought of the tattoo on Noah's arm. The one placing men over women. Maybe Noah had inverted the normal order by supporting feminist causes. That could be seen as a betrayal.

I glanced up as Bandoni came in. He looked better. Either the errand had done him some good or he had actually taken a nap. I flagged him down. When he stopped at my desk, I filled him in on what I'd spent the last half hour learning.

"Good work on Lynch," he said. But then he frowned. "But ColdShip? I sent off the warrant request to the North Platte PD. I thought we were waiting on that."

"I figured we'd want those recordings as soon as possible."

"You have them?"

"It hasn't yet—"

He leaned in and lowered his voice. "All you did was give those guys a heads-up that we want to take a look at their operations."

Clyde lifted his head, alert to the edge in Bandoni's voice.

I thought of the articles I'd just read in the newspaper, and my heart sank. All I cared about was a couple of stowaways, not whether ColdShip was hiring undocumented workers.

Around us, the room had gone quiet. Everyone appeared to be raptly attentive to their computers or the paperwork on their desk. But even though Bandoni had lowered his voice, they knew I'd done something to screw the pooch. My cheeks burned.

Bandoni crooked a finger. "Let's go get a Coke."

Meaning he'd chew my ass in private. I signaled Clyde to stay and followed Bandoni through the maze of desks and out into the hallway.

"We still don't have the warrant," I pointed out. It sounded defensive. Almost worse than making a mistake was not admitting it. "But it was my bad."

"This ain't a fucking game we're playing."

"I know. But be honest, Bandoni." It sounded like a whine, but in for a penny, in for a pound. "Were we really going to sit on our thumbs waiting while the North Platte PD got everyone to sign off on the warrant, then wait again for them to raid the place and confiscate their recordings? Or were we going to do exactly what I did? Call and ask nicely and mention the warrant in case they said no?"

"You gonna tell me what we would or wouldn't do? Well, let me tell you this. We do things by the book, Parnell. That way, no fancy-pants defense lawyer is going to make us out as fuckups. Or worse, get some perp kicked free because we can't even do police work right. You got that, Golden Girl?"

On one level, I knew Bandoni was being unfair. I'd read enough reports during my training period to know that cops often asked nicely before resorting to a warrant. It made things faster and kept some judge from deciding a cop was too warrant-happy.

But I was just a rookie. And whether or not to get a warrant wasn't a rookie cop's call. Lobowitz's warning sounded in my ears.

You're to be on Bandoni's ass like wet toilet paper. Unless he specifically tasks you with something, you don't do it. You especially don't do it if it's your idea and he hasn't okayed it.

I closed my eyes. Opened them.

You're a cowboy, Detective Parnell.

Bandoni was still waiting for my answer. The worst thing about all this was the disappointment in his eyes.

"I got it," I said. Worse than a sailor with a case of clap.

CHAPTER 16

Life, rookie, is an accumulation of heartbreak.

—*Len Bandoni. Private conversation.*

I tucked the Tahoe into the parking lot of an abandoned strip mall a couple of blocks from Leopard's Den. Bandoni and I would wait here while Boz and Cooper watched the venue for the gutter punks. The clouds had lowered, and the sleet morphed into a gloomy dusk shredded by periodic rain squalls.

Don't like the weather in Colorado? Give it a minute.

Bandoni crossed his arms and sank his chin onto his chest, a posture that invited no conversation. I tuned the radio to the channel we'd agreed on. Then, while Clyde curled up in his crate in the back and Bandoni appeared to nap, I stepped out into the purple light and called crime scene detective Ron Gabel.

"I'm calling for some good news," I told him.

"Bad day?"

"Won't give it a victory parade."

"I'm afraid I'm going to add to your misery," Gabel said. "I finished running all the samples from the nursing home, looking for a match with the sample from Carolyn Jackson's rape kit."

"A whole lot of nothing?"

"You're familiar with the vacuum of space?"

"Crap."

"I'm sorry, Sydney. It was a long shot, anyway."

But Noah Asher's case had raised another possibility—an angle the original detectives might not have considered. "What about cleaning companies?"

"Come again?"

"We've been assuming that the rapist was someone internal. Or at least someone who was there on a regular basis, like the cafeteria staff."

"Right."

"But a lot of businesses contract with cleaning companies. And while most of the night janitors are women, the companies also hire men."

"That's a good thought, Sydney. I'll find out if the facility used outside cleaners and get back to you."

I got back into the Tahoe, pushed my seat back as far as I could, and popped open my laptop. Using spreadsheet software and the five hundred rape-kit files I'd scanned and loaded onto my hard drive, I started sorting data from the kits. I looked at names and dates along with the type of assault, the location, and the age and race of the victim. Some of the assaults were clear outliers—either they were one-offs or the rapist had moved on. In some cases, as with Cohen's victim the previous day, the victims had chosen not to press charges. Their rape kits sat in mute testimony to their fear.

But when I sorted by the victim's age, eliminating every woman under the age of seventy, a clump of similarities emerged. With two exceptions involving home invasions, every victim over the age of seventy had been attacked in elder-care facilities. And all the women except Carolyn Jackson—the earliest case in the profile I was generating—had been Latina.

And—here I hesitated as an ice-cold hand slipped down my back—two of the women had reported that their attackers had yellow eyes.

Who the hell had yellow eyes?

Dana's voice sounded in my mind. *There are a lot of yellow-eyed supervillains in the comics world. Nightcrawler. Trigon. Gamora . . . Apocalypse.*

I stared out the window. Light from the streetlamps threw watery globes on the wet pavement. A cat darted across the street, narrowly missing disaster as a car roared past.

I drummed my fingers on the steering wheel.

Human brains hunted down patterns like mosquitoes heat-seeking for blood. We found the image of the Virgin Mary in our tea leaves and human faces carved into the surface of Mars. So maybe I was spinning ectoplasmic spiderwebs out of wishful thinking. Maybe the elderly women had been as delirious and demented as the police reports suggested.

Or maybe the rapist had been a comics fan.

I puffed out a breath of air and studied the data on the screen, my pulse slamming in my throat, unsure where, in all the data, the actual spider lurked. No one had made the nursing-home connection between the cases before because, of the seven assaults, five of them had occurred in municipalities like Aurora and Englewood, which had their own police departments. And while some of the cases had been clumped together in time, others had happened months apart. I hadn't spotted a connection, either, because the nursing-home locations hadn't popped up during my initial go/no-go search for rape kits that could be retested.

Now I shot a text to Gabel.

SEVEN NURSING-HOME CASES IN METRO DENVER. POSSIBLE PATTERN.

He answered, SERIAL RAPIST?

WHAT I'M THINKING. CAN WE COMPARE DNA FROM THOSE SEVEN KITS?

I'LL MAKE IT HAPPEN.

THANKS.

I stepped out again and made one more call, this one to Denise Jackson. Strictly speaking, I was supposed to go through the victim advocate. But Denise had broken that chain before I had.

When Denise answered, I asked if she could go to her mother with one very specific question: Had she noticed anything unusual about her attacker's appearance?

But Denise said, "I don't need to ask her that. She told me the man had yellow eyes. I think it was why the police didn't pay all that much attention. They thought she was batty."

Now the ice-cold hand wrapped fingers around my neck. *Make that* three *attacks. Maybe more.*

I thanked Denise, pocketed my phone, and got back in the vehicle to stare at the data, looking for additional connections. Nothing popped out. I'd let my subconscious work on it. I set aside the laptop and did a Tahoe version of a stretch, arching my back and rotating my head to get out the kinks. Bandoni scratched his left ear, then settled back into his coma.

The radio buzzed softly. It was Boz, who was monitoring text messages from his partner.

"Fox is in the den," he said. "No sign of Patterson yet."

"Roger that," I said.

Bandoni gave no indication he'd heard. While my subconscious chewed away at both mysteries—Noah's death and the nursing-home rapes—I entertained myself playing a solitary game of I Spy using a flashlight. I counted twenty-six empty beer bottles, two tennis shoes— nonmatching—eight separate piles of rubbish, the carcass of what might have once been a squirrel, and a cracked commode. Alphabetically, I was on *K* and having zero luck—no ketchup bottles or busted-up kegs or stray keys—when the radio popped again.

"Street Cred is in the hole," Boz said. "Looks like he's ordering a pitcher of beer for him and his pal. Street Cred has lost his rooster tail.

And Damn Fox has tattooed his ugly mug. Anything that covers up that kind of nasty is an improvement. Cooper is sending photos."

My phone lit up. Four photos, dim and shot at an angle. But the punks would be easy enough to make. Street Cred might have shed his rooster tail, but now he had a red buzz and an immense silver ring dangling from his nose, suggesting that eating was more of a recreational sport than a necessity.

Damn Fox had a fresh-looking tattoo of a red devil on his left cheek. He also had a black eye and swollen lip. The blank flatness of his stare brought up thoughts of roads that led nowhere.

"Our boys are heading for the back door," Boz said. "My money says they're just gonna take a whiz. Music's like a chain saw on speed, but they're digging it. I'm following them out."

I started the Tahoe and pulled out of the strip mall as a few raindrops pattered on the windshield and thunder rumbled in the near distance. Sensing action from his place in the back, Clyde barked. Bandoni opened his eyes, and I passed him my phone with the photos of the punks.

"How long'd I sleep?" he asked.

"Just to *K*."

"The fuck is that supposed to mean?"

On the radio, Boz said, "Our guys have company. Another male. Looks like a little entrepreneurial activity going down behind Leopard's Den. I'd sure as hell love to bring them in, but it's your show tonight. You two want to wait until our guys are alone?"

Bandoni picked up the radio. "Don't want them slipping down a rabbit hole. Why don't you and Cooper stick around while we make our move? In case things get complicated."

"You got it. Hold on, something is—" The radio squealed. "Fuck! Kelly just took off. Repeat, Kelly is rabbiting. Cooper ordered him to halt, but that works never. He's heading south. Patterson and the third male took off in the opposite direction. Cooper's going after Patterson. I'll run Kelly down."

I grabbed the radio from Bandoni. "Boz, go with Cooper. We'll use the K9 on Kelly."

"Roger."

I slammed to a stop in a private parking lot across the street from the Den and opened my door just as a figure sped by at the far end of the lot, heading toward a gap between the buildings. While Bandoni got on the radio to set up a perimeter, I opened the back and ordered Clyde out.

Belgian Malinois, the backup plan.

"Fass ihn!" I cried, flinging out my arm in the direction of the fleeing punk. *Get him!*

Clyde took off like a shot. I ran after him, grateful I'd swapped my pumps for sneakers before we'd left the station.

"Stop!" I yelled at Kelly as he reached the edge of the building and spun right. "Dog in pursuit!"

Clyde turned the corner. I followed as the skies opened up and dumped rain.

Kelly was halfway down the path between the buildings. He was moving like he was trying out for the Olympics, arms pumping, feet kicking.

I yelled again. "Halt, or my dog will take you down!"

Kelly reached down deep and put on an extra bit of speed. But it was impossible for him to outrun Clyde. Clyde leapt, and man and dog hit the pavement. Fox screamed as Clyde's teeth sank into the punk's ass.

I shouted, "Out!" to Clyde, grabbed his collar, and told him to guard. Then I slapped handcuffs on Damn Fox, pulled on gloves, and patted him down while he howled in pain.

"He hurt me!" he screamed.

My lungs bellowed. Rain poured down my collar.

It was never a K9 cop's first choice to use their partner as a weapon. But I had no sympathy for Damn Fox, whether or not he was guilty of Noah Asher's murder. According to the radio chatter that was coming in, Cooper had caught up with Patterson, but Patterson and the third man had escaped after Patterson hit Cooper with a set of brass knuckles.

"I told you not to run," I muttered under my breath, feeling metal in the right pocket of Damn Fox's jeans.

Gingerly, I slid my gloved hand into his pocket and pulled out a set of brass knuckles, heavy and dense.

"Who'd you plan to use these on, asshole?" I asked.

Kelly's shrieks were inarticulate.

I got on the radio and called for an ambulance. Nearby, lightning flashed, followed by the slow roll of thunder.

Bandoni limped up and surveyed the damage. He shook his head at Kelly, who continued to scream, then eyeballed Clyde.

"Right in the ass?" he said. "Remind me not to get on his bad side."

"Maybe you should kiss him and tell him you love him."

"Only after he brushes his teeth."

The nurse adjusted a surgical light in the emergency room bay while Damn Fox lay on his stomach, shouting vitriol at us.

The ER doc was a laconic forty-something black man with a salt-and-pepper beard and a look that said he'd seen it all. Given that the Denver Health Medical Center was known as the Knife and Gun Club, he probably had. Or at least a representative segment of the evil that men do. He introduced himself as Dr. Morris, then waited while Officer Petzky, the uniform who'd accompanied Kelly in the ambulance, hand-cuffed Kelly's wrist to the bed railing.

"All yours, Doc," Petzky said.

Dr. Morris put on a pair of readers and examined the wound.

"He needs stitches. A lot, if I'm any expert. Which"—he smiled—"I am. Shepherd?"

"Belgian Malinois."

Kelly's rage devolved into a soft sobbing.

"What about the facial injuries?" Morris asked. "Those related to the arrest?"

He was doing due diligence, and I applauded him for it. "The facial scrapes are from hitting the pavement. My guess is there will be more on his arms. But he had a black eye and swollen lip before we caught up to him."

"Make a note," Morris said to the nurse.

"You gotta knock him out for those stitches?" Bandoni asked. "We need to have a little chat before he goes night-night."

"I can use a local. Give me half an hour to clean him out and stitch him up, then he's all yours." He looked at me. "Dog up to date on his shots? I'll need the records."

"They're on file. I'll see that you get them."

The nurse waved us out of the room, waiting until Officer Petzky stepped inside before drawing the privacy curtain. We went looking for whichever bay they'd stashed Cooper in.

We found Boz around the corner of the U-shaped space, stalking back and forth along the hallway, his hands balled and his face creased with fury.

"What's the word?" I asked.

Boz forced himself still. "Loose teeth, crushed lip. The worst of it is he bit his tongue almost in half. The fucker had brass knuckles."

We were silent a minute, appreciating the severity of Cooper's injuries.

"Your dog nearby?" Boz asked me. "I want to shake his paw for bringing down Kelly."

"He's sleeping it off in his crate," I said. "You can meet him later."

Bandoni took a seat in one of the plastic chairs lining the hallway. He squeezed the bridge of his nose with his thumb and forefinger. Under the fluorescent lights, his scalp looked raw. "What happened?"

"Patterson and Kelly must have made Cooper when he was scoping the two of them inside the club. When they spotted him outside, they took off. Cooper caught the third guy. But while he was reaching for his cuffs, Patterson came back. When Cooper looked up, Patterson coldcocked him. Both of those punks got away."

"Son of a bitch," Bandoni said.

"I'd've gotten there before it happened if I hadn't done a fucking face-plant in the mud," Boz said. "Cooper was expecting me to back him up."

But Bandoni was probably thinking what I was—that Cooper had been careless exposing his back when one of the men was still unaccounted for and before his partner had gotten on scene. Probably he figured Patterson was long gone and Cooper was approaching fast. Reasonable guesses.

But guessing could get you killed.

As if reading our minds, Boz said, "It wasn't his fault."

"I know." Bandoni nodded. Now was not the time to sort out how things had gone down. He slapped his hands on his thighs and pushed himself out of the chair. "I'm gonna get some coffee. You two want anything?"

"I'll come with you," I said.

Boz shook his head. "Cooper's wife is on the way. I'll wait here."

Bandoni found a vending machine at the end of the hallway. He got two coffees, black, and handed one to me.

"Cookies?" he asked.

"No, thanks."

He shrugged, seemed to consider the chocolate chip for a moment, then moved away. His face was gray in the overbright light, and bags had collected under his eyes like luggage at an airport carousel.

He said, "You thinking what I'm thinking?"

"These guys like hitting cops," I said. "Patterson actually got away and then came back to nail Cooper. Which makes me wonder how things went down in that field when Heinrich was hit. If it was our gutter punks, maybe Heinrich was intent on one guy and didn't hear the other man coming."

"I thought we were focusing on these guys as witnesses for Noah's murder."

"The fact that they bragged on the street about seeing a murder doesn't eliminate them as suspects for Heinrich's assault. They might have panicked when they saw him, figuring he'd make them for the murder."

Bandoni nodded like I'd passed a test.

"That's the angle we take," he said. "If Kelly thinks we want him for Heinrich, he's got nothing to lose by admitting they saw a man get killed. What else are we considering?"

"That they might be the killers."

"Don't lose sight of that." Bandoni sipped his coffee, then spit it back. "Son of a bitch, that's hot."

I pulled out my phone to send Cohen a text that I'd be home late. Then I remembered he'd be heading to Denver International to pick up his cousin, who was coming in on a red-eye from Chicago.

Late night for all of us.

"You ever meet Cohen's cousin?" I asked. "Evan Wilding?"

"Sure."

"What's he like?"

"Brilliant." Bandoni grinned, his teeth caffeine yellow. "You finally meeting the fam?"

"I guess. Any advice?"

"Don't underestimate him."

"The fuck kind of advice is that? I thought we were partners."

"I cannot guide you down all paths, grasshopper."

The doctor appeared at the opposite end of the hallway.

Bandoni stood with a grunt. "While we're talking to Kelly, remember what I told you. We keep firing questions at him. Bounce around. Don't let him find a pattern."

◆ ◆ ◆

Kelly lay on his side when we walked in, one hand still handcuffed to the bed railing, the other tucked between his legs. He was pale beneath his tattoos, but his gaze was hot.

Bandoni and I took a second to look through Kelly's belongings, which Petzky had bagged. The brass knuckles. Forty-three dollars in cash. A light-rail pass. And two joints.

Bandoni dove right in. "Where'd your asshole partner go to ground?"

"I look like his mommy?" Kelly said.

"Tough guy. Here's the thing, Kelly. Patterson's in the wind. But we got you. Resisting arrest. Those brass knuckles. Arrestable offense right there. Plus, our cop's a little fuzzy on who actually hit him."

"Say what? What kind of bullshit is that? You can't charge me for that cop getting hurt."

"Depends on which cop we're talking about. Did you hit a railroad cop a couple of nights ago?"

Kelly's gaze went from Bandoni to me and back, his eyeballs jittering in their sockets like windup toys.

"What are you talking about?" His voice wobbled.

"It gets worse, though," Bandoni said.

"Whaddaya mean?"

Bandoni leaned back, jammed his fists in his armpits. "Why'd you run tonight?"

"Instinct, dude. Self-protection. Smart, huh? My face looks like pepperoni pizza." His eyes darted to me. "Thanks to that bitch."

"I have a different theory. You want to hear it?"

Kelly rubbed his free hand along his thighs. "I want my phone call."

"You're not under arrest, asshole. Not yet."

"I want my call."

"By all means," Bandoni said. "You want to make that call right now? Call your fancy-pants lawyer? You've got one, right? Or do you want to find out what you're looking at first?"

"I'm the one with the complaint. That psycho dog. I had my hands up. She sicced the dog on me anyway."

Bandoni looked at me with an eye roll. "That true?"

"You ever see a guy surrender by running away?"

"You hear that, Kelly? Your word against hers. Or maybe not. Half those businesses you ran past have cameras."

That was bullshit. But Kelly probably had no idea.

"You want that phone call now?"

His gaze dropped. "I'll wait," he muttered.

"Where's your partner in crime, Kelly? Help us out, maybe we'll forgive a few of your indiscretions."

Kelly rubbed his nose on the plastic ID band on his wrist. "Fuck you."

"That a no?" Bandoni said. "I'll go ahead with my theory, then." He swung a plastic chair around and planted a foot on the seat. "I think you made that cop and that got you to thinking about something else you did. Something worse. And *that* got you worried about why the cop had eyes on you. You panicked."

"The only thing in my head was how I had a pair of *dicks* following me around."

Bandoni tossed his empty coffee cup into the trash and dropped an elbow to his knee. "You're looking at some serious time, Kelly. You and your partner. You know what I'm thinking?" Bandoni directed this question toward me.

"What are you thinking?" I asked.

"I'm thinking this guy has something he's trying to hide. Something even worse than hitting a railroad cop. That true, Kelly? You do something so bad you don't want us to know about?"

Kelly licked his lips. "I didn't hit any cop."

"You want to know what the really bad thing is? I'm talking murder, Kelly. Cold-blooded murder."

"What?" Kelly started up from the bed, then squealed when he rolled onto the stitches. He collapsed back onto his hip. The handcuffs clanked.

Bandoni's grin was a shot of ice. "Now you feeling me?"

Kelly's good eye was wide now. The black eye looked like a pit. He rubbed his thigh with his free hand, and the bed squeaked. "What are you talking about? I don't know a damn thing about a murder."

"Noah Asher."

"Who?"

"The guy you and your asshole friend beat to death. Tell us what happened, Kelly. It's always better when you cooperate. Judges like that. Juries, too. Did this guy get on your train? Try to muscle into your turf?"

Kelly stared through us. His mouth was a thin line.

"That how you get that black eye and the lip?" Bandoni pressed. "Noah hit you?"

"Why don't you kiss my pimpled ass?"

I leaned forward. Drew in a breath. "You know what you smell like, Kelly?"

He sniffed, then sneered at me. "All I can smell is cop pussy."

I looked at Bandoni. "He smells like *fowl*."

"Fowl. As in chickens." Bandoni took a sniff. "You're right. He smells just like the inside of that poultry car."

"What?" Kelly's gaze went from my face to Bandoni's, back and forth. "What are you talking about?"

"Let's see your hands," I said.

Kelly flinched and curled his hands into fists. "You got me hand-cuffed, case you forgot."

"It's not like we duct-taped that wrist," Bandoni said. "Hold 'em out. Or do we need to get the dog again?"

"You can't do that," Kelly said. But he held out his hands, palms down.

I gestured for him to turn them over.

Kelly sighed the sigh of the aggrieved. But he rotated his hands. The palms and fingers were splotched yellow and black.

"A bitch, isn't it?" I said. "Getting spray paint off your skin."

Kelly tucked his free hand back between his legs. "Nothing illegal about me having paint on my hands."

I held up my phone, showed him the photo I'd taken of the tagging on the reefer car. "Vandalism's a minor charge. Three to twelve months in jail. Nothing next to murder."

His eyes darted to the curtain the nurse had drawn across the bay, like he was measuring the distance from his bed to freedom. "What is this murder shit you keep talking about?"

Bandoni leaned in. "Word on the street is that you saw a murder. But we think you're more than just a witness."

Kelly pulled his gaze back to Bandoni, then let it slide sideways. "That's bullshit."

"And there's the railroad cop. You tried to silence him. But it didn't work."

Kelly's tongue flicked out. He licked his lips. "Lies."

I walked to the other side of the bed. Kelly rolled his eyes, trying to follow me. I pulled out the picture of Ami in the milkshake shop and held it up.

A flicker in Kelly's eyes before he looked down. He knew her. Or at least recognized her.

"Who is she?" I asked.

"Beats the fuck out of me."

"And this guy?" I pulled out Noah's drawing of the yellow-eyed man near the train.

Kelly got busy plucking at the plastic ID on his wrist. "A man near a train. The fuck do I know?"

I stuck the photo of the Superior Gentlemen under his nose. "And these guys?"

"Looks like a bunch of fags."

"Riley Lynch," I said.

"Who?"

"Todd Asher."

"The fuck you talking about?"

"And Craze. Who's Craze, Kelly?"

Something slithered into Kelly's eyes. His skin took on a gray cast. Bandoni caught the change and leaned in. "He a friend of yours?"

Kelly held up his middle finger.

I folded my arms. "Here's what you and I and Detective Bandoni all know. When the techs finish processing that reefer car, they're going to find your fingerprints. And your DNA. All it takes is a single hair, Kelly. Did you know that? A few skin cells. And then we're going to place you at the scene of the crime."

Kelly had stopped moving as soon as I said *fingerprints*.

"We know you were there," I said. "And we know you're an asshole. A real, genuine, bottom-of-the-barrel asshole." I leaned over the bed. "But I'm not as convinced as my partner that you're a killer. What I think is that you saw something that scared the crap out of you. Maybe someone even beat you because of it. And now you're afraid to talk."

He snorted. Kept his eyes down. "So what if I was on that reefer? I'm not saying I was. But if I was, so what? That ain't murder."

"Here's what we're going to tell a jury. You and your pal Patterson caught out in North Platte so you could get to Denver and your favorite band. You picked the chicken car because the door was open. At some point, probably in Ogallala, you tagged the car because you wanted to tell the entire world how fabulous your band is. Kill the Normies."

Bandoni picked up the story. "By then the chickens were starting to reek. Must have been a real stink fest. But you were too stoned to care."

"Plus, relocating in a heavily patrolled rail yard is risky," I added. "Cinder dicks everywhere. You stayed put."

"Then, outside Denver, the train stopped," Bandoni said. "And here's where things could go either way. Maybe you killed a guy . . ."

"Or"—I snapped my fingers, and Kelly jumped—"maybe you saw him killed."

Bandoni jutted his chin forward. "Which is it, band boy?"

Kelly tucked his chin to his chest and stayed silent. His breathing rasped in and out. Black ink on his forearm read *Jesus raves*.

From the other side of the curtain came a continuous stream of chatter and the whoosh and beep of machines. Nearby, a curtain slid on metal hooks. Someone walked past with the squeak of rubber soles on tile. A man said, ". . . myocardial infarction. It means we have to . . ."

Bandoni's phone buzzed. He glanced at the screen, then excused himself and went out into the hall.

A single bead of sweat caught on Kelly's hair and splashed onto the bed.

"Who *did* land one on you?" I said softly. "Was it the same guy who murdered Noah? Did he tell you he'd kill you if you squealed? Tell you he'd beat your head in while you were sleeping?"

"Fuck you." Another bead of sweat dropped.

"Was it Craze?"

Silence.

"We can protect you."

Petzky came in.

"Your partner wants you," he told me. "I'll watch this guy."

"Last chance, Kelly," I said. "You want to tell me what really went down out there?"

He gave me the finger again. But the gesture was half-hearted.

"Why don't you sleep on it?" I said and blew him a kiss.

On the other side of the curtained doorway, Bandoni was still on the phone. He gave me a nod and finished the call. Then he pocketed his phone and dropped into a chair, his bowling-ball head sunk into his shoulders like it now weighed fifty pounds.

"We got a second victim," he said.

The hallway took a small twist, a warp in space that only I could see. And suddenly Noah Asher stood beside Bandoni.

He was a ghost with a face now, courtesy of the DMV photo. Pale skin, kind eyes. That innocent-looking black cowlick.

He pressed a hand to his heart.

Bandoni stuck his head into the bay where Kelly sat. "Petzky, book this asshole. Possession of an illegal weapon."

Kelly's howl of protest followed us as we headed toward the exit.

"Fill me in," I said.

"Smith and Wesson were up on rotation," Bandoni said. "But as soon as they saw that someone had used the corpse as an Etch A Sketch, they called us."

The emergency-room doors whooshed open, blasting us with cold air.

"The body's on the altar of a church," he went on. "Redeemed Life."

I gave him a startled glance. "Todd Asher's church."

"Right. Someone's on the way now to pick up Todd. Riley Lynch, too, while we're at it. Our victim's a white male. Midtwenties. No ID yet. The killer wrote across his chest, 'Vengeance is ours, we will repay.'"

"The Bible. Like Noah."

"Romans twelve nineteen, according to Weston, but with a slight change."

"The killer used the plural," I said.

"Right." Drops of rain darkened Bandoni's coat. "Not 'Vengeance is mine, I will repay,' but—"

"Vengeance is ours. Meaning we have more than one killer?"

Bandoni grunted. "Meaning we don't know shit yet."

I unlocked the Tahoe and looked through the window at Clyde. He wagged his tail in greeting. I owed my K9 partner a good belly rub when we got home.

While Bandoni heaved his bulk into the passenger seat, I started the engine and cranked the heat. The police-issued parking permit fluttered on the dash.

Bandoni pulled out his cigarettes, tapped the pack on the back of his hand. "That wasn't all. The killer—"

"—or killers—"

"—carved up or wrote on every square inch of this guy. Stuff about God not playing fair and anger being a good thing." He stuck a cigarette in his mouth. "Weston was talking so fast I couldn't keep up."

I stared through the glass into a night gone silver bright with the rain. The hospital's red **EMERGENCY** light rippled like blood down the glass.

Bandoni said, "One more thing."

An ambulance squealed into the lot, lights flashing. It jerked to a stop, and the driver leapt out and ran to open the back doors while two nurses in scrubs hurried out from the hospital.

Bandoni put his eyes on me. "They castrated the kid."

I drew in a breath. Held the air in my lungs.

"*And* they cut off his right hand." Bandoni took out his unlit cigarette, stared at it. The lights washed his face red.

I glanced back toward the hospital. Noah Asher stood at the door, staring at us through the rain.

"Fucking world," Bandoni said.

CHAPTER 17

*If trauma is the darkness that knocks us off our path, then life
is about finding our way home.*

But first we must learn to navigate the dark.

—*Sydney Parnell. Personal journal.*

Redeemed Life Church was a new, no-expense-spared construction set
smack in the center of a middle-aged Denver neighborhood, a peacock
lording over a gaggle of 1950s-era homes and decades-old businesses.
A monolith of concrete and angled, rust-colored beams, the structure
punctured the cloud-thick sky like a phallus. Stained-glass windows
glowed orange-red in the rain.

Bandoni whistled. "It's like Home Depot found God."

I parked, and we stepped into the rain. The responding officers and
Smith and Wesson had established two perimeters: an outside zone that
encompassed the entire church and two outlying buildings along with
all entrances and walkways. And an inside perimeter that blocked off
the walkway leading up to the sanctuary and included the sanctuary
itself.

"You take lead on this scene, Parnell," Bandoni said.

"Come again?"

"Don't worry. I'll step all over you soon as you fuck up."

"Right." I drew a deep breath. "Okay."

I went to the back of the Tahoe, where Clyde watched me, tail wagging. As much as I hated exposing my K9 partner to a corpse, it was now our job to get down and dirty with mortality. Dogs carried around the olfactory equivalent of a sixty-terabyte database of odors they could pull up and ping off as needed. Clyde might pick up a scent here that he recognized from the first crime scene.

Or add the killer's scent to his database.

Another upside to exposing Clyde to this body was that Clyde's trainer had assured me my partner's death fear would ease with continuous exposure.

As long as I didn't succumb to my own fears.

"It's for our own good, buddy," I told him as I opened the hatch. I snapped on Clyde's lead, and Bandoni and I ducked under the tape while Clyde pranced forward, tail waving, ready to work. A crowd of onlookers had gathered along the outside perimeter, and a Channel Nine news van pulled up as Bandoni and I were signing in with the uniform standing guard.

"Is someone taking pictures of the crowd?" I asked the cop.

The uniform, a stocky, freckled man whose name badge read *Murphy*, indicated his cell phone. "Taking a snap every few minutes."

"You're the first responder?"

"Yeah. My partner and me. A woman who teaches Bible studies here called it in. Soon as we saw the body, we called dispatch and closed off the area."

I pulled out my notebook. "And the caller's name?"

"Marcy Pitlor. Detective Smythe's talking to her now."

We went under the interior-perimeter tape. Clyde immediately lost his enthusiasm. His tail drooped, and he leaned into me.

"We're still good, buddy," I whispered.

But Bandoni had caught it. "What's up with the mutt?"

"Too many dead bodies."

He gave me a sharp look. "You ever think maybe you picked the wrong career?"

"Every day for three weeks now."

At the door to the chapel, Bandoni and I pulled on booties and gloves under the eyes of a second uniform, a woman named Vasquez. I knelt and snugged specially made booties around Clyde's paws. I took his head in my hands and poured my soul out through my eyes, knowing he'd get my silent message.

We're still good.

Clyde's tail lifted a little.

Vasquez pushed open the door for us.

"Stairs on the right lead to a balcony on the second floor," she said. "The two doors straight ahead go into the chapel. The body is on the other side of the altar rail."

She opened another door. Light poured out from the chapel.

"Were the lights like this when you got here?" I asked.

She shook her head. "We turned them on for Smith and Wesson." A flush. "Smythe and Weston."

"I want to see the scene the way it was when you found it."

"Of course. I'll get the lights."

She vanished, and moments later, the light softened to a dim glow.

I signaled Clyde to stay close, and we went through the doorway and into the gloom of the sanctuary. Bandoni wedged his bulk in beside us, and we stood silently, taking in the scene.

At the far end of the space, Detective Weston and a trio of crime scene detectives stood between us and the body. Flashes from a camera illuminated the semidarkness like bursts of lightning as the photographer worked. Pop, fade. Pop, fade. In between flashes, I made out Ron Gabel's familiar form. He glanced over his shoulder. When he saw us, he gestured for the others to stand aside.

I took my time. I wanted the environment first. Then the body.

The space was somber and hushed. And vast. Over a hundred pews. Unlit chandeliers hung from the lofty ceiling. Small, high windows marched down each wall, and at the far end, above the altar, an immense stained glass window depicted a series of images—Christ's crucifixion and resurrection. The red and blue glass glittered like a king's treasure.

"Not much like the inside of a boxcar filled with chickens," Bandoni said.

"Not unless you consider that trains and churches are both a form of passage to somewhere else."

"Getting philosophical?" He grunted. "You heard the story about the rich man and the camel and the eye of the needle?"

"Sure. That it's easier for a camel to pass through the eye of a needle than for a rich man to get into heaven."

"You ask me, we got a lot of rich men trying to squeeze themselves through that eye."

"How so?"

He spread his hands and shrugged. "It's just a feeling. I used to patrol this neighborhood. Solid working class. Lifeblood of America. But the last five years, there's been a big push for gentrification. Housing prices have reached the heavens faster than anyone who sits inside this place. The poor bastards who grew up here can't afford to stay."

My eyebrows rose in surprise. "You do care."

"Don't start spreading rumors."

We started down the aisle, Clyde hugging my side. Weston came to meet us.

"Thanks for the call," Bandoni told him.

Weston nodded. "A head bash ain't nothing like getting your balls cut off. So the MOs don't match. But . . ."

"The words," Bandoni said.

"Right. The words."

"No ID?" I said.

"Not on the body," Weston said. "But Ms. Pitlor thinks it's a kid from their youth group. Dashiell Hammett Donovan. Better known as Dash. We'll get a confirmation on fingerprints. Guys are working on it now."

Another grunt from Bandoni. "Who the hell names their kid Dashiell?"

"Someone who loves crime fiction," I said.

Bandoni scratched an ear. "I ain't tracking."

"Dashiell Hammett. Crime writer." I looked at the men. Blank expressions. "Sam Spade? Nick and Nora Charles?"

Weston made a face at Bandoni. "She like a professor or something?"

"Something," Bandoni said.

I said, "I'm ready to see the body."

Weston stepped aside and waved an arm toward the altar. "Have fun, kids."

As Bandoni and I approached the altar, the body emerged, pale and scarred, from the murk.

"Fuck me," Bandoni said.

The man lay on his back. His head tipped onto the stairs that separated the altar from the rest of the church, revealing a gaping throat wound. Blue eyes, cloudy with death, stared at something beyond the high ceiling of the sanctuary. His killer had slashed his throat so deeply that the spine shone white within the red gore. His penis and scrotum had been hacked away, leaving a ragged, bloody ruin. Carved on his chest were the words *Vengeance is ours, we will repay.*

Blood had spilled down the altar onto the stairs and pooled near the railing. Which meant they'd killed him here, in the church.

Man as sacrifice.

I stared at the ruin of the victim's manhood.

Shade it black.

My fingers curled into fists, and I heard my own breath rasp in my ears, my heart and lungs coupled into a fast rhythm like a pair of runaway horses. The church vanished, and the plywood walls of Mortuary Affairs threatened to close in. Half-heard, wholly imagined, the rotors of a Black Hawk helicopter thumped the heavens outside, bringing the dead.

My counselor's voice echoed in my head. *I'm not talking just any death, Sydney. This is the worst kind.*

I rested my hand on Clyde's head as he leaned his weight into me. The helicopter fell silent.

We're still good.

The photographer's flash flared. Black ink seemed to scurry like beetles over the victim's body, leaping outward in brilliance, then falling back as the light dimmed.

"Words and more words," Bandoni muttered. "Some carved. And some in ink. Like the guy's a damn whiteboard."

Words. Lines and spaces. Tightly printed letters riding in columns down his arms and legs, circling in tight coils around his arms, tripping across his blood-streaked stomach. Thousands of letters, hundreds of lines, scores of words. I caught *god is unjust* and *we are filled with rage* and—simply—the word *unfair.* All written over and over. Across his stomach was *our anger is righteous.* And near his ruined groin, *payback is hell.*

It was a torrent of lettered rage. An entire dictionary of hatred.

In the beginning was the Word, and the Word was not with God, and the Word was not God.

We all jumped as a hymn blared over the sound system and echoed through the vast space.

Abruptly the music stopped. The silence of the sanctuary descended once more.

"Nelson," muttered Weston. "I sent him to switch the lights back on. About gave me a heart attack."

The photographer took yet another photo. The victim seemed to jerk in the flicker-frame while written screams poured down his gaping throat.

◆ ◆ ◆

For the next two hours, Bandoni and I worked the scene. Emma Bell arrived and broke her usual reserve to tell us that the cause of death was almost certainly the severed throat and that the removal of his hand and the words carved into the victim's skin, unlike Noah's wounds, had been done posthumously.

Except the castration. He'd been alive for that.

Within an hour we had a confirmation on the victim's name and had gained emergency access to his social-media accounts.

Dashiell Donovan was a twenty-one-year-old college student from Twin Falls, Idaho, enrolled at Denver University. His online activity showed him to be a highly competitive tennis player as well as an outdoors enthusiast—rafting, hiking, rock climbing. He'd listed himself as unattached, although there were plenty of photos of Donovan with young, attractive women. He had a self-professed 3.7 GPA, a position on the university's swim team, and two thousand social-media friends.

Everything a young man could want.

Except a future.

"Our victims have got nothing in common other than being white, twenty-something men," Bandoni said. "Can't find one damn thing so far that links Donovan to Noah."

"Todd plays tennis," I reminded him.

"We got that." Bandoni palmed his skull. "And speaking of Todd, the young Mr. Asher is MIA. Not at home. Not at the hotel with his parents."

"We also have 'our anger is righteous.' On Donovan's chest and—"

"The sign over Noah's computer." Bandoni turned his bloodshot eyes to me. "Which fucking side was Noah playing? And what did he and Donovan do to piss in the killer's cornflakes?"

His phone buzzed, and he answered with a curt, "What?" He listened for a minute, then said, "Damn," then, "Good." He disconnected and frowned.

"Riley Lynch is in the wind. A couple of guys from the squad are talking to his neighbors now and tracking down friends. They'll take the city apart stone by stone, if they have to. Maybe finding Riley will net Craze, too."

I nodded, but hope wasn't exactly springing eternal.

While one of the crime scene detectives began the laborious process of typing the killer's words from the victim into a document file, and Bandoni and the others continued with the crime scene, I took Clyde outside to see what we could learn.

Ron Gabel and Detective Smythe had determined—based on mud on the floor and a single smear of blood—that the killer had brought Donovan in through a back door at the rear of the church and likely exited the same way. According to the woman who'd discovered the body, only five people had a key to the door. She was one of them—the other four were the church pastors and the facilities director. It was also the only door without a camera, suggesting that the perpetrator had information on at least some aspects of the church. To the woman's knowledge, the last time the door had been used was three days earlier, when one of the pastors led a marriage-counseling session.

Which meant that if we got lucky, Clyde would be able to pick up a scent from the altar and track it through the door and into the neighborhood. If we were even luckier, someone in the neighborhood had seen something.

After Gabel had cleared Clyde and me to walk through the crime scene, I led Clyde to the altar and gave him the seek command. Clyde seemed to have decided to ignore the dead body—who said dogs couldn't compartmentalize?—and sniffed calmly around the corpse. Then his tail came up like a flag, and he trotted toward a door that led out the back of the sanctuary and into a hallway.

Game on.

"Good boy," I said as Gabel and I followed him.

Clyde trotted down the hallway, jogged left when the hallway split, and led us to the back door. I removed Clyde's booties while Gabel opened the door, then Clyde surged through the opening.

The back door opened on to a below-grade stairwell that led up to a narrow alley. I flicked on my flashlight as Clyde raced up the stairs and Gabel and I pounded behind him. At the top I told Clyde to wait while I shone the beam around.

The alley ran between the church and a seventies-era office building. The office windows had a clear view of the alleyway and the church.

The paved lane was pockmarked with dumpsters, which would have to be searched. Trash—flattened soda cans, empty cigarette packs, fast-food containers—had snagged against the base of the trash bins, and a waterlogged stack of old newspapers slid out of the nearest dumpster.

The air smelled heavy with ozone. Moisture filled the night with a fine mist that collected on Clyde's coat and glimmered in our hair.

I gave Clyde his head. He went left, trotting down the alley.

My heart beating fast, I followed while Gabel lagged behind, observing our path and making note of places he'd return to later to look for evidence. Clyde went briskly and without hesitation, turning north into the office building's side parking lot. In the middle of the lot, he circled. A few seconds later, he stopped and lay down.

"End of the trail," I said to Gabel as he approached. I slipped Clyde a treat for a job well done.

"Looks like our perps parked here and either walked Donovan down to the church or carried him." He looked back along the alley. "Good job, Clyde. Maybe we'll get lucky and find something else."

Gabel set a marker next to Clyde. I looked at the office building, hoping to spot a camera. But the structure gave off a deserted air.

"I'm going to check out the building," I told Gabel. "Maybe someone's working late."

He nodded. "I'll start setting up lights in the alley."

While Gabel headed back toward the church, Clyde and I went around to the street side of the office building. As we drew closer, I spotted a FOR LEASE sign in the window.

"No help here," I murmured to Clyde.

Clyde gave a soft growl. I glanced down. My partner's hackles were up, and he'd pricked his ears, staring down the street. At the same time, the hair rose on the nape of my neck as a familiar feeling coiled in my gut.

We were being watched.

I pulled us against the building and followed Clyde's gaze. Cars lined both sides of the street—no cargo vans that I could see. In the houses across the road, dark shadows pooled beneath trees and under eaves where the streetlights and porch lights didn't reach.

I considered freeing Clyde to run down our watcher. But the night was too dark, the watcher possibly armed.

Then the moment passed. Clyde's hackles smoothed, and he wagged his tail as he sniffed at the door to the office building.

Damn it.

I pushed off my unease for the moment and focused on my partner. He looked at me, catching my eyes. He wanted inside the building.

I tilted my head back. The office building rose three stories. Maybe the killer had used the high windows to run surveillance of the church.

Maybe they'd even held Donovan here.

I rattled the latch on the front door, surprised when the handle turned. I looked at Clyde to confirm that he was curious and not reacting to any kind of threat. Then I raised my flashlight and pushed open the door.

A small lobby, empty, opened to a hallway with an elevator. Clyde and I eased inside, and I phoned Gabel.

"Clyde's hit on something in the office building. From his behavior, the building's deserted. But there's something here that's caught his attention."

"On my way," he said.

I put on booties and slid the K9 booties over Clyde's feet. I raised the flashlight.

"Find 'em, Clyde," I said. "Seek!"

Clyde leapt forward, and I hurried after him. He trotted through the lobby and down the hall, then stopped at the elevator, waiting for me to open the door so he could continue. He was on the hunt, but still not alarmed.

Still, I signaled him to stay close as I moved off to the side. Then I reached over and punched the button.

The door slid open. Silence.

Clyde stayed quiet.

Slowly, I peered around the edge of the door.

A pair of metal handcuffs dangled from the hold bar. Above the handcuffs, someone had scratched four words into the paneling.

Smile! I'm watching you!

Etched in the paneling below the words was the outline of an erect penis.

Exactly like the one someone had drawn on the door of the Tahoe.

CHAPTER 18

We are all linked. By stardust. By dreams. By the wild miracle of life on this small planet.

A murder is the dark note that plucks the web and breaks the strand.

—Sydney Parnell. Personal journal.

Later, after more detectives had been rousted from bed, after Gabel examined the elevator with the handcuffs and the words and image scratched into the wall, after Clyde and I looked over the rest of the office building and found nothing but dust-streaked windows and stained carpet and toilets that refused to flush, after all that, my partner and I fled back into the night.

The earlier mist had condensed into fog. The atmosphere was more San Francisco noir than Rocky Mountain high.

Just like my mood.

If I had a stalker, as the van and the doll and the images of the phallus were starting to suggest, what did he have to do with the murders of Noah and Donovan? How had some weirdo who'd latched on to me managed to leave his message near the site of Donovan's murder?

How could he know I'd be here to get the message?

Unless the stalker and the murders were linked.

Whose scent had Clyde hit on?

Clyde and I skirted around the church, heading toward the front door. I spotted Cohen standing next to Officer Murphy on the outer perimeter. Surprised, Clyde and I jogged over.

"Hey," Cohen said as we approached. "I was just sending you a text."

"You here for your murder fix?"

The words came out harsh. Cutting.

"Sorry," I said. I was spooked, working to convince myself that the words and phallus in the elevator and the carved-up bodies of two young men had nothing to do with each other.

Cohen didn't blink. He was used to my moods. "You okay?"

Moisture pearled in his dark hair as his eyes took me in.

"Sure." I found a nod, gave it a try. "Everything all right with your cousin?"

"He's good," Cohen said. "He had to take a phone call."

I tugged Cohen out of earshot of Officer Murphy. "Not that I'm not happy to see you. But . . ."

"Why am I here?"

"More or less."

"Evan and I were on the way back when I heard about the case. There was chatter about a lot of writing at the crime scene."

I nodded. Waited.

Cohen's fingers brushed my hand. "Evan's specialty is forensic semiotics."

"Semi-what?"

"Semiotics. It's the study of signs and something called sign process and a bunch of other things that are so far beyond me I don't even live in Evan's universe. But he's spent years analyzing the writing of suspects and known killers."

I pictured Dashiell Donovan's body, sprawled on the altar. The dizzying spiral of words.

"Sign process," I said flatly.

"It's not woo-woo stuff, Sydney. Evan's got a PhD in semiotics from Oxford. He's found killers when the detectives have given up."

I hesitated. I wanted the help. But I didn't know Evan from a sheet of drywall. Except I knew that drywall never talked to the media. "You say something to Bandoni yet?"

"He told me you're the lead, it's your decision. But he went ahead and cleared it with Lobowitz."

So not really my decision. But at least Bandoni was going through the motions.

"By the way." Cohen narrowed his eyes at me. "What'd you do to get Bandoni to play second fiddle? Take his Ossa Knifefish hostage?"

"His what?"

"Len's a collector. Exotic fish. Shall I get Evan?"

Exotic fish and Audemars Piguet watches. Bandoni was full of surprises.

"As long as Evan knows how to keep his mouth shut," I said.

"He consults with the FBI. And Interpol. I suspect he's on the payroll of the CIA and the NSA. The guy is a paragon of discretion. If *they* can trust him . . ."

"Well, then." I straightened my shoulders, willing away my exhaustion and the trickle of unease at meeting the esteemed Dr. Evan Wilding. If he found me wanting, there wasn't a damn thing I could do about it. "Bring him on."

Cohen sent a text. A moment later, a car door opened and closed down the street, then a child approached us along the sidewalk.

I gaped. "He's a kid?"

"He's in his thirties," Cohen said.

Bandoni's words came back to me. *Don't underestimate him.* My partner's warped sense of humor shining through.

No wonder he'd acted like a man with an inside joke.

Evan reached us where we stood in the glow of a streetlight and held out a hand. We shook. Cohen's cousin had thick, curly black hair and a gentle expression anchored by vivid green eyes, which came almost to the level of my chest. To his credit, his gaze was fixed on my face.

Which was good. It felt like bad form to deck a dwarf.

Wilding took in my expression, which I worked to keep neutral, then turned to Cohen.

"Why do you persist in springing me on your friends," he said, his deep voice rich with the accent of the British elite, "without warning them I'm a few feet short of an NBA career?"

Cohen spread his hands. "It seemed like a small thing."

Wilding turned back to me. "I have a condition that causes dwarfism. I stand just a hair's breadth under four-feet-five, although I prefer to round up. Most certainly child-size, you could say."

My cheeks flamed. Wilding had heard me. "I'm sorry. I didn't know."

"Of course you didn't," Evan said. "Michael loves to do that. Pop a dwarf on the unsuspecting. Bit of an ass that way, aren't you, cousin?"

Cohen pretended to be offended. "You're the one who likes surprising people."

"That is true." He eyed Clyde with apparent delight. "A cop near my level. Does he bite?"

"Only if you're the bad guy."

"I hope he has a very narrow definition of bad."

Clyde yawned.

"You seem to have passed the test, Dr. Wilding," I said.

"Excellent, then. And please, call me Evan. So it is all right with you if I have a look?"

"Yes. Please."

"Then it is time to put aside our personal failings and focus on evil men." His face turned somber as he looked past me toward the church. "The night is passing quickly, and for some the day will never break."

My eyes met Cohen's. He shrugged. "Evan fancies himself a poet."

"I wouldn't presume," Evan said, heading toward the church. "I'm merely a scholar."

I followed. "In signs and symbols."

"More than that." He slowed as Officer Vasquez opened the door, spilling light into the darkness. "In the poetry of madmen."

Chapter 19

Think of me as being infinitely large. But on the inside.

—*Evan Wilding. Conversation with Sydney Parnell.*

Evan said nothing again for a long time.

He stood first near the entrance to the sanctuary, quietly observing, much as Bandoni and I had done. But from what Cohen whispered to me about Evan's process, I suspected the linguist was mentally excavating the scene, digging down through layers of time. He would start with the arrival of Officers Vasquez and Murphy, and before them, Marcy Pitlor's discovery of the victim. Then further back in time. The killer—or killers—departing. Before that, his form bending and twisting as he staged Donovan's body. Donovan's murder. The killer arriving at the church.

Maybe all the way to a quiet, undesecrated church.

I watched him, wondering what pictures formed in his mind. Did he build scenes from the vibrations of the air, the memories of molecules? Did he read a strange calligraphy from the body itself, images imprinted on skin the way men once believed a killer's visage remained in his victim's eyes?

Next to me, Clyde whined in his throat. I rested my hand on his head.

"I know, boy."

After a while, Evan approached the altar. He walked around the victim, eyes moving everywhere as he read the words carved into and written upon the fleshy canvas of Donovan's body. Now and again he pointed out something to the crime scene detectives, who jumped into action at whatever he said, taking pictures.

Bandoni watched all this, his arms crossed, one ankle hooked over the other as he leaned against a wall.

Finally, Evan came to a halt and motioned us over. We gathered at the railing. The crime scene detectives began packing up their tools.

"I'll give you my thoughts," Evan said. "Take them for what they're worth."

"We're listening," Bandoni said.

Evan clasped his hands behind his back. "I believe you have multiple killers. Dashiell Donovan is their canvas. He's the start of their manifesto."

The doors to the sanctuary opened. A woman rolled a gurney down the center aisle. Another woman came behind her carrying a canvas bag.

"Manifesto . . . like they're making a declaration," Bandoni said.

"That's how it appears."

"And multiple killers." The now-bright lights tugged shadows across Bandoni's face. "I know there's all that 'we' and 'ours' shit. But serial killers usually work alone."

"I don't think you're dealing with a serial killer," Evan said.

I glanced at Cohen. His eyes met mine, and he gave a faint nod, like *Didn't I say he'd be helpful?*

But Bandoni scratched his scalp. "I see one victim on that altar. There was one victim in the train car. That says serial killer to me. What am I missing here?"

The women lifted the gurney up the altar steps. The taller of the two women slipped, and one end of the gurney banged to the ground.

Evan watched them for a moment before turning back to us. "Mass murderers will sometimes kill single individuals as they test their own commitment to a larger act. A sort of trial run, if you will. In my opinion, that's what you're dealing with."

Bandoni sputtered. "Mass murderers?"

I turned away as one of the body crew unpacked a body bag. Electric sparks burst inside my skull at Evan's words. Other terms tumbled through my brain—*mass killers, school shooters, workplace violence, going postal.* I knew how authorities generally defined mass murder: the indiscriminate killing of four or more people in close geographic proximity, with no cooling-off period between the slayings.

But I still had trouble wrapping my head around the idea we might have a mass murderer of our own.

"You're a professor." Bandoni scowled at Evan. "But I'm just a fucking cop. You gonna explain how you know that?"

Someone grunted as Donovan's body was maneuvered onto the gurney.

"Of course." Evan stared up at the image of a ruby-red Christ in stained glass. Cleared his throat. "How long do you have?"

The devil's hour of 3:00 a.m. had come and gone when Bandoni and I pulled in behind Cohen and Evan in front of the Walker mansion. The fog had lifted, and cold stars shone down. When Bandoni and I got out, our breath hung in the air. Clyde jogged toward the front door, his tail high like a flag. I grabbed his bowls and kibble and followed.

Inside the house, Cohen directed Evan up the stairs, to a room he'd prepared. Bandoni tailed after him, carrying the professor's suitcase.

Cohen turned to me. "You want to start a fire in the library? I'll get us something to eat."

"I feel like I could eat an entire cow. And then I'd throw it all back up."

"Spoken like a true murder cop."

"You didn't mention this part when you were telling me how great it is to be a detective."

"You mean the whole death aspect of being a murder cop?"

"Sarcasm."

Cohen pulled me close. "Maybe a little."

For a moment I melted into him, inhaling his scent, reveling in the solidity of his shoulder beneath my cheek.

Then he pulled away and headed toward the kitchen. The space where he'd just been felt cold.

In the library, I set Clyde's dishes on the tile next to the sliding glass doors and gave my partner food and water. I got logs blazing in the immense stone fireplace, then cleared a space on the football-field-size coffee table for whatever food Cohen brought. Finally, I filled a bucket with ice from the mini fridge, grabbed four tumblers from the bar, and opened a bottle of Johnnie Walker Founder's Blend.

If death could come for you at any time, why save the good stuff?

The room ready, I stood in front of the fireplace with Clyde, shifting edgily from foot to foot. Clyde watched me a moment, then stretched out on the carpet with a sigh.

"That's right, buddy," I said. "Rest while you can."

He closed his eyes.

In the flickering shadows from the fire, I took in the room, my favorite in the house.

The library would be the envy of any bibliophile, with floor-to-ceiling mahogany bookcases stuffed with leather-bound tomes and a vast assortment of more modern hardbacks. A ten-foot wood-and-brass ladder moved along a track, allowing access to the highest books. On one wall, large windows overlooked the back gardens, illuminated by lights along a flagstone path. The only other interruption to the books was the occasional piece of art. I moved to stand in front of an engraving of Egyptian ruins.

"Ramses the second," Evan said from the doorway. "André Dutertre. He traveled to Egypt with Napoleon as part of his *Commission des Sciences et des Arts d'Egypte.* Napoleon wanted conquest. Instead he found beauty and history. And tragedy."

I took in the engraving. "It's haunting."

"It's rumored to be the inspiration for Shelley's poem 'Ozymandias.'"

I nodded. "Look on my works, ye Mighty, and despair."

"Indeed. Is that whiskey I see? Shall we drink?"

"God, yes." I returned to the table. "Your accent. You're not American?"

"I am. But we can't escape our childhood." Evan chose an arm-chair near the fire. "My father's a bit of a toff. My mother—Michael's aunt—is firmly a Yank. After my parents' marriage failed along with my mother's health, she took my younger brother and fled back across the pond. I followed some years later."

A note of pain underlaid Evan's words.

I took a seat catty-corner to his and splashed whiskey into our glasses. "A pleasant childhood."

"Oh, it was pleasant enough. I had a good nanny."

We lifted the tumblers and clinked.

After a cautious sip, Evan downed the contents of his glass. "That is magnificent."

I poured more.

"You are a saint." He took a long swallow.

I forced myself to nurse the alcohol. "How did you come to be an expert on the writings of murderers?"

He set down his empty glass. "I stumbled into my line of work in much the way many of us do. An impulsive decision coupled with a modicum of talent."

"I suspect you have more than a little talent. Cohen describes your range of knowledge as . . . I believe at some point he used the word *breathtaking.*"

Evan laughed. "That's generous. But the impulsive decision *did* come when I was six. I spotted a Rongorongo board from Easter Island and learned that their language had never been deciphered. I was hooked."

"And you deciphered it?"

"Now *you* are being generous. I spent the tender years of six to eleven turning sallow skinned and weak-eyed under the lights of the British Museum's book room, trying with the desperation of youth to crack the code. I returned to it in college but, alas, I remain stumped to this day. It's simply too small a database. Or perhaps the genius who will solve it hasn't been born. Anyway, once I grew up—in a manner of speaking—I turned to crime to pay the bills. It is my great fortune that so many murderers feel compelled to capture their thoughts on paper."

"Why do they?"

"It depends. Ego for some. For others, a craving to create some kind of order out of the chaos of their minds."

A light patter of rain struck the windows. Cohen came into the room with a wooden cutting board stacked with cheese, cold cuts, nuts, and fruit. He was trailed by Bandoni, who set plates and napkins on the table and dropped into a chair next to Evan. For a few minutes we put aside the case and ate. Clyde pattered over to see if there was anything interesting. I slipped him a piece of prosciutto.

"So," Bandoni said, reaching for the whiskey. "Ready to explain, *Dr.* Wilding, how your brilliant fucking mind figures that we ain't got a serial killer? Like that's not bad enough for you?"

Evan glanced at me. "Don't let Bandoni's penchant for crudity mislead you. He's actually rather fond of me."

Bandoni rolled his eyes and slopped whiskey into his glass and Cohen's.

I looked back and forth between Evan and Bandoni. "I've heard you two know each other."

"The way a dog knows its own ass," Bandoni said.

"With Bandoni, I presume, being the ass," Evan said. "We worked two difficult cases together back in the day. After that, we were practically brothers."

Bandoni raised his tumbler. "Twins separated at birth."

"I can see that," I said.

"And so you see the man I could have become." Evan tipped his whiskey toward Bandoni's hulking form. "If not for a small problem with my zygote."

"To family," Cohen said. "Regardless of blood."

We clinked glasses. Drank.

"Okay." Bandoni wiped his mouth with the back of his hand. "We all love each other. Now let's get hammered or get focused. I vote focused, since we have killers running around." He tipped his glass toward Evan. "Start talking."

"I can tell you what the research says." Evan refilled his glass and settled back in his chair. "The writings of serial killers are different from those of mass murderers. Both types of killers are concerned with entitlement—their rights over those of their victims. But in general, a serial killer's writing focuses on his target. He documents what he did or plans to do. He might, like the Zodiac Killer, taunt the police with his success by sharing details only he would know. Also, a serial killer often recognizes that his acts are evil and defends himself by saying he was compelled by external forces. H. H. Holmes claimed he was born with the devil inside of him. Son of Sam said he was forced to kill on the orders of Father Sam. I'm sure you're familiar with other cases."

We nodded. The rain fell heavier, pelting the windows. In the garden, trees rattled as a sudden wind gusted. The smell of damp seeped into the room.

Evan went on. "Mass murder, on the other hand, is about victimhood and ideology. Think about the messages on Donovan's body. Words like *righteous rage* and God being unjust. 'Vengeance is ours, we will repay.' They are explaining themselves. For them, murder is

231

self-defense. Based on what Michael shared with me, your first victim was accused of betrayal. In the eyes of his killers, a betrayal would have justified—even demanded—his death."

"If Noah was murdered for committing some form of treachery," I said, "what did Donovan do to anger his killers?"

Bandoni grabbed a slice of cheese. "Right. The killer wrote nothing on his body about betrayal."

"But he wrote the words *payback is hell.* And—" I looked at my notes. "The owner of the comics store where Noah taught said that Noah told her the work he was doing was going to bring payback. She said whatever it was, he was scared."

We considered that for a moment, while the flames hissed and shadows rustled in the corners of the room.

Evan stirred. "We have to consider not only the words, but the significance of *where* the killer wrote those words."

"On Donovan's castrated groin," I said. "Are we back to the sexual angle?"

Cohen leaned forward, fisting his hands. "Noah was feminized. The rape. The dress. But Donovan had his manhood taken away. Which suggests that while both of them angered the killers, it was in different ways."

Bandoni grunted. "Well, other than treating our victims like writing pads, nothing I can see connects the two of them except Noah's brother. Todd Asher's a member of the church where Donovan was killed. And he and Donovan maybe ran into each other playing tennis."

"Fratricide is biblical," Cohen said. "God rejected Cain's sacrifice but accepted Abel's. You could argue that Cain killed his brother as a form of jealous self-defense."

"But if either brother had a reason to be jealous, it was Noah." I skimmed through my notes from our interview with the Ashers. "The father mentioned they raised the sons *as if* they were both theirs, although Noah was adopted. In the eyes of Hal Asher, Todd was the favored son. And depending on how you measure things, Todd also won the roll of the genetic die. He's good looking, extroverted, apparently successful. Based on his oh-da—" I looked at Bandoni.

"Audemars Piguet," he filled in. "Kid's got money."

"And he's tall, I imagine," Evan said.

"Just like Donovan." Bandoni tossed a fistful of nuts into his mouth. "Doesn't explain the sex angle."

"Who is God being unjust to?" Cohen murmured.

"We also have the subversive Riley Lynch," I said.

Bandoni glared. "Who is also missing."

Evan turned his bright-green gaze on me. "Tell me about Riley."

"Noah's high school friend. He and Noah were members of a group of pickup artists who called themselves the Superior Gentlemen. Four men. Maybe five with the photographer. But Noah had gotten interested in social causes and started dating someone. A couple of months ago, he dropped out."

Bandoni brushed crumbs off his suit coat. "That's a betrayal."

Cohen looked pensive. "What I know about pickup artists is their groups are fluid. Men join and drop out all the time."

At my feet, Clyde raised his head and cupped his ears. Curious about something, but not alarmed. An animal somewhere nearby. Or something blown by the wind.

I let my gaze rest on Cohen. A late-day beard shadowed his jawline, and his expensive suit was rumpled. A man who insisted on cutting his own hair, he'd obviously taken scissors to his thick locks since the last time I'd paid attention. Now, his gaze had turned inward, and I knew his mind was out ahead of ours, following unknown paths like a bloodhound on the scent.

He set down his drink, and my eyes caught on his forearms where he'd rolled his sleeves.

I sat up. "Noah's tattoo. The one his killers carved."

In an instant, Cohen was back. "The symbol of man placed over that of woman. It's not on Donovan's body. It's yet another suggestion that he wasn't killed for the same reasons."

"The clues don't add up because we're missing their ideology," Evan said. "Mass murderers have a system of belief, and their choice of targets will line up with that dogma. We have to look at all the components— how the men were killed, what was done to them, where their bodies were placed."

"A train and a church," Bandoni said.

"A rape and a dress," I added. "Against Donovan's castration."

"And all the religious elements," Evan said. "The biblical language. The body on an altar."

"What about them chopping off his right hand?" Bandoni glowered. "The hell does that mean? Ideology, my ass. I'm starting to feel like we ain't even dealing with the same killers." He pulled out his phone and glanced at the screen. "It's the lieutenant. Probably wanting to know when we're bringing the killers in."

He stalked out of the room.

Clyde's ears swiveled. A moment later, a great boom reverberated from somewhere in the house, the sound ricocheting through the library. We all jumped, and Clyde scrambled to his feet.

A bomb, I thought, reaching for my gun.

Cohen touched my shoulder as he stood. "Just the front door slamming shut. Bandoni must have gone outside."

Trust a Marine to go straight to the dark place. I relaxed my hand.

Cohen headed toward the hall. "We'd be drowning in sirens now if I'd set the alarm. But he will have locked himself out. I'll be right back."

He vanished into the gloom.

Evan turned to me. "Tell me about the tattoo."

I kept my eyes for a moment on the hallway where Cohen had disappeared. Unease stirred in my gut. Talking about mass murder would do that. I glanced at Clyde, who had his dark eyes on mine. I took a deep breath, willing calm for my partner's sake. After a moment, his ears softened, and he began circling on a rug near the hearth, readying himself for a nap.

No worries there.

Evan's voice broke through. "Sydney?"

"Sorry." I pulled up the mark the killers had left on Noah. "They tattooed this on his arm around the same time they carved words into his flesh. A day or two before they killed him."

He studied the photo and nodded. "Man rightfully over woman. Unfortunately, not an unusual conviction. You mentioned a girlfriend. What does she say?"

"We haven't found her yet." I gripped my glass, watched the crystal shimmer with reflected light, the amber liquid within deepen toward crimson. "But there's something else. When Noah drew Ami, he sketched a symbol on her shirt. Would you take a look? One of our detectives tried to find it in our tattoo book, but no luck."

"You had me at *symbol*."

I placed the drawing of Ami and the photo of Noah's tattoo on the coffee table. Evan picked them up.

"It might be a representation of the letter *P*," he said. "Do you have something I can write on?"

I grabbed paper and pen from the writing desk near the windows. Outside, the trees were hunched before the wind like old men. I glanced at the doorway. Still no sign of Cohen or Bandoni.

I returned to the chairs.

Evan knuckled his hand under his chin. "What do you know about this woman?"

"Only that her name is Ami, spelled with an *i*. And she might have worked cleaning houses."

"She's Latina?"

"From El Salvador."

"Ah. Interesting." Evan picked up a pen. "I'm just theorizing, you understand?"

"I live for conjecture."

"Aminta is a common Salvadoran name. It means protector. The word for protector in Spanish also starts with the letter *P*. *Protectora.* Since this emblem is on her shirt, much like the Superman logo, perhaps we can imagine it is intended as the letter *P*. Because"—he drew a curved line on the paper—"it is identical to the Semitic, or Phoenician, form of the letter."

"Why would they choose a letter from the Phoenician alphabet?"

"Creativity, perhaps. Or curiosity. Or because it is the oldest verifiable alphabet. The Semitic form of *P*, or *Pe*, is the origin form for the letter *P* in all other alphabets. Greek. Latin. Even Cyrillic."

"Maybe they were making a superhero origin story."

"That is one possibility."

"If they were creating their own superhero, the Protector," I said. "Who did they intend to protect?"

Evan spread his hands. "That, I have no hypothesis for."

My mind plucked at the various strings of the investigation, trying to pull them into a hummable tune. A housecleaner from El Salvador. Her boyfriend, a man who'd gone from geek to pickup artist to feminist. A man who called himself Craze, who'd taken over Noah's pickup artists and who inspired disgust in Todd and perhaps fear in the gutter punk Kelly, a.k.a. Damn Fox.

Then there was the handsome, athletic Donovan. I sighed. What, if anything, did he have to do with these other strings?

Ami the housecleaner. Kaylee had said she didn't recognize her in Noah's drawing. But even if Ami had worked at Top-A, she might have quit before Kaylee moved into the supervisor's position.

I pictured the three women at Top-A Cleaning. Helen, Lupita, and Erica. Erica glaring over privileged white men. Firmly denying she'd been harassed even as the heat in her voice said otherwise.

Evan cleared his throat. "I fear the house has swallowed our compatriots."

I pulled myself back into the present. "Clyde and I'll go see what's keeping them."

He slid off his chair. "Not without me."

I touched Clyde to get his attention. When his eyes were on mine, I said, "Find Cohen!"

The hallway was a labyrinth of shadows, lit only by softly glowing sconces. But Clyde trotted confidently toward the other end of the house. We passed the front door, now closed. Soothing green lights glowed on the alarm panel. The marble near the door was wet, and raindrops had left ghostly prints on the walls. Two pairs of damp footprints led away, into the gloom.

A few feet along, a glow appeared.

"The kitchen," I said.

Clyde rushed ahead.

When we entered, Cohen and Bandoni were huddled over the center island, looking at something.

I noticed first that they were both drenched. Next, that their hands were gloved. Then my eyes moved past them to the island where a fist-size rock, a crumpled piece of paper, and a thick rubber band marred the otherwise empty expanse of granite.

Written in block letters on the paper were the words *Have a nice day!*

Bandoni rubbed his jowls. His bloodshot eyes met mine. "I saw a light near your Tahoe and went to check it out. The rock was in the driver's seat, wrapped up with the paper."

"But the car was—" Realization dawned. "He broke a window."

"Sorry, rookie. We looked around, but the asshole was gone."

"The rain was too heavy for the camera to catch anything," Cohen said. "But there's been a run of minor vandalism in the neighborhood. Smashed mailboxes. Broken lights. It's either someone local or someone coming in over the neighborhood's perimeter wall."

"The seats—" I began.

"We taped plastic over the hole." Cohen's dark hair was plastered to his skull, his white shirt transparent with rain. "It'll hold until the glass-repair guy gets here. He's on his way."

The elevator with its scratched note and dangling handcuffs rose like a vision in front of me. The phallus carved into the paneling. And drawn in the dirt on the door of the Tahoe.

The naked Barbie doll tied to the chassis.

And a dark-blue cargo van.

Smile! I'm watching you!

Bandoni eyeballed me. "This note put you in mind of the words left near the Donovan crime scene?"

I nodded.

Cohen frowned. "What words?"

My hands had drifted up to grip my upper arms. "A pair of hand-cuffs were left in an elevator next to the words *Smile! I'm watching you*. Along with a sketch of a penis. The guy was no Michelangelo."

Cohen held on to his frown for a moment, then stared down at his hands braced against the counter. I knew he was riding a line between his desire to protect me and the fact that I was a fellow cop who could and should take care of herself.

I drew in a breath and told them almost everything. The doll. The phallus. The dark-blue cargo van I'd spotted in the garage and outside Cherry Hills. And near the comics store.

But I didn't mention the man in the grocery-store parking lot. Or my sense of being watched. As the only woman on the team, I could not appear paranoid or weak. Certainly not in need of protection. I'd ask the lab to prioritize checking the doll for fingerprints and DNA. It was all I could do for the moment.

Evan broke my reverie. "You have photos?"

"From the elevator, yes."

"Why"—Cohen lifted his gaze—"didn't you say anything?"

I put heat into my voice. "Hello? Marine."

Cohen's expression went flat.

"I'm okay, Mike," I said, more softly. "I can handle it."

I passed Evan my phone, and he zoomed in. He studied the image for a few moments before handing my phone to Cohen.

"Well?" Bandoni eyeballed the professor. "You got an opinion?"

"I'm rarely without one," Evan said. "These are small samples, so take what I say with the proverbial grain of salt. But we have the same simple, declarative sentence structure. And there are other similarities. The use of exclamation points. The way the letters *y* and *g* extend far below the baseline, while the middle-zone letters barely rise above it. And the tails of the *y* and *g* in both exemplars form large triangles. Which, by the way, suggests repressed anger toward women." He looked at us, his eyes in shadow despite the bright light. "I'd say the odds are better than fifty-fifty these notes are linked."

"Shit," Bandoni said. "The killers are watching Parnell?"

Cohen said, "Can you tell if the same person wrote these words and the ones on our victims?"

"Not without more time. It's difficult to compare styles across different mediums even when dealing with a larger sample size. If I had to take a wild stab, I'd say no. The writing on the victims is much more sophisticated. Then again, I, at least, am confident we're dealing with at least two killers."

We let Evan's words sit between us while the wind collapsed in upon itself, sinking to a throaty whisper. In the far distance, a dog bayed, and Clyde paced to the windows. My heart tripped over its own unsteady beats.

"Okay, I'm in on the whole 'two or more killers' thing." Bandoni folded his arms. "I buy that we got mass murderers. But if Noah and Donovan were the warm-up, who are the mass targets? Anybody got an answer for that?"

Cohen shook his head. Evan stared at something invisible just past the six-burner gas stove. I turned multiple possibilities over in my mind and came up with nothing I felt ready to offer.

The wind did a reversal and slammed into the walls, shaking the house.

"Okay, then." Bandoni put the rock and the note in a plastic bag from Cohen. "You youngsters keep at it. I gotta get some shut-eye. You"—he pointed at Cohen—"keep an eye on the rookie."

"Why don't you stay here?" Cohen said. "Save you the drive time."

But Bandoni muttered something about feeding his fish and asked if he could borrow Cohen's car. The three of us walked him to the front door and watched him hobble down the stairs through the rain. He stopped halfway across the cobblestone driveway, hunched his back to the weather, and lit a cigarette. He took a couple of drags before he crushed it under his shoe.

"Fucking rain," he said. His voice was faint, tattered by the wind.

The rain turned to sleet.

Chapter 20

Too often, my skin feels like a prison.

—*Sydney Parnell. Personal journal.*

Near dawn, I woke from a dream in which I was drowning. Shivering, I reached for Cohen's warmth.

My hand found only cool emptiness.

I jerked upright and threw off the covers. On the floor beside the bed, Clyde scrambled to his feet.

"Cohen!"

My voice echoed back, followed seconds later by the sounds of my lover moving in the kitchen, and the sweet, sharp aroma of coffee. Voices murmured; he had the radio tuned to local news.

"Damn it," I muttered.

I yanked up the covers and sank back onto the pillows. It was 5:52 a.m. While Clyde trotted out of the room to find Cohen, I worked to recapture the thoughts the dream had lifted out of the murk of my subconscious.

It had been nighttime. I'd been thrashing in deep, icy water, trying desperately to move my arms and legs, to keep my head above water. As I struggled, someone—a dark shape in the murky distance—snapped photos, over and over.

My phone buzzed. I checked caller ID.

Tom O'Hara. My contact at the *Denver Post*. My heart gave a long, slow thump, forcing a sludge of blood through my veins. I managed to grunt something into the phone. So Bandoni-esque.

"Were you sleeping?" O'Hara's voice rang bright with caffeine.

"No, no." I propped myself up against the pillow. "Just getting a mani-pedi."

Clyde trotted into the room, followed by Cohen, who carried two mugs of coffee. Cohen slipped into the bed next to me, and gratefully I took the cup he offered.

"Life of a murder cop, huh?" Tom said. The sound of a clacking keyboard came through the connection. He had me on speakerphone. "Sorry. Look . . . we . . . we got . . . something weird. Here. At . . . the office."

"Stop trying to multitask."

"I'm not. I'm hyperventilating."

Cohen clicked on the bedside light, and a soft glow lit the sheets and ushered shadows to the walls. Wide awake now, I put my own phone on speaker.

"Go ahead," I said.

"I'm working a story and couldn't sleep. Decided to come into the office and start going through yesterday's mail. There was a small box. Postmarked from Longmont. Inside was—well, I think it has something to do with that man killed in the church. Dashiell Donovan."

Tom's voice had an edge I hadn't heard before. Not even when he'd been following a kidnapping case with me.

"I'm all ears," I said.

"Funny you should say that. Like van Gogh. There are, um, two things. The first is what looks like pages to a graphic novel. You know, drawings. Panels. Speech bubbles. Superhero shit, only this is definitely not about superheroes."

Goose bumps rose on my skin. Cohen's arm came around my shoulders, and his warm fingers squeezed my cold flesh.

"There's a line written on one of the pages," Tom said. "'Vengeance is ours.' Doesn't that link with your body from last night? I know you're on that case."

The fact of the writing hadn't been made available to the press. "Who's your source, Tom?"

"You jealous?"

I put aside my concern about a leak for the moment. I swung my legs over the mattress and reached for my sweats. Clyde's moist nose brushed my knuckles.

"What's the other item?" I asked.

"It's . . . look, Sydney. Just—you need to come in."

◆ ◆ ◆

A short time later, four of us stood around Tom's desk wearing latex gloves and paper masks. Tom, Cohen, Evan, and me. Bandoni was on his way. Clyde lay half-under Tom's desk, unconcerned for the moment with the affairs of humans.

We stared down at a shriveled, severed penis.

"That's so wrong," Tom murmured.

The penis was in a plastic bag, the heavy-duty kind with a zip pull. Tied around what we guessed was Donovan's manhood—we'd have to run tests to be certain—were several long, thick strands of hair, like a macabre bow.

An ugly thought: *Ami is dark haired.*

And a worse one: *Ami is dead.*

On Tom's desk next to the plastic bag was a stack of comic-book pages—heavy paper, the drawings and lettering in dark ink like that used on the bodies of Noah and Donovan. With gloved hands, I picked up the first page.

"You touched this?" I asked Tom. "Or did you just shake things out on your desk?"

Tom's unease over the phone had morphed into a sparking curiosity. A dog on the scent. I'd have to kennel that enthusiasm soon.

"Sorry," he said, only half-rueful. "I touched everything before I realized what it was. The pictures and the bag." His lips pursed in disgust. "The *outside* of the bag."

"Well, that's something. We'll need to get your prints. And we need coffee." I smiled at him. "Coffee first."

"I see what you're doing."

"Just give us a minute."

He held my eye, then finally nodded. "Quid pro quo," he murmured as he turned away.

Evan leaned over the drawing. In bold lettering at the top were the words *The Coming Dark: A Vendetta*. Below that, five panels marched down the page. Five portraits of naked, malformed human males, each standing solitary in an arctic wasteland, their faces and genitals partly obscured by shadows.

Most startling were the yellow eyes.

Once again, I recalled Dana Gills's words as we stood in her comics store. *There are a lot of yellow-eyed supervillains in the comics world. Nightcrawler. Trigon. Gamora . . . Apocalypse, who was intended to lead the Alliance of Evil.*

As I studied the pictures, a memory worked to worm its way up through my sleep-fogged brain. Something about a man standing on ice. Next to me, Cohen leaned in, his gray eyes glinting. I knew that look—a thirst, a *need*, to understand.

"It looks like Noah's work," I said. I'd brought his drawings, and now I set out the one of the yellow-eyed man near the train. "The comics-store owner said yellow-eyed villains were cliché. She was surprised at Noah's drawing."

Evan and Cohen studied Noah's drawing, then turned back to the new pages.

"Vendetta," Cohen said. "Nothing good about that."

Evan dipped his head in agreement. "From the Latin *vindicta*, meaning vengeance. An appropriately mid-nineteenth-century Italian word, its appearance concurrent with the rise of the *mafie*. A blood feud. A retaliatory back-and-forth of murderous acts. Men like these are big on symbolism. And Donovan's manhood is deeply symbolic."

"But who is retaliating against whom?" I stared at the images, still trying to hunt down the sense of familiarity. "Who seeks blood?"

"Blood is often associated with sex," Evan said. "Which seems to be a recurring theme in the cases before us."

Cohen frowned. "The killer wrote on Noah's skin that the life of the flesh is in the blood."

Evan gently tapped the desk next to the bag with the severed flesh. "Sending us a clue. Wanting us to understand." His hungry expression mirrored Cohen's. In that moment, they looked very much like cousins. "Blood feud, bloodlines, blood brothers. One of our suspects is the brother of the first victim, yes? And look at the title they chose. *The Coming Dark.* In the quote from the first victim . . ." He turned to me.

"The life of the flesh is in the blood," I said.

Evan brought his fingertips together. "In the original Hebrew, you can translate the word for life, *nefesh*, as soul. 'The life of the *soul* is in the blood.' And the greatest threat to the soul is an eternity spent far from the light of God. Perhaps they are suggesting that they intend to cast the souls of their victims into darkness."

"Sounds ominous," Tom said, approaching with a pot of coffee and a stack of cups.

"The ambrosia of gods," Evan said. "Bless you."

We all looked up at a noise—Bandoni barreling through the door. He paused in the entryway and shook himself like a dog, scattering raindrops. Mud spattered the hem of his navy slacks.

For an instant, I saw him as a stranger would—gray, overweight, with a face sagging like an ice sculpture halfway through its melt. Then his gaze met mine. Maybe he saw the pity in my face, for his frown deepened, and an angry light switched on in his watery eyes. He sped toward us, a stone loosed from a slingshot, his bowling-ball head leading the charge.

"The hell is this about?" He glared at the items on the desk. "You call Crime Scene yet? And what"—he jabbed a finger at Tom—"is he doing here?"

"You *are* standing in my place of employment," Tom said.

"Then," Bandoni boomed, "get us a conference room."

Five minutes later, we'd relocated to one of the *Post*'s meeting rooms. While Cohen and Evan laid out the pages, I blocked Tom at the door.

"We'll cut you in later," I said. "Right now, you have to sit on this."

He put on his battle face. "It's important information."

I waved him into the hall and pulled the door closed behind me.

"Tom. No. It gives away details known only to the killer. You share it, you'll eliminate a way for us to narrow our focus to the right person."

"But the public—"

"*And*—" I held up a hand. "What about all the nutcases out there who will see this manifesto as a call to arms?"

Tom planted his feet. "The public has a right to know."

"The public has a right to be safe."

"Plus," he went on, "the package came *here*. To *me*."

"And you rightly called us. Let us handle it."

We glared at each other.

I'd once been firmly on Tom's side, believing it was the public's right to be informed and the media's duty to give them that information. But not in this case. Nothing superseded our hunt for the killers.

"You'll have the inside scoop," I said. "Have I ever let you down?"

His shoulders dropped, and I knew I'd won.

"Just swear you'll keep me in the loop," he said to me. "Quid pro quo."

"Quid pro quo."

Evan opened the door and peered out. "Say, do you have a footstool?"

◆ ◆ ◆

In the flickering fluorescents of the conference room, we spread the twenty pages of the vendetta across the table. A story of five men—victims decried by society, laughed at by the beautiful people. Taunted by women and belittled by men.

Victims made into self-proclaimed losers by a cruel roll of the genetic dice. The five men were pudgy and plain, with bad skin and worse haircuts. In panel after panel they approached women in bars, at grocery stores, in offices and theaters.

And each time, the women laughed or sneered or fled.

Then, on the fifth page, one of the five was visited in a dream by a stern figure with dark-feathered wings and fiery eyes.

Cohen read out loud. "'Raise up yourselves,' commanded the angel. 'Be not as God intended, but as you yourselves wish to be. When you are risen in my image, then you must smite your enemies and cast down the world. Our anger is righteous.'"

"Told what to do by an angel," Bandoni said.

A crease appeared between Evan's eyes. "Or by the devil."

"Either way, these douchebags have a pretty high opinion of themselves."

In the next panels, the men set about raising themselves up. Sessions at the gym, language classes, lessons in the art of conversation. They cut their hair and shrugged off their ratty T-shirts and appeared in clothes that looked straight from a *GQ* fashion shoot.

"Noah's transformation," I said. "His pickup artists."

Bandoni smacked the table. "The fucking Superior Gentlemen."

"They never quite show their faces," Cohen said. "Never enough to identify them."

Transformed, the men began fighting back. They came together to vow payback against their tormentors. They pledged to murder the men. And to seize the women, who were rightfully theirs. Beautiful, fair-haired women delivered casually to their doors with that night's pizza.

Bandoni flattened his hands on the table, his gaze moving from one picture to the next. "The sex angle again."

I rubbed my neck. "One of Noah's students, Markey Byron, said that sex should be something you could buy in bulk at Costco."

We looked at each other.

"That," Bandoni said, "is just weird. Is there anything we know of that links Markey to the Superior Gentlemen?"

I shook my head.

And finally, the last panel. A final portrait of a single man, standing on the ice. It was similar to the men on the first page. Except a giant red X had been slashed across the image.

The elusive familiarity finally surfaced. "They're like the creature from *Frankenstein*."

"Ah," Evan said. "You're right."

The furrows in Bandoni's brow deepened to ditches. "Explain."

"In Mary Shelley's novel *Frankenstein*," I said, "Victor Frankenstein sets out to create the perfect human. But instead, he creates a monstrosity. Horrified, he rejects his own creation and flees. The monster, who is described as sensitive and emotional, realizes it will always be denied love through no fault of its own. It retaliates by murdering everyone Victor loves."

Cohen nodded. "I'm reaching all the way back to my English lit class, but yes."

Bandoni growled. "Talk slow for us nondweebs. You're saying that these guys are killing people based on some old book?"

"*Frankenstein* is a big part of popular culture," I said. "And look at the first page of this manifesto. The artist, presumably Noah, portrayed the men as monsters, alone in the ice."

"Yeah. So what?"

"Once Frankenstein's monster had ruined his creator's life, he promises to kill himself and flees into the ice near the North Pole."

"It fits with much of what the killers wrote," Evan said. "That God the creator is unjust. The righteous anger."

"And the comment about payback being hell," Cohen added.

A vein throbbed in Bandoni's forehead. "You're telling me that these drawings mean our dickwads are going to kill a bunch of people and then off themselves? You get all that from pen and ink?"

Evan held up a hand, David soothing Goliath. "It's possible, Len. Mass murderers almost always take their own lives once they've committed their ultimate act."

Bandoni glared at all of us, as if we were responsible. "What you're saying with all this Frankenstein bullshit is that these guys are sensitive, emotional, sex-deprived monsters who are going to kill a bunch of people because they feel rejected. And then they're going to kill themselves?" He aimed his gaze on Evan. "Is she right?"

"It's possible that's what we're dealing with. Yes."

"Then who's this creator that they're getting back at? Noah and Donovan aren't *creators*. They're kids. A software geek and a student."

The overhead fluorescents hummed and flickered. We looked at each other. None of us, apparently, had an answer for that.

Bandoni grunted and folded his arms.

Cohen perched on the edge of the table. "What if the Superior Gentlemen are something darker than pickup artists?"

"Todd told us that Craze had taken over the group," I said. "Maybe his arrival is what started the men down a darker path."

Cohen snapped his fingers. "They became Forced Celibates."

"Which means," I said, "Donovan is a Chad."

"Exactly."

"Ah, Jesus," Bandoni snarled. "The fuck are you talking about now?"

Cohen ran an absentminded thumb along his jaw. "In the online communities, Forced Celibates are involuntary virgins. Men who believe they are too unattractive or socially awkward to attract women."

"And Chads—" I began.

"Hold on, rookie. One thing at a time." Bandoni scraped a hand over the stubble on his scalp. "How does being unable to attract women make these celibates different from the rest of us poor schmucks who can't get a date?"

"Plenty of people are sexually frustrated," Cohen said. "But these men feel shame at their failure. And that shame fuels their rage."

"Worse than pickup artists?"

"Much worse."

"They start shooting things?"

"Most don't. But some of them develop a profound hatred of the women they believe are depriving them of sex while simultaneously bestowing their sexual favors on more attractive men."

"So basically, they think everyone but them is getting a little?"

"Right. They both desire women and revile them. And sometimes, shame over their lack of sexual prowess inspires extreme rage against both the women who reject them—whom they call Stacys—and the men who get in their way. The so-called Chads."

Bandoni looked at me. "*Now* tell me what a Chad is."

"They're good-looking, charismatic men who can easily get dates."

"Okay." Bandoni chewed his lip. "Donovan's good looking. Athletic. We can see on his social-media accounts that he ain't hurting for women. If you say that makes him a Chad, I'll buy it. Could explain why they cut off the poor kid's dick. But what about Noah?"

Cohen nodded. "Where does he fit in?"

"He got the girl," I said. "Ami. That might have been all it took."

"Ami broke up their bromance?" Bandoni grunted. "Maybe. And going back to Donovan. Why'd the killers pick him out of all the other Chads we got walking around? What makes him so special outside of some possible link to Todd Asher? And"—he stabbed a finger at us— "why kill him at Redeemed Life Church?"

"If our killers are the Superior Gentlemen," I said, "we need to figure out where their lives overlapped Donovan's. Learn what drew their attention to him."

"We got a whole damn busload of theories and pretty much nothing that's concrete." Bandoni shook back his sleeve and glanced at his watch. "I filled the lieutenant in on Evan's theory about mass murderers, and she's asked us to brief her in half an hour. Let's move."

As I gathered up the pages of the manifesto, Evan leaned over and read the final words in his sonorous BBC voice.

"What the world took from us, we shall take from the world. We have gone to darkness. So shall the world."

CHAPTER 21

Sometimes I walk at night, searching in the dark for my mem-
ories. I hear all the normal sounds. Leaves rustling with the
whisper of paper outside the windows, the whir of the garage
door of a late-night neighbor, the bones of the house settling
around me in a soft rumble of creaks and groans like an old
woman making her way to bed.

I listen more closely and realize these sounds are antechambers
to the past.

All I have to do is follow them.

—Sydney Parnell. Personal journal.

"Mass murder," Lieutenant Lobowitz said from the other side of the desk as Bandoni finished his summary of our case.

Evan nodded. "That is our concern. Based on the killers' writings."

She squeezed her eyes shut. Probably hoping we'd go away.

We were gathered in a half circle on the other side of the lieutenant's desk. Our four plus Detective Ron Gabel, who'd provided us with an update of the crime scene work completed thus far. As always, the wheels of justice, hampered by the limitations of science and manpower, ground slowly.

The lieutenant didn't seem impressed with our progress.

I half rose from my chair and reached for a Boston cream out of the box Cohen had picked up on our way in. Bandoni beat me to it, forcing me to detour to a maple glaze. As I dropped back in my seat, Clyde stretched his chin across my thigh and gave me his best hungry-dog look.

"Sorry, pal," I whispered and signaled him down. Clyde's days of doughnuts and French fries were over. If I was going to ruin anyone's health, it would be my own.

Lobowitz reopened her eyes.

Her earlier shock had been replaced by narrow-eyed hunger. This was what cops lived for, regardless of rank, department, race, color, creed, or religion: catching bad guys. The more the better. The worse the better.

Evan's proclamation about mass murderers delivered the promise of both.

She tapped her pen on her desk. "How much time do we have before these guys act?"

"Very little, I think," Evan said. "When they sent the manifesto to the *Denver Post*, they knew they were opening themselves up to a broad investigation by law enforcement. Any delay increases their chance of getting caught. They won't want to risk that."

She held up the photograph of the Superior Gentlemen. "Let me make sure I understand. You believe that a group of men who call themselves the Superior Gentlemen are behind two murders, with a plan to cause the deaths of God knows how many more."

We nodded.

"But one of these so-called Superior Gentlemen is a victim. Noah Asher."

"Our guess is Noah wanted out," Bandoni said. "The group didn't like that."

"And Dashiell Donovan?"

"We're still looking for a connection."

She replaced the photo on the desk and gave us a narrow look. "But pickup artists? Aren't these guys just looking for a good time?"

"There are plenty of fringe elements floating like satellites around the more mainstream groups," Cohen said. "The factions that advocate violence operate mostly online, part of an echo chamber of mutual rage and entitlement. But I think in our case, these men found each other in the real world."

Evan said, "Like touching a lit match to gasoline."

"With a bunch of innocents standing in their way, if you're right." She sighed and leaned back in her chair. "Based on the first page of the manifesto sent by the killers—the drawings of five men—we have at least four surviving Superior Gentlemen. But of the five men in the photo, you've only identified three. Our victim, Noah Asher. His brother, Todd Asher. Who is missing. And the guy with the bleached hair, Riley Lynch. Also missing. The man in the T-shirt and jeans we know only as Craze." She tapped her chin with two fingers and frowned. "The man standing next to Craze remains unidentified. And, of course, we don't know who took the picture."

Bandoni cleared his throat. "That's correct."

Lobowitz glared at Gabel, who didn't appear to take it personally. "What kind of backlog do we have on the DNA from the crime scenes?"

"DNA testing is running months behind. Even with priority status, we're looking at a week, minimum."

"How can I help?"

"Get me access to one of those rapid DNA machines. And more manpower."

"Dream on," Bandoni muttered.

But Lobowitz jotted a note in her spiral pad. "Let me see what I can do. The FBI has been testing the interface process between the automated machines and the DNA index system, and they need material. Our investigation would be a good test case for them."

"Thanks."

She dipped her chin at Cohen. "Michael, I spoke with your lieutenant this morning. Based on the sexual nature of the crimes, he's given his approval for us to borrow you for a couple of days. You good with that?"

"Whatever you need."

She swiveled toward Evan. "Can you continue to help us out?"

"Of course." He was writing rapidly in his notebook. He didn't look up. "We have five writing exemplars. The two victims, the message scratched in the elevator, and the one left in Sydney's car. And now the manifesto. If you can get exemplars from our suspects, that would be helpful. I'll start building a profile of our demented scribes."

"Perfect. I'll find a place for you to park." She scooped her hair off her neck. Her face was flushed. "What about possible targets? Who do you think these killers might go after?"

Evan clipped his pen on his notebook and looked up. "At this point, it's impossible to guess, both regarding the targets and the scale."

"Men calling themselves unwilling celibates have killed before," Cohen said. "They've shot sorority sisters in Berkeley and yoga students in Florida. A guy in Toronto mowed down a crowd of people in a van."

Bandoni cleared his throat. "Parnell's spotted a cargo van three times since this investigation started. No plates that we've caught, but it's got a bull bar mounted on the front. Which is a pretty efficient way to take out pedestrians."

"You think that's what the killers are planning? Running down people in a van?"

"In the world of Forced Celibates," Cohen said, "the Toronto killer is considered the leader of the coming revolution."

This time the lieutenant closed her eyes only briefly. "I'm requesting assistance from the Feds. If we're really lucky, the FBI is already aware of these guys and knows something we don't."

"Like those assholes will share," Bandoni grumbled.

"Guess you'll just have to rely on your inexhaustible charm to convince them, won't you, Len?" Lobowitz said.

He stuffed the rest of his doughnut in his mouth and simmered.

"World's full of soft targets," she said. "And now we know these guys are watching us. Stay alert." She smacked the table with her notebook and stood. "Okay, people, let's get on it."

◆ ◆ ◆

Outside the conference room, Major Crimes was frenetic with conversation, television commentary, ringing phones, and a jittery energy that felt like a bone saw against my raw nerves.

The murder business was humming.

"I can't hear myself think in here," Bandoni said. "Powwow in the break room."

While Lobowitz and Evan went to find a place for him to work, Cohen, Clyde, and I tailed Bandoni into the room set aside for lunch and coffee breaks. Cohen and I poured coffee while Bandoni snagged a Mountain Dew from the refrigerator. He leaned against the appliance, his bulk looming over the old Whirlpool.

"Here's what I'm thinking," he said. He lifted his soda in Cohen's direction. "I want you to check out the church. See if you can find anything that links Redeemed Life to anyone in Noah's circle—his students and Riley Lynch. See if there's anyone in the church who belongs to one of these pickup lairs. You know the drill."

"I do," Cohen said mildly. "I'll see who might have gotten access to a key, as well. And while we're looking for all possible connections, I'll cross-check the church membership with the names of employees from Water Resources."

"Good thought." Bandoni tipped the Mountain Dew toward me. "What you and Fido are going to do is find Ami. Alive. Dead. Getting her nails done. On a rocket to the moon. Whatever. Find her."

I nodded. "I'll see if my contact in the FBI was able to get me a last name off the TPS registry. Outside of that, the only possible link

I've got is Top-A. The warrant came through, so I'll take a look at their records, see if Ami worked there and if they've got an address on file." I took a sip of the coffee and made a face. "Plus, I swear the women I talked to recognized her when I showed them Noah's drawing. I'll lean on them."

"Good. You hear anything from North Platte's detective's bureau about the warrant for ColdShip?"

I flushed and shook my head.

"I'll follow up on it." He took a long swallow, set the can on the counter. "I'll have patrol bring in Markey and Rivero. Make sure their alibis check out. And see if they have other names to add to the pot. I'll talk to the comics-store owner, too. Dana Gills. Then have another whack at Damn Fox. And keep kicking over stones for Riley Lynch and Todd Asher."

He went back to the refrigerator, pulled out a cellophane-wrapped chocolate Ding Dong.

"Bandoni," I said, pointing at the Ding Dong. "Seriously?"

Bandoni stared at the small cake as if he wasn't sure how it had gotten into his hand. Then he shrugged. "I've never been more serious about anything in my life."

He opened the Ding Dong and took a bite.

One of the detectives leaned around the door. "Bandoni. You got a call on your landline. 'Cause I'm your fucking secretary."

"Stay in touch, rookie," my partner said over his shoulder, his words mumbled around the chocolate. He swallowed. "Unless you hear otherwise, we all powwow at the Black Egg later this afternoon. Donovan's autopsy after that, special thanks to Emma Bell and her willingness to go the length for us. And what is it you jarheads say?" He slapped the doorframe. "Eyes in the back of your head. You see that van or any, I dunno, naked Barbie dolls, you call me. Got it?"

"Got it."

As soon as he was gone, Cohen and I faced each other.

"I don't like it," Cohen said.

"Which thing specifically?"

"Your possible stalker."

"*Our* possible stalker."

He snorted. "You picture anyone outside the IRS stalking Bandoni? Or me?"

"The only place I'm going right now is a cleaning company. If they try to abduct me at broom-point, I'll sic Clyde on them."

Cohen knelt and took Clyde's head in his hands. "You watch out for her."

Clyde made a noise, as if in agreement. Then again, it might have been the fact that he knew Cohen carried treats in his pocket.

Cohen held out a hand. "Shake, fur ball."

The fur ball complied, and all seemed right.

For just a moment.

But then my heart faltered. Something in this case was wrong. *To put it mildly*, I chided myself, thinking of Noah and Donovan. Even so, beyond the mutilated bodies of our victims and the possible threat of mass murder, a high-voltage threat seemed to pulse in the air. An electricity that made the hair lift on my neck.

Smile! I'm watching you!

Marine paranoia? Or a Marine's sixth sense?

Have a nice day!

When Cohen stood, I leaned into him and pressed my hand to his cheek. He turned his face to kiss my palm, his lips soft against my calloused skin. He smelled clean and good. Of soap and shampoo and the underlying scent that was his alone. The world couldn't be all bad. Not with people like Michael Walker Cohen in it.

I wrapped my arms around him and squeezed. I'd resisted him for a long time. But I'd finally come to the realization that Clyde and I wanted the sweet domesticity he offered. The calm. A place to call home. Cohen was an antidote to war and trauma.

We needed him.

I needed him.

And there was the fact that he was great in the sack. Sometimes a girl needed that, too.

"I'll be careful." I ran the pads of my fingers over the scars on his hands. "You be careful, too. We should all stay frosty."

"Deal." With his foot, Cohen kicked the break-room door closed. He wrapped his arms around me and moved his lips to mine.

For two glorious minutes, the world went away.

Then the door banged open. Bandoni. "Forgot my—" He stopped. "Ah, jeez. Get a room."

I stopped at the lab to ask Gabel to prioritize testing the Barbie doll and to give him the note left the previous night, then headed to Top-A.

Kaylee's Volkswagen convertible sat in an otherwise empty parking lot. The place looked forlorn. Wind gusted through the pine trees and rattled a lone tin can down the street. The picnic table where'd I talked to Helen, Erica, and Lupita was empty. A single candy-bar wrapper fluttered against the metal leg of the table.

I killed the Chevy's engine. My phone buzzed as I was reaching for my coat. Mac McConnell, my contact in the FBI.

"I was about to give you a call," I said.

"Good timing, then," she said. "I just got a possible name for your girl."

"If the name gives me a lead, I'm restocking your liquor cabinet."

"A drink at Joe's Tavern will do," she said. "A woman named Aminta Valle could be your Ami. She and her father, Cesar, came to the United States almost six years ago when Aminta was thirteen. They were granted temporary asylum under a Temporary Protected Status designation."

"You have any details on why they got the asylum ruling?"

"It's a way too familiar story. When Aminta was twelve, thugs from *Calle Eighteen* tried to conscript her brother into the gang. When he refused, they swore they'd rape and kill Aminta and force the boy to join anyway. The police just looked the other way. Aminta and her father and brother fled for America the next day."

"Fucking world sometimes," I murmured.

"It gets worse. The boy's appendix ruptured. Nothing like a hard kick from the universe when you're already down. Enrique died in a camp in Mexico. Aminta and Cesar tried to return home to bury him, and the gangbangers came after them. They fled again."

Tragedy piled on tragedy; heartbreak visited upon people guilty of nothing more than being born in the wrong place at the wrong time.

I pressed a button and lowered my brand-new window to let in a gust of chill air. In the back, Clyde slobbered on the glass, his tail wagging. He was ready for action.

"Thanks for the information, Mac. You have an address for Aminta and her father?"

"Valle senior passed away a few months ago. Ami lived for a time in North Platte, Nebraska. But she returned to Denver at some point before her father's death. Now she's listed as residing at their home in Globeville. I'll text you the exact address. Anything else?"

North Platte. Home to our poultry cars and ColdShip. "That's it for now, Mac. Thanks."

"Call when you're ready for that drink."

And she was gone.

I stared out at the empty picnic table and imagined the women who'd been sitting there, angry and frightened, braced for whatever additional calamities the world would unleash on them. I was sure that for Ami, and maybe for the other women as well, disaster had come in the form of the Superior Gentlemen.

I got out and opened the back for Clyde.

"Let's see if we can right some wrongs, partner."

Clyde's tail fanned the air, and he looked up into my face as if to say, *Damn straight.*

◆ ◆ ◆

When I walked into Top-A, the front room was empty. Maybe it was Candy's day off. I made my way to Kaylee's office. The door was open, and when I rapped on the jamb, she looked up with wide eyes and a mouth rounded with surprise.

"Oh!" she said as Clyde and I walked in. "I thought the door was locked."

"Good to see you, too, Kaylee." I took my old chair across the desk from her. "Nice sweater set. Pink today."

"Um." Her ponytail swished. "Thank you?"

I leaned forward and parked my forearms on my thighs. "So, Kaylee. Did you get a chance to talk to your boss about letting me look at those names?"

She blinked. "Names?"

"Names. And phone numbers. For whoever cleaned Mr. Asher's home. Remember that?"

"Oh." More blinking. "I forgot."

"It's okay." I placed a piece of paper on her desk. "I have a search warrant now."

She frowned, picked up the warrant. Studied it. After a moment she dropped the paper as if someone had just informed her it had cooties. Her chest heaved with her sigh.

"Fine," she said.

She went to work on the computer. In three easy minutes she had the name of the woman who had cleaned Noah's home. If I didn't have better things to do, I would have found a reason to slap handcuffs on her and haul her down to the station. Technically, her earlier refusal had been legal. But maybe I could get her for pissing off an officer of the law.

There were more than a dozen dates of service for Noah's home, November through February. And the same cleaner each time. Aminta Valle.

Excitement fizzed in my blood.

"I need whatever information you have for Miss Valle," I told Kaylee.

Kaylee went back to typing. After a few seconds, she gave me a shrug no one would mistake for apologetic. "She's been purged."

My throat threatened to close at Kaylee's word choice. "Purged, as in . . . ?"

"Deleted from the system. She must have chosen to end her relationship with Top-A. Or perhaps she was fired. I can't tell because she's been—"

"Purged. Let's move on to your customer database." I was operating purely on instinct now. "I need to see the files for some of your other clients. I'll write them down."

I grabbed a notepad on Kaylee's desk and made a list.

- **DASHIELL DONOVAN**
- **RIVERO MARTINEZ**
- **TODD ASHER**
- **RILEY LYNCH**
- **MARKEY BYRON**

"Fine." More typing. "Nothing for Dashiell Donovan."

Disappointment smacked. I'd been sure I'd found the common thread.

"Or Rivero Martinez. Or Todd Asher." She rolled her eyes at me. "Keep going?"

"If you would."

More typing. Then: "Riley Lynch and Markey Byron are customers. What do you want to know?"

Everything. I kept my expression neutral. "Who cleaned their homes?"

"Looks like . . . hmm." Even more typing, faster now. Apparently, we were clear of what Kaylee considered dangerous territory. "Looks like it's Erica Flores. Both men have a long-standing request for her. Erica is one of our best team members."

"So you *do* allow your customers to request a specific cleaner."

She swiveled toward me and sniffed. "It's only because Mr. Lynch and Mr. Byron are friends of Kurt's."

Now the excitement popped in my veins like champagne bubbles. "Kaylee, do you know about the Superior Gentlemen?"

"You mean Kurt's friends?"

"Yes. Kurt's friends. Is Markey one of them?"

A crease appeared in her smooth forehead, but she nodded.

"And Riley Lynch."

"Yes."

Markey was one of the Superior Gentlemen. I'd had the little shit in my hands and let him go.

I kept my voice level. "What other Top-A customers are friends of Kurt's?"

The crease deepened, and she shook her head. "Just Markey and Riley. And I guess Noah was, too. But all our other customers are businesses."

Which left Craze as our mystery man. "I need to talk to Kurt. Call him, and tell him to get down here."

Her chin came up. Defiant. "Kurt's on vacation. Kona. That's in Hawaii."

An uneasy prickling started in my gut. It didn't feel like the morning's doughnut. I sat up. "Yeah?"

"Yeah."

"You're positive."

"I'm a very positive person."

I couldn't argue. Everything in the office decor reinforced the idea. Stay positive!

Kaylee's chin rose even higher until she had to look down her nose to make eye contact. "I drove him to the airport myself."

"Must be true, then. Kaylee, are you familiar with what it means to make false statements to a detective?"

The flawless skin of her forehead wrinkled. "You mean lying?"

"Exactly."

"But I haven't!"

"Maybe your memory just slipped a little." I pulled out the photo of the Superior Gentlemen and set it on her desk. "I showed you a photo the last time I was here. Now I want you to look at it again. And this time I want you to look very, very closely. Do you see anyone you recognize?"

There was a shadow in Kaylee's eyes now as she gaped at me. Probably thinking that orange wouldn't go with her skin tone.

"Don't look at me," I said. "Look at the picture."

She complied, bending her head so that her ponytail swung around and covered one eye. When she looked up again, her cheeks sported a vivid shade of pink that clashed with the sweater set.

"Kurt," she whispered.

"Kurt who?"

"Kurt Inger."

"Can you please point to Kurt in the photo?"

Up came a manicured finger. Kaylee pointed to our unidentified Superior Gentleman. I allowed myself a small smile. Now we had Noah Asher, Riley Lynch, and Kurt Inger. Perhaps Markey was the photographer. Or maybe he simply hadn't been there that night.

But we had our Superior Gentlemen.

Only Craze remained a mystery.

And the missing Todd Asher. Whom I was beginning to worry about.

"Just to be sure," I said. "You're pointing to the man in the middle, the one with shoulder-length dark hair and the black ankle boots."

"Chukkas," she whispered. "The boots are called chukkas."

"Chukkas. You drove Kurt to the airport."

"No."

"No?"

"I don't really think he's in Hawaii," she confided.

"Where do you think he is?"

As if a dam had broken, her eyes filled with tears. She shook her head wildly until her ponytail seemed to fly under its own power and soft strands drifted free around her face. Her resemblance to a songbird caught in the clutches of a hawk was startling.

"Kaylee, tell me. I need to know." I spoke slowly, as if talking to a child. "Where is Kurt?"

"I don't know," she wailed. "I. Don't. Know. He made me promise I wouldn't even tell anyone he was gone. You can't arrest me for not knowing!"

Clyde's ears came up at Kaylee's distress. I kept my own voice soft. "But maybe you have some ideas. A friend he might stay with. Or a favorite town where he likes to vacation."

"I don't think he's on vacation. I think . . ." She hugged herself and leaned across the desk toward me. "I think he's, like, hiding out."

"Why would he want to hide?"

"Drugs, maybe?"

"Drugs. As in dealing? Or as in he's off somewhere on a bender?"

"I don't know! He just said—" She stopped. Started again. "He just said that I was to tell anyone who asked that he was in Hawaii."

"It's okay, Kaylee. Take a deep breath." Another lesson from Interviewing 101. Be friendly. Sympathetic when appropriate. Use the subject's name often. "When was this?"

"A few days ago."

Right around the time Noah was trapped somewhere, being tortured.

She said, "He said I wasn't to tell anyone anything. Then he got in his van and just—"

"What van?"

She looked at me like I'd lost my mind. "His *work* van."

"Let me guess. A dark-blue cargo van."

"Sure."

I shot off a text to Bandoni. DARK-HAIRED MAN IN S. G. PHOTO IS KURT INGER, MANAGER AT TOP-A CLEANING. HE DRIVES A DARK-BLUE CARGO VAN. MARKEY ALSO ONE OF THE SUPERIOR GENTLEMEN.

A few seconds later Bandoni texted back. I HAVE SOMEONE ON KURT. CHATTING NOW WITH RIVERO. FIGURES RE MARKEY. WE CAN'T FIND HIM.

Which meant every member of the Superior Gentlemen was either dead or missing.

I returned my attention to Kaylee. "Go on. Kurt got in his van . . ."

"And drove away. And that man!" Kaylee stabbed a wild finger at the photo. "He came looking for Kurt."

My heart leapt.

"Which man, Kaylee?"

"The man in the jeans." She pointed.

Craze.

"He was very nice," Kaylee babbled. "Brought me flowers, even. I was in the parking lot, getting ready to head home, when he walked up and just handed me the flowers. For being beautiful, he said. He'd stopped by to see his old buddy, told me he and Kurt went way back."

"He tell you his name?"

"Just said I should call him Craze. That everybody called him that."

"Did Craze come by before or after you and I talked?"

"After. He came by yesterday."

266

"And he was on foot? No car?"

"I didn't see one."

"What about how he looked?"

"He was dressed kind of like he was in the picture. Beat-up jeans and a T-shirt. And an old leather jacket."

"Any accent?"

"No."

"What about tattoos or jewelry? A watch maybe? Anything stand out to you, Kaylee?"

"No." More tears. "I wasn't really looking at him. It was dinnertime. I needed to eat."

A world regulated by Kaylee's dietary needs. I kept the frustration out of my voice. "What did you tell him about Kurt?"

"Well, like I said, he seemed like a nice guy. I almost told him the truth. That Kurt wanted people to think he was in Hawaii, but he really wasn't. But that's when I saw it."

I felt like I'd kept walking after Kaylee had stopped. "Saw Kurt?"

"No-o. This dog. Just trotting down the street, sniffing things."

I was completely at sea. "And?"

"He had a knife."

"The dog?"

Kaylee gave me a cops-are-so-stupid look. "Hel-lo? Craze."

I stopped trying to row and just went with it. "Craze had a knife."

"And he called the dog over. Whistled and held out his hand like he had a treat. And the dog—the dog—" She shuddered. "It came over, and Craze scratched it behind its ears and it was happy. And I thought maybe the knife was just, like, for show. You know, weird, but sometimes guys *are* weird. But then all of a sudden, Craze—he grabbed the dog, and he cut off its tail. The dog thought Craze was his friend. But Craze *cut off its tail.*"

I hadn't thought I could think less of our mysterious Craze. I was wrong. "What happened next?"

"He kept holding the dog. It was whimpering, and Craze was *smiling*. He told me that dog could be me."

"Meaning he'd hurt you."

"Uh-huh. He tilted his head to one side like he was *studying* me. Like I wasn't, you know, human. I thought he'd hurt me. So I told him Kurt wasn't *really* in Hawaii."

"What did he do?"

"Just kept looking at me. Then he said to let Kurt know he was looking for him. He let go of the dog, and the dog ran away. Then he left."

"Are there cameras outside?"

"Yeah. But just for show. We never connected them."

"Did you see where he went?"

Another wild headshake. "I got in my car and drove away. I was terrified. I almost didn't come to work today. But of course I had to give the women their assignments for the day. Helen and Erica and Lupita. And then I remembered that we become what we think about. So I didn't think about him. Other than to lock the door this morning. Which I guess I didn't . . ."

I had to squeeze my eyes shut. Just for a moment.

Then I said, "Kaylee, I need you to get out of here. And not come back until I say it's safe for you to be here."

"I can't, I—"

"But first, I need you to go to police headquarters and make a statement. I'll get someone to escort you there."

"What? No. I'll lose my job! He was just some weirdo. Kurt will clear everything up when he gets back."

I used my dog-training voice. "Grab your purse and anything else you need."

"Things like this can't happen to people like me. Craze. And the police. I have an MBA. I graduated *cum laude*."

"Congratulations. Pack up. Right after you tell me how to find Erica. And the other women. Helen and Lupita."

"You can't bother them. They're working."

"That's okay. I still need their numbers."

Kaylee stared at me for a moment, then shook herself and turned to her screen. She scribbled three phone numbers on a sticky note.

"Just one more thing," I said. "I need a list of addresses for all your clients."

A sniffling sigh followed by more typing. "There. It's printing now."

I signaled Clyde to wait, then stepped into the hall and called for a squad car. When I returned, Kaylee was putting herself back together with a compact mirror and a tube of lipstick.

"Kaylee, I'm going to give you some advice. One woman to another."

She placed the lipstick in a drawer. "Okay."

"A police officer will be here soon to escort you to headquarters. Follow him in your own car. When you're done, don't come back to work."

"But—"

"No. Go home. Lock your door. Call Candy and all your other employees and tell them to stay away. Because the man with the knife is a very bad man. You can't simply will him away with positive thoughts."

"What if Kurt comes back, and I'm not here? He'll think I'm a terrible office manager."

"Oh, Kaylee," I said softly. I touched her hand. Her fingers were cold. "Better than being a dead one."

CHAPTER 22

*Someone once told me that murder cops are the foot soldiers
in the battle between good and evil.*

—*Sydney Parnell. Personal journal.*

I leaned against the Tahoe and watched as Kaylee drove away, her
Volkswagen close behind the departing squad car. A tap of brakes, the
brush of tires on loose gravel, and both vehicles turned the corner and
disappeared.

Clyde stared up into one of the pine trees, ears swiveling, his gaze
fixed on a crow as it clung to a branch and croaked its rage at our
intrusion.

I crossed my ankles and fisted my hands in my pockets. I felt as
though we definitely now had the *who*. Our killers were the Superior
Gentlemen. Markey, Riley, Kurt, and Craze.

But we didn't have the *why*. Why had they murdered their friend
Noah? And had they done something with Ami? Most immediately
important, who else did they intend to hurt?

And who the hell was Craze? If he was their leader, why had he
come looking for Kurt?

The crow flew higher into the tree. Clyde pranced around the trunk.

What was Dashiell Donovan's connection to the Superior
Gentlemen? Why and how had he become their target?

I wondered, too, if I was missing something important in the men's link to Top-A. Had Kurt simply talked his friends into using his cleaning company? Just a few pickup artists who wanted their homes to look as spiffy as their clothes?

Before they turned to murder, that was.

And what *about* Kurt? Was he my stalker?

It was like tuning in to a distant radio station. The occasional burst of words, then more static.

I pulled out my phone and started making a round of calls.

Lieutenant Lobowitz promised she'd rustle up the manpower to park an unmarked near Top-A Cleaning. Two cops in plainclothes on alternate shifts. I didn't really expect Craze to show. But maybe we'd get lucky.

Next, I dialed Erica, who had cleaned the apartments of both Riley Lynch and Markey Byron. Straight to voice mail. I tried Lupita. Voice mail. Then Helen.

The voice-mail trifecta.

Silence, apparently, was trending. Maybe the women would return my calls when they went on break.

At least Bandoni answered. He grunted through my recitation of the conversations with Mac and Kaylee. When I was done, he said, "So we add Kurt Inger and Markey Byron to the list of the missing. If Evan's right, we now got four pissed-off, sexually deprived, dickwad killers hiding out somewhere plotting mass murder."

"But if these guys are in it together, why was Craze sniffing around the cleaning company looking for Kurt?"

"We ain't exactly talking the A-Team here. Most of these asswipes probably ain't interested in playing second fiddle. My guess is we got a little internal difference of opinion. We get lucky, these guys will blow each other to kingdom come without us having to lift a finger. Hold on."

Over the connection came the sound of voices murmuring and Bandoni saying something about buying Rivero whatever he wanted for lunch in order to keep the kid close and talking.

Then he was back on the phone. "Rivero's alibi checks out. He says Markey is a brilliant *artiste* and that was why he kept his trap shut about the Superior Gentlemen when you talked to the two of them. Didn't want to upset genius, apparently."

"Nothing else?"

"Nothing else. You heading to the address your feeb friend gave you for Aminta Valle?"

"That's my plan. And I'll keep trying to reach the other women. When are you having a sit-down with Damn Fox?"

"Right after I finish with Rivero and put on a hazmat suit. Stay in touch."

I disconnected and slid my phone into my pocket.

Clyde had given up on the crow and stood facing into the gusts, his mouth open and tongue lolling. His tail swept back and forth like a sail in a high wind. He sniffed around my pocket for his hard rubber Kong, the pot of gold at the end of every working dog's rainbow.

"You ready to catch some bad guys, partner?" I said in Clyde's favorite high-pitched voice.

Clyde's tail wagged harder. I opened the passenger door and gestured for him to get inside. He hopped into the passenger seat and waited while I used the K9 harness to buckle him in.

"Soon, buddy," I said, ruffling his ears. "You might get to run down an entire platoon of baddies. And then we'll buy you a case of Kongs."

◆ ◆ ◆

Clyde and I pulled up in front of a small tan brick bungalow with a patch of winter-brown yard and a once-white picket fence. Dead twigs from nearby poplar trees crunched beneath the tires as I rolled to a stop.

I zipped my jacket, and Clyde and I got out beneath a low-hanging sky. A flock of starlings wrestled past us in a headwind.

The warrant for Ami's house was in process, but I didn't need it to do a casual search. If necessary, I could break in based on our need to conduct a well check. The rooms, closets, beds, pantries, basement, and attic—any place that could conceal a body was fair game.

I'd kept the lock-picking kit in my pocket. But it turned out I didn't need it. The front door was closed up tight, but when we went through the gate and around to the back, we found the rear door standing wide open, a rock the size of a car battery shoved up against the kickplate.

I ignored the way the skin on my back crawled. I paused on the concrete slab with its charcoal grill and weathered table and chairs and peered into the gloom of the living room while Clyde sampled the air. A drift of last autumn's leaves had blown in and plastered themselves to the rain-soaked carpet, releasing a sad whiff of decay. The rest of the room was tidy—a gold-and-brown sofa with tasseled pillows tucked in the corners. An empty coffee table and a silent television set—a throwback console that had to be from the eighties. On the wall above the television hung a large metal cross with decorative scrollwork, surrounded by family photos.

Wind worked cold fingers down my collar. I glanced toward the neighbors—houses on either side, and one across the back fence. But rows of poplars and several immense blue spruce trees obscured their view of Ami's house. I'd get patrol to do a canvass, see if anyone saw anything. But my gut told me it would be pointless.

Clyde's eyes were on mine, waiting for instructions. His body language assured me we were alone.

"Good job, boy." I dropped my hand from my holstered gun and leaned into the house. "Hello? Denver PD. Anyone home?"

My words bounced off the far wall and echoed back.

"Okay, partner." I snapped on gloves. "Let's check it out."

I went quickly through the house and confirmed there were no skeletons in the closet or anywhere else. Like the front room, the rest of the home was neat but threadbare, with old-fashioned furniture and little decor. Ami's room was a bright spot with its pink bedspread and white furniture—carryovers from her youth, presumably. A student desk held a stack of drawing books and sketch pads and a large plastic cup brimming with colored pencils. The young Ami had been a budding artist who drew horses and lions and lots of sketches of a girl in a Superman cape.

Ami the Protector. Ami and Noah, wanting to save the world.

But from what, exactly?

I returned to the living room and looked through the photographs on the wall. Most were of Ami. Birthday parties. Her Catholic confirmation. Prom, where she wore a bright-blue gown and stood next to a beaming teenage boy. High school graduation—here she flashed a thumbs-up and a wide grin as she held up her diploma. Some of the photos were of a smiling man as he passed slowly from early to late middle age—Cesar Valle, Ami's father. His pride in his daughter showed clearly in every photo where the two were together.

But Cesar also carried sorrow in his eyes, a layer like winter ice over a lake.

Grief for his son, Enrique. For his lost country. Maybe many other things.

I found Enrique in only one photograph—standing with his father and sister outside a modest, whitewashed home. A little older than Ami, he'd been gangly and awkward, with unruly black hair and his sister's fierce expression. A boy with two choices—join a violent gang and take on their murderous ways. Or flee.

Two photos lay frameless on the floor, perhaps blown from atop the television set. In one, Ami sat with a group of women at a picnic table. I recognized two of the women—Erica and Lupita. The women had been lying when they'd told me they didn't know Ami. Their friendship went all the way back to Nebraska. I knew because I recognized the concrete patio and the black outdoor ashtray, which I'd seen when I zoomed in on ColdShip during my Google search right after Noah's death.

I studied the wariness in the women's eyes.

All three women had worked at ColdShip before relocating to Denver. Had they lost their jobs after the ICE raid and moved together to Denver and Top-A? The idea made perfect sense. Ami, at least, had ties to Denver. Perhaps the others did as well.

But the coincidence of Ami's boyfriend, Noah, ending up on a ColdShip car—that was harder to swallow.

Why would the Superior Gentlemen care about ColdShip?

I let my thoughts wander, looking for a connection between dots that refused to line up. But after a minute or two, I shook my head. If there was something there, I couldn't see it.

I used my phone to record the photo, then picked up the second picture. Ami's father. In contrast to his robust health in the earlier photos, this one showed Cesar thin and ill, with hollowed cheeks and deep lines etched around his grieving eyes. His black hair had faded to thin, gray strands. Sitting next to him, Ami wore a brave smile that didn't get within shouting distance of her eyes. Presumably, the picture had been taken shortly before Cesar's death and after Ami had returned to Denver from North Platte.

The weight of the loss endured by father and daughter settled into my heart. From gangs in El Salvador to predatory men in America and the very ordinary specter of a natural death. I pulled in a deep breath. Shadows rustled in the dimly lit house, as if the gloom of Denver's reluctant spring had crawled in through the open door and now held sway inside.

Change, of course, was our only constant.

"Let's go, Clyde," I said.

I shoved the rock onto the patio and closed and locked the door. At the Tahoe, I paused with my hand on the door latch. The now familiar feeling dropped on me like a hand pushing down on my neck.

Our watcher was close by.

But he wasn't near enough for Clyde to sense danger. My partner eyeballed a squirrel in a tree high above while he waited for me to open the door.

I glanced around. The neighborhood lay empty. Gloomy. The only movement came from the fleeing squirrel and the swaying branches and the glossy-winged starlings, which had found perch on the eaves next door—they were irritable and raucous in the cold. The wind suddenly gusted, sending trash skittering down the street, tugging strands free from my braid, and knocking against the houses as it whirled past.

It felt as if Clyde and I were alone in the world.

Just us and an invisible madman.

CHAPTER 23

*It took me a long time to make this distinction: The past is
not my enemy. It's my fear of the past that brings me down.*

—*Sydney Parnell. Personal journal.*

The Black Egg Diner was a panacea for loneliness and paranoia.

The restaurant catered to the blue-collar crowd, and today it was
packed with its usual after-work throng of cops, construction workers,
highway-department grunts, landscapers, and mechanics. The smells
of paint and plaster and tar fought against those of grease and coffee.
The din of voices, clinking flatware, and the cooks shouting, "Order
up!" hovered around the decibel level of an orchestra of jackhammers.
The stools at the counter were taken, and every table was either filled or
being bused by harried waitstaff. But Suzie Blair—an angel in a waitress
uniform—managed a miracle and got Clyde and me into our usual
booth in the back. She started Clyde on some bacon and me on some
coffee without wasting her breath asking.

After she left, I sank into the seat, sucked in the fumes, and let my
heartbeat slow to a brisk trot.

Then I pulled out the client list from Kaylee and opened my laptop.

Our killers had spent days torturing Noah. Wherever they'd taken
him must have felt secure—no nosy neighbors or prying eyes. No risk
of someone walking in.

Helen had said that most of Top-A's business was cleaning offices. An empty office building could serve as a hideaway for men plotting mass murder, as long as the structures were empty.

Kurt Inger, in his role as the supervisor at Top-A, would know which properties fit the bill.

I started down Kaylee's alphabetized list.

But by the time Suzie refilled my coffee and left the pot, I had nothing. Comparing Kaylee's client list with online real-estate listings indicated that all the office buildings cleaned by Top-A were occupied.

I flipped to the last page of the list.

One of Top-A's clients was Water Resources. They were ensconced in a high-rise in downtown Denver. Julia Asher had mentioned that Noah found new digs for Water Resources, but I couldn't find a previous address for the company. I called Julia, assured her we were working hard on her son's case, and asked if she knew where Water Resources had been located before their move. She did not. I asked if she'd heard from Todd. She said no to that as well.

I apologized for bothering her and disconnected.

Maybe Erica or one of the other women would know where they'd been located. If they'd ever answer the phone.

I looked up when I heard a grunt and a snarl and spotted Bandoni elbowing his way through the mob. He shrugged out of his jacket and hung it on the brass hook next to the booth, then scowled at Clyde and dropped into the seat across from me.

"Having a good day?" I asked.

He rolled his eyes. "Where's Mike?"

"On his way." I'd called Cohen from the Black Egg parking lot. "You want coffee?"

"Some questions you don't have to ask."

I turned over a clean coffee cup and filled it from the pot. Bandoni took a cautious sip to test the heat, then closed his eyes and drank down most of the cup.

I poured more. "Where are we?"

"David Kelly," he said. "A.k.a. Damn fucking Fox."

"Please tell me he decided to cleanse his soul."

"That would take industrial bleach. I got nothing out of the guy. Nada. Nil. Fucking zero. Whatever that punk is scared of, it's something worse than a murder charge. I tried everything short of slapping some sense into him." Bandoni flexed his sausage fingers. "And trust me, the thought crossed my mind."

"So what scares a guy like Kelly?"

"Something worse than he is."

"Like Craze."

Bandoni zeroed in on me. "Yeah. There's Craze. He's our wild card. What'd you learn at Ami's house?"

I filled him in on the open door. The threadbare furniture. The dying father and dead brother and the sketches of a girl in a hero's cape. "Maybe what her family went through in El Salvador inspired her to live up to her name, protector. Also, one of the photos in the house shows Ami with two of the women from Top-A, Erica and Lupita. They worked together at ColdShip."

"Speaking of ColdShip, we got no video. A detective took the warrant in. Their security guy showed him around, then showed him the door."

"You think they erased—"

"Water under the bridge, rookie. We're already ninety-nine percent sure that Damn Fox and Street Cred hopped on the train up there. And that Noah didn't. Keep talking."

I took a breath, nodded. "I think ColdShip is covering up that they hire undocumented workers. They've gotten in trouble before. My guess is that if they do have videos, that's why they erased them. But . . ."

"But . . . ?"

"It's about the women. Something made them relocate to Denver. It could be just that they needed jobs and Ami wanted to be close to her father after he got sick."

"Makes sense."

"It *does* make sense. What I'm struggling with is the fact that the boyfriend of one of those women ended up on a ColdShip reefer."

"Back up a few steps. You think our bad guys put Noah on that reefer on purpose?"

"I'm just saying, it feels odd."

Bandoni folded his arms. "How would our killers even know that the train was going to stop where it did? And that there would be ColdShip cars?"

"All they'd need is a railroad scanner. They could listen in on whatever the maintenance crews were discussing. With some effort, they could also piece together what kind of cars the train was pulling."

"What about the fact that the door was open? You're saying they planned that, too?"

I tapped my spoon on the table. "I guess it's possible, but *that*, I think, was just a lucky break for the killers. Otherwise, they would have had to cram Noah onto the exterior refrigerator unit or haul him up to the roof."

"The door just happened to be open."

"It happens more often than you think." I kept tapping the spoon as I thought things through. "ColdShip hires undocumented workers and then does a crap job with safety regulations. I got that straight out of the *North Platte Telegraph*. Whoever jammed that plug door open was just being smart. And, sadly, also giving our killers both a murder weapon and a place to leave Noah's body."

"But *why*?" Bandoni leaned back in his chair. "Why would his killers go to all that trouble?"

"I'm thinking." ColdShip and Top-A both hired undocumented workers. Ami, Erica, and Lupita had worked at ColdShip, then gone to work for Top-A. Ami had cleaned Noah's house and become his girlfriend. Erica had worked at the homes of Markey and Riley. Which meant—what?

Bandoni huffed. "Still thinking?"

"Yeah." The *North Platte Telegraph* article had mentioned an immigration attorney. It was time to give him a call, see if he could shed any light.

"You're giving me a headache with that fucking banging," Bandoni said.

I set down the spoon. "We're missing something."

He scowled. "You figure out what it is, you let me know. Moving on, Lobowitz got the holy grail for Ron Gabel."

"The rapid DNA machine?"

"Exactly. He's been running through DNA like an addict slamming pills, and he's got good news for you. He asked me to pass it along."

"I could use that about now."

"He linked the DNA from all the nursing-home rapes. It's the same perp. Still no ID, but this is real progress. He said to tell you congratulations."

I refilled my coffee, checking to see if my hands held steady as a happy dance of adrenaline and feel-good chemicals pirouetted through my veins. We were breathing down the neck of a man who'd been torturing women for years. Maybe the next incident would break the case open.

"Good work, Parnell," Bandoni said. "We might make a detective out of you yet."

Suzie appeared at our table. She gave Bandoni the evil eye. "Where's Michael?"

Suzie had been on me for years to find Prince Charming. In her mind and mine, Cohen was the spitting image. Bandoni, apparently, did not fit the bill.

"Cohen's on his way," I said. "This is my partner, Detective Bandoni. Bandoni, meet Suzie."

"Ah." Suzie's frown vanished. "Well, then, it's a pleasure. What's your poison?"

I ordered a green-chili burrito to share with Cohen. Bandoni asked for a second pot of coffee, Mountain Dew, a cheeseburger, and sweet potato fries.

"Coming right up," Suzie said and melted back into the crowd.

"Sweet potatoes?" I said.

"Getting my vegetables."

"And ketchup, I suppose."

"*Two* vegetables." He spread his hands over his gut and looked pleased with himself. "Picture of health."

"You are *such* a cop, Bandoni."

"You ever look in the mirror? You got the disease, rookie. I can see the hunger in your eyes."

"Yeah, right."

"You're hooked. And now you'll spend the next forty years trying to decide if it's the best job in the world or the worst. Here's some advice." He planted his elbows on the table and leaned in. His breath smelled of coffee and cigarettes and peppermint. "Soon as you lose faith in what you're doing, you quit. 'Cause after that you're nothing but a fucktard sucking up precious air."

Bandoni was right. I had the hunger. I'd had it since I found the shrine to Noah in the middle of a field.

But faith that I was the right person for the job? Or that the job was right for me?

The jury was still out for deliberation.

"Now," Bandoni said, "I want you to hang on to that hunger. 'Cause I got bad news, too."

"And I was feeling really great there for a minute."

"Gabel tested your Barbie doll. No fingerprints. But he did get DNA."

"That sounds like good news."

"The DNA from the doll matches that from the nursing-home rapes."

I jolted upright. My hand caught the coffee mug and tipped it over. Bandoni grabbed napkins.

"That's not possible," I said. "It's a mistake. The samples got contaminated."

"Anyone but Gabel, I'd agree. But not him."

"Something wrong with the machine, then."

He finished mopping up the coffee. "The samples are linked, rookie."

"But it makes no sense. Kurt—Kurt has a dark-blue cargo van. He's the one who's been following me."

"Which kind of suggests he's the rapist."

"He's too young."

"No, he's not. After your call this afternoon, I checked. He would have been seventeen or eighteen when those rapes happened. Old enough. But these so-called gentlemen are working together. Maybe it was one of the others."

I pictured Riley and Markey and Craze and tried not to go where my thoughts wanted to take me. My stomach twisted. "Is that supposed to make me feel better?"

"What it is."

"Don't tell the others," I said. "Not yet."

"Why the hell not? They need to know."

"Cohen will worry. Or try to put me under house arrest. Just wait until we're sure it's true. Okay?"

In the next second, Clyde shot out from beneath the table and unleashed the might of his wagging tail, almost taking out a man in an Xcel Energy uniform. All for Cohen, who was working his way toward us through the crowd. Dog's best friend. I scooted over in the booth and felt my lover's fingers grasp mine as he slid in beside me.

Evan was a few paces behind, creating a stir as he weaved through the cops and laborers. He squeezed in beside Bandoni's bulk.

"Mohammed comes to the mountain," he murmured.

"Your hands are cold," Cohen said to me.

I caught Bandoni's eyes and gave my head a faint shake. *Not yet.*

He frowned but nodded and folded his hands on the table. "What have you two geniuses got for us?"

Cohen shrugged out of his coat. "We've got a definite link between Donovan and Noah."

We all looked at him.

He said, "It's tennis, like you speculated. But the connection is through Markey, not Todd."

I used the mental equivalent of a backhoe to bury thoughts of the doll and a serial rapist. "Noah and Markey played tennis?"

"Markey did. But it's really about his dad, Ralph Byron."

"Can we skip the foreplay?" Bandoni said.

"The Byrons aren't members of Redeemed Life. Ralph is actually a pastor at another church, down in Colorado Springs. A real fire-and-brimstone kind of guy, apparently. Which probably says something about how Markey was raised. Anyway, Ralph had served as guest pastor at Redeemed Life a few times, so he had a key. And a couple of weeks ago, he was invited to become a full-time pastor at Redeemed Life."

I remembered the words the killer had written on Donovan. *In the beginning was the Word, and the Word was not with God, and the Word was not God.*

"The key is good. But—" Bandoni looked skeptical. "Markey hated the idea of his daddy preaching there so much that he decided to kill Donovan on the altar? And the fuck does that have to do with tennis?"

Cohen said, "Markey already hated his dad. And it's at least partly because of Donovan."

"Foreplay, then a strip tease." Bandoni groaned. "Can we just move on to the sex?"

Cohen shot him a grin. "The fact that you're in such a rush, Len, suggests to me there's a reason why you don't have a girlfriend."

"Fuck you."

"Fuck you back. I also talked to the DU tennis coach, who knows not only Donovan, but Markey as well. And his dad. The coach said Donovan was his star player. The kid was conference champion and a nationals qualifier his first two years. Probably had a real shot at winning the nationals this year, according to his coach. If he'd lived. Truly gifted."

"Let me guess," Bandoni said. "Markey, not so much."

"Right. The coach took Markey on, no doubt because of daddy's money. But he called Markey a nonroster practice player. Meaning he got to practice with the team, but he never qualified to compete. Markey stayed on at DU, but he quit the team after his first year."

Bandoni had that look again—the cat who caught the canary. "I can feel the dots starting to connect."

"Frankenstein," I said. "Markey's father is the creator who rejected his own creation. So Markey—the monster—struck out at those whom his father loves."

"And because this kid Donovan was a Chad, the others went along with it," Bandoni said.

"Markey's a gifted artist," I said. "Doesn't his father care about that?"

Cohen turned to me. "Even the coach mentioned Markey's gift. The kid used to make funny sketches of the guys on the opposing team. His teammates loved it. But that didn't impress his dad, apparently. And it gets worse. Donovan was at Denver University on a tennis scholarship. You want to guess who created the scholarship fund for the school five years ago?"

"Ralph Byron," Evan and Bandoni said.

Cohen nodded. "Like I said. Tennis."

"It fits with the manifesto." I reached for the coffeepot. "Frankenstein's monster was cast out of the paradise of human affection through no fault of its own."

"Not that Markey is a good kid," Cohen said. "He's never been officially charged with anything, but he's gotten his wrist slapped more than once. Mostly for letting his hands find their way uninvited onto women's bodies. A year ago, he got smacked for upskirting—taking pictures up a woman's dress. The woman's boyfriend decked him, and a cop wrote them both up. Neither side pressed charges."

"It's possible," I said, "that since Markey and Noah already knew each other, they started the Superior Gentlemen together. But I still feel like we're missing something. Why would Markey and the rest turn on Noah so viciously?"

"You mean other than the fact that Noah got a girl and left the group?" Bandoni said. "And was a better artist, presumably, than his student? Could be our guy's a little oversensitive after years of beatdown from Daddy."

"Maybe."

"Let's stick with what we do know." Bandoni glowered at Evan. "Your turn, genius."

Evan opened his mouth just as Suzie appeared at our table. She offloaded our food and Bandoni's soda, then took Evan's order for eggs and a side of bacon before disappearing again.

I'd lost my appetite after Bandoni brought up the Barbie, but I sliced the burrito in two unequal halves and slid the larger half onto the extra plate for Cohen, then pretended to dig into mine. Bandoni busied himself drowning his fries with ketchup. Maybe he was hoping to squeak out three servings of vegetables. Then he picked up his cheeseburger and aimed it at Evan like a weaponized Frisbee.

"Talk," he said.

Evan stole one of the fries and said, "We've got two scribes. First, the man who left the notes in the elevator and in Sydney's car. Her stalker. This man's writing is loose and uncontrolled. He changes the size and slant of the letters from one word to the next. There's no fixed baseline."

Bandoni's gaze slid to mine. "Which means what?"

"It suggests a lack of self-control. A tendency toward impulsive behavior. Not surprising in a stalker. Also"—he pulled out a photo of the words scratched in the elevator—"notice how much more deeply he carved the letter *t* in the word *watching*."

"It's thicker than the other letters," Cohen said. "It looks like a cross."

"Exactly. It might have been subconscious. But he's signaling that religion, specifically Christianity, is in some way important to him. Maybe he feels God is always watching and judging him. It fits with the biblical phrasing in the writing of the second scribe. Now"—he looked around at us—"be aware that while handwriting analysis is based on science, interpretation is an art. But in my opinion, this first gentleman is what we might generously call a few cards short of a full deck."

"Someone like Markey, is what you're saying," Bandoni said. "Guy with a history of aggression toward women. Maybe even up to and including rape."

"Possibly."

Cohen's leg pressed reassuringly against mine.

Bandoni sucked up half his Mountain Dew. "And the second guy?"

"In terms of pathology, I find him more frightening. Spacing is important, and all of you saw how tightly he spaced his words on the bodies of our victims. The letters touch, which suggests he lacks boundaries. And the way the words line up precisely, along with the well-defined letters . . . I'd say this man knows exactly what he's doing, how much harm he's inflicting. His rage is tightly controlled, as are his actions." Evan propped his elbows on the table and fisted his hands.

"This man isn't insane, like our first scribe. He's deliberate. Some might say evil."

Abruptly, the diner fell silent. It was a weird temporal anomaly during which, for an instant, no one spoke. No one rattled their forks or set down their glasses. The cook and waitstaff quit calling out orders, the grease fryer in the kitchen paused in its popping.

The four of us stared at each other.

Then the din fell back into place, a soothing reassurance that life went on. Suzie appeared with Evan's eggs and bacon. Evan grabbed the pepper.

"Let me see if I can summarize," Bandoni said. "We've got a nutcase and the devil working together to destroy the world. They probably have minions. All of them are hoping to kill as many people as possible before they exit stage left. That sound about right?"

Evan dug into his food. "I'd say that sums it up nicely."

"Long as we know what we're dealing with," Bandoni said. "Now eat up, kids. It's time for the rookie and me to get a move on. Dashiell Donovan awaits."

I turned to Cohen. "You mind taking Clyde home so he doesn't have to wait in the truck during the autopsy?"

"Bachelor night." He leaned over the table, and Clyde licked his face. "Hey, fur ball. What do you say we get pizza and beer and do a bunch of farting?"

Outside, day shaded toward evening. Clouds bunched over the mountains, and an icy wind breathed winter into the March air. I knelt and took Clyde's head between my hands.

"Be a good boy, Clyde," I said. "I'll see you in a few hours."

Clyde looked tired, and for a moment I hesitated. My partner wasn't a puppy anymore, but his energy usually outlasted my own.

He studied me solemnly as I got back to my feet.

"Clyde might be a bit under the weather," I said to Cohen. "If he vomits or gets diarrhea or a fever—"

"I'll rush him to the vet. Then I'll call you."

"Thanks." I gave Cohen a quick kiss. "See you in a few hours."

"I'll keep the home fires burning," he murmured.

"And if anything changes—"

"I've got the vet's number memorized."

Clyde made a low moan in his throat as I walked away and got into the Tahoe. I started the engine. Cohen and Evan waved. They looked sad and oddly worried. The price for working a case like this. I gave them a thumbs-up out the window.

Bandoni pulled past me and onto the street.

I followed.

CHAPTER 24

Some try, through violence, to control a world that seems to have passed them by. To satisfy their hatred for what they cannot have. And their hatred for those who have it.

—Sydney Parnell. Personal journal.

Attending the postmortem of Dashiell Donovan was, as Bandoni put it, nothing like a family picnic. The similarities between Donovan's autopsy and Noah's were agonizing—young men brought down in the prime of life, each the victim of rage-fueled torture followed by a singularly violent coup de grâce.

Hardest of all was the way in which the killers' fury had been made manifest in the words they'd carved into their victims' flesh—an engraved testimony of madness.

There were differences, of course. The cause of death. The form of torture. The locations of their bodies. But the final result was the same—a cold steel table in the autopsy suite, the body of a young man laid out beneath surgical lights.

Emma Bell clipped the red tag on the body bag. Pulled down the long, heavy zipper. She and her tech slid Donovan's corpse free.

Somewhere in the distance, Donovan's parents were on their way from Twin Falls, flying into the ruination of their lives.

Closer by, Noah Asher's family sat hunched inside their own grief. I wondered where their second son had gone. And if we should be worried.

Detective Miller snapped photos of Donovan while Bell recited a litany of injuries.

The room grew colder. I looked up and saw Noah standing behind Bell, his ghostly image wavering under the harsh lights, an expression of deep sorrow on his face. He did not speak, but I heard his words anyway.

Fix this. And, *Find Ami.*

"I'm trying," I whispered behind my paper mask.

Bandoni glanced at me. I looked down.

When my phone buzzed in my pants pocket, I jumped. I fished it out and checked caller ID.

John Yaeger. The immigration attorney I'd read about in the *North Platte Telegraph*'s article on ColdShip.

I'd called Yaeger on the drive over and left a message, asking for a callback. Now I held up my phone, showing Bandoni.

"I need to call this guy back," I said. "I'll be in the lobby."

He regarded me gravely for a moment above his thin paper mask. Then he nodded and turned back to the autopsy table.

I grabbed a couple of three-ring binders on my way to the front. Because both the inner and outer doors would automatically lock behind me, I propped the binders in place to keep the doors from latching.

Then I went out into the cold. A glance up and down the street showed only empty pavement. No cargo vans. No stalkers. I relaxed.

The lobby, my ass. What I needed was fresh air and nicotine.

The March night had come on hard, the threat of frost silvering the air. I zipped my coat, turned up the collar, and—against my better instincts—pulled out the cigarettes and lighter I'd purchased on the way to the medical examiner's office in a fit of pre-autopsy anxiety.

I lit up while Yaeger's phone rang.

A click, and then a man said, "Detective Parnell. We've been playing phone tag."

"Thanks for returning my call." I snapped the lighter shut and stuffed it in my pocket. "I pulled your name from an article in the *North Platte Telegraph* concerning an ICE raid on a distribution warehouse. I'm wondering what you can tell me. About the raid and the fallout."

"That goes back a bit. Eighteen months, isn't it?" Yaeger's voice was thin, with a light tremor. I pictured him white haired and frail. "ICE got an anonymous tip that ColdShip was hiring undocumented immigrants. The tip turned out to be right. In response, the company laid off a third of its employees and promised to clean up its act. I entered the picture when I filed a lawsuit against ColdShip on behalf of some of the workers. Unsafe working conditions, mainly. But also sexual harassment."

"Your firm handles labor-law cases?"

"We usually don't. But because some of the plaintiffs were undocumented, we took it on. It felt like a chance to make a point—that everyone deserves to work unmolested and in a safe environment."

"What was the outcome?"

"Like most cases, we settled out of court. A shame, because we had a good case. But the undocumented workers got cold feet, and there went half our plaintiffs. Not that I blame them."

"It might help my case if you'd share the plaintiffs' names."

"Sorry. Nondisclosure was part of the settlement."

I made my way down the steps and into the thickening dark. My cigarette flared and faded. "Any idea who tipped off ICE?"

Yaeger was silent so long that I thought the connection had broken. I checked my screen. The call was still open.

"Mr. Yaeger?"

"Yes." A phlegmy cough. "At first we thought it might be a disgruntled worker. When that didn't pan out, we looked into the possibility that the call came from a male employee accused of sexual harassment. Maybe he decided if the women wouldn't sleep with him, he'd cost them their jobs. Get some of them deported. But . . ."

"But . . . ?"

"It turned out the truth was a little stranger."

I took another drag and tipped back my head. Diamond-point stars glittered in the deep vault of the heavens. "Strange in what way?"

"Well." He made a sound between a chuckle and a sigh. "I say *strange*. And it was. But I suspect it had more to do with the helplessness and terror these women feel rather than with the truth."

"I'm listening, Mr. Yaeger."

"Some of the women told me they'd been threatened by a man who didn't actually work for ColdShip. They said he rode the trains and raped migrant women in the boxcars. Which, of course, is sadly and horribly believable. But they also told me that the man was a giant with yellow eyes. That he could fly. That he could walk through walls and appear out of nowhere. The women called him crazy. Named him *el diablo*. The—"

"The devil." My gaze fell away from the stars. *Crazy.*

Craze.

In North Platte. With Ami.

"The women swore he appeared in their apartments as if out of thin air. Sometimes to hurt them. Sometimes to threaten. He wanted them to sell themselves while he watched from the darkness. I don't think it was even for the money. It was just plain ugliness." Yaeger's sigh held a whisper of unease. As if deep in his reptile brain, the wild stories rang true. "I doubt that, in their heart of hearts, they thought he was supernatural. But with the hold he had on them, he might as well have been."

My heart fragmented. The pain one man could visit upon the world. But I kept my voice deliberately brisk, trying to separate my detective self from the part that was breaking. "He sounds like a real prince."

"Indeed. The women also believed that, like many evil spirits, *el diablo* was vengeful. Some of them were sure he'd tipped off ICE as punishment when they refused his demands. That he was flushing them out of hiding and back onto the trains where he could hurt them at his leisure."

I turned back to the medical examiner's office, fixed my gaze on the faint light falling through the windows.

Craze. Leader of the Superior Gentlemen. Almost certainly the tall, heavily built, yellow-eyed man who walked next to a train in Noah's drawing. And, quite possibly, a serial rapist, given the common DNA on the doll left by my stalker and the nursing-home rapes.

The devil, indeed.

"You understand this information about *el diablo* is hearsay, right?" Yaeger said. "Nothing we could use in our suit. Plus, only one woman was courageous enough to go to the cops."

I flashed to the picture of Ami at ColdShip with Erica and Lupita. The symbol of the Protector on her shirt in Noah's drawing.

"Aminta Valle," I said.

Another long pause. "I'm not at liberty to say."

"That's okay. You don't have to." I dropped my cigarette, ground it under my heel. "What did the cops do?"

"There was nothing to be done. This woman was the only person willing to press charges, and our so-called devil hadn't actually done anything to her beyond offer threats she had no proof of. She was trying to help her friends, guard them from this guy."

Ami, the Protector.

"Detective Parnell," Yaeger said. "Is this related to a case you're working now?"

"A double homicide. Two men."

A pause. "Then I think there's something else you should know. The woman who stood up to *el diablo*, the one whose name you might have just mentioned. She called me from Denver a month ago. She told me she and a friend had been pushing for the rights of domestic workers—janitors, caregivers. She asked about restraining orders. How effective they are."

A month ago. That would have been around the time Noah had mentioned to the comics-store owner Dana Gills that he was worried about payback. That he was scared.

"What did you tell her?" I asked.

"The unfortunate truth. A restraining order won't help if someone really wants to get to you."

"Just tell me one more thing," I said. "Did the women ever use another name for this *diablo*? A real name?"

"Not that they ever told me. They just called him the devil incarnate."

"I suspect, Mr. Yeager, they were closer to the truth than you and I can know."

After we hung up, I pulled out another cigarette and smoked while I ran through scenarios. I imagined Ami fleeing Craze after the police told her they couldn't do anything to stop him. Erica and Lupita would have joined her. The three of them buried themselves deep inside Denver, far away from *el diablo*.

And for a time, things were okay. Or somewhat okay. Ami nursed her sick father until his death. Erica and Lupita got busy building new lives. All three women found jobs with Top-A.

Then things started to go off the rails.

It was impossible to know which came first—Top-A Cleaning or the Superior Gentlemen. But either way, Kurt got his friends—Noah, Riley, and Markey—to sign up for cleaning services with Top-A. I recalled Erica's anger at privileged white men, her hint that she had been sexually harassed. Maybe, as the pickup artists slid into something darker, became Forced Celibates, they decided that targeting undocumented workers who couldn't risk going to the police was a safe way to gain access to sex.

Except Noah didn't become a Forced Celibate. Instead, he fell in love with Ami. Grew a conscience. Wanted to get out of the group.

Sometime during all this, Craze showed up.

Craze, furious with Ami's defiance, had traveled to Denver to find her. The city was a place he knew well—he'd raped here before. Maybe he met the Superior Gentlemen through Noah and his work with the gutter punks—Yaeger had said that *el diablo* rode the trains.

If so, for Craze, meeting Noah and finding the Superior Gentlemen must have felt like destiny.

He took over the Superior Gentlemen. A serial rapist, he was a lit match to the fuel of the Forced Celibates—formerly isolated loners finding each other in a perfect storm of rage and entitlement.

Noah and Ami fought back. They knew the risk they were taking. It was why Ami had asked about a restraining order. Why Noah had confided to Dana Gills that he was worried about payback.

But they were superheroes. Ami was the Protector. They thought they could win. Against Craze. Against the Superior Gentlemen and their abuse of women.

Only they didn't win. Noah was killed. And Ami was God knew where.

Placing Noah's body on a ColdShip car hadn't been a quirk of fate or a coincidence. Craze had been sending the women a message only they would understand. *You can run. Run as fast and as far as you like. But you ColdShip bitches can't hide. Not from me.*

For I am the man who walks through walls. The man who can fly.

I am el diablo.

Another thought struck. What if the final remaining coincidence—the reefer door being jammed open—wasn't? *Damn Fox,* I thought. *And Street Cred.* They could have slipped into the yard at ColdShip and wedged in the pipe. Or paid one of the workers to leave it in place.

No wonder the gutter punks wouldn't talk. They weren't just witnesses. They were accomplices.

I shook myself. After Noah, the men went after Donovan. Because Donovan had mattered to Markey's father in ways Markey couldn't. Donovan was a Chad. Charming, athletic, easy with women. He was everything Markey wanted to be.

I could not guess at the relationship between Markey and Craze. Not who had led whom into murder. Nor if their reasons for committing murder even aligned. Maybe Markey had an agenda to avenge his wrongs, while Craze simply wanted to destroy. All I knew was what we'd learned from Evan's analysis of their handwriting. That, at its simplest, one of them was insane. And the other was evil.

As for Riley and Kurt—perhaps they were part of the murders. Part of the plan to kill many more. But I suspected that Kurt, at least, had panicked and gone into hiding when Craze and Markey turned murderous. Maybe Riley, too, had fled.

I found my hand on the butt of my gun. "Who the fuck are you, Craze?"

Behind me, the lights of the Denver Medical Examiner's office shone like a brilliant oasis in this pasture-and-warehouse area of Denver. In the distance, a motorcycle revved its engine. An owl hooted in the field across the way. As I stared into the darkness, Kaylee's words swam into my mind.

He tilted his head to one side like he was studying *me. Like I wasn't, you know, human. I thought he'd hurt me.*

And in a flash, I had it. The man who'd approached me in the grocery-store parking lot. Who'd asked me out for a drink while he studied me, his head tilted in a way that had seemed menacing for reasons I couldn't then articulate. But hearing Kaylee, I understood.

He was studying me like I wasn't human.

I scanned the street—still empty—then ran across to the Tahoe. Inside, I locked the doors and scrabbled through the photos and drawings from Noah's house until I found his sketch of the yellow-eyed man by the train. And the photo of Craze with the Superior Gentlemen.

They were the same man.

The same man who'd approached me in the parking lot. I'd rejected him. And he had been following me ever since.

Because what these men hated more than anything else was rejection.

Time to get back to the autopsy. To the safety of lights and locked doors and Bandoni.

I stepped out of the Tahoe. Started across the road.

All around, an angry wind kicked up and rolled over the land. Nearby, metal clanked on metal. Then a sharp bang as the lid on a dumpster crashed closed.

Closer still, a voice whispered, "Sydney."

I sprinted. Reached the far side of the road.

A laugh that seemed to come from all around. "You can run, Sydney Rose Parnell. But you can't hide."

I sped up the stairs to the glass doors, then jerked to a stop. The binders I'd placed to keep the inner and outer doors open were gone.

On the door, someone had written in black marker: TAG! YOU'RE IT!

I yanked on the handle. The door didn't budge.

I spun around, half expecting yellow eyes to stare me down.

But only pitch blackness glared back.

I texted Bandoni. LOCKED OUT. HURRY!

CHAPTER 25

If we are wise, we are afraid of the dark.

—*Sydney Parnell. Personal journal.*

"You okay, rookie?"

Bandoni stood sweating in the dim light of the lobby. He'd shoved his mask down around his neck and now he gulped air like a swimmer coming up from the deep.

"I'm fine." Under my coat, my heart was in full gallop. "Thanks for coming so fast. For a minute I really thought . . ."

"Thought what?"

"Nothing."

I glanced past Bandoni toward the door. Night breathed against the glass.

He said, "I thought you were going to be in the lobby."

"I changed my mind."

Bandoni glared at me and mopped his face with the paper mask. "Let's go take a look."

But I touched his arm. "They're long gone. They were just sending another message."

I steered him toward the chairs and told him about my conversation with John Yaeger and my theories about Craze and ColdShip and the train. And about my stalker. When I finished, he shared his own news.

"The lieutenant's been working with the Feds. Our FBI friends have come up with a couple of possible targets in case Evan's right and these guys really are planning to make a move in the next few days. There's a women's leadership conference scheduled for the day after tomorrow at the Crowne Plaza Convention Center."

"That's close to where we found Noah's body," I said.

"Yup. And students from Denver University are holding a pro-women's march in LoDo bright and early tomorrow morning."

"DU is Markey's school."

"And Donovan's. Can't you just picture all those kids packed into a shopping corridor where vehicles aren't supposed to go?"

I closed my eyes, envisioning a van with a heavy-duty grill mounted on the front as it plowed through a crowd of pedestrians.

I was saved from the image when my phone buzzed.

Helen from Top-A. Finally.

"Helen," I said. "Thanks for calling me back."

"They're gone," she said. Her voice was thick with tears.

"Who's gone?"

But of course I already knew the answer.

"Erica and Lupita," she said. "And Ami. They've taken them. And God only knows what they're doing to them."

◆ ◆ ◆

Helen was at the home of Father Thomas, a priest at Our Lady of Guadalupe Church. Ami and Erica and Lupita's church. Helen had gone to Father Thomas with her fears, and he'd urged her to call the police. She'd finally agreed.

Now Bandoni rode with me to the priest's house. I found myself looking in the rearview mirror for Clyde, but the back of the Tahoe was silent and empty. Since I'd heard nothing more from Cohen, I was sure that by now my men were sacked out and snoring.

After my experience outside the medical examiner's office, Bandoni was taking no chances. He verified that the address Helen gave us belonged to Sean Patrick Thomas, and he checked Thomas's DMV photo. Then he called for a patrol unit to meet us at the priest's home and to wait outside while we talked to Helen. Patrolmen Ryson and Olmer were already there when we pulled up.

The man who opened the door to our knocks was ginger haired, with pale freckled skin and a grave expression. He wore black slacks and a black shirt with a clerical collar. As cautious as Bandoni, he checked our IDs before ushering us in.

"Helen is in the basement," he said after he'd locked the door. "Not the most comfortable room in the house, I'm afraid. But it's where she feels safest."

We followed the priest into a hallway and past framed photographs from other countries—images of rural villages set in forests or farmland. Families posed before modest homes or next to donkeys and primitive farm equipment.

"You've been in Latin America, Father?" I asked.

"Many times. El Salvador. Guatemala. Honduras. The Catholic Church is very active there."

Father Thomas opened a door and led the way down a narrow flight of stairs, the wooden steps creaking beneath us. A bare bulb created a patchwork of light and shadow, and the smells of cigarettes and epoxy and the sharp burn of a soldering iron rose to greet us. Faint beneath it all lay the musk of concrete and the recent damp.

"If you're wondering about the smell," Father Thomas said over his shoulder, "my hobby is stained glass."

The stairs ended at a sharp turn to the right, and we followed the priest into a long, paneled room. Two chairs, a sofa, and a coffee table created a seating area. Beyond stood a large work bench covered with colored glass, soldering irons, and tools I couldn't name.

Helen stood in front of one of the chairs, her face white, her hands clenched into fists. She wore the same uniform I'd seen her in before—khaki slacks and a blue polo shirt. Her pale-blue eyes were red and wet. She'd pulled her hair into a loose ponytail; a few strands clung to her damp cheeks.

I introduced Bandoni to Helen, and Thomas gestured for all of us to sit. Bandoni and I took the sofa, his bulk making the springs shriek in protest. He tipped his head toward me in a "go ahead" gesture.

I placed my phone on the table and tapped record.

I began. "Helen, can you—"

Helen overrode me. "You've got to find them."

"Of course. We understand your concern, and we're as anxious as you are to locate the women. But we need you to start at the beginning, so we have a complete picture."

Helen freed her bedraggled ponytail, scraped back her hair, and pulled it through the loop again. She straightened her shoulders. "All of this started with Kurt Inger."

Kurt, she told us, had realized that hiring undocumented women offered benefits to the company. Lower pay, longer hours, an ability to cheat the women out of overtime and sometimes out of entire paychecks.

"Then he realized the biggest benefit of all," she said. "Free sex."

She picked up a pack of cigarettes from the coffee table and shook one out. Father Thomas rose and struck a match for her. She closed her eyes as she puffed. "Thank you, Father."

She turned back to us. "Kurt hung out with a group of like-minded assholes. They called themselves the Superior Gentlemen. Ha. They wouldn't know a gentleman if one walked up and introduced himself." Her pale eyes snapped at me through a cloud of smoke. "That photo you showed us. That's them."

I set the picture of the Superior Gentlemen on the table. "Can you identify them for us?"

"Happy to." She aimed a finger at the men like a gun. "Kurt, of course. Riley Lynch. And Noah Asher, who started the group with Markey Byron. That was before he met Ami. Before she helped set him straight."

"They were in a relationship," I said, curious what Helen would say.

"They were in love. But it was Romeo and Juliet from the start. The girls—Erica and Lupita—they didn't trust Noah. And those assholes"—she gestured again toward the photo with her cigarette—"they were pure poison."

"And the fifth man? Who is he?"

Helen's eyes narrowed. Her free hand rose to her chest, and she rubbed the tips of her fingers against her skin, a self-soothing gesture. "That's Craze."

I leaned in. "Do you know his real name?"

She shook her head.

I held my disappointment. "What do you know about him?"

Helen pulled hard on her cigarette. She held it the way you would hold a joint, pinched between her thumb and forefinger. Her knuckles were red and peeling. Cleaning chemicals and elbow grease.

"He was terrorizing the girls. Erica and Lupita. Ami. Five or six others. Ami was the only one who stood up to him."

I feigned ignorance. "How'd she do that?"

"She went to the cops. And they didn't do shit. Craze, though, when he heard what Ami'd done? He swore he'd kill her. So she and Erica and Lupita moved here. And for a time, things were fine." Her face went tight with fury. "The three of them got jobs cleaning offices. Top-A didn't care about their immigration status. And they liked the work okay. It was a hell of a lot better than processing chickens at ColdShip. Then—"

She sucked on her cigarette and exhaled, waving away the smoke.

"Then what, Helen?"

"Kurt Inger moved from customer service into the management position. He'd always been a creep, forever hitting on Erica and Lupita. Didn't take him long to get the idea the girls should offer 'bonuses' to special clients."

"Meaning what, exactly?"

"Meaning they should provide sexual favors for his friends. Unless they wanted to get reported to ICE. I swear, there's a place in hell for him. And now—" Her eyes went bright with tears, and she blinked them away angrily. "Now he's got Erica and Lupita. And Ami."

"He kidnapped them?"

"Him and Craze and the others." The hand holding the cigarette shook. "I'm sure of it. That was the promise Craze made—that someday those girls would belong to him. I don't know how he got the others to go along with it. Even I didn't realize Kurt was *that* much of an asshole. But he did."

"You're saying the Superior Gentlemen are kidnappers?"

"Kidnappers. Rapists."

"What about murderers?" I said softly.

She blinked at me. "You think they killed Noah Asher?"

"What do you think?"

"Oh, dear God." She pressed the heel of her hand to her forehead. "I don't know. But Noah was the only decent one among them. He never went along once things started getting crazy." She dug into her pants pocket and pulled out a wadded tissue, blew her nose. "I know Erica and Lupita would have called if they were just sick. Something's happened."

"You hear anything about a falling-out between these guys?"

She shook her head.

"Okay," I said. "Let's stick with Craze. Anything else you can tell us about him? Where he lives, any friends?"

"Friends." She snorted. "I know three things for sure. He likes to hurt women. That's one. Sometimes he rides the trains like a hobo.

That's two. And he puts in yellow contacts when he hurts people. You know about that?"

My eyes met Bandoni's. The nursing-home rapes.

I said, "We've heard about the yellow eyes."

"Ami called him a supervillain. Like in the comics." She picked up an ashtray and mashed out her cigarette. "Now, what about my friends? What are you going to do?"

"When did they go missing?"

"Ami's been gone almost a week. We didn't know because she and Noah were going on vacation, a four-day weekend in Vegas. But she didn't show up for work yesterday. Before you came by, we were hoping she and Noah were so happy together she just decided to take an extra day. Call me an optimist."

"What about Erica and Lupita?"

"They disappeared sometime between when we clocked in this morning at seven and when they were supposed to clock out this evening at four." The tears rose again; she furiously dashed them away. "I was afraid to call you because of their undocumented status. I went to Father Thomas, hoping something had scared the girls into asking for asylum."

Bandoni and I looked at Father Thomas, who shook his head. "I haven't seen Erica or Lupita since Sunday mass. I'm as worried as Helen."

I turned back to Helen, who was tapping out another cigarette. "Any idea where the men might have taken them?"

"I figure it's one of the properties we clean. We did a couple of move-out cleanings this month, but I don't know if the places are occupied now. Or maybe they took the girls to one of their homes."

We'd already eliminated that possibility. I pulled out the client list from Kaylee and passed it to Helen. "Here's Top-A's list of clients. Any of these seem like a prospect?"

Helen flipped through the list. "Where's the rest?"

My scalp tightened. "This isn't everything?"

Her laugh was bitter. "You got this from Kaylee, I'm guessing? No offense, but that pretty little airhead needs GPS to find her way home every night. Kurt must have deleted some of the properties. Kaylee would never even notice."

"Why would he do that?" I asked.

"Probably so we can clean the sites off the books, and he can pocket the money. But . . ." Her eyes were heavy. "Having the girls go missing changes everything, doesn't it? One of these places might be where he's got them."

Bandoni hefted his bulk forward. "Which properties are missing?"

"Let me look." Helen went back through the list more slowly. "An office complex near the Four Seasons, for one. We did a move-out cleaning there last month, so it might still be empty. Also a few places down south are missing. Near the tech center. But those are occupied."

Bandoni and I looked at each other. The Four Seasons Hotel was less than half a mile from the pedestrian walkway where the Denver University students were going to march. If the Superior Gentlemen were planning an attack there, then holing up nearby made sense.

"That's enough for me." Bandoni hefted himself to his feet. "Father, you got a place where I can make some calls?"

"Of course." Father Thomas stood. "My study will work."

After the men left, Helen lit another cigarette and fell into silence, her gaze far away.

I thought about Ami.

I imagined her, having been taken prisoner along with Noah, escaping her captors long enough to signal the engineer and leave a shrine for the man she'd loved. A shrine with her necklace of the Virgin.

Or maybe she hadn't escaped. Maybe, knowing she had nowhere to run, the men had let her free long enough to create the shrine. It would have amused them to watch her grief and devotion. But they'd been careful to wipe out the message she'd written in the dirt.

Ami, though, must have hoped the Madonna heard her.

I heard the floorboards creak under the priest's footsteps, heard the muffled growl of Bandoni's voice. He would be talking to the lieutenant—arranging backup and preparing the cavalry. Deciding whether we'd go in sirens wailing or if it would be better to slip in like shadows. If we were lucky, the women were in the offices near the Four Seasons Hotel and we would rescue them and arrest the Superior Gentlemen. If we were really lucky, it would go down without a single shot being fired.

I thought about Noah and Donovan.

We hadn't been very lucky so far.

Helen sighed and leaned back in her chair. Closed her eyes. Smoke drifted lazily up from her cigarette.

Exhaustion rolled over me like a black tide. I recognized the fatigue for what it was—with the case apparently drawing to a close, my mind was loosening its hold on my body, sending a signal that it was okay to relax.

I shook myself out of my stupor. I imagined what Bandoni would say to me: *We ain't done until we've connected all the dots.*

I made sure the recording app was still running, then touched Helen's knee. Her eyes popped open.

"Helen, did Top-A clean Water Resources' original office? I don't see it on Kaylee's list."

She shook off her own fatigue and nodded. "We had the contract for that place for almost two years. It's east of here, near the old Rocky Mountain Arsenal. The owner sold the building, and another business moved in. Erica and I did the final cleaning."

"Water Resources moved out because the building sold?"

She shrugged. "That's not something anyone tells the help. I do know Noah was a hero for finding that place for them downtown—I got that from Ami. But we lost the cleaning contract. The owners of the new place had an agreement with a different cleaning company."

"How did Noah find the place?"

"Through Kurt. Which was odd. We had twice weekly cleanings at the old place—it pulled in a lot of cash. Steady work for Erica and me. But Kurt never said why he told Noah about the new office. He just had us do a final cleaning. We did what we could, but there was still a bunch of crap out there."

"Like what?"

"Junk left by the employees. Old printers. Paper files. Half-dead potted plants. A few months back, Kurt brought in something like fifty of his own cardboard boxes. He made a deal with Water Resources to let him store his stuff in two of their offices."

"Did he have to remove the boxes after the sale?"

She looked thoughtful. "I don't know that he ever did."

My scalp prickled. "What was inside?"

"Cleaning supplies. Kurt said he'd gotten a sweet deal on the inventory from another company that was going out of business."

"So he might have left the boxes there?"

"All I know is they were still there when I turned out the lights and gave Kurt the keys." She lit a third cigarette from her second. Her chapped hands trembled. "You gotta find those girls, Detective Parnell. They're like daughters to me."

We stood on the sidewalk in front of the priest's house. Officers Ryson and Olmer had gone. The wind had eased off, and the nearby houses were dark. Somewhere in the distance a dog barked, answered a moment later by a volley of nearer, higher-pitched barks.

"It's the feebs' case now," Bandoni said. "Domestic terrorism. They own it."

When he broke the news that the takedown was no longer ours, adrenaline had gone shooting through my system like a pinball without an exit. Now, still furious, I smacked the hood of the Tahoe with the flat of my hand.

"Yeah." Bandoni sighed. "I know."

I rubbed my palm. "What is their plan?"

"They're going to send SWAT into that office building. It'll be the fucking apocalypse. And we're going to miss it. Unless you want to go down there and watch from a distance along with Lobowitz and the rest."

"I guess the fucking apocalypse is a good thing."

"Sure. Long as it gets the job done."

Bandoni patted his pockets. Swore. I handed him my cigarettes and lighter, and we lit up together. Bandoni stared off down the street.

"I feel like a fucking appendix," he said.

I got it. My earlier rage had simmered down to a low boil. But I had nowhere to direct my energy.

"I do have one idea," I said.

He glared at me. "Lobowitz said we were to hold off, wait for the Feds to do their thing."

I shrugged. "Okay."

Thirty seconds went by. Bandoni threw his cigarette in the gutter. "Fuck it. What's your idea?"

CHAPTER 26

When a dog has a chance to bite, he will.

—*Len Bandoni. Private conversation.*

"You know how to use the internet?" I asked Bandoni as we headed east on I-70 in a light rain. The wet road flowed like a dark river beneath us.

Bandoni said, "Fuck you."

"I'll take that as a yes. My laptop's under the passenger seat. Why don't you—"

"See what I can learn about the company that bought the building near the Rocky Mountain Arsenal? Because we'll need the owner to let us in? Is that what you're thinking?"

"Sorry."

He grunted as he pulled out the computer. "Always a good day when the grasshopper tries to tell the master how to do his job."

I shot him a quick look. He was already tapping like a madman. A few minutes later he was on the phone, talking to the owner.

"Yeah, it's an emergency," he said. "You think I fucking want to poke around a goddamn office building in the middle of the night?" Pause. "No shit?" Another pause. "That's right. See you soon."

He hung up.

"Did you really just talk to a member of the public like that?" I said.

"That wasn't a member of the public. That was Lloyd."

"Lloyd."

"Lloyd Shumacher. A long time ago, he was one of us. Financial crimes. Then his wife's parents left them a shitload of money, and he went into real estate. He's like a fucking tycoon now, owns buildings all up and down the Front Range." He scowled. "Could have been me."

"How's that?"

"Lloyd offered to cut me in. But I was too busy trying to save the world."

"You're still trying to save the world."

"For all the good it's doing. We're chasing fucking snipe. *Maybe* boxes and *maybe* crap left in offices. What's that going to give us? A chance to write in our reports that we kicked over every rock. Detectives of Paper. Masters of Forms. Meantime, the feebs are the heroes."

"Maybe we'll get lucky and the whole place will be crawling with mass murderers."

"I haven't had that kind of luck in years."

"And anyway, is that really what matters to you?" I said. "Being the hero?"

He laid his eyes on me. His gaze was heavy. "Word is, that's your job, jarhead."

I heard the bite of steel in his voice and was surprised at the sudden burn of tears behind my eyes. Denver newspapers had made me into something I wasn't. A hero. A golden girl. A woman who—according to the media—rose from nothing to rescue men, women, and children and single-handedly save the world.

"Screw that," I said.

A streetlight shot a flare of gold into the cab, then left it in darkness as we drove on.

"Don't diss it," Bandoni said. "You got legacy, rookie."

"So do you."

He barked a laugh that turned into a smoker's cough, deep and harsh. When he could talk again, he said, "A legacy's only good if you leave before the shine comes off. I'm like one of those beat-up old lions.

311

Scarred and toothless. Worthless in a fight. But too stupid to crawl off into the savanna and die."

"That's not what—"

"Fuck it." Bandoni cut me off. "Let's move on. Lloyd says our address is three stories, but only the first floor is rented out. He lives close by, so he'll meet us there." He stowed the laptop. "I'm starting to feel better. This whole thing feels hinky. I'll bet my pink, puckered ass that if those boxes are still around, they ain't filled with cleaning supplies."

"That's an ugly visual," I said. But I was thinking, *You go, partner.*

He pulled his gun, checked it. "Anything looks weird, we call in backup. No cowboying."

"Stay strictly inside the lines."

"Like this is a coloring book and we're the crayons." He rapped the window with his knuckles. "Why don't you call lover boy? Tell him to meet us out there with Fido. Might be evidence he can sniff out."

I was all in on that, assuming Clyde felt better. I dialed Cohen. No answer. I ignored the uneasy feeling in my gut, left a message with the address, and disconnected. They were fine. Everything was fine.

"And when we see him," Bandoni said, "you're gonna tell him all about the Barbie doll and the rape kits. Because the only kind of partnership worth having is an honest one."

"Okay," I said. "Partner."

"Damn straight."

We drove on in the rain, the tires hissing beneath us and the wet turning the world into a wash of gray and black.

GPS directed us north off I-70 and onto a two-lane blacktop. We passed turnoffs for residential areas. Then a fast-food joint, a tire store, and a gas station where a woman stood hunch-shouldered by a car with New

Jersey plates and more rust than metal. I hit the gas, and the lights dropped away as we rolled into darkness—open fields on both sides. Rain glimmered in the headlights, falling harder now.

Two miles farther on, the Tahoe's lights caught a sign, DENVER EAST OFFICE PARK. I turned onto a private road and drove up a low, grassy hill and down the other side. A parking lot with a single streetlight appeared through the rain-streaked glass.

Bandoni pointed. "There he is. Bastard's got a Cadillac Escalade. Turn here."

I pulled into the otherwise empty lot and parked near a red SUV with vanity plates—OFICE4U. No one was inside.

I killed the engine.

Ahead rose a 70s-style, tan-brick building with windows on the top two floors and a main entrance approached by a covered walkway. An illuminated sign in front read TYRELL INDUSTRIES, the words fractured in the downpour. Landscaping consisted of a row of evergreen trees along the walk and encircling the building's lower floor.

"There's Lloyd." Bandoni opened his door.

A fit-looking man in his midfifties wearing jeans and a navy-blue polar-fleece jacket stood just inside the door. He waved.

"Guy looks good," Bandoni said. "Fucking real estate. The hell was I thinking?"

He got out and slammed the door.

I hesitated for just a second. Then I pulled my lock-picking kit from my pocket and replaced it with a couple of ammo magazines.

I got out. The rain was shifting to sleet; silver pellets dive-bombed the asphalt. The ammo mags slapped against my hip.

Bandoni stood on the walkway. "You coming?"

I pulled up my hood and ran after him, my pumps skidding on the slick concrete.

Lloyd pushed the door open and called Bandoni's name. As soon as we were inside, he grabbed my partner's hand and shook it vigorously.

"Damn good to see you, Len," he said. "But you look like shit."

"What I get, serving the public. How the hell are you, Lloyd?"

"Good. Great." He eyeballed Bandoni's gut, then looked at me. "He still eat like he's hoping for a heart attack?"

"Total garbage disposal." I dried my hands on my slacks and held out my right. "I'm Sydney Parnell."

"Pleasure." Lloyd's handshake was warm and firm.

Bandoni said, "The rookie's so new she don't even know how to find the can yet."

Lloyd slapped his hand to his heart in mock horror. "And they stuck her with you?"

"Nothing like learning from the master."

Lloyd grinned at me. "Bet he's got you going through the paces."

"Like being on a treadmill," I said.

"Well, Len's the best. He'll get you up and running in no time." He stepped back. "Now, what is it you guys want to look at?"

"A couple of things," Bandoni said. "We want to rifle through anything left by Water Resources. We heard there were cardboard boxes stored in two of their offices. We need to take a look."

"Hmm." Lloyd's brow wrinkled. "I don't recall any boxes. But then, I haven't been in the building in months."

"When did the new guys move in?"

"Oh, they're not here yet." He locked the front door and pocketed the keys, and we walked with him into the lobby. "Not until April. Tax day, actually."

I said, "Really?" as a faint unease trickled into my stomach.

Bandoni had a handkerchief out and was drying his face. "The building's been empty since Water Resources moved out?"

"Almost a month now."

"And you haven't had any issues?"

Lloyd came to a stop in the middle of the lobby, his gaze on Bandoni quizzical. "I've never had any trouble with this building. I get good renters, and it's a quiet neighborhood. Bit off the beaten track. But." He frowned and stuffed his hands in his pockets. "I guess you never get over being a cop."

Bandoni tucked the handkerchief away. "Which translates to what, exactly?"

"Since the place has been empty, I've had one of my security guys come by a couple of times a week. Walk the property. Rattle the doors."

"Nothing ever caught his attention? Cars that shouldn't be here? People?"

"Nope." The frown had reached his eyes. "What kind of trouble you expecting to find?"

"None." Bandoni sighed. "We're just pounding the pavement, crossing some t's for the reports."

"Ah," Lloyd said. "Thanks for reminding me why I quit."

"You quit 'cause your wife's parents dumped untold millions in your lap."

The frown vanished. "Well, there is that."

"So now that I feel like shit, let's get back to business. You're telling me no one has moved in since Water Resources moved out."

"Right."

"They ask you to hold on to anything?"

"Nope."

"Which means everything in the building can be considered abandoned."

Lloyd spread his hands. "I can sign a consent-to-search form if you want, but as far as I'm concerned, anything you want, you can have." He laughed. "Of course, I'd rather you left the furniture."

"I'll send the movers home." He scraped a palm over his chin. "Where did Water Resources have their offices?"

"Third floor. They wanted the view." He pointed down a hallway. "Elevator's down there. When you exit on the third floor, take a right, and go all the way to the end."

"You're not going to hold our hands?"

"With the likes of you? I'm going to hang out here and make phone calls."

"Big-shot Realtor, huh?"

"You know it." He rocked back on his heels and tapped Bandoni's belly. "Sure you wouldn't rather take the stairs?"

"You always were an asshole," Bandoni said.

On the third floor, the elevator opened on to velvet darkness. I used the flashlight on my phone to find the light switch, and fluorescent bulbs hummed to life. A long, windowless hallway came into view. Following Lloyd's directions, we turned right, opening doors as we went. Bathrooms. A janitor's closet. Two conference rooms.

A door at the end of the hall opened on to a large space divided into cubicles by soft-sided partitions. We walked through the area, noting metal desks and empty filing cabinets that probably didn't fit in with Water Resources' upscale digs downtown. The desks held scattered paper clips and thumbtacks, rubber bands, and pencils worn down to nubs.

Some of the cubicles still had name plates on them. I found Noah's office near a window.

A metal desk. Filing cabinet. I went through the drawers. Paper clips and thumbtacks and an entire box of mechanical pencils. I dropped to the floor and peered under the desk.

A piece of paper. I stretched out my hand and caught it with the tips of my fingers. I stood and set the paper on the desk.

It was a photo of Noah and Ami in front of a pavilion in the Denver Botanical Gardens. A foot of snow lay on the ground, and Noah and Ami wore bulky coats and knit hats. They were facing into the sun, their faces bright and happy.

Noah had his arm around Ami.

For a moment, they'd had a future.

I slid the photo inside my coat and went to find Bandoni.

He'd gone back into the hallway and was on the phone. When he hung up, he said, "SWAT has cleared the building near the Four Seasons. Nothing. But a security cop found a dark-blue cargo van with a bull bar on the front parked in a garage near Fourteenth Street. Belongs to one Kurt Inger. The Feds aren't taking any chances. They've set up a perimeter, deployed snipers, and got plainclothes special agents on patrol along the pedestrian walkway. Soon as our douchebags pop out of hiding, they'll nail 'em."

"I'm still excited about hunting for cardboard boxes. Aren't you?"

"Beats hemorrhoids." He heaved a sigh and put his phone away. "Let's keep looking."

We walked through the rest of the third floor but found nothing of interest.

Back at the elevator, the lights above the door showed that the elevator was stopped in the basement. I pressed the call button.

Bandoni said, "Second floor next?"

"Got nothing better to do."

"Thanks for the reminder."

The elevator was still in the basement. I pressed the call button again.

"Maybe Lloyd started moving things out from down there," Bandoni said. He put his phone to his ear.

I slipped my hands in my pockets, stared at the lights over the elevator, waiting for them to change. I wondered if I should call Cohen and tell him not to bother coming out.

My idle gaze caught on a mark on the wall just to the right of the elevator door near the call button. A hooked line inside an upside-down triangle, drawn with black marker. A casual mark, of no consequence.

Unless you'd seen it before.

A shepherd's crook. The Phoenician letter *P*.

Adrenaline exploded into my blood like an electrical current hitting water.

The Superior Gentlemen might be hiding somewhere near Denver's Lower Downtown, waiting for the start of the student march. The discovery of Kurt's van just about guaranteed it.

But the women were here, in this empty building, where no one would find them. Where, I shuddered, no one would hear their screams.

"Lloyd ain't answering," Bandoni said. He pressed the call button.

"Ami," I whispered and pointed to the mark. "She's in this building."

"What are you talking about?"

The lights went out.

CHAPTER 27

"What makes a real hero? You're asking my opinion?" Gunny leaned back with his cigar. "A real hero knows when he's finished. When his sanity's gone MIA and his body won't do what needs doing and he's hanging on by a thread that's seriously unraveling. A real hero knows when to walk away and make room for someone whose balls are still swinging free. 'Cause here's the deal." Gunny leaned forward and stabbed the cigar in my direction. "Walk away at the right time, and you might have a chance of coming back."

—Gunnery Sergeant O'Rourke, Habbaniyah, Iraq.
Private conversation.

"Fuck," Bandoni said.

Above the elevator, the emergency lights shone. The *B* glowed a steady red.

I said, "Bandoni, look."

I used the flashlight on my phone again and shone it at the mark on the wall.

He grunted. "Noah's tattoo."

"And the symbol on Ami's shirt. What if they're holding the women here?"

"Wouldn't it be more straightforward to figure Ami drew it when she cleaned the place for Top-A?"

"Helen said she and Erica always cleaned this office. Not Ami." Adrenaline made my head light. "That's why Kurt told Noah about the new office space for Water Resources, even though it cost him a cleaning contract. It was so the Superior Gentlemen could move in *here*, away from prying eyes."

My light caught Bandoni's angry, startled face.

"Okay, good thought," he said. "Let's find Lloyd, and then we'll figure out the rest of it."

I gave the call button a final furious stab. "We'll have to take the stairs."

Bandoni groaned. "My lucky day."

We started down, our shoes squeaking on the tile, the light from my phone tossing our shadows against the wall.

Behind me, Bandoni's breath rasped in and out like a bellows. Even with the help of gravity, he was moving slowly. As we approached the second-floor landing, he lost his footing. I spun around fast, but he'd caught himself, both hands white-knuckling the railing. Sweat glistened on his red face.

I climbed back to him. He had a hand pressed to his chest.

"Is it your heart?" I said.

"Indigestion."

"Let's rest for a minute."

Another labored breath. "If you insist." His suit rustled as he sank to the steps, and then he groaned. "Shine your light over here."

He had a tiny bottle in his hand—brown glass with a blue screw cap. He opened it and shook out a miniscule white pill, which he placed under his tongue.

"What is that?" I asked.

"Nitroglycerine."

"For your heart? Jesus, Bandoni. When were you going to tell me?"

"Now."

"I'm calling an ambulance."

He held up a finger. Seconds ticked by. Then he said, "Here's the plan. In about five minutes, I'm going to feel like a new man. As soon as I do, we're going to get down these stairs and find Lloyd. Then we'll look for the women."

"Then you *do* think they're here."

"It's as good a guess as any. What I can't figure out is why Lloyd—" He groaned. "Why he didn't answer his phone. Maybe *he's* having a heart attack."

"Is that what's happening with you?"

"No. It's angina. Had it for years."

For a minute, the only sound I heard was my blood, roaring in my ears.

"They'd have the women in the basement, right?" I said. "No windows. Controlled entrance and egress."

"Yeah."

"So why is the elevator stuck down there?"

Bandoni said nothing.

"And what about the lights?" I added.

"What *about* the lights?"

"What if Craze and Markey and the rest aren't hiding near Lower Downtown? What if they're here?"

"Then, rookie." He grunted. "We'll get to be the heroes."

Another minute went by.

"I swear." His voice was hoarse. "I'm never going to *look* at a Ding Dong again."

"Scared straight?"

"For the moment. Shine the light again?"

He had the bottle out. "Sometimes it takes a couple."

But I'd had enough. I tapped the phone app to call for backup and an ambulance but couldn't get a signal. I stood and held the phone higher. Nothing. Panic flashed and then disappeared. It was the stairwell. I just needed to get to a different place.

"Bandoni." I sat back next to him. "I can't get a signal in here. Probably the walls are too thick. I'm going to the first floor, and I'll call for backup from there."

I didn't mention the ambulance.

"Just give me another five minutes," he said.

"I'll be back in half that." I offered him two of my four ammo magazines. He took one of them. I said, "Two minutes. Don't you fucking die on me."

"Furthest thing," he gasped, "from my mind."

◆ ◆ ◆

I slipped off my shoes and went down the remaining stairs fast and silent. Just before the last turn and the final set of steps, I stopped and shone the light around the corner.

The bottom of the stairwell was empty. Straight ahead were two doors at right angles to each other and maybe ten feet apart. One presumably to the basement, the other marked FIRST FLOOR.

A narrow passage on the right led to the space beneath the stairs. A perfect place for an ambush.

But the stairs blocked most of my view.

I turned off the light, pulled my gun, and toed my way down each step in the inky dark. At the bottom, I stopped and listened. Silence. I spun around and, with my gun aimed at the shadows under the stairs, walked backward toward the door that led to the first floor. Beneath my stockinged feet, the floor turned suddenly wet and sticky, and the rusty-nail stink of blood hit my nostrils.

Lloyd.

They were here. The Superior Gentlemen.

I kept walking, feeling my way in a dark so thick I couldn't see my gun. The skin between my shoulders was cold and tight; I expected to feel a bullet punch through flesh and bone at any second.

Or maybe it would be Craze's knife.

When I bumped up against the door, I felt behind me for the knob. It wouldn't turn. I jiggled it. Pulled. Tried turning it the other way. No go.

I paused for three heartbeats, contemplating a run back up the stairs, to Bandoni, and then beyond, to the third floor where I should be able to get a signal. I sure as hell wasn't going into that basement without an M4 carbine and a platoon of Marines.

And whatever they'd done to Lloyd, I suspected he was beyond my help.

I'd taken two steps toward the stairs when the lights came back on, irradiating the stairwell, bathing everything in harsh, blinding brilliance.

In front of me, the floor was streaked with thick lines of blood, now smeared where I'd walked through it.

Go, I told myself. *Look under the stairs. Maybe he's alive.*

And another thought. *Maybe he's not alone.*

My left hand spasmed, a reflective reaching for Clyde. And then a matching spasm of my heart for Cohen and Clyde and what they might walk into if I didn't find the killers first.

Assuming Clyde was okay. And that Cohen had gotten my message.

I crept along the passageway toward the space beneath the stairs. Just before the gap, I gripped my pistol hard to stop the shakes, drew in a breath, and pivoted.

Kurt Inger stared at me from out of the shadows.

A shotgun blast had destroyed the Top-A supervisor's chest. Drops of red patterned his chin and cheeks. His hands lay clasped in his lap, as if in his last moments, he'd begged his onetime friends for his life.

Next to him lay Lloyd, tossed on his back like garbage, his throat cut ear to ear.

Fury rose in a black wave that swamped my heart and roared like a flood in my ears. Shaking with rage, I spun back toward the stairwell, my gun up, finger on the trigger.

I wanted, with a fierce, savage rage, to kill something.

Don't get mad, Corporal, the Sir whispered in my mind. *Get even.*

I nodded and sucked in air. Waited for the black tide to wash away. A faint sound reached my ears. For the briefest second I thought it was the wind—that the storm had gotten strong enough to penetrate the building's thick walls. Then I realized it was the sound of a woman. Weeping.

The basement door opened.

Lupita—small, fragile Lupita—stood in the doorway. Shudders shook her body. Her wild and terrified eyes found mine, and her lips formed a word. *¡Ayúdame!*

Help me!

A form appeared behind her. A man with pale skin and soft, brown hair that flopped over his forehead above his one visible eye. He wrapped an arm tight around Lupita's throat and dug his fingers into her shoulder. In his other hand he held a knife.

Markey Byron.

"Drop your gun, Sydney," he said. "Or I kill the bitch."

His steel-edged voice contained nothing of the boy-man I'd met at the comics store. Nothing soft or uncertain. Markey Byron wasn't cherub or lap dog or frustrated artist.

He was ice.

I kept my gun up. "Fuck you, Markey."

His shoulders moved as his hand dropped and did something behind Lupita.

She screamed.

"You don't want to make me angry," he said. "Every time I'm upset, I take a little more of her flesh."

Lupita sobbed. *"Por favor, no, por favor, no."*

"I'm a cop, Markey. I can't put down my weapon. It's against—" Lupita shrieked.

"But," I said, "maybe we can make a deal."

Markey's knife reappeared, blood shimmering on its length, and he smiled.

"That's better. Here's the deal. You put down your gun and come with me, and this little bitch goes free. And who knows? Play nice, and I might even spare your fat fuck of a partner."

I wondered if Bandoni was already dead.

Markey raised his voice. "You hear that, you old, fat fuck? Or has Craze already cut your throat, too?" His eyes were hot on me. "We listened to the two of you coming down. Denver's finest. What a joke."

Think about Bandoni later, I told myself. *Keep this one talking.*

"Why'd you kill Kurt?" I said. "I thought he was one of you."

"Kurt lacked vision. Just like Noah and Riley. I thought at first they were prophets, that they'd help us bring in a new world order. But it turned out they were worms." His voice thickened with hate. "Just like every other pathetic soul walking this planet."

"The Feds found the van, Markey. They know about you and Craze. It's over."

He snugged Lupita closer and sneered.

"The van was just a decoy. And it worked, didn't it? Let me guess— the Feds are swarming all over downtown Denver. And they have no idea you're here. By the time anyone comes looking, we'll be long gone."

I kept the Glock high, looking for a gap between Markey and Lupita, a wedge of skin where a bullet could slide in without hitting her. But while Markey was a cold-blooded asshole, he wasn't a stupid one. He kept himself well covered. Taking a shot was too risky.

For the moment.

I said, "Let her go, Markey. You don't want your father thinking he was right about you. That you're the bad son. Show him that you're better than that. Better than he is."

The knife vanished, and Lupita shrieked. The shriek rose and rose until I wanted to slap my hands over my ears and run. Then it sank into a deep bubbling moan that made me think Markey was cutting out one of Lupita's lungs.

She sagged, and he shook her. "Don't you fall, bitch."

Drops of blood spattered the floor at her feet.

He looked at me. "Bad idea, talking about my father."

"Okay, okay." I made my voice soft and shaky. It didn't require a lot of acting. "Don't hurt her."

"I *am* the bad son. I'm the monster he created. And now that he knows what I am, he'll have to live with that knowledge forever. The blood on my hands is on his, too."

"I understand your anger, Markey." *Keep him talking.* "But why hurt Noah? He was your friend."

"Noah betrayed me. He and that bitch. *He* got the girl. Then he tried to take away *my* girl. Erica belongs to me."

I nodded, going along. "She's here, isn't she? Waiting for you."

"She can't get enough of me. But who wants chopped beef when there's filet mignon on the menu? You're so beautiful, Sydney Rose. And so strong. You think you don't need a man. But that's exactly what you need. We'll make you see that."

Fury and revulsion tore through me like a double tap to my chest. I rode it out, kept my voice calm. "Then let's talk about that deal. You let Erica and Lupita go, and I'll stay."

"Do you remember that night at the Seven Grand?" Markey plowed on. "I bought you scotch, an *expensive* scotch. Had it sent to your table. And you told the bartender thanks, but no thanks. Forty-two dollars a glass, and you turned it down. I thought maybe when you came into the comics store, you'd remember me. I was even a little worried. But pretty damn fast I realized that to you, I was just another loser. Just some sad, sorry asshole not worth your time. You didn't even fucking remember me."

"I just—" I groped for words, trying to remember someone sending me a drink at the Seven Grand. "I didn't know it was from you."

"And then. Then!" He sniggered. "You rejected Craze. Bad move, bitch. Nobody rejects Craze. Ask those old ladies in the nursing homes. You think you're too good for us. So far above what we can hope for. Well, pretty soon you'll be beneath us. *Right* beneath us. First me. Then Craze. We'll see how you like that. Payback is hell, bitch."

I edged ever so slightly to the right, still looking for an opening.

"Don't move!" he shouted.

I froze.

"We've been watching you for a long time, Sydney Rose. We know everything about you. All about your fuckboy and your dog. We know about your grandmother and your weak, stupid cousin and how you take flowers to your mom's grave."

A lake of ice filled my stomach. I wrapped my fingers more tightly around the gun, as if it were an anchor that would keep me from drifting away.

Markey went on.

"We know what kind of cereal you like. We know about the old Marine T-shirts you wear to bed and what your tits look like and that your fuckboy reads to you at night like you're a little girl."

I said, "You son of a bitch."

"We have a special room prepared for you. A very special room. I'll take you there myself. And just an FYI. If you think your fuckboy and the dog are coming to save you, well, flush that thought. Your little doggy's not feeling too well tonight, is he? That's because I left a treat for him outside your house."

I ignored how the ice tried to reach into my legs. *Don't think about Clyde. Clyde's okay.* I risked another slight shuffle to my right, looking for a better angle.

Markey adjusted Lupita, his human shield.

Get him angry, I thought. *Force him to make a mistake so you can take the shot.*

"You know your problem, Markey?" I said. "You *are* a sad, sorry loser. You think you can win a woman just by sending over an expensive drink. And she's so shallow that a little flash of cash will make her spread her legs. But women can sniff out creeps, Markey. We can smell them a mile off. You'll never get what you want."

"Shut up!"

"Your father and God let you down, isn't that right? Neither of them gave you what you needed, the looks and charisma to seduce women. Erica doesn't belong to you. You had to force yourself on her. You're a rapist, just like Craze."

Beads of sweat popped out on Markey's forehead. "Shut. Up!"

In his rage, he loosened his hold on Lupita. His left ear and cheek popped into view. I sighted.

But then Lupita thrashed, and he jerked her close again. The gun was turning slick in my sweaty hands. Maybe I should try for his eye. And pray.

No. Better to get Lupita away from him. Get a clear shot.

In Spanish, I said, "Lupita, when I tell you, bite his arm as hard as you can. He'll let go. Then run."

"No!" Markey yelled. The patch of his forehead that I could see was red with rage. The single eye bulged. "Stop! What are you saying to her?"

"I'm telling her to stay calm. I've told her that she and I will trade places, and she'll be free. You win, Markey." To Lupita, I said, *"¿Lo entiendes?" Do you understand?*

Lupita's eyes were on me now. Focused. She gave the slightest dip with her chin.

But Markey tightened his hold on her neck. The veins in his forearm popped as he pressed her throat, the force lifting her off her feet.

Her eyes bulged, and her feet kicked as she fought for air. Any more pressure and he would crush her larynx.

"Drop your gun *now*," he said, "and kick it over here."

The moment of truth.

Shit.

His wolfish laugh rang off the walls.

Then a gunshot boomed from up the stairs, and a bullet whined off the wall near Markey.

He jerked at the sound.

I screamed, *"¡Ahora!"* and Lupita sank her teeth into his arm and broke free.

Markey surged into the stairwell, stepping clear of the door. I could see him plainly now, dressed in black tactical clothes, one hand clenched around a large knife, the other reaching to swing around an AR-15 on a sling. The insanity in his eyes glowed like flames.

I raised my gun. But then Lupita was running straight for me, her body blocking my aim.

He'll kill her, I thought. *Then me.*

Lupita reached me, threw her arms around my body.

Another boom from the top of the stairs. The round caught Markey in the gut.

And then another. *Boom!*

Markey's forehead exploded. He took a single step back and sank to the ground, as if he were making himself comfortable. His remaining eye looked soft and surprised.

Bandoni came down the steps. He stopped at the bottom and stared at Markey's corpse.

"They killed Lloyd," I said.

He glanced over at me, then back at Markey. He toed the body so that it tipped over and sprawled in the blood pouring onto the floor.

"Good riddance," Bandoni said. "Courtesy of the old, fat fuck."

CHAPTER 28

When some of us look inside ourselves, we find a whole lot of ugly.

—*Sydney Parnell. Personal journal.*

Death metal music began to blast from the basement. Low-tuned guitars, distorted drumming. Vocals that sounded like the devil quarreling with himself.

Craze, I figured. Putting out the welcome mat.

Bandoni sat on the bottom stair, gun up, watching the open door to the basement with the demeanor of a hawk hunting roadkill—disgust and anticipation pulling his heavy features into half-lidded predation.

"There's a wide hall in the basement with twelve rooms," Lupita told us, her voice raw and hoarse, her throat bruised. "Six to the left of the door and six to the right. But there might be more. They kept us locked away, so I didn't see everything."

She and I sat on the floor near the stairs. She was shivering. Markey had carved long lines into her back, and her dress clung to the wounds.

I shrugged out of my coat, removed the extra ammo mags from the pocket, and settled the coat over Lupita's shoulders.

I slid the mags into the pocket of my suit coat.

"Where are the women?" I asked.

"Sometimes they keep us together in a room at the far end, on the right. But usually we are held apart. He will kill them now, you know.

If you don't hurry." She pulled on the coat, cried out as it brushed across her injuries.

"What about weapons?"

"I saw them with guns. But Craze . . ." She shuddered. "He prefers the knife."

I looked over at my partner, who nodded to indicate he was listening.

I turned back to Lupita. "What kind of guns?"

"I don't know."

"Small ones?" I asked. "Like mine?"

"Yes. But also big guns. Long ones. Like that one." She tipped her head toward the AR-15.

"Okay." I stood and helped Lupita to her feet. "You ready?"

She took a shuddering breath, coughed. Straightened her shoulders. "I'm ready."

I led her over to the stairs and watched her hobble up. With her right hand, she gripped the railing. In her left, she held my phone.

At the turn in the stairs, she looked back at us, her face pale, her eyes as large as plates in her small face. She gave me a thumbs-up and disappeared around the corner.

She was heading for the third floor, where she should be able to get a signal. She'd dial 911 first. Then Cohen.

Bandoni sighed and made as if to stand before thinking better of it. His face had gone from red to gray, and a hollowness had found its way into his cheeks.

"You aren't exactly a new man," I said.

"Close enough."

"You didn't see Craze up there?"

"Nah. That was more of Markey's bullshit. If that dickwad had shown his face, I would have removed it. He's in the basement. Like any good troll."

I turned toward the open door where the light flickered and danced.

I blinked.

Blinked again.

The light shone steadily.

The Sir shimmered into existence beside me.

Don't lose your nerve, he said over the sound of death metal.

"No." I bent and picked up Markey's rifle. It was a dangerous weapon to use when clearing a space because it was all but worthless in close quarters. I walked over to the gap under the stairs where the killers had stashed Lloyd and Kurt and hid the gun behind their bodies. Then I went back to Bandoni.

I offered him my hand. "You ready?"

To my surprise, he grasped it, let me pull him up.

"Thought you'd never ask," he said.

A flight of steps ended in a T-intersection that split off to the left and the right.

We stood at the top of the stairs, just outside the door. With the music throbbing below our feet, Bandoni leaned close and yelled into my ear.

"When we hit the bottom step, we go right. I'll take lead. We'll clear any unlocked rooms on our right, then come back down the left side. Keep checking your six. If we find the women, we don't stop. Understand? If we find Craze, shoot first, ask questions later. Center of mass, rookie. 'Course, they probably taught you that in the corps."

"Every Marine a rifleman."

Bandoni snorted. "Ooh rah. We'll take it slow and deliberate, make sure we've cleared each unlocked room before we move on. Craze will probably want to play jack-in-the-box, so keep your head on a swivel." He looked me in the eyes, then leaned back in. "You got it?"

I nodded while the music screeched about violent death.

"Craze might have company. You see anything with a dick, shoot it." He frowned. "Present company excluded."

Again, I nodded.

My mind was slipping into the zone, shutting down the parts of my brain that were trying to tell me that going into the basement after Craze was the dumbest fucking thing I'd ever done.

"Eyes in the back of your head," Bandoni said and pivoted into the doorway, his gun aimed down the stairs. He hit the first step and kept going. I stayed close behind. At the bottom, he cleared the immediate area and turned right.

I tucked in my elbows, Glock at the ready, and followed.

A wide concrete hallway stretched before us, maybe thirty yards long, with closed doors on both sides. The space was dimly lit by overhead fluorescents, half of which were dead.

Other than the doors, the hall was empty. Featureless. Benign.

Beneath our feet, the floor thrummed with the music. My bones vibrated.

We reached the first door. No hinges were visible, which meant it opened inward. Bandoni crossed to the far side and nodded. I put my hand on the knob, tested it.

Locked.

We moved on, hugging the wall, continuously scanning the doors, waiting for one to pop open so that Craze could take aim while we stood like targets against the wall.

But Craze, Lupita had said. *He prefers the knife.*

We could hope.

My heart thumped with the music, and my mouth was so dry that swallowing felt like eating sand. But a calm had descended, a form of detachment I'd adopted in Iraq where the choice was to either suck up the fear or run wailing into the wilderness.

Craze had dragged us into war. But war was what I understood.

Bring it on, motherfucker.

We reached the next door. Again, Bandoni crossed to the far side, and I grasped the knob. When it turned, I pushed on the door with enough force to open it wide.

Inside was Riley Lynch.

One glance told us he was dead.

We cleared the room. Then we turned back to Riley.

Noah's high school friend was naked, tied hand and foot to a high-backed wooden chair. His head was propped upright by a knife embedded in his throat, his expression the kind you saw only on the faces of those whose last minutes on earth had been a nightmare.

I ignored the fracture in my heart, and we exited the room.

The next door was locked. This was the room where Lupita said they sometimes kept the women. But if Erica and Ami were inside, we couldn't hear them over the music.

We moved on.

The hallway ended at a concrete wall on which hung the remnants of a workplace safety poster.

WORK SAFE! 0 DAYS ACCIDENT-FREE!

The zero had been written in by hand.

We started down the other side.

Bandoni had slowed. Sweat darkened the back of his skull, and the hollows in his cheeks had turned into canyons. I got the sense the only thing holding him up was willpower.

Don't die on me, partner.

The next door opened on to living quarters. Six bunk beds. A television. A tiny kitchenette with refrigerator and stove. There were clothes on the floor, an overflowing trashcan, and the remains of a meal on the table. A pegboard next to the door was meant for keys, but it was empty.

We slipped back into the hall.

The door of the next room was covered with Markey's pornographic art. Women doing things to men that only certain kinds of men dreamed about.

I opened the door. Bandoni pivoted into the well-named fatal funnel of the doorway, and we cleared the space.

The dimly lit room held a bed, a crude toilet, and a chair.

And a woman, curled in a fetal position on the sheets. She had long, dark hair, dark eyes, and an expression that had once been fierce.

Aminta Valle.

Ami.

I closed the door. Bandoni frowned at me, but then he collapsed into the chair and fumbled in his breast pocket for the nitro.

"Five minutes," he said.

I turned to Ami and said her name.

She gazed past me with dull, flattened eyes. Her face was mottled with bruises. A crust of old blood ran from her swollen left eye to her ear. She wore a filthy blue bathrobe, and her hair was tangled and dirty. Her fingernails still bore traces of long-ago pink polish. A leftover from better days, when those things would have mattered to her.

"I'm Detective Parnell," I told her. "And that's Detective Bandoni. We're here to get you out."

She didn't move. Didn't so much as blink.

"I saw the mark you left upstairs. The letter *P*. Protector. You were so smart to write it on the wall."

No response.

My eyes went again to the chipped nail polish. Strange how something so innocent, so everyday, could feel like a knife to the heart.

I said, "I have something for you."

I pulled out the photo I'd found of her and Noah and held it in front of her eyes. She made a dry, clicking noise in her throat. I longed again for Clyde, who might have gotten through to her in a way another person couldn't. Ami needed a hell of a lot more than dog therapy. But it might be a start.

I reached out a hand to touch her hair, but she flinched.

I lowered my hand. "We can't stay. But we'll come back for you."

A tiny crease appeared between her eyes. She made the clicking sound again.

"It's going to be okay," I promised. Like it was something she could take to the bank. Like that and a bottle of pink nail polish would erase everything that had happened in this room.

I placed the picture on the bed next to her and turned to my partner.

He looked like he needed a hell of a lot more than five minutes to recover. But he nodded and heaved himself to his feet, and we returned to the door.

Don't think about Ami now. Don't worry about Bandoni.

Keep moving.

My hands were shaking when I reached out to open the door. Ami's presence had destroyed my warrior calm. I took a deep breath.

Cool. Detached. You are a machine.

Bandoni and I stood to the right of the doorway. I raised my gun and opened the door. Pivoted into the fatal funnel. I intended to step quickly out into the hall and move to the right so that Bandoni could follow.

Instead, a red-hot spear slid into my left thigh just above my knee.

I screamed as my leg folded under me and I tipped forward, out into the hall. The walls turned sideways. I clung to my gun as I scrabbled to push myself up.

The walls stayed sideways.

Bandoni stood where I'd been only a second ago, leaning out through the doorway, firing wildly and shouting at me to get back in the room.

Words bubbled up from my Marine days.

To protect your fellow Marine, lay down repeated rounds of suppressive fire so that the enemy cannot fire without risking mortal injury.

Good old Bandoni. Laying down suppressive fire.

Only it didn't work.

Another hot spear sliced along my right shoulder, and the Glock dropped from my hands.

It seemed important that I tell Bandoni to leave me. To get back into the room with Ami. To hide there until help came. But when I opened my mouth, the only thing that came out was a moan.

Bandoni grunted. My eyes fastened on him as he fell back into Ami's room in a spray of red.

Something grabbed me by my right arm, yanking it, and I shouted with the pain. The walls righted themselves, but now they sailed past as I bumped and bounced along the floor, my leg and shoulder on fire, my head smacking concrete, my blood leaving a bright-red smear on the dark cement.

A gunshot echoed, and the grip relaxed its hold. I shook myself free, scrabbled onto all fours, and skitter-crawled into the nearest room.

I rolled onto my back and kicked the door closed with my good leg. It must have locked automatically, for a second later the doorknob rattled, and then the entire door shook when something slammed against it.

Not something.

Someone.

I dragged myself to the side of the door and fell against the wall.

The music screeched and growled as fire rolled from my shoulder and my leg and began to eat its way along my bones, devouring flesh. A deep, black sinkhole opened in front of me, and I felt myself tip forward, falling toward the blackness.

I moved my leg, and the pain jerked me back to consciousness.

I leaned my head back against the cold concrete and waited for the fire to slow. As I panted, my breath fogged in the air; the room was frigid.

Or maybe it was me.

I am cool. I am detached. I am a machine.

I looked at my leg through the ripped slacks. Blood ran from a deep, narrow wound. I shrugged out of my suit jacket, crying out as I twisted my injured shoulder, and used the sleeves as a tourniquet. I tied it as tightly as I could above the wound.

The flow slowed to a seep. Adrenaline surged, and the flames banked to embers.

Now your shoulder.

I looked at it. Sliced muscle. A great deal of blood.

I tipped my head against the wall again.

My own face gazed back at me. I blinked. Sat up.

My image was everywhere. The walls were covered with my picture. Photographs from the paper and snapshots taken while I was completely unaware. I heard Markey's voice.

We know what kind of cereal you like. We know about the old Marine T-shirts you wear to bed and what your tits look like and that your fuckboy reads to you at night like you're a little girl.

My stomach twisted, tried to crawl up my throat.

The rest of the room came into focus. It was unfinished, as if the builder had simply run out of money after he'd gotten this far. Bare walls seeped water, bare pipes ran overhead. A rusting drain breathed out the reek of dead things. There was a bed and handcuffs dangling from the ceiling and plastic sheeting on the floor and other things both shiny and dark. Things with edges and points.

We have a special room prepared for you, Markey'd said. *A very special room.*

I turned my head, vomited.

Next to me, the door burst open. A man stormed in, as tall as Bandoni but leaner, bare arms bunched with muscle, his chest wide and strong, tendons thick as rope in his neck, his long hair a viper's nest around his shoulders. He was naked, his body marked only with stripes of thick, black paint. And blood, streaking from a wound in his upper arm.

Bandoni's last shot.

The man stopped. Turned to look at me.

I knew him. From the photo at Noah's house. And from the few minutes we'd spent together in a parking lot one cold winter night. His face had been mostly covered that night, his eyes in shadow. But he'd loomed over me then exactly as he did now, his head tipped slightly to one side.

Now I could see his eyes. They were yellow.

He kicked the door closed, then reached down and grabbed my shirt and hauled me to my feet. He spun around and drove me back, onto the bed, pressed his weight into me.

"Sydney," he said. "At long last."

Pain sent up flares that sparkled and burst behind my eyes.

"I've been watching you for months," he said. "Your violence. Your anger. We are so much alike."

His voice was thick, harsh; it was a physical thing, penetrating, like the root of an obscene tree snaking deep into the ground.

I flailed and managed to sink my teeth into his flesh. But he pressed my injured arm back until I screamed.

Then he pushed some more.

"Yes. Fight me, Sydney. Hurt me if you can. You and I, we live for the fight. For the pain."

I heard a *snick* and felt the cold press of steel around my left wrist. The handcuffs. With my free hand I flailed behind me, searching for anything to use as a weapon. But I found only air.

He thrust out his tongue and laid it hot upon my throat, dragged it up along my jaw and over my cheek and pushed it into my ear.

I gave up my search and worked my fingers into my pocket, praying for a miracle.

Anything at all.

My fingers closed around the lighter I'd purchased a million years ago, on the way to Donovan's autopsy. I wriggled it out, snapped the wheel.

A tiny yellow flame appeared.

I held the fire to the wound in his arm. At first, he didn't react, just kept pushing his tongue into me. His weight was crushing, squeezing my lungs, forcing my sobs back into my throat.

Then he jerked and reared back. His eyes fell on the lighter, and he smacked it out of my hand. I heard it hit the wall with a dull clank.

He leaned back in. A knife appeared in his hand. The light in his eyes was wild and distant. Nothing remotely human dwelled there.

I would be raped and murdered by a monster.

"Why?" I whispered.

I wasn't asking why he did the things he did.

I was asking why it was possible for a man such as this to exist in the world.

He pinned my legs with his, grabbed my blouse, and used the knife to slice it open. His hand went to my pants. Fabric fell apart. I twisted, trying to heave off his weight. The wound in my leg began to bleed again in a rush, pain dancing up and down my nerves. I shoved the heel of my hand against his face, working to get a thumb into his eye. I found something soft. Pushed. He bellowed and knocked my hand away. The distant light in his eyes turned darker, drew nearer. He gave a slow, heavy-lidded blink and peered at me the way a lion might examine a downed gazelle, wondering how long it would take to stop kicking.

He wrapped one hand around my throat; with the other he brought the knife to my eye.

"This will make your pleasure greater," he said. "And mine."

A great, thundering crash sounded behind him—the door slamming open—and air rushed into my windpipe as Craze threw back his head and roared in pain. I caught a glimpse of black-and-gold fur, and then the bed shuddered as the force of Clyde's attack drove it against the wall. The handcuffs jerked, and I felt a sickening pop as my shoulder dislocated.

Craze released me and spun around, the knife held high, as Clyde danced away, preparing for another leap.

I watched as Craze's wrist cocked, ready to flick the knife.

"Clyde!" My voice was raw. *"Geh nach links."* Go to the left.

Clyde skittered to the left, and the knife smacked into the wall where he'd been only seconds before and clattered to the floor.

My partner lunged forward and buried his teeth in Craze's leg. The two of them shuffled around the room like old boxers, Craze trying to reach the knife, Clyde locked on.

Enraged, Craze threw himself at the wall, smashing Clyde against the concrete. He backed up, did it again. Clyde's growl changed to an odd, soft whimper.

"Out!" I coughed. "Out!"

It must have taken everything Clyde had to release his target. But he pulled away. Circled to Craze's right and made as if to lunge forward before dancing back.

The movement of the bed when Clyde leapt had driven it closer to the objects I'd noticed before. The sharp, ugly things laid out on a table. While Clyde darted in and out and Craze lunged, trying to get his arms around him, I grappled again for a weapon.

My hands closed around cool plastic. I hoisted up a red-and-gray drill. Printed on the side was the word CRAFTSMAN. And below that: 350 FT-LBS MAX TORQUE.

A half-inch diameter bit protruded a foot from the drill.

Craze landed a kick on Clyde, and my partner flew backward, slamming into the wall. *El diablo* whirled back toward me. I read death in his eyes as he leaned in close and reached once again for my throat. He found it, laid his thumbs against my larynx, and closed his eyes in ecstasy.

I raised the drill, pressed the point of the bit to his temple.

I said, "Adios, fucker."

And pulled the trigger.

EPILOGUE

We are all trying to create a good place in the world. That
place where maybe we give a little more than we get.

—*Sydney Parnell. Personal journal.*

I sat with Clyde in the chill quiet of the fog-drenched beach, waiting.
We had come here every morning for a week so that I could celebrate
one small fact.

That the sun would rise, and the world would go on.

The sand was damp beneath us; moisture dewed my skin, beaded
on Clyde's fur. Mere feet away, the Atlantic alternately rumbled and
hissed in the darkness. The air smelled of salt and seaweed and fish.
Primal things.

Soon, dawn would seep into the world.

Clyde leaned into me, and I wrapped my good arm around him.
He nosed my palm, then licked my fingers. I ran the fingers of my other
hand gently over his ribs. He didn't flinch.

"That's my boy," I whispered. "Stronger every day."

Between the bruised ribs caused when Craze slammed him into
the wall and the food poisoning, Clyde had been miserable for a few
days. But he'd bounced back quickly. My partner had been through a
lot worse. And he was tough.

I was working to be just as tough. The truth was that while I was
supposed to be Clyde's teacher, more often he taught me.

The molecules of the air shifted ever so slightly, parting to let in a faint pewter light. The miracle of a coming day.

I tightened my hold on Clyde.

As with the last six mornings, I'd left Cohen sleeping in the beach-front cottage he'd rented for my convalescence and come down to the Massachusetts shore to wait and sit with Clyde and to think about everything that had gone down four weeks earlier. I'd been doing a lot of thinking lately. That, and physical therapy and eating lobster and watching old comedies on TV with Cohen, my body curled into his on the couch and, later, our bodies entwined in bed as heat and sweat rose from our skin and were erased by the ocean air.

I'd been doing a lot of dreaming, too. Those things we could not resolve in the daylight followed us into the night, urging us to find answers. To find a way to lay our ghosts to rest.

The answers were slow to come.

A month after I'd put a drill to Craze's skull and killed him, we still didn't know who he was.

We'd learned a few things about him, confirmed others. We knew he'd been in Noah's home under the guise of friendship. That he'd raped women in assisted-living facilities throughout the Denver metro area after taking a brief job with a cleaning company under the name John Smith.

We had linked him to at least fifteen rapes.

Carolyn Jackson now had a picture of her mother's attacker. It was the best we could do. None of the details we dug up gave us a name or offered insight into *el diablo*.

This man isn't crazy, Evan had told us. *He's evil.*

Those words followed me into my dreams.

Whatever Craze might have been, he was at least in the system now. Maybe someday a detective with a name and a bit of DNA from an old robbery or an assault would enter them into a database and discover he'd stumbled onto a serial criminal. A rapist. A killer. And just like that, a name would be attached to all those other crimes.

Or maybe the clue would come from familial DNA—an aunt or a cousin creating a family tree and unwittingly leading the police to Craze.

I had to believe it would happen.

A light bobbing down the beach caught my attention. Maybe a shell hunter. Or someone walking their dog.

But Clyde and I got to our feet. I watched the light from the corner of my eye and continued my rumination.

Kurt's and Riley's deaths sat in my dreams, too. Along with the knowledge of what the surviving members of the Superior Gentlemen had planned. When police and federal agents found Kurt's boxes in the basement where Markey and Craze had gone to ground, they discovered terrible things beneath carefully packed toilet brushes, cleaning rags, and scrubbers.

Rifles with sniper scopes and night-vision goggles and maps of hotels and schools and churches. The makings of bombs and photographs of their targets. Everything needed to destroy the worms.

The *why* of that did not leave me. Nor did the horror of what happened when unhappy loners found each other and decided to spread their misery.

Damn Fox and Street Cred had confessed to their roles in propping open the ColdShip refrigerator car, but swore they had no idea what Craze had planned. A jury would decide if they were telling the truth.

Todd Asher was a bright spot in all this. While we'd been tearing apart the city trying to find him, he'd been hiding from the world at his girlfriend's house, emerging astonished and relieved at the news that his brother's killer had been found.

And that he was dead.

The bobbing light drew closer. Clyde and I backed away from the water's edge, went to stand near a tumble of rocks. A few minutes later, the light resolved into a flashlight, and soon a father walked by with his young son. The toddler wore rubber boots and carried a plastic pail. The father whistled a tune under his breath. They held hands and smiled. They passed on by, never seeing us in the gray gloom.

For many, the world was still a safe and sane place.

And that was how it should be.

I leaned against the rocks and—finally feeling ready—reached into my pocket for the letter that had arrived three days earlier from Noah's mother, Julia Asher. I slid my finger under the flap, opened the envelope, and eased out the folded pages.

> Dear Sydney,
> Forgive my boldness in addressing you by your given name, when I know you have worked hard to earn the title of detective. But what I want to say to you feels better when shared between women.
> First of all, I've been spending a lot of time with Ami.

I paused in my reading while the wind fluttered the edges of the paper.

Ami. She of the long silences and downcast eyes. The obvious wounds, and the deeper, hidden scars.

> She's doing as well as we can hope. Erica and Lupita and Helen have all moved into Ami's father's house with her. Helen is a mother hen with those girls. They need each other. I actually spend a lot of time there. Lupita taught me how to make *pozole rojo*.

The writing blurred in the salty air. Pearl-pink light spread over the unending swells of the ocean. The sand beneath my feet turned russet.

I've filed for divorce from Noah's father. For years I was okay being Hal's step-and-fetch. Running the household, entertaining the wives of the men who worked at his company. Planning his parties. Making his goddamn martini every night. But not anymore. Not after what happened to Noah. I have to do something that matters. Something that makes a difference.

The flashlight bobbed on the beach again. The boy and his father making their way back along the shoreline. Seagulls swooped and wheeled overhead, and the boy shouted in glee.

Some families made it. Some didn't.

Now I'm working as a victim advocate. And next fall I start back to school—I'm going to become a lawyer, doing work that supports victims' rights. Not only the young have a social conscience. I know Noah would be proud of me.

I pushed myself off the rock and started down the beach. Clyde trotted alongside me in the surf, a puppy again. I knew if he could speak, he'd ask me why I'd waited so damn long to show him the ocean.

I stopped by the station to see Detective Bandoni, but I was told he was out on short-term disability. How is he doing?

That was another thing that entered my dreams every night. While Bandoni had been laying down cover fire for me, he'd taken a knife in the chest for his troubles. The blade had cut through his pectoralis muscle and shattered his clavicle on its way past. Despite that, he'd managed to get off one more shot, the one that hit Craze. But the shock of his injury had triggered a heart attack. Only the fact that Lupita had already called 911 saved Bandoni's life. He'd been quickly stabilized and undergone a triple bypass the next day. Stitching up the knife wound had been almost incidental.

His doctor predicted a full recovery and a return to the detectives' squad. Bandoni himself insisted that the heart attack had saved his life. Time for a little overhaul in his diet, he'd said. Maybe some exercise.

Cut down on the Ding Dongs.

But whatever he might say, something in Bandoni had shifted.

I thought I understood.

Bandoni had looked into the abyss of his own death. But he'd also looked into the abyss of profound madness and evil. Murder cops do their best to give that void only a passing glance before they bury themselves in interviews and reports and the minutiae of crime scenes. They keep the void in their peripheral vision, knowing the darkness is *right there*. But they try not to look too deeply.

Bandoni had looked. Good and hard.

And when you look into the abyss, the monster stares back.

I kept walking while Clyde darted in and out of the water, then came running back to me to shake himself dry.

"Bandoni's strong," I said out loud. "He's going to be okay."

> I hope you'll look me up someday. I'd love to thank
> you in person. I've enclosed something for you from
> Ami. I know you're going through your own personal
> hell right now. I hope this helps.
>> Warm regards and best wishes,
>> Julia

I returned Julia's letter to the envelope but held Ami's paper in my hand and kept on limping through the sand, the grains clean and cool beneath my feet, the sky steadily lightening, the mist burning off. Clyde spotted Cohen and took off like a fur-covered rocket.

Sometimes, usually at night, I found myself back in that room with the reeking drain and wet walls and air so cold it froze my breath. Yellow eyes watching from the dark.

Each time I found myself there, I was terrified.

In the dream, just as in real life, I didn't know that Cohen and Clyde were closing in. That Clyde had caught my scent and surged ahead, and that Ami—still and always the Protector—had roused herself enough to find the keys and let Clyde through the door, where he was panting and scratching, desperate to reach me.

In the dream, the drill was suddenly in my hand, and I pointed it toward the yellow eyes, and a fierce happiness rose in me, lifted me out of the room.

When I woke from these dreams, I wondered if I, too, had gone to darkness.

Back in the real world, Clyde bounded back to me, Cohen jogging close behind. On my right, the sun lifted over the edge of the world, shafting its light across the ocean and filling the air with gold. Clyde paused and turned toward the light, head up, ears cocked. Then he abruptly spun around and knocked into Cohen.

The two went down into the sand together, Cohen laughing, Clyde mock growling as they tussled.

Half-afraid, I unfolded the paper from Ami.

It was a drawing of two women sitting at a table, drinking milk-shakes. One of the women was Ami, although her countenance was less stern than it had been in Noah's drawing. The second woman had long, braided hair and wore a fierce expression. Emblazoned on the front of both women's T-shirts was a shepherd's staff inside an inverted triangle. The emblem of the Protector.

The woman sitting at the table with Ami was me.

At the bottom of the drawing, Ami had written, **NEVER GIVE UP, NEVER GIVE IN.**

I lifted my head. In the surf, Cohen had gained his knees. Clyde barreled into him again, Cohen shouted, and back down they went.

Everything else dissolved.

And with utter certainty, I knew that this could be the sum total of my world if I let it be.

A good, righteous anger swept through and then past me.

Never give up, never give in.

Never let the darkness win.

I moved toward Cohen and Clyde.

Thinking that for now, for this moment, I was still good.

AUTHOR'S NOTE

In writing this novel, I took certain liberties in how I portrayed some of the counties, cities, railroad tracks, and institutions. The world presented here, along with its characters and events, is entirely fictitious. Denver Pacific Continental (DPC) is a wholly fictional railway. Any resemblance to actual incidents and corporations, or to actual persons living or dead, is entirely coincidental.

That said, some of the groups and organizations mentioned in this book are very real. If you're curious about pickup artists, I recommend starting with Neil Strauss's entertaining introduction to the seduction community, *The Game: Penetrating the Secret Society of Pickup Artists.* For information on the darker aspects of the manosphere, a simple Google search will suffice.

Evan's theories about the differences between the handwriting of serial killers and mass murderers owe a tremendous debt to the authors of *Murder in Plain English*, Michael Arntfield and Marcel Danesi. My thanks to these gentlemen for their articulate and entertaining study of murder through the written word. Evan also owes his job description to Danesi, a renowned semiotician and founder of the branch of semiotics called forensic semiotics.

ACKNOWLEDGMENTS

As always, I am grateful for the continued support of so many.

To my critique partners and fellow teachers, the wonderful writers Michael Shepherd and Robert Spiller. You guys always come through. And you're always brilliant. Thank you.

To my beta readers, authors Michael Bateman, Deborah Coonts, and Chris Mandeville. You make my writing so much better, and I am immensely lucky to have both your friendship and your wisdom. Thank you for making room in your lives for my books.

To Patricia Coleman, for all the hours in coffee shops and at the library. Mission accomplished.

This novel would not be possible without the professionals. Thank you all for your time and wisdom. Jessie Donaldson, Vietnam veteran and retired technical expert (railroad maintenance of way equipment and rail repair). Meredith Frank, MD, Denver Office of the Medical Examiner, who patiently and generously answered my many questions. Retired crime scene detective Ron Gabel, Denver Police Department, who generously gave his time to make sure I got the facts right, and who lent his name to the crime scene detective in this book. FBI Special Agent Matthew S. Harris—a scholar and a gentleman. Britta Lietke, who once again helped with Clyde's commands. Forensic handwriting examiner, instructor, and mystery author Sheila Lowe, who helped Evan do his job properly. Candy Muscari-Erdos, CEO of Mountain High

Service Dogs, and the amazing working dog Count Nathanael Athos. I learned up close and personal how much Nate loves a Kong! And retired homicide detective Lieutenant Jon Priest, Denver Police Department.

Any errors in this book are strictly my own.

Ongoing thanks to my agent, Bob Diforio of the D4EO Literary Agency, and to the always terrific Liz Pearsons, Charlotte Herscher, and the fantastic team at Thomas & Mercer. They make a wonderful job even better.

To Cathy Noakes, for her brilliance and for her unflagging pursuit of all that makes life worthwhile. To Lori Dominguez and Maria Faulconer for their wisdom and friendship. And, as always, to my family: Steve, Kyle, and Amanda Nickless. You are the center of my universe.

About the Author

Photo © 2017 Trystan Photography

Barbara Nickless is the *Wall Street Journal* and #1 Amazon Charts bestselling author of the Sydney Rose Parnell series, which includes *Blood on the Tracks*, a *Suspense Magazine* Best of 2016 selection and winner of the Daphne du Maurier Award for Excellence; *Dead Stop*; and *Ambush*. *Blood on the Tracks* and *Dead Stop* won the Colorado Book Award, and *Dead Stop* was nominated for the Daphne du Maurier Award for Excellence. Her essays and short stories have appeared in *Writer's Digest* and *Criminal Element*, among other markets. She lives in Colorado, where she loves to cave, snowshoe, hike, and drink single malt scotch—usually not at the same time. Connect with her at www.barbaranickless.com.